GW00692308

The Bells of Westminster

Also by Leonora Nattrass and available from Viper

Black Drop
Blue Water
Scarlet Town

The Bells of Westminster

LEONORA NATTRASS

First published in Great Britain in 2024 by Viper
an imprint of Profile Books Ltd
29 Cloth Fair
London
ECIA 7JQ
www.profilebooks.com

Text Design by Crow Books

1 3 5 7 9 10 8 6 4 2

Printed and bound by
CPI (UK) Ltd, Croydon CRO 4YY

A CIP catalogue record for this book is available from the British Library.

Hardback ISBN 978 1 80081 7012
eISBN 978 1 80081 7005

The Cloud capt Tow'rs,
The Gorgeous Palaces,
The Solemn Temples,
The Great Globe itself,
Yea all which it Inherit,
Shall Dissolve;
And like the baseless Fabrick of a Vision
Leave not a wreck behind.

From Shakespeare's monument,
Westminster Abbey

Cast of Characters

THE DEAN AND CHAPTER OF WESTMINSTER ABBEY

Mr Bell, Dean of Westminster
Mr Bray, Canon-treasurer
Mr Slater, Canon-steward
Mr Turnbull, Canon-almoner
Mr Suckling, Sacrist
Mr Lamb, Chanter

ABBEY SERVANTS

Henry Ede, Verger
John Catling, Verger
Benjamin Fidoe, Clerk of Works
Thomas Corbett, Searcher of the Sanctuary
George Slemaker, Porter
James Michelson, Gardener
Also sundry sweepers, scullions, bell ringers, butlers,
laundresses, workmen, &c.

THE ABBEY LADIES

Susan Bell, daughter to the Dean
Mrs Bray, wife to the Canon-treasurer
Mrs Slater the elder, mother to the Canon-steward
Mrs Slater the younger, wife to the Canon-steward
The young Miss Brays, daughters of the Canon-treasurer
The grown-up Miss Turnbulls, daughters of the
Canon-almoner

THE SOCIETY OF ANTIQUARIES OF LONDON

Robert Delingpole, Lawyer
Thomas Alnutt Esq., Antiquarian
Henry Quintrel, Librarian at Lambeth Palace
Louis Durand, visiting antiquary from France

OTHER PARTIES

His Majesty George III, Sovereign Visitor to the Abbey
Major-General Thomas Desaguliers, Equerry to George III
Major-General Edward Mathew, Equerry to George III
Princess Elizabeth, the king's daughter
Lindley Bell, nephew to the dean and cousin to Susan Bell,
just returned from his Grand Tour
Thomas Ffoulkes, a friend Lindley made while on his Tour
William Blake, an apprentice engraver, employed to draw
the tombs in the abbey
Sir Horatio Mann, nephew of the Envoy Extraordinary to
the Tuscan Court in Italy
Dame Elizabeth Yates, widow of Sir Joseph Yates, lawyer
Admiral, Dame Yates's dog
Cuthbert, Susan Bell's parrot

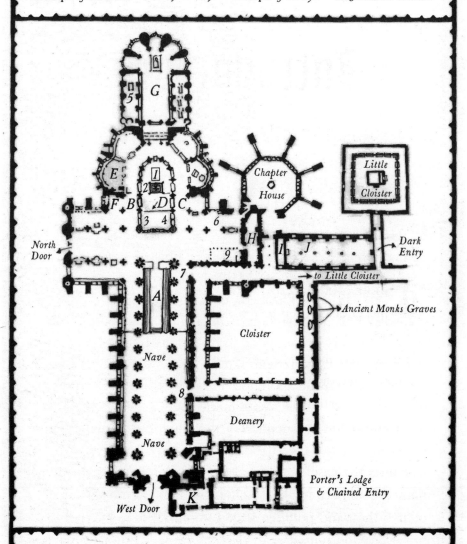

A. Quire   B. North Ambulatory   C. South Ambulatory   D. High Altar

E. Chapel of John the Baptist   F. Chapel of Abbot Islip   G. Henry VII Lady Chapel

H. Chapel of St. Faith   I. Abbey Library   J. Chapel of the Pyx   K. Jerusalem Chamber

Little Cloister

Chapter House

Dark Entry

North Door

to Little Cloister

Ancient Monks Graves

Cloister

Nave

Deanery

Nave

Porter's Lodge & Chained Entry

West Door

1. Shrine of Edward the Confessor   2. Tomb of 'Longshanks' Edward I   3. Tomb of Aveline de Forz

4. Tomb of Edmund Crouchback   5. Tomb of Queen Elizabeth   6. Poets' Corner

7. Entrance to East Cloister   8. Entrance to West Cloister   9. Muniments Gallery (upstairs)

Introductory

THE DEANERY

WESTMINSTER ABBEY

THE YEAR OF OUR LORD 1774

THERE ARE TWO solemn maxims with which my father has endeavoured to impress me over the years of my girlhood.

The first is that although he has neglected the worldly matter of amassing money (so that he must remain Dean Bell of Westminster until his death, merely to keep a roof over our heads) I shall not starve on that unhappy but inevitable occasion.

This is the case because, along with a large grey parrot named Cuthbert, my late mother has also left me a fortune of two thousand pounds, settled upon me so securely that not even God himself can part me from it. After Father's death the money will be invested in the funds and Cuthbert and I shall always have an income to live upon.

Not a great income, however, Father says. We might need

to live something in the manner of a greengrocer, with about the same amount of ready cash at our disposal. I do not know if Cuthbert would like it, but I must say this prospect does not entirely dismay me. At church fairs, when I inveigle myself on to some stall or other, I always much enjoy the feeling of *filthy lucre* in my palm. Coins are a delight to me, for I am so seldom in their presence or they in mine. The world of bills and payments happens elsewhere, out of sight – in Father's study, I suppose, or at the kitchen door of the Deanery.

Father's second maxim (*query*: do I really mean *maxim*? Or is it more properly called a *dictum*?) is that if I do not wish to live like a greengrocer, I had better marry, give my two thousand pounds to some deserving gentleman, and continue for ever in my current, happy ignorance of money matters and tradesmen's bills.

He advises against a clergyman, however. (I believe fathers often warn their children away from their own professions.) A churchman's stipend is shocking, he says, and a clergyman quite as subject to the whims of his superiors as any politician. It would therefore be unfortunate that I scarcely meet any other kind of gentleman, if it were not the case that Father's dearest wish (though he does not absolutely say so) is that I should marry my cousin, Lindley Bell. Lindley is presently staying with us at the Deanery, between returning from his Grand Tour on the Continent and going home to the family seat in Leicestershire, where he is to settle down and be a country gentleman at the ripe old age of twenty-one.

Meanwhile, I have two maxims (or dictums?) of my own, which are more pithy, if no less sincere.

First: a deep and solemn love of bonnets and gowns is not incompatible with common sense or even genius. I often have my profoundest thoughts when concentrating upon the sewing of a very fine seam. The truth of this is self-evident, since the clergy of Westminster Abbey, in their golden gowns, are more gorgeously arrayed than I could ever be, and never seem to think themselves the slightest bit frivolous.

Second, my strictest and most absolute *dictum*: never remain in any space, large or small, alone with Mr Suckling, the sacrist; curator and keeper of the said gorgeous clerical robes, along with the abbey's collection of chalices, candlesticks, altar cloths, *et al.* He will infallibly propose, if given any opportunity to do so, and I cannot in any possible circumstances be known as Susan Suckling.

Or, at least, it is to be hoped that Mr Suckling will propose. I sometimes think he might dispense entirely with such preliminaries and instead proceed directly to carnal pleasures. He has a special leer I believe he reserves only for me, which always puts me in mind of Roman emperors in general, and Caligula in particular. (And everyone knows how *he* carried on.)

To be fair to him, Mr Suckling is always smiling in some way or other. A pious dreamy curve to his full lips when he conducts Evening Prayer and what I would call an oily simper when the archbishop comes visiting. It is common knowledge that Mr Suckling supported the archbishop's preferred candidate for Dean against the king's choice to appoint Father (or desired the archbishop's favour, which is much the same thing) and as a consequence takes pleasure in all of Father's little trials and tribulations.

7

And of these there are unfortunately many, for the dean oversees all the various doings of the abbey. What with the vergers and the clergymen, the sweepers and the gardeners – along with the abbey watchman, the searcher of the sanctuary and the army of workmen who keep the ancient fabric from falling on our heads – Father has the care of what amounts to a large and thriving village.

But beneath these various obstacles to tranquillity there is, nonetheless, a soothing rhythm to abbey life. The daily round of services and prayers; the weekly round of maintenance and sweeping and arranging flowers at the altar; the seasonal feasts of the Church year, which come one upon the other at intervals of a few weeks. The practising of the choir: the singing men making the roof ring with their deeper voices beneath the boys' soaring sopranos; the boys from across the yard at Westminster School looking as pious as cherubim in the new-built choir stalls, while at other times making a great hullabaloo about the gardens with their footballs.

And then there is me. I try not to be another burden on Father's shoulders, but the abbey is my home after all, and the cloisters my garden where I take my daily walks. No one cautions me against haunting the abbey for my recreation either (there is, as I have said, always a great deal going on and even the vergers may not positively eject a young woman from church, especially if she makes sure to pray at regular intervals) and I have made it my place of business, too. Viz. I arrange the flowers on a Sunday and record any matters of particular interest pertaining to the abbey in this journal.

The second bible in this place is a volume entitled *An Historical Description of Westminster Abbey, its Monuments and Curiosities*, much beloved of the vergers, who make a considerable amount of *filthy lucre* of their own, showing visitors around the abbey. I once thought my journal might supplement this worthy work, in a new edition to be published under the suitably sexless name NASUS BELL (which, if you study it, you will find a very cunning stratagem). But lately the *curiosities* have grown rather more curious than is comfortable, and a truer title might now end with the words: *its Monuments and Murders*. Whether we shall ever get to the bottom of the business remains to be seen, and there is a lofty personage very anxious, along with Father, that the report will not reach the press (Father being above all things afraid of the archbishop's spiteful tongue).

This being so, alas, Nasus Bell will likely remain forever unborn, along with my literary fame. But for my own satisfaction, I shall preserve the account of the affair as it unfolded in my journal, beginning on a morning in early May when the events surrounding *its Monuments and Murders* had their first commencement.

1

SATURDAY 7 MAY

MY COUSIN LINDLEY was already at the table when I came into the parlour this morning, with a book propped against the teapot. He did not raise his eyes when I came in, nor greet me, so I busied myself cutting a slice of cold meat for my own breakfast, and giving Cuthbert a very wrinkled apple from last autumn's store for his. Within a month there will be strawberries and, in another month, grapes from the hothouse, but Cuthbert liked his apple and commenced peaceably dismembering it on his perch.

The sun was shining through the windows, showing in scrupulous detail the egg yolk trickling down my cousin's chin, and the butter glistening amid the boyish wisps of hair on his upper lip as he bent, transfixed, over his book. The manner in which a man eats his quail eggs may not be an infallible window into his soul, but I did wonder how I should tolerate the yolk, *&c.*, if confronted with it every morning of my married life as Father wishes.

In one way, Lindley is a perfect example of a secular young gentleman destined to inherit his family's affluent country estate. He is well-dressed, well-combed and slightly scrubbed looking, as though he has only just escaped from his nanny's managing hand. I know nothing bad of him (though, quite besides the yolk, &c., he has a propensity to stare at one with a strange unblinking gaze and his ears protrude and turn pink when he is excited). Father likes to joke that our name has a ring to it, and there is certainly much to be said for remaining always Susan Bell, one way or another, at least for the length of this earthly existence. (*Query*: are there surnames in heaven? Are there names at all? And if not, how is conversation to be carried on without confusion?)

But in his own way Lindley is quite the curiosity himself. He is lately returned from Europe where, instead of spending his time examining the marvels of antiquity in Greece and Rome as most men do (and as a man with so milk-and-water a name as Lindley really *ought* to do) he betook himself to Holland (of all places) to talk to men of science. He has carried home a trunk full of souvenirs, but rather than pleasant things like silks and statues, he has instead brought back odd bits of metal and glass, and a number of strange machines.

His father does not know he is staying with us. There was some terrible quarrel between Father and my uncle when I was small, and Father quitted the family living in dudgeon. He subsequently made his way in the world quite alone (and, I might add, with great success, having risen so high as Dean of W. without the usual money or connections). But

I suppose Lindley is curious about us, being a curious kind of youth, and Father is extremely eager for a reconciliation with his brother. (*Query:* does Lindley know the reason for their falling-out? His father is a worldly man and must have done something very bad to make Father break with him. But it is typical of Father's gentle nature that he should also be the one to wish to heal the breach.)

I am afraid my own character is more resentful, a trait exemplified over breakfast, as I tried to repay Lindley for ignoring me with a show of equal indifference. In this I had rather less success than he did, for I had forgotten to bring my own book to the table and Cuthbert, so talkative at other times, was wholly preoccupied with his apple. Father had been called out early, but by his plate a small parcel lay waiting. It was his birthday and the package was my gift to him. I was morally certain he did not know it was his birthday for he is always far too busy with his various enthusiasms to remember such trifles. I therefore also knew he would greet the discovery with delight at my thoughtfulness, and self-deprecating amusement at his own absence of mind.

'What are you reading?' I asked Lindley eventually, after a protracted inward tussle between maintaining a dignified silence and finding out what subject could be so riveting as to make him utterly dead to all other considerations. Lindley looked up at me as if clambering out of a very deep, dark hole – which, as it turned out, was rather apt.

'A very interesting disquisition on coal.'

'I beg your pardon. Did you say *coal?*'

'That black stuff your Father keeps in his fire grate, for making the flickering orange lights which we commonly call flames.'

And this is why it is generally better to mind my own business and leave Lindley to his. Though our fathers were estranged long ago, I do have fragments of memories of the Parsonage on the family estate in Leicestershire. The pattern of a cushion. The way light fell in through the glass door to the garden. Breaking Lindley's toys and him biting me.

'I expect you find yourself very droll,' I said. 'It is lucky for you, since no one else does.'

'It is hard to amuse a spinster aunt,' he answered, squirting golden yolk on to a slice of rather charred cold toast as he cut into another tiny egg. 'Her interests must naturally be jaded by so many long and disappointed years.'

'Lindley,' I said, 'I am twenty-three.'

'And I pity you, dear Miss Bell, from the depths of my heart, I really do.'

Here's the dean, Cuthbert announced, stretching a leg and a grey wing, and it was certainly lucky that Father came in then, or to relieve my feelings I might have wiped the butter from Lindley's chin with his own eggy toast.

But Father looked unusually fretful. He didn't even sit down, nor notice my parcel at all. 'I am deuced annoyed,' he said, picking up a bath bun and pecking at it irritably. He is very small and very round, like a robin in his scarlet cassock. Perhaps it is Cuthbert's doing, but I always think we Bells are birdlike. I suppose I am a thrush, being brown-haired and freckled and somewhat larger than Father is. And Lindley, being all eyes and ears, is an owl.

'What's the matter?' I asked. 'Not old Dame Yates again?' (Surely only something so dreadful could elicit the expletive 'deuced' from Father's lips.)

'No, no. I almost wish it were,' he said. 'This is something much worse.'

'Worse?' I echoed. 'What could possibly be worse than Dame Yates?'

'Susan, my dear, that is not very kind.' Father now sat down and buttered his bun, still oblivious to my waiting parcel. 'But any interruption is certainly a nuisance this week.'

Holy Thursday was almost upon us, when the great and the good present themselves at the abbey for the Ascension Day service, including the king our patron, and the numerous members of his family. The king stood out against the archbishop and appointed Father as his dean, which he was perfectly entitled to do, the abbey being what is known as a *Royal Peculiar* – more or less the king's private church and no one's business save his own.

'But now the antiquities are in the north transept, causing a terrible fuss,' Father was going on. 'We shall have to close the abbey and rearrange all our rehearsals, merely for their convenience – I might even say, for their trivial amusement.'

'Antiquities? Making a fuss?'

The abbey is certainly brim full of antiquities; there being so very many tombs and monuments it is like living in a city of the dead. Battalions of pale, carved men and women loiter about (some striking highly unlikely poses) or doze on top of their monuments as brazenly as if they were at home in their own beds. Their faces are various, but most wear a look of bland, soulful despondency, though among dead people they are pretty well off, being spared the horrors of the grave and dusted weekly. On the whole, a rebellion seemed unlikely, and in this it turned out I was right.

'The *Society* of Antiquities, I mean, my dear, or at least some of them,' Father explained.

Lindley was still reading his book, but, as always, Cuthbert was listening to the conversation with his head cocked on one side. Catching Father's fretful tone, he loudly opined that the Antiquities in question were *bad old birds* and then tolled the chime of the sonorous abbey clock, three times, with some ominous meaning.

'But what exactly do they want?' I asked, sipping my tea, and trying to exude calm as I always do when Father begins to fuss.

'To open a tomb, if you will believe it. Now, at this very hour, without any forewarning at all!'

'Then tell them to go away,' I said. 'Strange gentlemen cannot come in and rummage through our tombs just as they please.'

He looked unhappy. 'I told them that if their authority came from the archbishop they were mistaken, for he has no sway here. But they had already found that out and are come properly armed with a letter from the king.'

Bad birds, bad birds, dong, dong, dong, Cuthbert reiterated with some energy, while Lindley finally raised his head from his book and stared at Father, a slight look of interest dawning in his owlish face. 'What tomb do they want to open?'

'King Edward the First. Edward Longshanks, as they called him. A very tall and, some say, disagreeable man who was making endless wars against the Scots and Welsh in the late twelve hundreds. You will have seen his very plain marble coffin behind an iron grating in the north ambulatory, I am sure. It has "Hammer of the Scots" embossed upon it in rather faded gold lettering.'

I wasn't sure I had seen it myself and was therefore pretty certain Lindley hadn't. 'What does his effigy look like?'

'He has no effigy at all, my dear. As I say, it is just a plain coffin – very odd, in its way, lying among the other medieval kings who are so very ornate. I gather that is partly why they wish to open it.'

Lindley wiped his chin and stood up. 'They are going to open it now?' he said. 'Well then, what are we waiting for?'

2

WHEN FATHER AND I hurried out of the Deanery Court, Lindley's figure was already well ahead, flickering in and out of the arches as he flew along the other side of the cloisters towards the door to the south transept of the abbey.

Father turned the other way, past Michelson the gardener peacefully weeding the borders, towards the door to the nave (the distance to the north transept being pretty much of a muchness, as I have established from long experience. In general I prefer the route Lindley had taken, as it gives me the opportunity to bid good morning to the three ancient monks who, after more than six hundred years, lie almost worn away to nothing among the paving slabs against the left-hand wall.)

Inside the abbey, we found a small clutch of gentlemen waiting in the gloom by the quire, hats in hand, while a trumpeter practised his cheerful fanfares for Ascension Day from a platform somewhere above our heads. As we drew nearer, the group proved to be composed of four gentlemen of varying ages. Their leader was a sensible-looking man of about forty, neatly dressed in a bottle-green waistcoat, who introduced himself as Mr Robert Delingpole before naming the others to Father with tremendous politeness, despite being obliged to speak very loudly above the warbling trumpet. He first presented a very old, very thin man called Mr Alnutt; next, a scholar with long hair and a dirty neckcloth by the name of Quintrel; and finally an acquaintance of Mr Quintrel's, a visiting antiquary from France by the name of Louis Durand. Antiquary seemed too grand a title for the lad in question, who was dark-haired and good-looking and appeared scarcely older than Lindley. (But then Lindley likes to call himself a *natural philosopher*, which is just as ludicrous.)

Mr Delingpole was holding their letter of authority from the king and, having made these introductions, wasted no further time in pressing it upon Father.

'You will see His Majesty requires all accommodations to be extended to us, Dean, but there should be very little difficulty for you, I hope. Being so plain and simple, the tomb will be easy to open with the assistance of your workmen, and we think the abbey need only close for about an hour. We have arranged with Mr Basire, the engraver, for his apprentice to make some sketches to record the occasion, for the boy is here already, working on some drawings of the monuments for Basire's new book.'

I knew who he meant. I had seen the lad about the abbey these several weeks, always working on some tomb or other; a youth of about seventeen, stocky with practical hands but large, dreamy eyes which I sometimes thought followed me as I passed him.

'But I don't understand why it must be today.' Father thrust the letter back at Mr Delingpole. 'Indeed, I don't know why it must be at all. What business has the Society of Antiquities to rummage through our tombs just as it pleases?'

It was gratifying to hear Father echo my own words in this way, since as far as all the gathered gentlemen were concerned, I might just as well have been a pigeon perching in the rafters.

'We were emboldened to request the permission of His Majesty by your own very interesting researches, Dean,' Mr Delingpole answered. The trumpeter was catching his breath and a moment of blessed peace descended upon us. I thought Mr Delingpole seemed a nice sort of creature, for his voice, now reduced to a normal pitch, was steady and deep, and his manner towards Father was tactfully soothing. 'We have long heard of your interest in the antiquities of the abbey and your own investigations into the tombs. You really should join our society – which is, in fact, *Antiquaries*, not Antiquities, which makes us sound rather antique ourselves,' he smiled good humouredly, 'for we would be delighted to hear all about your findings.'

But Father is not the sort of man to sit writing scholarly articles; indeed the only accounts of his researches are the ones recorded in my own hand in this journal, so if they ever do reach print they will be the work of Nasus Bell. Nevertheless, Mr Delingpole was quite right to take Father as a good precedent for opening tombs. Seized by the latest of his enthusiasms, he has recently had half the floor up, with the help of the abbey's clerk of works, Benjamin Fidoe, in a quest for James I, who seems to have gone unaccountably missing sometime in the last one hundred and fifty years.

When he watches Fidoe's pickaxe prise up the floor slabs, Father looks exactly like a robin waiting for the gardener to turn up worms.

'My *researches*, as you call them, are underpinned by prayer,' Father said primly, as the trumpeter started up again with a series of fine, pealing flourishes. 'We cannot open the last resting place of any man – still less a king – without all due reverence.'

'Oh, we'll be as reverential as you like,' Mr Quintrel, the shabby scholar, put in with a rather cynical smoky laugh. The thin old man, Mr Alnutt, cast him a reproachful, trembling glance before turning eagerly to Father, but he was forestalled in whatever he was going to say by a sudden shout from above our heads. When we looked up, Benjamin Fidoe was leaning out of an arch in the triforium gallery fifty feet above us and waving down at a couple of workmen, who saluted in answer and shambled off, presumably on some special errand.

Father turned his eyes reluctantly from the workmen back to Mr Delingpole. 'It is all highly inconvenient and the king ought to have known better. He is to be here himself on Thursday and should remember we are taken up with preparing for the ceremony.' (For myself, I think it far more likely that it never crosses the king's mind that the marvellous occasions from which he flits, one to another, are the result of so much labour; but being only a pigeon I did not venture to say so just then.) 'We are installing some lamps in the gallery for a new effect never before attempted,' Father added.

'We need not interrupt those works,' Mr Delingpole answered pleasantly. 'Your man is so far above us that he will not be able to see or hear what we are about.' He squinted up at Fidoe, who was now sitting with his legs dangling out of the arch. 'But, dear me, that looks a very precarious perch. What do you call that high gallery now? A *triforium*, I think?'

Father didn't answer, being distracted by Fidoe making more cabbalistic signs, this time to him. He raised a hand and Fidoe scrambled to his feet and withdrew into the triforium's shadowy depths.

'What can have been its purpose, I wonder?' Mr Delingpole's eye was now scanning the length of that lofty arcade which runs round the three sides of the transept. 'Whatever did the original builders intend to do with it?'

'Some say it was to be a range of private chapels,' Father answered. 'But the work was never done, and it has always remained abandoned, a dusty, dirty loft full of antique rubbish.'

Mr Delingpole's eyes positively lit up. 'One man's rubbish is another's treasure, you know, Dean. How does one get up there?'

'There is a very narrow winding stair, but no one dares go up except for my man Fidoe there, for the floorboards are quite rotten.'

The rest of the Antiquities (I find it is far too dull to call them antiquaries) were growing restive under these pleasantries. 'Are we ever to see Longshanks this morning?' the French lad asked, with some boyish energy, and Mr Delingpole smiled at him apologetically.

'Yes, yes, of course, Durand. Dear me, the abbey is quite the siren, is she not? So full of alluring secrets that one gets far too easily distracted. But if you will be so good as to empty the place, Dean, and summon some of your strong men to help us, perhaps we may begin.'

A group of visitors had just come in at the west door, in hope of a tour with a verger, but they were routed out, along with another unoffending set presently examining our collection of wooden kings and queens summarily stuffed in a cupboard. The trumpeter took his silver trumpet away, to continue practising elsewhere, and Basire's apprentice engraver sloped past us, probably assuming himself also banished. But Mr Delingpole called him back as the great doors of the abbey thudded closed, and Mr Suckling the sacrist, who always seems to know when great things are afoot, appeared among us, smiling as usual.

3

EDWARD LONGSHANKS' tomb is indeed a very plain one. It lies, dour and glowering, behind its iron grille in the north ambulatory, and is therefore only properly accessible from within the shrine of Edward the Confessor, which is a small room raised above the floor behind the high altar. (Two Edwards in one room! It is lucky they both have their nicknames, else I should never keep them straight in my mind. All I know about the Confessor is that he built this abbey in the first place and was the last – or perhaps next to last? – of the Saxon kings, before the Conqueror came in 1066 and shot someone in the eye. But if I am right, why then is the Confessor not called Edward I instead of this other, later one? Did kings not have numbers before the Conquest, only nicknames? And why does Edward Longshanks have both? Perhaps he was greedy as well as *disagreeable*.)

The Confessor's shrine has two marble doors set into the altar itself, along with a flight of wooden stairs from the ambulatory, which is always locked behind a low gate. The only decoration on Edward I's (Longshanks') tomb is the dull, gilt inscription in Latin that Father had mentioned. It may say *Hammer of the Scots*, for all I know – and when I looked closely I could make out EDWARDVS PRIMVS – but I am no Latin scholar and the rest was Greek to me. (Ha, ha!)

Father unlocked the left-hand door in the altar and we were soon all standing in the Confessor's shrine. Father had gestured to Fidoe to come down and help us, and a brief exchange between them resulted in the appearance of a dozen workmen, flexing their muscles. Their arrival made the shrine somewhat crowded, and Father looked crosser than ever, no doubt fearing the Confessor's displeasure at the invasion. But the saint leads a lonely life these days, cloistered inside his peaceful room when once it would have been thronged with pilgrims, so I thought he would probably enjoy the company.

Meanwhile, Mr Suckling was still smiling, evidently amused by this whole new irritation to Father's day. I really wish that, if he is to be so disagreeable, he would get himself a place with his beloved archbishop at once and be done with us. But, of course, *pace* Father's *maxim* or *dictum* on my marriage prospects, a clergyman is always the helpless receiver of preferment, and can never absolutely demand it for himself however much he might desire it (and however much his colleagues might wish to be rid of him).

Fearing to be noticed and sent packing, I fell back to a small distance, loitering in the friendly shadow of the Confessor's tomb. The workmen stood about sucking their teeth at Delingpole's request that they should remove the massy marble slab that lay atop Longshanks' casket. Fidoe was on the point of calling for a lever when they all seemed seized by some sudden inspiration, communicated one to the other without words, and braved the thing at a rush. The young Frenchman darted forward to assist them and Lindley, apparently not to be outdone, also lent a hand. (I do not think either of them, slight as they are, could have been much help.) There was much shouting and some regrettably blasphemous utterances that might have shocked the Confessor's delicate ears (though perhaps not his *disagreeable* successor). But before Father could protest the slab was off Longshanks' casket and had been set down on its edge against the side of the tomb, where, if it fell over, it would infallibly break everyone's toes.

From where I was standing I couldn't yet see inside the coffin, and the poor workmen were bundled out summarily before they could have a good look. Father said something to Fidoe and pointed to the roof, probably telling him that Mr Delingpole was content for the works up there to continue. After that, Fidoe departed and the select company made up of the four Antiquities, Mr Suckling, Lindley, Father, the engraver's apprentice and I were left in a sudden peace, all the more marked for coming after so much noise and bustle.

We all drew a step closer to the opened coffin, and Mr Delingpole ran his hand lovingly along its stone rim. 'I dare say we are all acquainted with something of Longshanks' history,' he said, 'at least to the extent that it is to him we owe the first unification between England, Wales and Scotland, he having *hammered* the Welsh into obedience with some enduring success, and afterwards attempted the same against the Scots. There, for all his hammering, the conquest would prove less permanent – though he brought their ancient coronation stone south to this abbey, where much to their chagrin it remains to this day.

'Which brings us to the reason we wish to open the tomb. On his deathbed, he left instructions that he was to be buried in this plain way, so that whenever England went to war with Scotland again, his body could be removed from the abbey to accompany the troops northwards on their march.'

Lindley's owlish eyes were more than ever like saucers and his ears decidedly pink. He glanced at Louis Durand, perhaps sensing in him some youthful kinship. 'How splendid! How macabre! Imagine his great long skeleton tied to the saddle and flapping about! By God, they should have taken him to Culloden. It would have scared the living daylights out of the Jacobites, for all their manly beards and plaid.'

Mr Delingpole smiled tolerantly. 'It certainly would, Mr Bell, though our army did well enough even without him at that battle, I believe. And I'm afraid the reality was to be rather more prosaic. The plan was merely for the troops to draw this coffin along with Edward in it.'

If those had been his wishes, I thought that his successors had let him down. It would take twenty horses to move the heavy oblong monolith an inch, and perhaps explains why the government had elected not to draw on Longshanks' aid in 1745.

'But though young Bell is being mischievous,' Mr Delingpole added, 'his picture of King Edward is nearer the truth than he supposes and is another reason for our interest in the tomb. Longshanks also decreed that his body be embalmed at regular intervals, to preserve it for any such adventure, and if his directions have been faithfully followed, we hope to find him a leathery mummy, rather than a mere bag of bones – a mummy which could indeed have ridden a horse just as Mr Bell supposes and whose height we can measure, to see if he was in truth the titan that legend claims.'

A great deal of this was beyond me then, the words *embalmed* and *mummy* being at that time strange to me. The first made me think of creams for the complexion (*query*: am I thinking of *embrocation*?) and the second of the apothecary shop, where I have seen *mummy* written on a jar but have never troubled to enquire of what the contents exactly consist.

'The practice of embalming Edward's body fell into abeyance, we think, in the later medieval period,' Mr Delingpole was continuing, 'and, of course, during the Civil War and Interregnum, it was completely forgotten. But we hope to find evidence, however slight, of some such procedure from an earlier date, which might prove the story true.'

It was at this point, unfortunately, that Father noticed me. 'Susan, my dear, I hardly think this a suitable sight for a young lady. You would very much oblige me by going to find a verger and preparing refreshments for these gentlemen in the Jerusalem Chamber.'

'Yes, Father,' I said, but his eyes had already turned back to the opened tomb, and I stayed where I was, merely taking a step to the left to put the engraver's apprentice between us. This was when being a pigeon proved most useful, and the lad looked at me and smiled, a conspiratorial smile of so much sweetness that I smiled back. We really neither of us had any right to be among these grave, learned gentlemen.

But, as yet, there was nothing to frighten me in any case, for the opened box had only revealed another, smaller stone sarcophagus lying inside it. This, I suppose, was the coffin they had really meant to draw behind the troops, and which was certainly a far more practical proposition.

'A dull yellow colour,' Mr Delingpole observed, tracing his finger across the lid of the sarcophagus. 'The remnants of gold leaf, I fancy. Well, gentlemen, I wonder if we can lift this inner lid between us, without the aid of the workmen? Shall we try?'

All the men started forward to help, except for Mr Alnutt, who was too old, and Father, who was too small and stout to lean over the rim of the outer casket without the aid of a box, of which there happened to be none at hand. Fortunately, the inner lid was much less heavy than the outer one, and even a handful of scholars, clergymen and well-dressed youths proved a match for it. They carried this second lid carefully away and laid it down against the neighbouring wall. Then we all stepped closer again.

There certainly was a body within. A very long body. Or, at the least, a long, body-shaped parcel, its head resting in a hollowed-out extension to the cavity carved out of the solid stone block of the inner coffin. Remarkably, a king's coronet had been placed about the wrapped head, and it gleamed dully in the gloom of the Confessor's shrine.

'Good Lord,' Mr Suckling said. 'Is that gold?'

But the metal was rather dull. Mr Delingpole leaned a little closer to inspect it, touching the crown with a cautious forefinger. 'Just some kind of gilding, I think, but it has lost its high shine being so very old.'

The old man Alnutt had also put out his hand, eager to touch the crown for himself. But Mr Delingpole straightened, mastering his own impetuous curiosity, and smiled at the old man. 'Wait a moment, Mr Alnutt. We must have it all properly recorded, you remember.' He turned to the engraver's apprentice. 'Blake, will you do a quick sketch of the tomb as we now see it?'

The young man did as he was bidden, balancing his paper on the edge of the outer coffin, his large eyes moving along the bundle within as his pen quickly sketched its elongated lineaments.

I confess that it did frighten me a little to see the outlines of the body within the wrappings, and at first I rather dreaded the opening of the contents to our view. But there was no smell at all, of course, the body being so ancient, and as the lad sketched on, my anxiety gradually subsided. On the whole, the yellowed package reminded me of nothing so much as an old letter, or an old book that had lost its covers, the sort of sorry thing one might find forgotten at the back of a cupboard.

'Mr Alnutt is a well-known medieval scholar,' Mr Delingpole was telling Father, 'and it is his scholarship that has led us to make this special request to the king.'

'And what a glory and wonder it is,' the old man said, his eyes still fastened on the wrapped corpse as greedily as his hand had reached out to touch the gilt crown. 'To discover the reality of a thing, only previously described on the written page, is surely the noblest of scholarly pursuits.'

'And what do you think we'll find inside the wrappings?' Lindley asked him. But Mr Alnutt only shook his head, seemingly too moved to speak further. Delingpole touched the old man's elbow gently.

'Come now, sir, tell the young man what you told me yesterday. About how Longshanks loved King Arthur above all else, and staged jousts and built a round table for his own followers.'

'He did, Delingpole.' Mr Alnutt nodded, his head trembling. 'Yes, yes, it is certainly thus recorded in the sources.'

'And how he went to Glastonbury,' Delingpole went on, 'where Arthur was supposed to be buried with Queen Guinevere; and how he exhumed their bodies, just as we are doing now.'

'He had a great tomb built for them in Glastonbury Abbey,' the old man said. 'They were reburied with all due pomp and majesty.'

'Which, though all very splendid, of course, can be well explained as convenient homage on the part of a foreign invader,' Mr Delingpole said to the rest of us. 'Edward Longshanks was a Norman by blood and probably meant to bolster his position as king by allying himself with his Saxon predecessors.'

Louis Durand had been listening to all this with a slight frown between his eyebrows, but now he smiled. 'Me, I should like to see inside Arthur's tomb. Suppose the 'oly Grail was buried with 'im! That would surely win me a place in the *Académie Royale*.'

'You can have the Grail, Durand,' Mr Quintrel said with a kind of cynical smile, fingering his grimy neckcloth. 'Since the whole Arthurian story is a fable, you are welcome to it. As you know, *I* am seeking something altogether more ancient, more precious, and more real.'

Mr Suckling had by now abandoned grinning, having been drawn in to all this scholarly treasure-hunting just as much as I was. (It was, I must say, most interesting and almost made me resolve to learn Latin after all and become the Society's first lady member.) Unsmiling, Mr Suckling's face was as convex and smooth as the back of a spoon. 'Something more ancient than King Arthur?' he asked. 'Whatever could be more ancient or precious than that?'

'Many things are more ancient.' Mr Alnutt's old body was still gently quivering with emotion, or age, or perhaps both. 'The story of these islands goes back far before the birth of Our Lord, sir; much further back, indeed, at least to the time of Troy.'

'And Mr Quintrel is the finest classical scholar among us,' Mr Delingpole added, nodding to the slovenly man. 'His interests in your abbey, Dean, are Roman. Isn't that so, Quintrel?'

'I have a point to prove, certainly,' Mr Quintrel said in his smoky voice. 'There's a Roman temple somewhere under the foundations of this place, all the written sources say so. But when Wren was Surveyor of the Fabric he said most disobliging things about it. Denied it point-blank, in fact. As if *he* ever dug down beneath the undercroft or the Lady Chapel sufficient to prove all the histories wrong!'

'A Roman temple?' Mr Suckling echoed. 'Under Westminster Abbey?'

It did seem a rather extraordinary, if not blasphemous, notion. But Mr Quintrel only shrugged at the sacrist's curiosity. 'Why not? The Christians have often buried former gods under holy stone and tile, to show their victory over the pagans, and very successful the stratagem has proved through many centuries.'

'And which old god do you propose is buried here?'

'I do not propose it. I *know* it,' Mr Quintrel said. 'According to all the chronicles, this was once a temple to the sun god, Apollo. And his light still glows somewhere under its floor, I am certain.'

Blake had unconsciously broken off his sketching to stare at Mr Quintrel, quite as captivated by this notion as Mr Suckling was, but now he remembered himself enough to go back to his sketch.

'It would certainly be a coup to prove Wren wrong,' Mr Delingpole remarked, as he glanced at the boy's drawing to see how he was getting on. 'And it would make a very fine paper for the Society, too, not to mention put all Wren's supporters' noses out of joint – as I dare say you'd enjoy, Quintrel.'

'I suppose you are all deadly rivals,' Lindley said. 'Ink spilled like blood over your desks, and intellectual jousts to the death at your meetings.'

Mr Delingpole laughed. 'And you seem just the right kind of man to relish it. Can I tempt you to apply for a fellowship as well as your uncle?'

'No, thank you, sir.' But though he shook his head, Lindley smiled and his ears flushed even pinker. I thought he liked Mr Delingpole even if he was an Antiquity and not a scientist. 'I'm afraid your historical squabbles seem as petty to me as the religious ones my uncle must contend with. There is no real bottom to any of your studies. No firm ground of experiment. Where is the proof that Britain's history goes back to Troy, for instance? Have you ever found a wooden horse?'

He was being flippant, of course, but Mr Alnutt answered him with a quavering scholarly excitement. 'The proof is in the name, sir. *Britain* is named for *Brutus*, who fought at Troy and came here afterwards in search of refuge and a new kingdom. He defeated the giants who had inhabited these islands from the beginning of time, throwing them off the cliffs at *Gogmagog's Leap*, which is somewhere near Totnes, we believe. It is all minutely recorded in the chronicles, I assure you.'

Lindley looked unimpressed, only bulging his large, round eyes at the old man. 'And who wrote the chronicles?'

'The only learned men of their day, sir: the monks.'

'The same monks, I suppose, who thought thunderbolts were God's anger, when we now know them merely to be discharges of atmospheric electricity? Who thought God sent the rainbow, when we now know it to be an optical illusion created by the refraction of light through water droplets? And has anyone ever seen a giant?' Lindley was being discourteous, and I wished he would leave the poor old man and his monks in peace.

'We are about to do so, I fancy,' Mr Delingpole said soothingly, 'for Longshanks could not have been so named for nothing. But Mr Bell, you cannot expect *electricity* – is that the word you said? – to be a matter of research in the Society of Antiquaries. Mr Alnutt's scholarship is of a former, much less mathematical age.'

If this was meant to make Mr Alnutt feel better, it failed.

'Less mathematical?' he quavered irritably, now trembling more noticeably like a leaf in a moderate breeze. 'What then of biblical chronology? Will you call that nonsense, Mr Bell, when your great Sir Isaac Newton devoted as much time to it as he did to his little experiments with apples? That he identified the year of Christ's crucifixion as 34 AD, and that he endorsed Bishop Ussher's date for the world's creation to the very hour?'

'And what hour was that?' Lindley was still somewhat insolent, either not having noticed Mr Delingpole's attempts at diplomacy or else boyishly disregarding them.

'Twelve noon, on the 23 October 4004 BC.' The old man was triumphant. 'Is that mathematical enough for you?'

It certainly took the wind out of Lindley's sails for a minute, and he looked to Mr Delingpole for confirmation.

'It's true.' Mr Delingpole answered his look with another mild smile. 'The bishop made that very nice calculation and no one has since rejected it, not even Newton – who was, as Alnutt says, also a scholar of biblical chronology. He wished to bring his mathematical genius to bear on a matter which will be, after all, of far more enduring importance to mankind than your *electricity*.' As he spoke he was fishing in his waistcoat pocket. 'And I hope we shall presently have a mathematical number for Longshanks' height, too, for I have brought a measuring tape. Blake, are you finished your drawing?'

4

I WOULD NOW HAVE been extremely vexed to be banished. I shuffled closer to the tomb, tucking myself in behind Blake where Father could not see me. On closer inspection, the parcel that enclosed King Edward Longshanks' mortal remains was more in the way of a shawl than anything else, a shroud passing under the body and wrapped together at the front.

'Yes, this is certainly a gilded piece,' Mr Delingpole said as he carefully removed the crown from the shrouded head. 'There is a very thin layer of gold laid over what seems to be an iron base, since rust is breaking through the trefoils at the points.'

He began to peel one layer of the shroud delicately from the other. 'I see this outer fabric is waxed,' he said, 'but I imagine that is merely an extra precaution. I have read extensively on the subject of embalming, in anticipation of this opening, and I expect to find the body wrapped far more tightly than this, in waxed strips of linen. The wax excludes the air and allows the body within to dry and shrivel rather than decay.'

But when Mr Delingpole pulled the outer wrapping back, we saw that any embalming strips were still well out of sight, beneath a fine red satin tunic and cloak, and a sumptuous cloth of gold wrapped about the body's legs. The tunic was old and faded like the outer wrapping, but no wonder: the tailor who had sewn its fine seams had been in his grave near five hundred years like Edward himself. The face of the corpse was covered by a very ancient and perished waxed red cloth, which had settled onto the features like a kind of death mask but only faintly hinted at the man hidden beneath.

Mr Alnutt was now tearful with joy. 'Edward's coronation robes, do you see, gentlemen? See the priestly stole, crossed at his breast; and look, he carries the coronation insignia in his hands. Good Lord, Good Lord . . . who could have imagined . . . ?' And the old man staggered a little so that Mr Delingpole had to support him by the elbow to stop him sinking under the weight of his own emotion.

Mr Suckling pointed to the bands of the stole, crossed over the chest, which were glowing dully in the morning light, like the gilt crown. 'And are those pearls? Are those diamonds?'

'Glass and beads, I imagine,' Mr Delingpole answered. 'Even medieval kings had more sense than to bury diamonds and pearls along with their predecessors.'

'Yes, yes indeed, we see many such things elsewhere in the abbey,' Father said eagerly. He had been drawn into the excitement and had forgotten to be cross. 'You have perhaps seen our royal funeral effigies, sirs, which I am sorry to say Mr Walpole once humorously called the *ragged regiment*, being so very old and neglected. They, too, wear paste beads like these, and carry the same imitation investitures.' He was pointing to the body's hands, which were leathery and mud-coloured like old gloves. In the left was a rod, made of the same gilt as the crown, surmounted by a small and exquisite green enamel dove. In the right, was a gilded sceptre topped by a cross made up of three trefoils.

The mummy was indeed very like the members of our ragged regiment, being a kind of simulacrum of the living man. 'A remarkable sight,' Mr Delingpole was saying, carefully lifting the rod and dove out of Longshanks' hand and holding it to the light. 'This is not heavy iron, like the crown, but a much lighter gilt piece, and along with the crown and sceptre must be an exact copy of the Confessor's crown jewels, since Edward's father made a point of it in his will that his son should wear them at his coronation. More bolstering of their Saxon connections, as I said before. It is a pity no one knew these were here when they remade the jewels for the restoration of the Stuarts. They had to use the other sources we find in old paintings and with your ragged regiment, not to mention that ancient painting of Richard II on his throne which hangs by your quire, Dean. The craftsmen charged with recreating the lost jewels were very vexed to find scarcely two pictures of the sceptre alike. They had to employ a regrettable degree of artistic licence in their reconstruction.'

I knew what he meant about the variety of sceptres. There are several about the abbey, and all of them differ. One is a huge flamboyant leaf, another is a simple fleur-de-lis, while Queen Mary II's is a plain cross, and Elizabeth has something similar but with added balls. I didn't know what Mr Delingpole meant by *lost jewels*, however, and would have asked, only old Mr Alnutt had now seized the rusty crown and was jabbing it at Delingpole in some excitement.

'No, no, Delingpole, you are not quite right. Whatever we may think of the other things, this is not the Confessor's crown. All the sources agree that the Confessor's crown was composed of gold wires, rising to a cross at the crown. I believe there were precious stones about it and two little bells. This is a much plainer piece.'

'Curious,' Mr Delingpole replied. 'I wonder why he wears this one instead? Perhaps they ran out of money for a copy of the other.'

'Or Monsieur Alnutt may be mistaken,' the young Frenchman said, almost as discourteous as Lindley had been.

'Indeed I am not, sir.' Mr Alnutt was vexed and trembling again. 'I think I am the best Longshanks scholar among us, and if this crown reminds me of anything it is Llewellyn's, the Welsh prince whom Edward defeated. Edward took his crown as a symbol of his conquest of Wales and brought it to Westminster. Like everything else, it was later melted down by Cromwell, after he beheaded Charles I, to pay for his ruinous wars. But I can well imagine Edward Longshanks might wear a replica in memory of that Welsh campaign, for it was a victory far more complete than any he achieved in Scotland.'

'The Welsh are less puissant than the Scots,' Louis Durand remarked.

'Dear me,' Mr Delingpole laughed. 'Have a care, sir. You never know what fierce loyalties may lie hidden in our hearts, beating away beneath our respectable waistcoats.'

He glanced at Blake, who had all this time been sketching busily but now had put his pen behind his ear. 'And finally,' Mr Delingpole said, 'for the countenance of a medieval king. Mr Alnutt, sir, as our greatest authority, I think it only right that you should be the one to reveal Edward I's visage.'

We all fell back to allow Mr Delingpole to support Mr Alnutt's tottering steps to the king's head. The old man paused a moment, as if in prayer, and then reached out his own thin arm which in the dim light of the sanctuary looked quite as withered as the dead king's. His gaunt old fingers scrabbled at the cloth over the face and Mr Delingpole shifted uneasily, as if fearful the old man's awkwardness might do the precious corpse some harm. But then the cloth came away in Mr Alnutt's trembling hand and, in a reverent silence, we all gazed on the ancient king's long-dead face.

Edward Longshanks was as peaceful in death as the stone figures on their coffins all about us in the abbey chapels. But instead of their smooth marble, his face was the same leathery dark brown as his hands. His head was bald, though whether from old age or the ministrations of the embalmers I didn't know. His large eyes were closed as if in sleep. His firm, slightly down-turned mouth was solemn. His nose was rather big. It struck me that (apart from the ears and lack of hair) he would have looked rather like Lindley.

'Yes,' Mr Alnutt said, his hand dropping to his side still holding the cloth. 'This is just how I pictured him. A hard man. An implacable foe, certainly. But a fair man, nonetheless. They called him Hammer of the Scots and conqueror of the Welsh, but he did much else in his time. Made fast the rule of law in his kingdom. Strengthened Parliament. Taxed his people fairly. And all this is to be clearly seen in his face.'

Lindley tutted softly at such a sentiment but everyone else nodded, while I regretted that my own thoughts on noses and ears had been so trivial.

'And yet he did 'ammer the Scots,' Louis Durand said, gazing down at the face with a boyish frown. ''Orribly killed the Wallace. And stole their sacred stone of Scone, just as he stole Llewellyn's crown. *They* will not forget or forgive, I think, whatever Monsieur Alnutt may say about Longshanks' virtues.'

'You are from Brittany, I surmise, and feel for your Celtic brethren,' Mr Delingpole said with a smile. 'I thought there was a trace of something in your accent, sir.'

The Frenchman only shook his head at this, upon which Father sighed and, seeming to think the whole business now at an end, hoisted his belly over the lip of the tomb with some difficulty. He placed his small hand on Edward's shrunken one and began to recite the Lord's Prayer. Above us, in the triforium, I could hear the dull thud of a hammer – Fidoe back at work.

But Mr Delingpole was not to be hurried away so quickly. 'Just one more thing, Dean, if you'll oblige me,' he said, stopping Father before he had even got to *kingdom come*. 'We opened the coffin to answer the question of the body's embalming, you remember, and though we can all see from its remarkable preservation that the procedure was indeed carried out successfully, we really should peer beneath the robes to see exactly how it was done. The wax strips I mentioned.'

'Very well then, if you will be brief,' Father said, his

face clouding. 'And reverent. As reverent as you may be. I confess I can't see how you are to undress the body with any decorum.'

Neither could I. To disrobe this man-sized, leathery doll could hardly be achieved without a good deal of rumpling to its kingly dignity. But perhaps they would just turn up its sleeves and roll down its stockings to see. (If there were, indeed, any stockings beneath the gold cloth about the mummy's legs. And if there were not stockings, there might not be breeches neither. I can only describe my feelings on that prospect as mixed.)

'I suppose we must remove the rod and sceptre,' Mr Delingpole said. 'Then we can get at the body more easily.'

Father still had hold of Edward's hand, the dead fingers wrapped just as tightly round the gilded sceptre in death as, metaphorically speaking, they had no doubt clung to power in life. Father hesitated a moment, then set his lips and tugged at the thing gently, to ease it from the corpse's grasp. It was really rather horrible to see the dead fingers resist and then slacken, and for the first time I looked away.

'Can you manage, Dean?' Mr Delingpole was asking. He had picked up the rod topped by its lovely enamel dove for another admiring look.

'Yes, yes, it's just a trifle awkward, that's all,' Father answered, glancing up with a helpless gesture at his own predicament, being perched precariously on his toes with his belly wedged on the tomb's rim. The Frenchman threw down his hat and started forward to help him, but then all of a sudden there was the most almighty crash from the triforium gallery above us, and we all jumped out of our skins.

43

My first thought was that Fidoe had had some terrible accident (rotten floorboards, *&c.*), but it was even worse than that. We had no sooner looked up, than Fidoe appeared at the gallery's precipitous edge, an agitated figure in his workman's apron, waving his woollen cap to us in an agony of alarm.

'Get out, sirs; for God's sake, get out!' he shouted, in a voice made hoarse by panic. 'The whole roof's coming down!'

There was the merest moment's hesitation among the startled scholars, then a burst of activity. Mr Delingpole laid Edward's rod hastily back in the coffin and whisked Mr Alnutt off to the north door, which was the nearest exit to where we stood. Mr Quintrel and Mr Suckling hurried after them without a backwards glance at the poor abandoned king. Monsieur Durand took hold of Lindley and pulled him away with a hand on his arm. Blake thrust his sketches at Father, then held out his own hand to me. It was firm and square as he tugged me away. Fidoe called out another anxious warning and there was a second mighty crash from above.

Only Father did not follow the rest of us out into the daylight. Instead, like the brave captain of a sinking ship, I saw him open the narrow door in the corner beside Edmund Spenser's memorial, which leads to the winding staircase up to the triforium and its rotten floorboards. I called out to him to leave everything to Fidoe, but he did not hear me, or if he did he would not listen.

5

As we spilled out of the north door, the non-ecclesiastical world was going about its business on the pavement outside quite as usual, and it spared us not the slightest glance, nor the army of workmen rushing in past us, with scaffolding boards and poles. There is always incomprehensible activity of some kind or other going on at the abbey, and the world in general disregards our affairs just as it might the passing of the clouds over the sun.

The apprentice's cool, hard hand dropped mine as soon as we were out of doors, and with only the merest respectful salute of farewell he wandered away. Unfortunately, I found my fingers immediately enveloped again, this time in Mr Suckling's moist palms. His face was still spoon-like, but now lubricated by an anxious sheen of perspiration, as if the spoon had been held over the spout of a steaming kettle. 'My dear Miss Bell, are you injured? Are you hurt?'

'No,' I said, though it was no thanks to him, he having scuttled off to safety ahead of me. 'I am not injured, nor hurt, I thank you. Just rather startled.'

I tried to pull my hand away, but his grip only tightened. 'And no wonder, Miss Bell, no wonder! Dear me, it is almost like the judgement of heaven on our blasphemy, is it not? We should certainly never have opened the tomb. The dean should not have permitted it. Whatever was he thinking?'

At this, I managed to wrench my hand from his grasp. 'My father had no say in the matter, Mr Suckling. Did you not hear? They brought a letter of permission from the king.'

He saw I was vexed with him and changed tack directly. 'But you yourself are not injured, you say? You are not hurt? Nevertheless, let me take you directly to the Deanery.'

'I can take my cousin home,' Lindley said from behind me. He had grasped hold of my elbow before I even saw him come up. 'You had much better go rescue your gowns and trinkets, Suckling, before they are buried in a mound of rubble.'

The sacrist didn't much like that, but some of the Antiquities were coming up to join us, and he was obliged to be civil. Deprived of my company, he took the old man Alnutt's arm under his own instead, and led him away around the abbey towards the cloisters. 'All so fascinating,' I heard him say as they made their way at Mr Alnutt's painful pace. 'I wish you would tell me something more about those ancient monks.'

'Poor old fellow,' Mr Delingpole said, watching them go. 'I hope the sacrist sits him down and gives him a cup of tea. It is the culmination of many years' work for him, and as you can see he is quite overcome.'

I now remembered that I had been supposed to provide refreshments in Jerusalem instead of gawking at corpses, and we had all reaped the rewards of my disobedience with a general lack of sustaining nourishment to revive us after the shock. Let this be a lesson to ladies more inclined to do their duty than I am.

'You are all very welcome to come to the Deanery for tea and cake,' I said to make amends, but Monsieur Durand shook his head, pleading another engagement, while his friend Quintrel had already disappeared. Mr Delingpole said he was eager to discover the cause of the accident to the roof but would join us presently. As a consequence, Lindley and I set off for home alone, in the same direction Mr Suckling and Mr Alnutt had just taken.

They were already gone into the cloisters when we came up to the dark archway that leads to the Deanery, tucked away in its little court and private garden behind an iron chain guarded by George Slemaker, the porter. Lindley had dropped my elbow as we went, for which I was grateful. There had been altogether too much grasping and squeezing in the past few minutes for my taste (though I must say I had rather enjoyed holding the apprentice engraver's hand).

'Well, that was a surprisingly entertaining episode,' Lindley said. 'How did you like your first corpse, cousin?'

'It was not my first,' I said, for a woman can hardly live to my age without seeing several dead bodies, often very dear to her.

To do him justice, Lindley looked sorry, probably remembering my mother. 'Uncle much enjoyed it in the end, whatever his first doubts.'

'Of course he did.' I nodded a greeting to George Slemaker as we passed into the Deanery yard. 'You know he is enchanted by the abbey's tombs and has been looking for James I under the Lady Chapel floor for weeks. It was only the unexpected intrusion he did not like, and the disruption to the abbey this week before Holy Thursday.' I had momentarily forgotten those coming celebrations. 'Lord, and now with the roof all falling down—'

'Oh, that can hardly signify,' Lindley said as we came to the Deanery door.

'Hardly signify? I assure you that it will be a terrible vexation to Father if he is obliged to mend the whole roof before Thursday.'

'If the *whole roof* really came down, the repairs would outlast both our little lifetimes, cousin.' This was hardly very comforting. 'But Fidoe was only talking of the ambulatory ceiling where he was standing,' Lindley added. 'He probably put his foot through the floorboards, which your father said were rotten. Of course he was frightened – I shouldn't fancy to have been in his shoes, thinking the whole floor was giving way beneath him above a drop of fifty feet. But *we* were never really in danger. Even if the ambulatory ceiling had collapsed, we should only have been enveloped in a cloud of dust from the falling rubble smashing off the paving.'

'And Fidoe smashing off the paving, too.'

We eyed each other sidelong a moment as I took off my bonnet, and to my inner gratification he grinned. I don't know why it was funny, but it was, and it took an effort to keep myself rigidly proper and shake my head at him. 'Hardly a matter for amusement, Mr Bell.'

'Ah – the spinster aunt returns,' he said. 'I thought she had gone missing, for *she* would never peer at old corpses with such obvious delectation. But she cannot be banished for ever, it seems.'

'Lindley, I have no brothers or sisters and therefore I never can be anyone's aunt.'

We were coming into the parlour again and Cuthbert perked up at our entrance. His apple was shredded all over the floor but he had not picked it up. He was rarely left alone so long, and he had probably been moping.

Bonjour, Mrs Bell, he said now, turning a circle on his perch and nodding his head vigorously. Cuthbert still waited vainly for Mother's return, and persisted in pretending I was her.

'No, Cuthbert. I am Susan, remember.'

'It must be your aged face that makes him think so. The lines of so many years.'

I couldn't help glancing in the mirror over the mantelpiece as Cuthbert squawked rudely and then exclaimed in a voice that was plainly Lindley's, *Good God preserve us!*

I looked accusingly at Lindley, but he only escaped laughing, taking his exhilarating tome on coalmines with him.

'You are very bad,' I told Cuthbert, scratching his head, after my cousin was gone. 'Mother would not have liked to hear such oaths, and Father will be upset. Lindley is a rascal to teach you such things.'

The bird looked despondent at my reproving tone and took himself off to his cage, where he sat with his back turned to me and my sewing, muttering, *Good God preserve us!* rebelliously under his breath, at intervals, until the maid came in and announced the arrival of a visitor.

6

IT WAS MR DELINGPOLE who came in, looking very capable. I confess I am not familiar with men such as these, for they do not gravitate naturally to a clerical career.

'I spoke to the workmen,' he said, as he sat down. 'It seems they had dislodged a keystone in the vaulted arch above the ambulatory, and a keystone being, as you might say, *key*, your clerk of works feared a catastrophe. But it turned out it was only loosened, not completely out of place, and the men are propping it up with a scaffold and resetting it with mortar. By tomorrow the roof will be quite safe again, they tell me.'

'Thank goodness.' I had rung for tea, and when the maid came in I bid her tell Lindley that Mr Delingpole was here. Mr Delingpole was smiling at me easily, like a father or an uncle, and I suppose he is technically old enough to be either, but he is still very young looking – very *good* looking – and even if he was oblivious to our being alone together, I found I wasn't. Until I am thirty and positively past all hope, all gentlemen that come across my path must be viewed in some wise in the nature of potential husbands. It cannot be helped. A man chooses a career, and with it a way of life. And just so does a woman when she takes a husband. The only difference is that she cannot absolutely seek one out but must wait for the said career and way of life to present itself to her – if it wishes.

In fact, I didn't know anything about Mr Delingpole at all, except that he gave off an atmosphere of kindliness, and that I liked his smile almost as much as Blake the engraver's. I didn't even know if he was married or single.

'You are at leisure from your business on a Saturday morning?' I asked, in an attempt to find out that I hoped wasn't too flagrant.

'I can be, when I choose,' he said as the tea and scones came in and I busied myself pouring the one and buttering the other, glad of an occupation. 'I live in chambers, so if I am at home, clients may always find me.'

In chambers! That certainly meant a single man, and being the wife of a successful lawyer in London had its attractions. One would go about and dine with the cleverest minds in town.

I stole another glance at him as I handed him the cup and saucer. I had thought him forty, but perhaps he was only thirty-five and, having been busy establishing himself in his profession, might be just beginning to think of marriage as a possibility. Such are the different ways the world dictates the paths of men and women, unless, like Lindley, they are born to money and can do just as they like.

'And you escape your clients by going to the Society of Antiquities meetings?' I asked him.

'*Antiquaries*, Miss Bell, yes, among other things.' He smiled at me again. 'Many things interest me, and I also have a sympathy with your cousin's scientific bent. I am a Fellow of the Royal Society, too, and have recently written a paper on the likelihood of man ever reaching the North Pole.'

'And will he?'

'At my urging, one expedition has already been attempted. Regrettably it ended in failure, but I have collated as many accounts of the region and former attempts as possible, which I hope will be of use to the next one. There is talk of a man named Cook making another attempt in a year or two. He has sailed extensively in the southern oceans and recently claimed a large land mass there for the Crown.'

I was a trifle awestruck at this sudden display of large ambitions. 'Do you mean to go with him?'

'No, no, I could not leave my chambers; and besides, I fear I would be of no practical use, being a man who thinks rather than acts.'

Cuthbert had been eyeing Mr Delingpole for some minutes, shuffling up and down his perch and bending double to examine the visitor from all angles, a performance to which Mr Delingpole had until now been oblivious. W*here's my coat?* Cuthbert now enquired in Father's voice, perhaps prompted by the mention of the North Pole. *Chilly for June.*

Mr Delingpole turned his head to look at Cuthbert, and Cuthbert scratched his own head affably, in a friendly gesture. *Here's a nut.*

'Your bird speaks,' he said, looking back at me.

'I'm afraid sometimes only too well.' (Which Cuthbert confirmed by exclaiming *Good God preserve us!* with much emphasis.)

'A male bird, I suppose?' At my nod Mr Delingpole looked pleased. 'I have also written extensively on birdsong and find that a female bird is far less musical, and far less prone to learn new songs.' He smiled gallantly. 'Which is not the same among human ladies, I know, whose musical accomplishments are always so remarkable.'

'Only the result of long study,' I said. 'And in that way no more remarkable than your fluency in Greek and Latin.'

He bowed his head. 'Quite so. Application is everything, of course. And this is what I found by experimentation. The songbird learns just as a human infant does, from hesitant beginnings to confident fluency within the space of a year. And if separated from birds of its own species, it will learn the songs of its new companions instead, just as your parrot learns your language.'

'Your interests are very wide,' I said, not sure whether I liked the dispassionate tone in which he spoke of birds in general and Cuthbert in particular. But it was only the same kind of scientific curiosity Lindley showed about everything and I could hardly call it reprehensible. I suppose a lawyer must also be a cool observer of facts and, in its place, such detachment will undoubtedly be useful.

At this juncture Lindley himself came in, sat down with a nod to Mr Delingpole, and poured himself a cup of tea before I could do it for him. 'Well, sir? Did you find out anything?'

Mr Delingpole conveyed the same information he had already given me: that Fidoe had feared the roof would fall but the workmen had managed to patch it up.

'A very interesting morning,' Lindley said, before stuffing a scone whole into his mouth, upon which Mr Delingpole politely relieved him of the necessity of further talk by making some observations about the excellent preservation of Longshanks' body.

'Mr Suckling – our sacrist – told me he feared the roof the judgement of heaven at our disturbing the tomb,' I said, when Mr Delingpole had concluded all his interesting remarks.

At this, he waved a polite, deprecating hand, but Lindley snorted. (Luckily he had by now swallowed his scone or the consequences would have been messy.) 'Suckling is a spy,' he said, 'and a most unpleasant greasy one at that.'

'A spy?' Mr Delingpole raised an eyebrow. 'A spy for whom?'

'The archbishop, though I dare say the great man doesn't thank him for it. Suckling has appointed himself in the role and doubtless rewards himself too, with self-praise even if not with preferment.'

I was astonished that Lindley had noticed so much, and that he had formed so accurate a judgement of the sacrist on such a short acquaintance. 'I told him it was the king's orders,' I said, 'and upon that he was obliged to be quiet, of course.'

Mr Delingpole emptied his cup and refused my offer of another. 'His Majesty meant to attend the opening himself, but unfortunately he was detained by other duties. He is very interested, of course, it being the tomb of a fellow monarch.'

'And what now?' Lindley asked as Mr Delingpole got to his feet. 'Are your enquiries over?'

'I think so. We saw almost everything we desired to see and have the valuable drawings Basire's apprentice made.

It was a pity we did not see the wax strips and I did not measure the length of the body as I meant to, but on the whole it was a remarkable morning and time very well spent. Thank your father for us, Miss Bell, and remind him he is always welcome at our meetings.' He took up his hat. 'By the by, I was very interested by the dean's mention of your funeral effigies. What was the droll name he gave them? The ragged regiment? I might look at them on my way out, if you will point me in the right direction.'

'I will show you myself,' I said, 'if you are quite sure the abbey roof will not fall upon our heads.'

7

Bishop islip's chapel is a very grand affair, being built over two storeys like a small house, under the abbey's vaulted heavens. It is here that the ragged regiment reside, stuffed in a cupboard – which is perhaps as well in their present state of repair but seems an undignified way for kings and queens to end their days.

Mr Delingpole, Lindley and I climbed the stairs to the chapel's upper chamber, where I opened the cupboard doors under the watchful stone eyes of Christopher and Alice Hatton, who sit on their tomb, heads together but not looking at each other. He has one leg casually crossed over the other knee. She has her eyes half-closed, as if wearied of his conversation.

As the cupboard door opened the regiment fell upon us like an ambuscade: tumbling out all ways and – being made mostly of solid timber – apparently bent on knocking us all insensible. 'Good Lord,' Lindley said, throwing up his arm against this woody onslaught. Then, on a second inspection of our assailants, he said, 'Good Lord,' again, but this time in a mingled tone of pity and horror. They are indeed a very strange set of creatures and some of them, to my mind, rather too uncanny.

'The old custom was to carry the effigy of the departed monarch alongside their coffin to the altar for the funeral service,' Mr Delingpole was explaining to Lindley as if he already knew all about it.

'Whereafter, the effigy hung about, beside its tomb, for a very extended period,' I added, feeling rather possessive of the story and not wishing to have my thunder stolen, 'until, I suppose, they began to look rakish and disreputable instead of royal and serene.'

The oldest effigies have lost all their clothes over the course of five hundred years. These medieval specimens are like naked, man-sized peg dolls, their bodies stiff as ramrods and their faces primitive carvings into wood which are, frankly, rather sinister.

Mary I, Elizabeth's older sister, is also a simple effigy of this kind, but with a red dress painted on her rudimentary body. ('Bloody Mary,' Mr Delingpole observed with a shake of his head as he looked on her. I confess the connection had hitherto escaped me, and I nodded my appreciation of his insight.)

'Poor James I – as well as being missing from the abbey and consequently the subject of Father's present excavations – has lost his head,' I said. 'And that seems rather like a prophecy of what befell his son. But to my mind, Henry VII is the worst of all, since his face is not wood but a plaster cast of his real, dead face, with every line and wrinkle. It looks far too real and makes me shudder.'

Lindley had glanced over the medieval peg dolls with Delingpole, but now turned his attention to the more recent and elaborate effigies, which still possess their costumes and their jewels. Queen Elizabeth's body is in a bad way, but it wears a full set of clothes, down to a very decayed corset. She also has a crown, an orb and the sceptre I have previously mentioned with its balls. At present, crown, orb and sceptre were tumbled into a corner of the cupboard unaccountably mixed up with those belonging to Queen Anne and our Orange monarchs William and Mary.

'The visitors are really disgraceful,' I said, burying myself in the cupboard to extract the various crown jewels from the muddle. 'But they always have been. The vergers tell a story that Samuel Pepys was very pleased with himself for kissing the lips of a shrivelled old body that lay about the abbey in his time.'

Lindley took Mary II's sceptre from me and turned it to the light.

'You see, it is different to Elizabeth's,' I said, 'not having balls.'

Lindley smiled mysteriously. 'Perhaps Orange Mary didn't need them, being in possession of a male fellow-monarch to provide those articles instead.'

Mr Delingpole frowned at him and returned to my former words. 'A shrivelled old body lying about the place?'

'Some lady's body which lay about the abbey for years, according to the vergers, never happening to be decently buried.' I saw their puzzled faces. 'No, I don't recall the exact details, but I am pretty certain they were unedifying.' I gestured to the tumbled mess of effigies at our feet. 'And from the state of everything here today, we must have had a party of visiting ladies and gentlemen trying on the crowns and braying at each other like fools, just like Pepys.'

Lindley immediately stuck the largest of the three crowns on his head and struck a regal pose.

'That is William of Orange's crown,' I said, as I examined my cousin's large eyes, his firm, slightly down-turned mouth and long nose. Again, I was struck by his resemblance to Longshanks. The crown made the resemblance even more striking, though it was entirely different to the mummy's plain gold one. It was padded with red velvet and richly jewelled gold wires rose to an equally rich jewelled cross.

'You see, it is just as Mr Alnutt described,' I said, plucking it from his head to show them. 'And so are both the others. See, this one belongs to Mary II and Elizabeth has yet another.' I dived into the cupboard again, while Lindley reunited the Orange crowns with their true owners' heads. I re-emerged with Elizabeth's crown, feeling rather dusty. 'They must all be copies of the Confessor's crown, as Mr Alnutt said.'

'And this lady?' Mr Delingpole was admiring a very gorgeous wax lady in a rich brocade dress. 'She wears a miniature crown of the same design.'

'That is the Duchess of Buckingham. She was James II's natural daughter, the vergers tell the visitors, and insisted on being treated as if she were true royalty both in life and in death.'

Mr Delingpole now dragged out the final effigy: the lady's husband, apparently peacefully asleep. He has a gilt rod clasped in his hands so long it reaches his feet. He wears a brown curled wig and is rather handsome, in a sentimental way that, on the whole, seems better suited to the name *Lindley* than Lindley himself is.

Mr Delingpole examined the gentleman's recumbent form as my cousin began to return the other effigies to the cupboard one by one, until all were in except for Charles II, who is really the most splendid of them all, even if he doesn't possess any jewels. He is remarkably tall and dressed in magnificent scarlet robes and silver breeches. His dark brown curls cascade halfway to his waist, and he wears the most splendid hat, very dashing and wide-brimmed with (according to the vergers) ostrich and heron feathers sprouting up from it in a great plume.

In fact, it was the effigies that had brought on Mr Suckling's unfortunate interest in me. I happened to mention their crowns and sceptres to him one day, he being professionally concerned with the abbey's precious objects. He told me they were only inferior gilt copies, but when I said I had a fancy to restore the poor creatures' costumes to their former glory, he began to look at me in a new light.

I have not yet done anything about it. Queen Elizabeth's fine old corset will need to wait for a day I can consult the staymaker, since the apparatus of bones and padding are too scientific a matter for me to tackle alone. But when Lindley passed me Charles's feathered hat, I saw that the moths had apparently found it irresistible, and the lovely velvet was a mass of tiny holes from their little champing teeth. Mending innumerable small holes with invisible stitches is exactly the kind of thing I like, and, moreover, well within my powers. I tucked the hat under my arm while Lindley carefully stowed Charles II in the cupboard and closed the door.

'Remarkable,' Lindley said. 'So now we know what the Confessor's crown looked like and Alnutt was right, it was certainly a world away from the plain one Longshanks wore.'

'And you see I was also right about the sceptres,' Mr Delingpole said, as we descended the stairs to Bishop Islip's ground floor. 'They are all different and, as I told you, were a terrible puzzle to the jewellers charged with recreating one for Charles II's coronation. Elizabeth's an ornate cross decorated with golden rounds, and Mary of Orange's as plain as could be.'

'And her husband's only a kind of scribble,' I said, 'rather like Richard II's, in his picture by the quire. Richard's sceptre has a leaf on top: a leaf that was never seen in any of God's creation, I am quite sure.'

Mr Delingpole wasn't listening, still thinking about Charles II's restoration. 'In the end Charles II's jewellers settled on a sceptre with a small, diamond-encrusted cross above a twisted golden shaft, very much more ornate than these models.' He cast a look at the plume of feathers protruding from under my arm. 'But then, as we have just seen, Charles II was a very ornate man himself.'

As we came out of the chapel, back into the body of the abbey, Lindley turned to the Antiquity. 'I am just returned from Europe with some interesting philosophical machines,' he said. 'I mean to demonstrate them to the whole Chapter at half past seven o'clock tonight, in the Jerusalem Chamber. If you'd like to come, you'd be very welcome.'

'I should be delighted.' Mr Delingpole then looked at me, with what I rather hoped was, despite his tendency to hog the conversation, pleasure at the prospect of a deeper acquaintance. 'Will you be there, Miss Bell? Are you also a lover of science like your cousin?'

'I know too little about it to say,' I answered. 'And unfortunately I am to learn no more of it, since I am called upon to entertain the Chapter's ladies.'

'A clever, sensible man,' Lindley said, as we watched Mr Delingpole stride away. 'There are not many such in London.'

'As ever, cousin, you show great humility in recognising it.'

He looked at me a minute before he took my meaning and shrugged. I suppose Lindley is clever, if not sensible, but I was a little vexed that he had not joined Mr Delingpole in regretting my forthcoming absence from his stupid little show.

8

AFTER THAT I SETTLED to darning Charles's hat, until Cuthbert's cry of *Here's the dean!* greeted the return of Father later in the afternoon, looking very tired and rather grimy. I gave up my seat to him by the fire (the Deanery being shockingly old and damp we must endure the dust and smog well into summer or else be rheumatic) and fetched him a glass of sherry. It is something he much enjoys before dinner, and seemed more than usually in need of now.

He gave Cuthbert a nut from the pocket of his cassock before sitting down. 'Dear me, Susan,' he said as he took the glass from me. 'I am quite worn out, my dear.'

'I gather the roof is not much damaged after all.'

'No, no.' He sipped the sherry and patted my hand where I knelt by his chair. 'All is well in that regard at least.'

'How did it happen? Did Fidoe put his foot through the rotten boards?'

'Perhaps he did.' Father frowned. 'I didn't ask. At any rate,' he brightened, 'we spent the whole afternoon up in the triforium, which turns out to be a remarkable place.'

'*You* were up in the triforium? I thought only Fidoe was allowed up there?'

Father smiled at me tolerantly. 'As I am the one who allows and disallows all things in the abbey, my dear, I think I was entitled to permit myself to go.'

'But it is so dangerous. You said so.' (Though if Lindley and I had thought Fidoe would smash off the paving, Father was frankly more likely to bounce.)

'It is certainly very disagreeable. The staircase alone is treacherous and the triforium itself shockingly dusty.' He looked at his grimy hands. 'I should really go and wash.' But in truth he did not seem too much disgusted with the dirt and dust. Instead, an excitement I knew of old had kindled in his beady eye. 'We could do so much up there, my dear. There are any number of rotten beams, quite besides the dreadful floor. Any custodian of the abbey worth his salt would have it all torn out and replaced at once.'

Yes, it was the waking of his usual destructive enthusiasm, which I suppose is a mark of commendable protestant zeal on his part, and which Fidoe takes it upon himself to temper with his own far greater veneration for antiquity. If Father had his way, the abbey would be stripped down to its shell, and all within new made. Fidoe has saved much, but he was not able to stop Father ripping out the old choir stalls (*quite four hundred years old, my dear, and worm-eaten right through*), replacing them with some very handsome but, to my eyes, soulless modern mahogany. It is very good of Fidoe to follow after him and curb his excesses, for Father often keeps him back at the abbey after all the other workmen have gone home. But Fidoe has a large family, and the extra pay is probably useful.

66

As the maid brought in the dinner, Father's thoughts turned to the coming service on Holy Thursday, and the installation of the new lamps in the triforium, to be lit at the moment of Christ's ascension into heaven. From what Father had told Mr Delingpole about the rubbish of ages, I feared a naked flame up there might lead to a grander blaze than either of them intended, but I hadn't the heart to dampen Father's spirits. In any event, he was soon absorbed in recounting the details of a disagreement between Mr Suckling and Mr Lamb, the abbey chanter, as to the order of the music. 'It is really none of the sacrist's affair, you know. He is a shocking busybody, but I suppose we must put up with him. After all, God knows best.'

'And what about Longshanks' tomb?' I asked. 'Did the workmen put back the lid?' He blinked his little robin's eyes at me, still apparently thinking only of his lamps and music. 'You are preposterous, Father. How can Edward's mummy have slipped your mind already?'

He smiled, quite as amused by his own foibles as I could be, and in all fairness there had been so much for him to do since then, while I had been quietly sewing (and interviewing husbands) in the parlour. 'Oh, of course, of course,' he said. 'And, as it turned out, the opening of the tomb was a truly splendid episode. A pity you were not there, my dear.'

I said nothing to *that*, only pointed to the small parcel beside his plate. 'But, see, I have not yet wished you a happy birthday, Father.'

'My birthday?' Again, astonishment, perplexity and then, finally, the expected delight. 'Is it really today? And how happy a day I have had, to be sure!'

'Apart from the nuisance of the Antiquities' visit and the falling roof.'

'Nonsense,' he answered, with a good imitation of Lindley's earlier tone on the subject. 'It all turned out to be something or nothing in the end.' His stubby fingers were busy at the string that tied the parcel closed. 'And this is really your gift to me, my dear?'

'Yes.' I watched as the paper came off to reveal a silver pocket-watch. Father's old brass one had stopped working a year past Christmas, a fact which had made him rather erratic in his timekeeping. Long-saved *filthy lucre* of my own being involved in the purchase had made the whole thing even more satisfactory to my mind.

He kissed me. 'Thank you, my dear. Now I shall never be late for dinner again. How well you know your old father.'

Thank you, my dear; thank you, Mrs Bell, Cuthbert echoed from his perch, where he was still busily peeling the cobnut Father had given him.

'I wish I could say the same for Cuthbert,' I said. 'I tell him I am Susan every day, but I'm afraid he persists in calling Mother's name. I'm sorry if it pains you.'

'I would never wish to forget your mother. How could I?' Nevertheless, Father looked wistful. 'But have you noticed how well he mimics the voice which taught him the words? Sometimes, when he greets me with *Here's the dean,* it is your mother's voice to the very life.'

This is quite true, and how I had detected Lindley's hand in Cuthbert's new oath. Nor can any of us creep into the parlour without Cuthbert crying out a joyful greeting. The bird shares everything he sees, and he speaks in the voice of everyone he hears. It is lucky we none of us in the Deanery have any secrets.

'I wonder where Lindley can have got to?' I said, the bird having reminded me of my cousin again. 'I suppose it is just more of his usual incivility to miss dinner.'

'No, no, I met him just now, coming in. He is arranging his scientific apparatus in Jerusalem for the demonstration tonight and has asked the cook to send him bread and cheese while he works.'

'I wish you would ask him to invite us ladies too, instead of banishing us to our knitting. He told me the queen once saw such a demonstration, and it has not harmed her feminine accomplishments.' (In fact, having produced nine living children in eleven years she can scarcely have been more accommodating in that regard.)

But before Father could answer, a verger came in, announcing the unexpected arrival of Dame Elizabeth Yates in the nave, requiring an audience with the dean as soon as might be convenient – which, in other words, meant as soon as he had stuffed down the rest of his dinner.

'She is a very demanding woman,' I said, watching him dab his mouth. 'I wonder she doesn't remember other folks have lives of their own to lead.'

'Not *demanding*,' Father objected. 'Merely eager that her husband's costly memorial is to her liking.'

'I wish she would employ an architect to see to it and leave us be.'

'She is lonely,' Father said. 'Her children are grown, like you are, Susan, and her house is very empty. It pleases her to watch over the progress of the works. It gives her an occupation. I confess I should be very lonely if you married and I did not have my duties here to fill in my days.'

'But I am not married, and you do have your duties,' I said firmly. 'Not to mention Cuthbert. *You* have no need to look for other companionship.'

Father didn't answer, only put down his napkin and hurried off through the cloisters to find the dreaded woman, as if he positively enjoyed her company.

9

THE DAME IS, at any rate, dreaded to me. She is a square woman with a square face and a very square conviction that her late husband was the greatest jewel to ever walk the earth, Jesus Christ probably not excepted. This would be an amiable and wifely partiality, if I did not suspect she was beginning to think the same about Father, which – though of course perfectly true in his case – was in danger of bringing many inconveniences in its train.

When we reached the apse, we found her examining the half-built monument to her husband. Fidoe was conferring quietly with the mason, just now carving the inscription on the stone casket housing Sir Joseph's imaginary bones (I think his actual body has gone to rest in Cheam, a village in Surrey).

The memorial is being built here, in pride of place, between the Confessor's shrine where we had spent the morning and the steps up to Henry VII's Lady Chapel, flanked by the tombs of medieval kings, who all desire to nestle close to the saint. How the dame has got her husband into such a favoured spot I am not sure, except that, as she never omits to remind us, she has given a lot of money to the abbey and expects a good return on her investment.

'The mason needs to sharpen his chisel,' she said, planting herself closer to the work in progress and raising her eye-glasses to her face. 'There is a definite chip on the letter J.'

'Beg yer pardon, ma'am.' Though the mason touched his knuckles deferentially to his forehead, he nevertheless spoke with some dogged meaning. 'A man can only work with what he's given.'

'Indeed!' Dame Yates straightened and fixed the man with a glare. She has reached that time of life where a woman (and especially a square one) begins to resemble a tortoise. 'I think you have been given the very best, my man. But perhaps your talents only extend to straight lines and you are defeated by the shapely and elegant name you have been given to carve.'

Father was watching Dame Yates, his brow once more furrowed into its habitual anxious lines. Mr Suckling had arrived among us again and was naturally smirking at this new unpleasantness.

'My dear Dame Yates,' Father said in his most appeasing tone, 'we will, of course, make sure that the inscription is to your liking by the time it is finished. The whole composition is really very fine, and with only a little more carving and the gilding of the inkpot, it will all be complete in good time and entirely to your satisfaction, I promise.'

Dame Yates seemed somewhat mollified by these earnest protestations. She looked with a little more complacency at the legal paraphernalia depicted on the tomb and then took Father's arm, leaning on him so heavily that his small, spherical body was in danger of becoming, like the world, somewhat flattened at the poles. (I wonder if Mr Delingpole would be impressed at my knowledge of the Arctic and Antarctic regions? My governess did teach me *something* other than the pianoforte, and I shall endeavour to display the fact to him next time we meet.)

It has occurred to me more than once that the dame's frequent visits to the abbey, and her endless harping on the vast sum she has spent on the memorial, are all contrived to impress Father with the extent of her fortune and persuade him to make her an offer. Being entirely reliant on his dean's stipend (a figure scarcely grander than my putative greengrocer's income, I fear, though of course he has the Deanery and all the comforts of its staff *gratis*), marriage to a wealthy woman presents the only certain possibility for Father to enjoy a comfortable retirement. Not that a marriage to Dame Yates would be so very comfortable, *I* think, or that she would likely allow him to retire. She is a very managing woman, and an abbey would be a delightful thing to manage after all.

'You are very kind, my dear Dean,' she was saying, 'but to my eye there is still something missing from the thing. I have pondered on it. Indeed, I have scarcely slept, the form and composition always preying on my inward eye. But last night the answer finally came to me – what was missing – and to think, it had been curled up on the counterpane beside me all this time!'

Father was a little slow. 'I don't quite—'

'Atop the monument,' she interrupted him, 'as if standing

guard. I have seen something similar in Cheam, on the Lumley tomb – in that case a solid silver horse. But Sir Joseph did not care much for riding, while he was very attached to Admiral, his most faithful and – next to myself – his most beloved companion.'

'A bird?' Father ventured, thinking perhaps of our own beloved Cuthbert.

'A bird? What a horrible notion. Nasty, feathered things.' At Father's continuing blank look she waxed impatient. 'Why, Dean, I mean his dog, of course! Are there not scores of dogs in the abbey? I know I have seen half a dozen lying asleep at their masters' feet.'

Once he understood her, Father looked extremely relieved. 'Why, yes, dear Dame Yates, yes of course. I am sure such a thing can be arranged. If you have a drawing made of the dog, the mason will be only too glad to carve it.'

'I'll need better stone,' the mason said briefly, from where he now seemed to be wrestling with the curves of the letter S.

'Stone! By no means.' Dame Yates clung even more tightly to Father's arm and looked as transported and spiritual as a square woman who much resembles a tortoise can reasonably do. 'My dear Dean, I am quite certain there must be money left enough for something far more splendid. Far more splendid than the Lumleys' silver horse. My dear, dear Dean, it must be gold; it must indeed.'

'Gold leaf, like the inkpot?' Father replied. 'Yes, certainly, that can be done.'

'No, no.' Dame Yates flushed a patchy purple in her extreme excitement. 'Not mere stone or wood, Dean, with

74

only a coat of paint upon it! *That* is the kind of thing the Lumleys have done in Cheam with their hideous green parrots.' She looked pitying. 'I dare say the Lumleys could not stretch to silver for everything. No, no, my dear sir, I desire real gold. *Solid* gold. I have spoken to my man of business about it this afternoon, and he tells me that gold is to be had at hardly more than four guineas an ounce. The most glorious statue cannot therefore amount to more than a thousand guineas; and what less could Sir Joseph possibly deserve?'

She evidently felt the burden of the Lumleys' supremacy in Cheam, whoever they were. (I must say, I liked them already for having parrots which, I am sure, are not hideous at all. Yet more evidence of the dame's entire unsuitability for our establishment.) But as there are so many such follies scattered about the abbey, Father could hardly object to one more. He looked a little harassed nonetheless – I like to think he was inwardly longing for the monument to be finished and her pestering at an end, whatever he might charitably say about her loneliness. (I wonder if he is as afraid of her intentions as I am? I hope so. He is exactly the sort of man to be hurried into something against his better judgement, and this is, of course, the source of my aforementioned dread. Growing into an old spinster, alone with Dame Yates as a stepmother after Father's *unhappy, &c.*, death, is a prospect far too horrid to contemplate. Especially now I discover she harbours a previously unsuspected antipathy to birds in general, and parrots in particular.)

Fortunately, Fidoe knows just how to smooth over such matters, and invited Dame Yates to expand further on her idea. With a brief, conspiratorial nod to Father, he led her around the monument, so that she could show him exactly where her nocturnal visions had placed the dog. He must have said something to amuse her, for she cackled a laugh as Father, Mr Suckling and I thankfully made our escape.

'How are the preparations for Thursday coming along?' Father asked the sacrist as we came into the south transept and paused by the Chapel of St Faith where the sacrist keeps most of the vestments and chalices.

'All in order, Dean. All the vestments are pressed and the silver polished.'

'Still, I'll come with you now,' Father said. 'It will put my mind at rest to see for myself that the preparations are in hand, and I think we must also bring up some items from the dark vestry.'

'As you wish.' Mr Suckling did not show any particular resentment at Father's interference – instead, he had turned his eye on me with that special leer of his. 'If Miss Bell was to accompany us, she might attend to one little matter for me: a very small tear in your cope, Dean, where doubtless you stepped on the hem.'

The abbey's copes are really too big for Father, and over time will be taken up by some tailor far more expert in the matter than I am. Moreover, Mr Suckling can sew a small tear himself, if he chooses, so I took this invitation, along with the leer, as more disturbing desire for my company on his part.

I do not much like the Chapel of St Faith either. It is a narrow afterthought of a room, with a sloping ceiling and looming wooden cupboards that look like doorways to hell in the dismal gloom. Only the dark vestry is worse: the crypt under the Chapter House where the most valuable things are kept in utter blackness.

I was opening my mouth to make some excuse, but Father saved me the trouble. 'I am sure my daughter would be delighted to oblige you, Sacrist, but it cannot be now. She has promised to entertain the abbey ladies this evening while we gentlemen amuse ourselves, and I believe she is wanted in the kitchen, to consult with the cook.'

It was a poor excuse, since I never consult the cook about anything, the Deanery having run in the same groove for fifty years and not likely to change on my account. But it was probably the best Father could manage on the spur of the moment and Mr Suckling could hardly argue.

Instead of going to the kitchen and the cook, I went directly to the library in the East Cloister and climbed the stairs to the musty old room with its shelves on shelves of ancient books. I always think it very likely that I am its only visitor, since the subject matter of the volumes is eccentric in its variety. The last Dean left his own personal collection to the place and, as he was a man very interested in French grammar, there is a positive swathe of books on the topic which no rational person could possibly wish to read.

I was, at present, in search of something that might shed light on the likely nature of Lindley's coming demonstration. I had little hope of success among our rather ancient collection, but at length I found one volume on Isaac Newton, written about thirty years ago, with a preface that informed me Newton *censured handling geometric subjects by algebraic calculations* and *considered the term geometry injudicious.*

I flicked through the very long and very dull poem to Sir Isaac's memory which followed, until I came to the table of contents. This was, if possible, even worse. If Lindley was to demonstrate the *perpendicular, oblique* or *curvilinear descent of bodies* I for one was not minded to watch. Nor did I think myself equipped to consider the movement of the planets, or to have much interest in the *refraction, reflection* or *inflection of light*. The only intelligible subject was something about rainbows, but as these were unlikely to appear at Lindley's command (whether *optical illusions* or not), I closed the book and put it back on the shelf.

Before I left the pleasant peace of the library I went up to the Muniments Gallery. It looks down on to the south transept, which the vergers like to call Poets' Corner for the benefit of their paying visitors. Being a pigeon, I very much enjoy this little eyrie of my own, halfway between the abbey floor and Fidoe's triforium above. Here I can roost and examine the passers-by below, oblivious of my watching gaze. Today I could hear the scrape of scaffold poles and the workmen in the north ambulatory shouting to each other about the damaged roof. Mr Lamb, the fussy little chanter, was hastening across the paving towards the quire, and an ugly white cat was slinking out from behind a tapestry at the altar unobserved.

As I crossed the Deanery yard, Lindley poked his owlish head out of the door at the top of the flight of outside steps that lead up to Jerusalem. He seemed to have ink all over his hands and an ink smudge on his beaky nose.

'Can you ask the cook for another plate of something?' he called out. 'I shall be busy here until they all arrive and am dying of hunger.'

I duly passed on this message to a very small maid at the kitchen door who looked alarmed and withdrew. There was a lot of shouting going on, accompanied by a tremendous billowing of steam from the ovens. But I am afraid it wasn't entirely charity to the poor child that made me take the plate from her and carry it to Lindley myself, for I thereby took the opportunity to climb the stairs to Jerusalem. (I dare say God will sort out the good and bad in my motives to his own satisfaction and chalk it all up for a later tally at the pearly gate.)

When Lindley opened the door, I peered over his shoulder for a glimpse inside. He had drawn the heavy velvet curtains against the evening sunlight, and the ancient room was lit with candles. It would all have looked suitably medieval, except that I could see the bounty of Lindley's trip to Europe laid out on the large table in the middle of the room and there was the strong odour of whale oil mixed with the scent of the beeswax candles. There was a strange glass globe mounted on a horizontal pole, rather like the abbey carpenter's lathe with which he turned the new finials for Father's choir stalls. Behind that, there seemed to be a large painting which I had never previously seen, hung above the grand stone fireplace in a very heavy gilt frame.

'Lindley, for God's sake, you have not been hammering nails into the walls? The vergers will go demented.'

He looked vexed at my tone. 'Never you mind.' And then, without even thanking me for saving him from starvation, he positively shut the door in my face.

10

AFTER THAT, I RATHER begrudged Father trotting off to Jerusalem at half past seven, while I braced myself for entertaining the Chapter's wives and daughters who are, at the same time, rigidly pious and brutally political in their jockeying for position. They all coo over Father (being pigeons too) for he is so very amiable that no one can possibly dislike him – except for Mr Suckling and the archbishop, of course. But being the most senior female among them, I am simultaneously an object of apparent homage and secret detestation which, as I never applied for the position of dean's daughter, I think is remarkably unfair.

The billowing steam had resulted in an enticing spread of edibles laid out on the table in the grand dining room upstairs, while a fire had been lit in the formal drawing room where no one ever goes except on such occasions and is therefore always cold. Father and I prefer the cosy parlour, not least on account of Cuthbert, who would be lonely if left to spend his evenings alone. Now I kissed the bird's beak and left the window ajar so that he could smell the evening scents of the garden without escaping. These familiar preparations acquainted him with his forthcoming seclusion and he watched me dolefully from his perch, not even bidding me farewell as I went up to the drawing room, hardly feeling more cheerful at the prospect than he was.

But it was pleasant, after all, to see the roaring fire and the jewel colours of the ladies' dresses gleaming in the candlelight. There were only nine of us in attendance, they being the womenfolk of the four other resident canons, and I knew them all pretty well. The canon-treasurer's wife, Mrs Bray, was a tired-looking woman of about forty, with two small daughters far too young to be out in society. Mr Turnbull, the canon-almoner, had two grown-up daughters who had been out and were come back in again, having failed to find a means of escape from their secluded lives in the Little Cloister, where their quiet days were only interrupted by the shouts of the boys in the neighbouring school.

The canon-steward, Mr Slater, had no daughters at all, only a wife and an aged mother, who were just now bickering with each other over the placing of their chairs (offering a salutary reminder of why I should not relish a life alone with Dame Yates). Only the canon-clerk had managed to marry off his daughter (coming from an old family who had taken her to Vauxhall Gardens and balls and all the other places husbands are generally to be found – places where clergymen are hopelessly disinclined to wander unless they think they might bump into the king or the prime minister to their own advantage). His daughter's husband had also been invited to Lindley's demonstration, and so she was able to grace our presence and thereby remind the canon-almoner's daughters of all their own failures.

Yes, we were a happy party. But, of course, once we had been together a half-hour, and general conversation had given way to little tête-à-têtes, human kindliness triumphed over abbey politics. As I moved from group to group, I could hear the young married lady declaring her intention to take the almoner's daughters to Ranelagh Gardens for the midsummer fete, while Mr Slater's aged mother was making Mrs Bray's young daughters laugh by telling them how her cat's aversion to the canon-steward had quite driven him from his own fireside.

Mrs Bray and the younger Mrs Slater had gravitated to each other, being a similar age and similarly worn out – one by her young daughters, the other by her mother-in-law. Seeing everyone else settled, I sat down with the two women and listened quietly to their talk.

'Mr Bray is lately very irritable,' Mrs Bray was confiding to Mrs Slater. 'I tell him it is only on account of his hay fever, and that he had better keep out of the College Garden, where he persists in walking up and down positively half the day. But he will never listen.'

Mrs Slater had evidently been keeping half an ear open for her detested mother-in-law's amusing tales. 'And I tell Mr Slater to turn the dratted cat out of his armchair, but *he* will not listen neither.'

They both shook their heads at their incomprehensible spouses. Then, their menfolk's foibles having being adequately dealt with, they turned to the more interesting matters of whom they would direct their said spouses to vote for in the coming general election, the cost of muslin for their summer gowns, and their own various ailments.

Mrs Bray is dreadfully prone to headaches, she told us, which may explain her habitual frown, which I have always taken as a sign of personal dislike. (From which discovery, I learn the humiliating lesson that another's frown might have nothing to do with oneself but be only the fruit of their own worries of which one knows nothing. *Addendum:* Lindley frowned at me horribly when he slammed Jerusalem's door in my face. I now rather hope this wasn't dislike either, but from some calamity with his experiments, preferably involving the scorching of his eyebrows.)

It was not another half-hour when, true to her word, Mrs Bray announced the onset of a very bad head, and took herself home. I went with her to the door, where the night air was perfumed by the pot of gillyflowers under the parlour window. I offered to walk with her to her house in the Little Cloister but she said she was quite well enough for *that*. Accordingly I left her and went back to the ladies upstairs while she wended her way home alone through the familiar darkness. (*Query*: was the whole story of her headaches feigned from beginning to end, merely to go home early and have an hour's peace and quiet without her husband and children?)

The remaining ladies repaired to the dining room and demolished most of the comestibles before the gentlemen came in full of laughter from their unusual evening. Mr Bray greeted his young daughters cheerfully, with no sign of either hay fever or irritation, telling them that the dean's nephew was a remarkable young man. (I devoutly hope Lindley did not hear him.)

Mr Delingpole found me by the coffee urn, while the other gentlemen settled on the remains of the repast like fattening locusts. 'An entertaining performance,' he said, with the smile I had already learned to like, 'and quite astonishing to the Westminster clerical mind. We have one or two clergymen in the Royal Society, but science has not penetrated here at all. I think some of them thought it witchcraft.'

I would have liked to know exactly what Lindley had done to provoke the canons into such astonished hilarity, but I was too proud to ask, and after a moment Mr Delingpole joined the other gentlemen. Meanwhile, Father was eating a pie and looking thoughtful, as though a whole new world had just opened up before his eyes. Given his general propensity to enthusiasms, he might easily become the eagerest scientist of them all, I thought, and as a consequence I should, at least, soon know all about it.

There was another young man present whom I did not recognise but turned out to be a friend of Lindley's. 'I met him on the Tour,' Lindley told me, as he presented the lad for my inspection. He was a good deal handsomer than Lindley, with green eyes and a curled wig that made him look rather like one of King Charles's cavalier spaniels, or indeed, like the sleeping effigy of the Duke of Buckingham in the cupboard, who was so much more a *Lindley* than my unromantic cousin. 'This is Thomas Ffoulkes, Susan. Thomas, this is my cousin, Miss Bell. She will be impertinent to you, and very scolding, but you must not mind it.'

'I shall brave it,' Thomas Ffoulkes said gallantly, 'merely for a flash of those remarkable dark eyes.'

'Oh, Lord,' Lindley said. 'Susan, do not mind him either.

85

He is an outrageous rake and has half a dozen married females panting after him at this very moment.'

'Only one,' Thomas Ffoulkes objected. He turned to me. 'And you must not think me a rake, Miss Bell, for it is a case of true love, I assure you.'

This was not the kind of talk I was used to at the Deanery. 'Oh dear,' I said helplessly. 'How very unfortunate for you both.'

'Unfortunate! It is a tragedy, Miss Bell. I met her on her wedding day. A week earlier and – who knows – everything might have been different.'

'But she must have loved the other man enough to have agreed to marry him?'

Thomas Ffoulkes looked mysterious. 'On the contrary, Miss Bell, she had never met the man at all before that day.'

Lindley was laughing at my astonished expression. 'It is certainly an enterprise beset with much difficulty, Tom, but of course that makes it all the more jolly in your eyes.'

Mr Ffoulkes ignored this jibe and looked at me meltingly. 'The worst of it is the distance, you know. My father is determined I shall settle down, but how can I, Miss Bell, tormented as I am by the memory of her loveliness?'

'The lady will have forgotten you entirely by this time,' Lindley said brutally. 'Depend upon it; she has a dozen suitors much more conveniently on hand. You may as well stay at home, save your money and avoid your father's wrath.'

'She has not forgotten me.' Thomas Ffoulkes was eager to contradict him. 'I had a letter from her last week.'

'Which, with the dilatoriness of the post, was probably sent the day after you left.'

'By no means. It was dated last week and brought to me by hand, by a particular messenger.' Thomas Ffoulkes now looked very triumphant. 'I gave him a bed for his trouble, and I shall send an answer back with him when he goes and pour my heart and soul into the production.'

Lindley grinned, not entirely good-naturedly, and slapped his friend on the shoulder. 'Come, Tom, you are incorrigible and it is very late. I must go to dismantle the equipment before the vergers complain at the mess. Did you enjoy my entertainment?'

'Tolerably. I would have preferred the opera or the ballet, but being obliged to humour you, I dare say it was well enough. But from your unaccountable aversion to carousing lately I surmise a love affair. Am I on the scent, Bell?'

'You are certainly a hound at sniffing out that sort of secret, Tom.'

'Ha! So I am. So all men say. And I fancy the attraction is close at home.' At this Thomas Ffoulkes smiled at me very gallantly.

'Come on, Tom,' Lindley said again. 'Time to go.'

Mr Ffoulkes bent over my hand with exaggerated ardour, his spaniel ears flopping. 'Your servant, Miss Bell.' He leaned a little closer and murmured, 'I see it every time he speaks of you, and I wish you joy with all my heart.'

'What are you whispering about to the poor woman, Tom?' Lindley asked, from his place at the door. For a brief moment I fancied he was slightly pink, though not (as usual) with enthusiasm, so much as a sudden and inexplicable embarrassment.

'Only things I am sure Miss Bell will find agreeable,'

Thomas Ffoulkes answered, as he followed Lindley out onto the landing. Lindley was thwarted in his purpose of going at once to the Jerusalem Chamber by Mr Delingpole engaging him in friendly chat. And so, with a boyish laugh, the two young men parted, and Thomas Ffoulkes ran lightly down the stairs with a nod to a passing footman.

11

SUNDAY 8 MAY

LINDLEY AND MR DELINGPOLE had still been talking when I took myself to bed, and so, first thing the next morning, I crept into Jerusalem before breakfast, in the hope that my cousin had neglected to dismantle his apparatus after all. In this I was disappointed, as the table was empty, all the candles cleared away, and the heavy window curtains drawn back to let in the sun. The vergers might never need to know Lindley had taken such liberties with the grand old chamber.

Except for that large picture he had hung over the fireplace, of course. I scanned the wall to see how badly Lindley's nails had damaged the ancient plaster, and if there was anything to be done to save him from the vergers' ire. But I need not have worried. The old plaster was as smooth and unblemished as alabaster, and there was no sign of any hole at all – not even a pinprick.

I could make nothing of this as I went into the abbey to

arrange the flowers on the high altar, as I always do before breakfast on a Sunday morning. I should like to do so every day, but there is a system jealously guarded by the Mrs Slaters and Mrs Bray, and my superior position only makes me doubly suspicious in their eyes, as a potential usurper of all their weekday privileges.

The flowers and the large silver vase were already on the altar, awaiting my attention, but I was distracted by the sight of the engraver's apprentice, Blake, back at his usual work, sitting some way above the floor on a scaffolding the workmen had rigged up for him in front of the memorial to Isaac Newton. He was apparently deep in conversation with an unseen interlocutor. For a moment I thought he must have a dog with him (or more likely, up on that perch, a parrot?) to whom he was addressing his remarks, but as I drew nearer, I saw he was quite alone.

When he noticed me, he broke off his mutterings and turned the same full, sweet smile down on me as he had done the day before. I must say it quite made my heart flutter, and also made me wish I had not pulled my stays so tight. Of course, I was pleased to exhibit a slender waist to the boy's downward gaze, but it would have been convenient to be able to breathe too.

I regretfully rejected an urge to climb the scaffold to join him. The stays would not have it and I would in all probability make a hash of things, not having climbed a tree since we left Leicestershire. Nevertheless, it would have been a splendid opportunity to display to him my white silk shoes laced with pretty ribbons, which are really far too delightful to be always hidden under my skirts.

'Who are you talking to?' I asked him instead.

'That damned cherub.' Blake jabbed his quill in the direction of the small carved relief that ran along under the large effigy of Newton leaning on his books and looking wise.

'What's the matter with it?' I peered up at the cherub. 'What's it doing?'

'Weighing the sun, according to the book.' Blake waved a tattered copy of the vergers' *History of W* at me.

'And why do you call it *damned?*' I repeated the blasphemy with a good stab at casual bravado.

'For its gall.' Blake still looked vexed. 'I was telling it that it takes too much upon itself, and that only God should know the sun's pounds and ounces.' He shook his head. 'In any case, who can say that the sun has weight or mass at all, and is not merely a glorious spiritual light from heaven?'

I thought Newton had said so with some confidence, but I looked at the other small, naked figures among whom the offending cherub was arranged. They were all busy and remarkably self-important considering they appeared to be about two years old.

'What are those others doing?'

Blake consulted the guidebook again. 'One is looking through a telescope. One is making money, for the book says Newton was master of the Mint. One is discovering gravity. And this one,' he pointed, 'is studying heaven through a prism.'

'What is a prism?'

'A piece of glass that traps the rainbow.'

I didn't exactly understand, but I could see the lad was

very displeased. 'And why do you dislike it all so much?'

'Because science makes everything so dreary. Did you not hear that man yesterday calling thunderbolts *electricity*, and rainbows an illusion? Perhaps he's right. And perhaps we could find out the weight of the sun if we wanted to. But why should we? When there is so much . . .' He shook his head. 'More.'

If I had known what *electricity* was, I might have been able to judge its dreariness or otherwise, but unfortunately the abbey library had been silent on that subject altogether. Nevertheless, I took Blake's meaning, and on the whole (from the evidence of Sir Isaac Newton's *descent of bodies* and *inflection of light, &c.*) I agree with him. After all, I am the daughter of the Dean of Westminster and have grown up in as spiritual an atmosphere as exists in London. The newspapers chide the Church and call it merely a profession, like the law or the army – a refuge for younger sons (and Father is indeed a younger son). But the ancient fabric of the church buildings is ingrained with the sublime, and one cannot help but absorb it, however much one may fail to act on it or render it back in such good deeds as the gospels require.

'*That man* is my cousin,' I said. 'And he is entirely taken up with science, I assure you. He has all sorts of nasty experiments he has collected abroad. But for myself, I much prefer poetry.'

'Do you?' Blake's large eyes gazed down at me, larger than ever, if that was possible. But whereas Lindley's large eyes were owlish (as if looking for mice), Blake's were softer, as if bent upon a hazy far horizon. 'Tell me a poet you esteem.'

'I like Mr Gray.'

'His "Elegy Written in a Country Churchyard"?'

'Ye-es, although . . .'

The choir had come in to practise their psalms before Morning Prayer, and as the boys' voices began to soar around us, to the very height of the roof, I remembered the flowers on the altar. 'Forgive me, I must go.'

Blake slid down from his scaffold and followed me through the quire to the high altar, probably relieved to get away from his troublesome scientific cherubs. '*Although*? Although what? For myself, I think it a splendid poem.'

'Oh, I know it is tremendously famous and all that,' I said, examining the flowers and picking up the scissors abstractedly. 'But the first line is poor. *The curfew tolls the knell of parting day.*'

'I think it fine.'

'It *sounds* fine. But what does it mean? A curfew is a bell rung at evening, is it not? And a knell is the sound of a bell. So beneath the mellifluous sounds, all the line really says is that "the evening bell rings the bell of the evening".'

I was almost as pleased to see Blake's reluctant smile at this as I had been to make my cousin laugh the previous day. I fear that, in my heart of hearts, I aspire to be nothing more than Cuthbert, a performing animal earning nuts as my reward.

'Yet beautiful words are the surest way past science to the real truth of life, just as beautiful paintings are,' Blake said, watching as I began to pick up the hot-house lilies one by one, trim their stems and put them in the silver vase. 'For myself, I cannot choose between them. I spend my days composing verses in my head even as I sketch, the silence and the beauty of the abbey being so very conducive to poetry.'

My heart sank, but I endeavoured to fix my face into an encouraging smile. Other people's poetry is lamentable at the best of times, and though we are all supposed to be cast equally in God's image, I am afraid He is far more sparing with His poetical gifts, as evidenced by the dreadful poem to Sir Isaac I had read yesterday.

'Last night I wrote a poem about Apollo,' Blake went on, coming closer to be heard above the choir's singing, so that I had positively to lean around him for the bunch of greenery that I thought would set off the white lilies to perfection. 'You remember, the scholar Quintrel talked of it? The Roman temple under the floor of this place?'

'I remember.'

'That is why the cherub so irked me. To call the sun a ball of mud, like the earth, to be weighed and measured! When it is really nothing less than the countenance of a god that brings warmth and fertility and new life to us every morning in his fiery chariot.' He was very close to me now, so close that I almost thought, in the spirit of the said fertility, he was going to kiss me. (And, apart from the disgrace attendant on being found kissing an engraver's apprentice at the high altar, I thought I should enjoy it very much.) The choir approached a crescendo as his mouth moved towards mine.

But then he probably remembered the indecorum of such a kiss in such a place – or the impossibility of a dalliance with me, which is just as unthinkable for him as for me to fancy marrying the Prince of Wales (and yes, the comparison is valid even if the present *P of W* is not yet twelve, for it is the principle which counts). He therefore drew back despite the stirring music and decided to recite his dratted poem instead. '*Let thy holy feet visit our clime . . .*'

Fortunately, at this moment, there was a tremendous bustle at the west door and I was spared the rest.

12

THE COMMOTION WAS caused by the entrance of Mr Delingpole, Mr Alnutt and Mr Quintrel of the Society of Antiquities, along with three other gentlemen, two in very handsome military dress and the third a tall man in a plain curled wig and a dark suit. It was the latter that caused most of the commotion because (I meant to draw out the suspense much longer for literary effect, but I find myself unequal to deferring my own gratification) it was *THE KING*!

Perhaps *consternation* is a better word than *commotion*, for it was mainly the vergers who made it. They scattered in search of dusters and polish lest His Majesty should begin to suspect that the atmosphere of beeswax he generally moves in is not the common lot of mankind.

The military men were his equerries, men with very sensible faces and keen eyes, looking about the abbey for potential assassins. Behind them came a retinue of workmen they had managed to round up about the place on this Sabbath morning.

'I'm afraid Father isn't here,' I said to Mr Delingpole

breathlessly, as I cut them off by Newton's tomb and simultaneously dropped a deep curtsey to His Majesty. I surmised the chanter must also have noticed the arrival of our illustrious visitor, for behind me the choir swelled to a new and rather urgent magnificence.

'I am sure the vergers are already gone in search of your father,' Mr Delingpole answered with a smile, and in this he was certainly right. I hoped Father would take the news calmly, but I doubted it.

'And we shall not be long,' Mr Delingpole went on. 'It is only that we were rushed away from our business yesterday before it was quite concluded.'

'I didn't know you were returning, and I'm sure Father doesn't.'

'I'm sorry for that. I told your cousin last night, but perhaps he did not pass it on. His Majesty, being at leisure today, desired to accompany us. We mean to open the tomb again to examine the embalming cloths and make some more detailed drawings of the body. I believe young Monsieur Durand may arrive at any moment. And you'll help us again, Blake?'

Blake had been hovering at my shoulder, his expression hard to read. Had he recognised the king? If so, he looked remarkably unimpressed. On the other hand, it would get him away from his horrid cherubs, and moreover he might have an opportunity to recite his Apollo poem to Mr Quintrel. At any rate, he nodded assent.

And for once in his life Mr Suckling was absent. I wasn't sure if I hoped the vergers would forget to tell him the exciting news, or whether I wanted him here to witness the king's favour towards Father and the consequent uselessness of all his oily resentment.

In the hurry of my feelings I spoke stupidly. 'But I'm afraid Father will not like it on a Sabbath morning. Not with all the day's services to come.'

'On the contrary, I am sure the dean will be only too gratified to meet all His Majesty's wishes,' Mr Delingpole replied with a warning frown at me to mind my tongue, which I duly remembered to do.

'Delighted ... quite happy ...' I babbled and made another curtsey so deep I nearly sat down with a thump (the very thought of how *that* would have looked still makes me scarlet).

'Come, gentlemen,' His Majesty said to his equerries. 'Let us rout out the little dormouse from his nest, what, what?' And before I understood his meaning, they were striding off into the cloisters in search of Father. I was a shade offended to hear my robin called a dormouse, for I am sure he never sleeps above six hours a night and is always busy.

At first I thought to follow the king, but there were the other Antiquities to think of, and they were now hurrying away in an unruly mob towards the Confessor's shrine. Mr Quintrel stepped over the low wrought-iron baluster about the Cosmati pavement and tried both the marble doors in the high altar with a startling degree of effrontery. They were locked. (They are always locked. I think only Father has the key.) Upon which Mr Delingpole took himself off to the north ambulatory instead. As I think I have previously mentioned, a second set of steps leads up to the shrine past Longshanks' tomb, and though its low gate is also always

99

locked, it is not so insuperable a barrier if a man does not mind risking his breeches in the attempt.

But in this Mr Delingpole was also thwarted, for a rope had been hung across the paving, preventing any access into the north ambulatory at all beyond Bishop Islip's chapel. This was explained by the sight of Fidoe threading chains through the arches of the triforium gallery above us, and three new lamps already dangling a dozen yards ahead. (Perhaps he and Father had also reflected that a naked flame in an attic full of debris might be rash and had decided upon this safer route to the same heavenly effect.) Mr Delingpole coolly unhooked the rope and walked through as the rest of the Antiquities came up behind us.

'Mr Delingpole, sir,' I said, hurrying after him. 'I'm sure the way is barred for your own safety.'

'I shan't walk beneath the works,' he answered. 'I am not such a fool as that, Miss Bell, don't fear.'

And now, for the benefit of future readers of *its Monuments and Murders,* I suppose I had better explain the exact circumstances of where we were standing at that moment, so that the events which followed may be properly understood.

As everyone knows, a church is built in the shape of the cross on which Christ died, the head facing east (to Jerusalem) and the foot west. The two arms of the cross are called the transepts, one running north, the other south from the body of the church. In the abbey, the altar and the shrine of the Confessor lie just east of the crossing place – at Christ's head, as it were – and the ambulatories are the pavements which lead around the outside of the shrine in a loop from north to south.

Edward I's tomb frowned darkly down over this pavement in the north ambulatory, from its place high in the Confessor's shrine. But just at present the rope discouraged any entry to the ambulatory and its maze of pillars, statues, memorials and arches, or the two semi-circular chapels to John the Baptist and St Paul which lead off it to the left, like protruding jewels on a sword hilt.

Mr Delingpole had gone a pace beyond the rope, and I had just glanced back to see if the others meant to follow him – and wondering what in heaven I should do about it if they did – when I saw a strange expression come across Mr Quintrel's face and he uttered an oath highly improper to be heard inside the abbey. Blake passed a hand across his eyes as if he thought he were dreaming. Finally (and all this you must understand happened in no more than the blink of an eye) Mr Alnutt gave a shrill old man's scream that made my blood thrill to my extremities and then rush pell-mell back to my heart.

I cannot say what I expected to see as I swung about to follow their gaze. Poor Fidoe, perhaps, fallen from his precarious perch and smashed on the paving as I had unfeelingly joked to Lindley. But it was nothing like that, though almost equally horrid. And now, I must try to describe exactly what I *did* see.

That maze of pillars and arches and statues ahead of us, which I have mentioned, were shimmering with a strange and sombre golden light. For a moment I thought it was Fidoe's lamps but no, they were still unlit, and then I saw it was not the *light* that was shimmering, but the pillars and arches and statues themselves. They bulged weirdly, seeming to press one upon the other; seeming, even as I looked at them, to shift and move. And then Mr Alnutt shrieked again, so shrilly that the hairs stood up on my arms. Something else was stirring.

Something that looked like a hand was groping out of the shimmering bulging air in the middle of the pavement below Longshanks' tomb, as if pushing its way through an unseen door from the invisible spiritual world into our own. Then an arm followed, clad in a dull white. But they were a hand and an arm unlike any human hand or arm that I had ever seen before.

A foot followed last and now the figure had fully emerged through the unseen door from nothingness. It was tall. Hugely tall. Its legs were like tapering tendrils, its body a streak of white. And all of it was wrapped in linen – the same waxed linen, I thought, that had wrapped Edward's body in his tomb.

I do not know if it saw us. It lurched away eastwards, horrible in its shuffling movements. As it passed the columns and statues and arches they bulged and shrank again, as if the pressure of another world was pressing upon them. Everything looked wrong, everything looked changed and uncanny. The very statues and pillars it moved among seemed altered, as if we were looking into another realm, like our own and yet subtly changed.

And then the figure swung about towards us of a sudden, and we fell back in alarm. I glimpsed its face, covered by the same crimson cloth that had hidden Edward's features yesterday – and about its shrouded temples was bound a crown. The figure bulged and shimmered back towards us for a half-dozen paces and then, reaching Edward's tomb once more, it climbed back into nothingness, with the same spider-like deliberation, and was gone.

The moment the vision disappeared Mr Delingpole came to his senses. 'Quick! After it!' he cried, and before I knew it he was gone to the stairs up to the shrine and Edward's coffin. He leapt over the gate, followed by the workmen and the other Antiquities. How Mr Alnutt got over I cannot say, for instead of watching I looped up my skirts and ran for Father. At the crossing I turned to look back and saw that the pillars and statues and arches were now stock-still again. The strange, dull gold light was gone, and the common, everyday gloom of the abbey had returned.

When I went out into the cloisters, Father was hurrying towards me, his small round figure looking even smaller and rounder between the tall figures of the king and his equerries. 'Your Majesty,' he was saying breathlessly, as he trotted to keep up with their long strides, 'I wish you had given us some notice of your visit. I might have been here to greet you, but as it is, on a Sabbath morning, we are really far too busy—'

If I had been Mr Delingpole I would have given Father the same warning look he had turned on my own untimely objections, but the king was only smiling tolerantly (I suppose he must be well used to fussing inferiors).

'Father,' I said, as I came up to them, in what I fear was a rather strangled tone. 'Your Majesty.' (I bobbed the most perfunctory curtsey HM has probably ever witnessed.) 'Something strange has happened. Something terrible.'

They did not slacken their pace and I was obliged to run

after them to the south transept door. 'Your Majesty, we have just seen something dreadful. I do not think it safe—'

But then, just as we came in to the abbey's gloom (the choir still singing, Mr Lamb the chanter still conducting, all apparently oblivious to what the Antiquities and I had witnessed), there came the most almighty cry from the direction of the Confessor's tomb: men's voices raised together in what sounded, more than anything, like surprise and consternation. I supposed that they had come face to face with the ghost, just as they had desired to do.

The king put on a tremendous spurt of speed while the choir's voices faltered and died, and the chanter turned at the sound of our clattering footsteps with his hand upraised, still unconsciously keeping time.

The king hurried to the right-hand marble door to the shrine and beckoned Father to hasten himself. Poor Father's hands were unsteady as he unlocked it. The king pushed past him, flinging the door back with some force, and Father and I followed, to find the Antiquities and workmen gathered, staring into Longshanks' open tomb. They had found the outer lid open a fraction when they came in and, having hastily shoved it further open at an angle, they had seen that the inner lid to the sarcophagus was missing entirely.

'He is abroad!' Mr Alnutt was gabbling to anyone who would listen. 'He is abroad!'

I had been transfixed in the doorway but now, stepping closer to look down into the tomb, I saw what he meant. The embalmed body of Longshanks, with its tunic and cloth of gold, its crown and rod and sceptre, were all gone.

'Unaccountable,' Delingpole was saying. 'Extraordinary.

And we have indeed just seen him walking! Is it possible . . . ?'

Father said afterwards that he didn't know if it was a curse or a blessing that they had come to the abbey that morning. (Though, for myself, I do not think he could have prevented them, the king's pleasure being law to all other men.)

Nevertheless, this second opening in the presence of His Majesty was certainly the opening of a Pandora's Box, bringing with it a world of trouble. On the other hand, as Father afterwards said, it behoved a dean to know when mischief was done in his abbey and, more than all the rest, it behoved us all to seek justice for a murdered man.

I am quite aware of the proprieties of literature. That dramatic events should be nicely spaced throughout the narrative to give the reader time to catch his breath and fully savour one marvel until he is ready for the next. Yes, Nasus Bell well knows that this is how matters should be arranged. Unfortunately, the narrative of real events makes no such provision for their proper enjoyment and in this case presented us with a dead body so close upon the ghost's heels that it is better, perhaps, to see it all as part of the same scheme.

Dead body? Murdered man? The reader asks, agog. Yes, yes, I am coming to it as fast as my pen will let me.

'Susan, my dear,' Father said. He had turned beseeching eyes on me, as if he hoped I might tell him the empty coffin was a mistake or a dream, but now his eyes widened strangely. 'Susan, my child, what has happened to your shoes?'

I had been too much dumbstruck to notice the half-dried stain I had paused in at the door as I had taken in the strange scene around the tomb. My skirts were still looped up from running for Father and, when I glanced down, I saw that strange rusty stains now sullied the white silk and trailing ribbon laces of my shoes. The equerry gave a bark of surprise and pushed past me to the door which the king had impatiently pushed back against the adjoining wall of the shrine as we came in.

The equerry pulled back the door. Behind, in the corner between the door and the wall, the young and handsome French antiquary, Louis Durand was sitting. His limbs were awkwardly splayed out before him and he looked as if he had just received some very bad news. In that he was certainly right, for there was a gaping hole in his throat, whence had issued the effusion of blood whose half-dried remains I had stood in. And, as a consequence, he was perfectly and incontrovertibly dead.

13

'GOOD GOD!' Father said faintly. 'What in heaven has happened here?'

'The old king's mummy is missing,' one of the equerries said with some excitement, 'and there is a dead man here in the corner,' which was certainly an answer to Father's question, but not a particularly useful one.

'But who has taken it?' His Majesty asked, his priorities seeming a little muddled. 'By God, who *could* have taken it, what, what?' And then, seemingly as an afterthought, 'And who the devil is this dead ruffian here?'

'A friend of mine, sire,' Mr Quintrel said. He did not seem particularly shocked, however, or much grief-stricken, which was somewhat explained by his following words. 'Or, I should more properly say, merely a recent acquaintance. I brought him with me to view Longshanks' mummy yesterday.'

For the few moments it took me to register the mummy was missing, see the dead body revealed and observe how the others reacted, everything seemed strangely unreal, just as it had done when the ghost walked. But that spectral exhibition was all forgot – at least for the present – a circumstance I could scarcely have imagined when I accosted Father and the king in the cloisters five minutes earlier.

While everybody else gradually gathered their wits together, my sense of detachment persisted – a thing of which I am not proud, but for which I am nevertheless grateful. It was horrible to see the handsome young man sitting there dead, who yesterday had been so full of life; but if I had fainted or screamed – as it surely behoved a well-brought-up young lady to do on such an occasion as this – it would only have added to the general confusion.

The poor lad was still very well-dressed and now, in my strange cold clarity, I noticed that his splayed hands were very white and his nails neatly polished. The equerry was bending to examine the wound that had killed him.

'He has bled to death, Majesty. But the wound was not made by a blade,' he said, turning to the king, all military expertise and, after the first shock, as detached as I was; though in his case likely from long experience of wounds and death. 'It is not a slit but a hole.' He actually put his fingers into the wound and felt about. 'Yes, it has been made by a round-handled weapon, like a pike or a spear. The point has gone right through and the haft followed, severing the artery. After the weapon was withdrawn the effusion of his life's blood would have killed him in scarcely more than two minutes.'

He stood up and looked about. 'The weapon is gone. The killer has taken it. But the first thing will be to call for the constable. You have your own abbey constable, do you not, Dean?'

Father nodded weakly and the king waved his permission. The equerry hurried out, followed by Mr Delingpole and Mr Quintrel. In their distraction, they quite forgot poor old Mr Alnutt, who hobbled after them, his tottering steps unsupported by any friendly hand. Meanwhile Mr Lamb, the chanter, had abandoned his choir and come to look, and inevitably Mr Suckling had finally come sidling in, with a look of damp, pious horror.

'You must close the abbey,' the king was saying to a verger. 'Go and lock the doors, man. No one must come or go without my leave.'

'We cannot close the abbey,' Mr Lamb bleated feebly. 'We cannot cancel worship on a Sabbath, Your Majesty. It has never been done, not even under Cromwell.'

'We will worship later, Chanter – if we can.' Father rallied himself with a visible effort, and whatever the archbishop might think of this episode (and Mr Suckling was certainly going to tell him all about it) I couldn't suppose the AB's favoured candidate would have done any better. 'Send the boys home, Chanter,' he added. 'We will call for them when we are ready for morning service. Whenever that might be.'

'Damn it, Dean.' His Majesty was also recovering from the first shock and more than anything he was now excited. 'You must gather your people in one place and quiz them at once, what, what?' Excited? He was positively aglow. Accidents scarcely ever happen to kings, I suppose, their lives being far too well managed for surprises, and any novelty consequently must delight them.

'I will, Your Majesty, I certainly will.' Father flapped again at the verger, John Catling, who had so far ignored his instructions, being too busy gawping at the dead Frenchman in the corner. 'Do as the king bids you, Catling, and close the doors. Then fetch the singing men from the choir, as well as every other member of the abbey staff. Direct them all to the Jerusalem Chamber. I will meet you there presently once His Majesty has departed.'

'Departed?' the king said. 'Bugger that.' A murdered man was not just a novelty but a cause, and it seemed the king was going to take it up. Everyone sprang into action, apart from the chanter, Mr Lamb, who was shaking his head at the king in apparent disapprobation of his regrettable language in the presence of the Confessor. (It would have been useless for him to voice his objections, however, since kings can do just as they like, saints or no saints.)

'And what shall I do, Father?' I asked, as the whole body began to move off, the one remaining equerry's spurs ringing on the paving as he followed the king's cheerful step to Jerusalem. 'Can I go back to the Deanery and change my shoes?'

Father hesitated. 'No, my dear, not yet,' he said after a moment. 'The king desires every possible witness at the meeting. If you can bear it, come as you are.'

'And what about the workmen?' Henry Ede, the other verger, was asking Father. 'What about that drawing chap? You even want *them* in Jerusalem with the king?'

Father looked unhappy but resolute. 'Yes, yes, everyone. Everyone must come to Jerusalem and account for themselves to His Majesty.'

14

HIS MAJESTY SAT down at the head of the large table in Jerusalem, the old chamber where the business of the Chapter goes on and important visitors are entertained. It has seen many remarkable events in its long history. I believe they wrote the English Bible here, and certainly the Prayer Book. Henry IV died here, too. Having been prophesied to die in the Holy Land, he had long resolved to go on crusade. One day, at prayer before the Confessor's shrine, he fell gravely ill (I suppose it was some sort of apoplexy) and they carried him here. *Where am I?* he asked. *Jerusalem*, they answered. *Then my hour is come*, he said and promptly expired. (*Query*: perhaps even on this very table?)

Meanwhile, the vergers had done a good job of rounding up the staff. They were all there, from the canons and their womenfolk to the lowliest kitchen maid. Those who had witnessed the scene in the Confessor's shrine looked shocked. The chanter wiped his forehead with his handkerchief, still bleating softly at intervals. The vergers seemed absolutely furious to have been so remiss as to let Edward's body disappear and another fresh one be inserted under their very noses, and angrier still to have been found out in such a dereliction of their duty in the august presence of the king.

Those who had not seen the body were perplexed at having been wrenched from their usual morning pastimes, not to mention abashed by His Majesty's presence. When the matter was explained to them, the gardeners looked suitably solemn, though I thought on the whole they probably viewed it as a pleasant and providential excuse to avoid the tedium of the canon-steward's Sunday sermon, with a king thrown in for good measure. Even the porter had been called away from the Deanery door and looked very out of place inside this lofty room, being a man I had only ever seen outdoors in all weathers or folded into his little porter's lodge beside the Deanery gate. Blake was sitting quietly at the far end of the table, apparently in some dream of his own, not attending to much. And the workmen, who had not only seen Louis Durand's dead body, but a ghost to boot, looked particularly knowing.

Meanwhile, Mr Suckling had managed to seat himself beside me. He drummed his fingers lightly on the table and looked from one face to another attentively, with only the ghost of his usual smile. Perhaps he dared not smirk at Father's discomfiture in the presence of His Majesty. Still, I could hear his soggy breathing and I inched my chair away a fraction.

'We must establish the exact events of the whole case,' the king said, as soon as we had ceased scraping our chair legs on the stone flags and muttering to each other. 'But we cannot make any guess as to who might or might not have killed this dead fellow until we know more about him, what, what?'

'We do know some things, Your Majesty,' Father said. 'As Mr Quintrel indicated, the poor young man was an acquaintance of his, a French antiquary who accompanied the members of the Society yesterday for the viewing of Edward's mummy.'

'A *Frenchman*!' the king exclaimed. 'God damn them, have they not yet learned we are at peace?'

'I don't believe the gentleman was bent on warfare, sire. But I thought at the time he seemed too young to be an antiquary, and perhaps I was right. It certainly seems now that he was there on some false pretence or other.'

I remembered Durand darting forward to help the workmen open the lid of the coffin. If he had planned to return later and open it again to steal Edward's body, it would have been useful to weigh the difficulty of the enterprise beforehand.

His Majesty nodded and looked wise. 'Very well then, a Frenchie witnessed the opening yesterday and then was found dead in the shrine this morning. It looks to me very much as if he came back later to steal the mummy, upon which someone else, presently unknown, stabbed him and took the mummy away afterwards, what, what? But who killed him, hey? And why? And when? We must find it all out and establish the exact whereabouts of everyone connected with the abbey at the time of the murder.'

'Heaven preserve us,' Father said. 'You cannot think any one of us was involved?'

'I cannot say anything as yet, Dean.' The king was suddenly magnificently offhand and regal. For his part, Father looked terribly anxious.

'Dear me, dear me. I am sure it is impossible. And whatever would the world say?' (*The world* in Father's mind was of course the archbishop, and what he would say was that Father was incompetent and had better be removed at once in favour of his own superior candidate.)

'It is quite as tiresome for myself,' the king answered, though he still looked sunny. 'I have enough trouble with the damned press as it is.' He looked at his equerry. 'Imagine the cartoons in the papers, Desaguliers, what, what? If anyone in my Peculiar is involved in murder I will never live it down.'

'But there is surely no reason to think anyone could be,' Father said. 'The young man was a friend of the Society of Antiquaries, not the abbey – as I have said, he was the particular friend of Mr Quintrel, in fact. We should speak to Quintrel as soon as he returns.'

'Returns? Where the devil has he got to?'

'He went for Corbett, the searcher of the sanctuary, sire, with your man.'

It is very unpleasant to realise that once one begins to doubt men's motives there are so many reasons to continue. Mr Quintrel is indeed, by his own admission, the Frenchman's friend, is unprepossessing to look at, and is therefore a man it is very easy to suspect. But he seems far too lackadaisical to thrust a pike or spear into another man's neck. And, surely, if he had done so sometime since the opening of the tomb yesterday, he would not have returned this morning along with the rest to discover the corpse – unless he was very cool indeed.

'By all means quiz Quintrel when he returns,' the king said, meditatively now. 'But even supposing he was the murderer, if he came to the abbey with Durand in the depths of night someone from the abbey must have let them in.'

'We do not know they came at night,' Father objected.

'You don't mean to suggest they were thieving and murdering each other in broad daylight, under the very noses of your vergers, Dean?'

'No, no.' At this Father looked wretched.

'Then let us begin at the beginning,' the king said, apparently bent on getting his money's worth of entertainment out of the business or, to do him more justice, to fulfil his heaven-sent role as Solomon the judge. 'Come on, Dean, out with it, what, what? Tell us all exactly what happened.'

Father did not immediately answer, a circumstance by which the sacrist lost no time in profiting.

'The dean is naturally a little discomposed,' he put in smoothly. 'Allow me to speak for him while he gathers his thoughts. As you know, Your Majesty, the whole affair began yesterday with the visit of your Society.' (From the way he said it, I thought he wanted to add *and what I consider to have been an ill-judged and indecorous act of vandalism that has led directly to this calamity*. But of course he did not say so aloud.) 'The antiquaries demanded that the abbey be emptied of all witnesses except the dean, his daughter, his nephew, myself, and that young lad there, who has lately been working in the abbey on a book of drawings.'

'Susan was not there,' Father said confidently.

Mr Suckling ignored him. 'The workmen were called in to open the tomb and were afterwards banished – which was, in hindsight, an efficient means of immediately communicating the contents of the tomb to the outside world.'

'All we saw was one coffin inside another,' one of the workmen protested, apparently too affronted by the sacrist to hold his peace even in the presence of his monarch. 'We sees coffins every day, don't we? Ain't nothing new to us. What we wants to know about is that there ghost. What did *that* signify? Must be something, stands to reason.'

'We then opened the inner coffin and examined the mummy,' Mr Suckling went on, ignoring him, too. 'Whereafter, there was an alarm in the triforium gallery, and Fidoe – our clerk of works, Your Majesty – advised us all to make haste and leave the building.' He looked around at those of us there assembled. 'Fidoe is not here, I see. Do we know where he is?'

'I sent him after the antiquaries to find the searcher,' Father said. 'He will be back shortly.'

'In any case, none of this is to the purpose, what, what?' the king said, with a marvellously disdainful look at the sacrist. 'We all know the mummy was there and the Frenchman alive at that time. It is later events we must investigate, Mr . . . ?'

'Suckling, sire. Simon Suckling, sacrist of the abbey.' Mr Suckling was unabashed by the king's manner. He sat back and tapped his palms together lightly. 'Very well, then: after the opening we all hurried from the abbey, leaving the coffin open and the mummy uncovered. For quite an extended period, there was no one left inside except for the workmen and their scaffolding.'

The workmen's spokesman was offended again. 'Gawd, Sacrist! Are you bent on blaming us for everything? I was there, Yer Majesty, and I can tell you we was far too busy holding up the roof with poles to spare any time thieving mummies.' He looked at us all with disgust. 'Nor murdering foreign gents, neither. It's that ghost what done it, mark my words.'

The king frowned slightly, perhaps at this word *ghost* mentioned twice in as many minutes. But as neither he nor Father knew anything about it, the workman was not likely to get any satisfactory answer just now.

'I myself also remained in the abbey,' Father said, and I remembered I had seen him going to the triforium as Blake hurried me away. 'But I did not see Monsieur Durand or anyone else again. However, I did see *you* inside, Suckling, not long after the first alarm.'

Mr Suckling bowed his head at this little dig and did not answer. I recalled that he had walked away with Mr Alnutt before I returned to the Deanery with Lindley, but their conversation had probably not been a long one. The sacrist had said he wanted to hear more about Mr Alnutt's studies, but the old man had probably been far too shocked by Fidoe's shouts for any lengthy recital then.

Father now took up the story. 'Once the roof was propped, Fidoe supervised the closing of the tomb before returning to his work in the triforium, resetting the keystone.'

'And at that time Edward's body was still within the coffin?'

'Yes,' Father said. 'Yes, of course. That is . . .' He was suddenly afflicted by doubt. 'I wasn't there myself.'

'I was,' the bad-tempered workman put in. 'The mummy was there then, all right. A funny old bundle of cloth, it were, when we put down the lid.'

(*Obs.*: so the workmen *did* see the body then and could have told others outside the abbey after all, if only later.)

The king was looking around the table. 'Very well then. So much for the tomb and Edward's mummy at that time. Where was everybody else, what, what?'

'My cousin Lindley came back to the Deanery with me,' I said, 'and afterwards he was busy in here, setting up his experiments to show the members of the Chapter.'

'I see he is not present, either,' Mr Suckling remarked. 'Do we know anything of his movements today?'

I hadn't seen Lindley at breakfast, it was true. I am inclined to think he must have been clearing away his exhibition from Jerusalem, having been kept from it last evening by Mr Delingpole. If so, he had gone by the time I looked in, on the way to arrange my flowers.

'My nephew can have had nothing to do with this,' Father said stiffly. Poor Father! *What* would the archbishop say if the culprit turned out to be one of his own family? And then I thought rather uneasily about Lindley's owlish eyes, excited pink ears, and his schoolboy mockery of Mr Alnutt. Would a man of science think himself justified in snaffling a mummy to add to his trunk full of curiosities? Would a schoolboy snaffle it merely for a lark? Perhaps he might, but I was fairly confident that a schoolboy would not go so far as to collude in this enterprise with a strange Frenchman, and even if he did he would certainly not have stabbed him in the neck with such vicious force.

'So then, we come to this morning,' the king said. 'Who was first here? And were there any strangers about then, what, what?'

'I offered Holy Eucharist at seven o'clock, Your Majesty,' the chanter said. 'For which, I regret, there was a very poor turn-out of congregation. But that very aged man among the antiquaries was present.'

'You mean Mr Alnutt?' At the chanter's nod Father looked interested. 'He must have come early, then, before the other antiquaries arrived. But we can hardly suspect *him*.'

It was certainly hard to imagine the papery old man tottering about with the mummy and all its accoutrements, and impossible to imagine him stabbing the young Frenchman.

The canon-treasurer and his wife had been whispering together for some minutes, and he now cleared his throat. 'If you'll forgive me, Your Majesty, Mrs Bray may have something useful to add.'

The king turned a smile on her, so dazzling it would probably give her a headache directly. 'We are all ears, dear lady, what, what?'

'I was at the Deanery last night, Your Majesty, while Mr Bray attended the scientific exhibition,' she said. Her breath was short, either from the unusual requirement to speak in front of so many faces or from too-tight stays like my own. 'But I left early with a bad head. About eight o'clock, I think it was, for I heard the abbey clock toll the hour.'

'You left the Deanery all alone, dear lady?' the king asked, with an attentive frown. (He is famously protective of his own womenfolk, I gather.)

'Yes, Your Majesty. It is no matter – only a step to my door in the Little Cloister from the Deanery gate, and the abbey is always locked at night so there are no strangers about.' She hesitated. 'No strangers usually. But as I walked home last night I did hear voices.'

'Voices?'

'I thought nothing of it then, but now I do wonder.'

'What manner of voices?' the king asked.

'Well, I wasn't listening, Your Majesty, at the time, but on reflection I think one of them might have been French.'

A rustle of gratified astonishment ran round the table.

'Durand!' the king exclaimed. 'God damn me, it must have been. And what about the other voice?'

She hesitated again. 'I don't know, sire. I suppose I thought I knew it, for it didn't strike me as a stranger's voice.'

Everyone was staring at her, expectantly. She looked at us all and threw up her hands. 'It was dark, I had a headache, and what more likely than I should suppose it just one of the vergers?'

The king pounced. 'You think it was one of the vergers?'

'No, Your Majesty, I only mean it could have been. It could have been anyone who wasn't in the Jerusalem Chamber with Mr Bell.'

At this moment, the door opened and Fidoe came in, looking hectic. 'The searcher's waiting outside the west door, Yer Majesty, with them gents from the Society,' he said.

His Majesty rose to his feet and nodded to John Catling the verger. 'Very well then, let the constable in. I shall go to him and tell him all our findings.'

Catling hurried off and we all followed the king out. We did indeed have *some* findings – the whereabouts of the mummy yesterday afternoon, and Mrs Bray's mysterious intruders at night – but not very much more. I confess, I now feel very bad to have let the poor woman walk home alone. I should have followed my better instincts and accompanied her – if only so that I could have heard these mysterious voices, too.

15

THE WEST DOOR creaked open to admit the Antiquities and Thomas Corbett, the searcher of the sanctuary, and then closed again with a thump. It was almost eleven, and the congregation would be kicking their heels outside, wondering at the delay, but it couldn't be helped, Father said to Mr Lamb's complaints.

I knew Corbett by sight but had never spoken to him, his remit being the ejecting of drunks from the abbey lawns, and the circumnavigation of the whole building once an hour to be sure no one was being murdered on the premises or disporting themselves in a manner unpleasing to God. In the former it seemed he had been, on this occasion, unsuccessful.

He did not notice the presence among us of the King of Great Britain and Ireland, and therefore cheerfully imparted the information that he had been eating a late breakfast in the Cock and Crown up Charing Cross (there being a shocking lack of taverns in Westminster, he added), which accounted for the delay in fetching him.

Mr Delingpole and Mr Quintrel were with him. Mr Alnutt, whom I had seen hobbling off after them, had apparently not hobbled back again. I hoped the poor old man was now sitting in the Cock and Crown himself, fortifying his old frame against the shocks of the morning with a breakfast of his own.

'We are obliged to you for coming,' Father said. 'We have discovered something regrettable – something very unseemly—'

'A carcass? Yes, yes, the gents have already told me all about it.'

'It is this way. We will show you.'

We all repaired back to the shrine of the Confessor (the saint must be imagining his great days are returned upon him). Mr Delingpole was white about the mouth and very grave as he looked again at the poor dead body, while the equerry was busy telling Corbett how to go about his business. The poor searcher had two voices at him, for Father was also twittering. 'We cannot account for it. We cannot, indeed. And what the archbishop will say—'

Corbett went straight to Louis Durand's body and after a cursory look at the wound began rifling methodically through the pockets of his fine suit. From one he produced a single coin and from another a well-stuffed moneybag. He handed both to Father, who held them helplessly until relieved of the one by Mr Delingpole and the other by the king.

'Ten guineas in gold,' the king said, closing up the drawstring bag and handing it to his equerry, who absent-mindedly put it in his own pocket. 'And what have you got, Mr . . . ?'

'Delingpole, sire. Something rather strange. A coin I do not recognise, but which bears the name of the Pope upon it.' He held the brass coin up to show us.

'The Vatican has its own currency, I believe,' the king said.

'But who was with him?' Corbett interrupted, getting up and scratching his head. He still didn't know he was in the presence of royalty, I was sure. 'Someone stabbed him and afterwards pinched this here missing skelington what the gents told me of. Murder, it must be, plain and simple, though not for money, else they'd have taken his moneybag. I'll go fetch the coroner.'

'Is that really necessary?' The king looked at the searcher kindly. 'We can all see the cause of death.'

Corbett was confidential. 'Yes, sir, but see, sir, there's rules what we got to follow, 'specially when a man's been skewered, like. Rules made by the king his own self. I can't stray, else I'll be turned off double quick.'

'Desaguliers,' the king said to his equerry, 'take this man out and explain the situation to him, will you? If the coroner is called, the press will be next and I don't wish it. Not yet, in any event.'

'Yes, sire.' And Desaguliers led the poor searcher away to be acquainted with his brush with greatness.

Meanwhile, the king had fixed his eye on Mr Quintrel with a severity that I myself should have found alarming but which seemed to leave the scholar entirely unmoved. He showed no sign of guilt, but no sorrow at the death of his friend either. If anything, he looked rather bored. He was a strange man indeed.

'And so you're the fellow that brought the Frenchman here, hey?' the king asked.

Mr Quintrel sniffed, and nodded, and scratched under his neckcloth as if he had lice.

'A particular friend of yours, I gather?'

'By no means.' Mr Quintrel peered up at the king from his habitual scholar's stoop. 'Scarcely knew him.'

'But you *did* know him? From where, what, what?'

Mr Quintrel looked evasive. 'I travel to France a good deal, sire.'

'Do you!' The king evidently thought there could be no very good reason for that. 'For what purpose?'

'I am in search of Roman fragments. Roman remains. Some trace of an old temple under the oldest part of this abbey, which is a remnant of the first cathedral built by the Confessor.' Unconsciously Mr Quintrel took out his pipe and fiddled with it, unlit. 'The only picture of the Confessor's abbey is on a tapestry they have in a French cathedral – a small place called Bayeux. It shows the death of Harold and the crowning of the Conqueror in the Confessor's new-built abbey. Like Edward Longshanks, being a foreigner, William the Bastard was eager to appropriate the kingly Saxon past.'

This was hardly politic, the present Hanoverian king being quite as much an interloper as the Conqueror to many minds.

Meanwhile the king was frowning. 'You have been to Bayeux, what, what?'

'Yes, a half-dozen times. A Frenchman commissioned a set of engravings of the tapestry which I took care to get hold of and publish in England under my own name.'

'The same Frenchman you brought here?'

'No, no. Another fellow who doesn't know me else he'd have caved my head in for stealing his work.'

'Mr Quintrel is speaking of academic rivalry, Your Majesty,' Mr Delingpole put in. 'Nothing more serious than that.'

'So where did you meet this here dead man?' the king asked.

'In Calais, the last time I was there.'

'And when was that?'

'About ten days ago. Delingpole had already written to you about the opening of Longshanks' tomb, Your Majesty, asking permission, and I told Durand so. It turned out he was coming to England to research the grail.'

'The what? What, what?'

'The Holy Grail.'

'God damn me,' the king said with some astonished feeling. But he was still enjoying himself. 'Carry on.'

'I invited him to our society meetings as a guest. It is a courtesy we extend to all foreign antiquaries who visit London and such a young man with an interest in history seemed worth encouraging.'

'Do you know where he was lodging?'

'Never asked.'

'And you did not see him again, last night, after the opening?'

Mr Quintrel shrugged a negative. He was making no effort to excuse himself from suspicion. The result was that I believed him.

The king now waved the antiquities away and turned back to Father, speaking low and confidentially.

'See here, Dean,' he said, 'a murder in my own Peculiar, under the eye of my own dean, for whom I stuck my neck out over the archbishop, would look very bad, what, what? We have only just got through all that unpleasant business with Pitt, and the press are still undecided if they like me or hate me. Of course, I don't much care – these days there are no Jacobites lurking around the corner to knock me off my throne – but I don't choose to look like a fool for bringing you in over the archbishop's man.'

'No, Your Majesty,' Father said humbly.

'I expect we can fob off enquiries for a day or two, and by then I'd be obliged if you had found out who let the Frenchie into the abbey and who killed him – if it ain't this dirty fellow, Quintrel, after all. I ain't so particular about the mummy – we can always say it was never there at all, and *that* whole story a fairy tale. But if you do find it, I dare say that will be all the better.'

'OPEN THE WEST doors, Ede,' the chanter said to the verger, as soon as the royal party had swept out, spurs clattering. 'It is well past eleven, and we must go to worship, we must indeed.'

And if we were to obey the king and keep the death quiet as he wished, it was, I suppose, necessary to let the day go on in its usual way. Henry Ede duly hurried off while Father locked the door to the shrine in the high altar. The choir were already processing up the aisle to their stalls again, with Mr Lamb trotting behind them, and the congregation coming in. It seemed Louis Durand's body was to remain where it lay at least for now.

I had let down my looped skirts to hide my bloodstained shoes just in time, for Lord Chatham, formerly Pitt, and the king's deadly enemy, was now upon us. 'All well, I hope, Dean? I have never known the place locked against its worshippers before.'

'No, no, my Lord, just a delay while we finished some works for Holy Thursday.'

As Lord Chatham joined the congregation, the service began and the rest of us retreated to Poets' Corner. Father leaned on the edge of Chaucer's tomb, looking suddenly as white as a sheet. After all my former cold clarity I now felt scarcely better, and I took hold of his sleeve, finding a sudden comfort in his sturdiness. The rest of the Antiquities talked among themselves in low voices while Mr Suckling listened, the smile finally back on his lips.

'Nonsense.' Mr Alnutt was among them again, his reedy voice rising above the others. 'He is not gone at all. We saw him not ten minutes earlier. We all saw it.'

'We saw a spectre,' Mr Delingpole said. 'Not the corporeal form, Alnutt, from which it differed very markedly.'

Mr Alnutt waved a hand. 'The spiritual realm was about it, that was all. I dare say angels would look much the same.'

He approached Father and took hold of his arm with trembling old man's fingers. 'Do you not see, Dean? Edward's body is not stolen. Yes, he has left his tomb, but not the abbey. We all saw him.'

I think Father really loathed the Antiquities by now. He shook off Mr Alnutt's hand with an irritable gesture and looked at me, probably hoping for some sense. Unfortunately I was obliged to disappoint him. 'We did see something before you and the king arrived,' I said. 'I tried to tell you, only then we found the dead body and afterwards we were

127

all bundled off to Jerusalem. I don't know what it meant, or whether the workmen were right that it had something to do with the death.'

Father frowned. 'I really think—'

'It was horrible, Father. Longshanks, wrapped in his shroud. Wearing his crown and walking.'

'Walking?' Father repeated, in a tone that made it clear he found himself unwillingly in an excitable company of lunatics.

'Lurching,' Mr Delingpole said. 'Lurching and shuffling more than walking. Very strange, Dean, and, as Miss Bell observes, very horrible.'

Mr Alnutt sat down suddenly beside Father as if struck by a new thought. 'By heaven, though! By heaven, though, sirs! It may have been dreadful, but it was Edward, nonetheless! Our unworthy eyes have been blessed with the sight of an ancient king of England.'

The rational reader who did not witness it all may disapprove, of course; but I confess I thought Mr Alnutt was right. So, too, remarkably, did the cynical Mr Quintrel. 'Praise be to God,' he said. 'And will we see Apollo next? Will he lead me to his temple? Everything is possible, now.'

'It is certainly a mystery,' Mr Delingpole said, not really listening. 'And it surely cannot be unrelated to the murder. With your permission, Dean, I'll creep around the ambulatory and see if the vision has left any physical traces.'

Father flapped an acquiescent hand, only too glad to be rid of them as they all departed in Delingpole's footsteps. The choir had begun to chant the *Venite* and, in the following quiet, as I held Father's hand, the ineffable peace of the abbey gradually sank down on us like a warm blanket of feathers.

'It will all be found out, Father. Don't fear.'

He looked at me, his little face very troubled. 'I dare say it will, my dear. I only hope that what is *found out* is not disgraceful to the abbey. I rather wish we might lay poor Durand in Edward's tomb and forget all about it.'

'You do not mean that,' I said soothingly. 'Depend upon it, young Durand was only a thief and he brought another one with him. No one can blame you.'

'Who can say? Who can tell?' But Father stood up and gestured towards the cloisters. 'Let us go home, my dear. If the antiquaries find anything out they will come and tell us.' He sounded bitter. 'I think we can safely rely on them for *that.*'

16

LINDLEY WAS IN the parlour, looking very satisfied with himself, reading the newspaper and eating bread and marmalade. Though I was eager to take off my bloodstained shoes, I felt ignobly pleased to linger long enough to puncture his contentment. 'You have missed an extraordinary amount of excitement,' I told him, 'not to mention the king his very self, with us all morning.'

Lindley looked up at us, smiling slightly at my tone, the slice of bread halfway to his mouth. 'Excitement? Whatever has happened?'

'King Edward's mummy has been stolen and that poor young Frenchman, Monsieur Durand, is murdered.'

'What?' Lindley's face changed and he dropped his bread marmalade side down on his lap. He jumped up, cursing. 'For God's sake, Susan, look what you have made me do. It is no joke.'

'No, it is not,' Father said sombrely, sitting down at the table and looking suddenly dreadful. 'It is a calamity, my boy, that I fear may involve us all in a dreadful scandal.'

Lindley stopped dabbing at his breeches and looked at Father with dawning alarm. 'It is true, what she said?' At Father's weary nod, he put down the cloth. 'Forgive me, sir, I thought she must be teasing as usual. I didn't expect to hear of such *excitement* as that.'

'I would not have believed it either, if I had not seen it with my own eyes,' Father answered. 'But what Susan says is unfortunately all true. Our best hope is that Monsieur Durand was merely a thief who came back to the abbey after dark to steal the mummy with an accomplice, a man with whom he argued in a manner fatal to himself.'

'An accomplice!' Lindley looked even more astonished.

'Mrs Bray, the canon-treasurer's wife, heard voices in the cloister last night,' Father said, 'while we were all in Jerusalem attending your performance. She thought she heard one of them speak French. But it was past sunset, and therefore if it *was* Durand then someone from the abbey must have let him in, for the doors were locked. The king is very vexed, as you may imagine, and the sacrist jubilant at my discomfiture.'

This was the first time I had ever heard Father admit Mr Suckling's personal dislike of himself, and it made me think things must be very bad.

'But where were you, Lindley?' I asked. 'Mr Delingpole said he'd told you they were coming back today with the king. Why weren't you there?'

'Delingpole told you?' Father looked at Lindley, surprised. 'Told you when?'

Lindley answered Father's question instead of mine. 'Last night as he left the performance, sir.'

'And it did not occur to you to pass the message on to

me?' Father was vexed, and it would certainly have saved him a good deal of embarrassment if he had been there to welcome the king that morning instead of hurrying in late, to find the body already discovered.

'I would have done,' Lindley said, now looking rather chastened, 'but by the time I had cleared everything away last night I could not find you. You were already abed.'

'And this morning?'

Lindley looked shamefaced under Father's evident displeasure. 'I'm sorry, sir. I was busy packing away my things from last night into my trunk upstairs. I had no idea about any of *this*,' he added with a helpless gesture.

I dare say we all looked more sombre than usual, but there was a new seriousness in Lindley's face that made its oddities somehow more interesting. 'I did think it was strange when I came out to find the porter away from his post and everything deserted,' he added. 'Then I found that old man Alnutt sitting outside looking rather ill. I asked him what the matter was, and he started babbling something about ghosts and empty tombs. I thought he was probably suffering an attack of senility – had perhaps lost track of time and thought it was Easter again – so I brought him in with me. I put him in your study, uncle, and went to fetch him tea and cake.'

So this is where Mr Alnutt had been while the others ran off for the searcher. I was glad to find he had not hobbled all the way to Charing Cross and back. 'He didn't mention the dead body?'

Lindley shook his head. 'Not a word.'

'Poor old man,' I said. 'I suppose it was more of a shock to him to see the mummy gone when it is so close to his heart.

He was still very excited when he reappeared among us in Poets' Corner.'

At this juncture the parlour door opened and Mr Delingpole came in.

'Nothing,' he said, at our enquiring looks. 'No remnant of anything to say the ghost was ever there. But I'll lay money on the fact it had something to do with the murder, coming so soon on its heels.'

'Ghost?' Lindley asked in a tone of renewed astonishment. '*Something to do with the murder?*'

But Mr Delingpole wasn't listening. 'Is it not obvious that the ghost walked in order to frighten us away? It was meant to prevent us from entering the shrine and discovering what mischief had occurred. Who else but the murderer would wish to do so? And therefore he must have returned this morning, to the very scene of his crime, with remarkable nerve.'

'How horrible!' I said with a shudder. But then I remembered the inhuman attenuated tendrils of the ghost's figure. 'But, Mr Delingpole, surely it is impossible that it was a man, even if such a giant even existed. How could a man look so like a monster?'

Mr Delingpole frowned. 'I myself thought there was something familiar about the ghost's figure, however strange, though I could not place it.'

That was even more horrible, and for a moment my mind flashed over all the men I knew. Who could possibly have played the ghost's part, if it were indeed the murderer's trick? Who was so tall and strangely thin? No one I knew; and of that I was exceedingly grateful. 'I cannot think it was human. It seemed wholly fiendish to me.'

'As I fear it was meant to, Miss Bell.'

'If someone does not explain all this to me at once, I shall go demented,' Lindley said, his new seriousness apparently warring with his old boyish enthusiasm so that his ears pulsed red and white by turns.

'Then you must ask your cousin about it, Mr Bell, for I must return to my chambers. But, while I think of it, Dean, I asked Blake if he still had the drawings he made of Edward's mummy – thank God for them, now – and he told me he had given them to you in the hurry of leaving the abbey when the roof was coming down. Do you still have them?'

'Certainly,' Father said, 'I put them in my desk, for safe keeping. I confess that in the muddle of all these happenings, I had quite forgotten them. You are welcome to take them, I am sure.'

Father took him into his study and Lindley turned to me. 'Susan, for God's sake, what is all this nonsense Delingpole is spouting about a ghost?'

'If you will call it nonsense before we begin, I cannot tell you.'

He was impatient. 'Oh, you know it is just my way. I don't mean anything by it. I am only ever teasing.'

I suppose I did know it. And, in that, I also supposed he was no worse than I was. But, then, I fear, I *do* mean something when I tease him.

Father popped his head around the parlour door. 'Susan, my dear, have you had those drawings?'

'No, Father. I never saw them.'

'Curious.' He withdrew again and I heard him tell Mr Delingpole that perhaps they were in Jerusalem, though he distinctly remembered putting them in his own desk. They went out together, their voices retreating.

'But the ghost,' Lindley prompted. 'Tell me precisely what you saw.'

He was an exacting inquisitor, and my vocabulary was tested to its limits by his questions (in fact, it was only now that I came up with the useful words *bulging* and *shimmering*).

My cousin frowned, looking rather preoccupied and far away. For a moment he lived up to his name, looking far more like a dreamy *Lindley* than he usually did, and to my surprise I found myself admiring the new, thoughtful creases around his eyes.

'But why does Delingpole suppose any of this is connected to the murder?' he asked.

'Why would he not?' I countered. 'After all, we have never had a ghost in the abbey before, and never a murder neither – or not since thirteen hundred and something, when people were rather more hasty than now.'

In normal circumstances Lindley would have been eager to hear that story and I would have been delighted to tell it. An escaped prisoner from the Tower took sanctuary in the abbey but, perhaps taking Thomas à Becket as a precedent, the king's soldiers disregarded religious niceties and murdered him in the quire along with a hapless, passing sacrist. (That latter detail is particularly satisfactory to my mind and I think would please Lindley, too. When all this is over I shall be sure to tell him, for I also like the way his eyes crease when he laughs in his more usual, unsentimental way.)

'In any event,' I added, 'since neither Father nor the king

saw the ghost themselves, they will never believe it, whatever Mr Delingpole says.'

'The king did not see it?' Lindley had wandered away to the window but now looked back at me, surprised.

'No, he had hurried off to find Father. It was only the Antiquities, myself and the workmen that were there to witness it.'

At this juncture, Father and Mr Delingpole came back in.

'The devil of a business,' Father said. 'The drawings are not in Jerusalem either. I have looked high and low, but I am certain I left them in my desk. Truly I am.'

Father's idea of looking high and low usually consists of opening the drawer in question and, if the item he desires is not in plain view, declaring it missing. Accordingly, I went to look myself. In this case, however, he had had everything out, tossed carelessly about on the desktop, and the drawings were certainly not there. (Though I did notice that the pocket watch I had given him for his birthday was among the muddle, wrapped up again in its paper packaging. I wondered if, despite his thanks, he had not really liked it, which, what with the saving up of *filthy lucre*, *&c.*, would be rather vexing.)

I looked into Jerusalem, but there was really nowhere the drawings could have been left, apart from the long table where we had sat with the king, and the mantelpiece above which Lindley had hung his mysterious picture.

I hurried back to the parlour to find Lindley quizzing Mr Delingpole more closely than I thought polite about the exact nature of the *bulging*, *shimmering* and *lurching* we had seen when the ghost walked. But when I confirmed that the drawings were really missing from Father's desk, and not in Jerusalem either, Mr Delingpole broke off answering Lindley's questions and looked at Father gravely. 'This is rather strange, Dean. How can you account for it?'

'I can't. Dear me, dear me, this is all far too much.' Father looked suddenly very pale and deflated under his scarlet cassock. I went to him and knelt at his feet, chafing his hands, while Cuthbert shuffled up and down his perch, alive to the atmosphere of mystery, muttering *Good God preserve us!* in an excitable undertone.

'Murdered bodies and wandering spirits,' Father said, his voice as faint as if he were at the bottom of Lindley's coalmine. 'Good grief! That tomb has lain undefiled for half a millennium until impious hands opened it.' He looked up at Mr Delingpole with a return of some energy and volume. 'I shall never forgive you, sir, if your meddling has brought all this disaster upon us.'

At this Mr Delingpole wisely elected to return to his chambers, and at Lindley's urging, Father took an unprecedented second glass of sherry.

17

I THOUGHT FATHER SHOULD go to bed, but he said there was no earthly possibility of sleeping a wink until the dead man was removed from the shrine and the whole business explained. So, as his colour was returning under the influence of the sherry, I suggested he go to Holy Eucharist instead, which would soon be starting and might comfort him more than anything. After that, I added, he should go and find Fidoe and soothe his mind in the Lady Chapel with his new hole in the floor.

Lindley examined me consideringly after Father was gone. 'You look in need of a sherry yourself, Susan.'

'Do I?' I was rather flattered by his attention, which was – as I have previously recorded – usually uncomplimentary. 'Am I very pale?'

'Green as Cuthbert's apple.' He stood up and held out his hand to me. 'But come, exercise will do you more good. Walk with me in the abbey.'

'I must change my shoes,' I said, raising my skirts to show him the bloodstains, which now, to my eye, looked more than anything like the rusted patches on the old iron crown the poor missing mummy had worn.

At the sight, Lindley's face changed again. I suppose, until then, the whole story had seemed so preposterous that, however serious he might have looked, he had still hardly believed it. The incontrovertible proof of the bloodstains now drove every vestige of banter from his expression. 'Good God, Susan. That is horrible.'

'I shall show you where the ghost walked,' I added, going to the door. 'I think Mr Delingpole must have been right that it was the murderer returned, and that too is horrible – really more horrible than this blood, since it means I have seen the murderer myself, face to face.'

'I don't believe it,' Lindley answered. He pointed to my rusty shoes. 'Delingpole is talking nonsense. No man, not even the deepest-dyed murderer, would be so stupid as to return and play ghost after *that*.'

'BUT WHATEVER CAN these stolen drawings have to do with anything, do you think?' he asked me, as we went back through the abbey where the sung Eucharist was beginning, with Mr Suckling as the celebrant. In this capacity his unctuousness is put to good use, for he beats his breast with lachrymose self-loathing, and melts to his knees with a humility so profound it is really pure vanity. There was no sign of Father. Perhaps he did not like to take the wafer from the sacrist's clammy hand. I certainly should not myself.

Lindley and I walked together up and down the nave and the ambulatories, the side chapels, and finally into the

Lady Chapel – where Father poked his head up from the hole in the floor which he and Fidoe had opened last Friday in search of James I. He looked a little more cheerful than before, for Fidoe had just opened Queen Elizabeth's tomb to reveal the great queen herself along with her sister Mary piled up in their coffins – Elizabeth naturally on top, Father told us. I was pleased to see he had recovered some of his usual cheerful spirits and I silently blessed Fidoe, whose good-natured voice I could hear from the subterranean vault even if I couldn't see him. There was going to be a world of trouble and grief, but I really couldn't see where we were to begin in the enquiries the king had ordered.

Lindley, however, was more optimistic (even if, by the same token, more alarming). 'There are nooks and crannies everywhere in this place where a murderer could hide,' he observed rather too cheerfully, as we dived off past the Chapel of the Pyx towards the Little Cloister, another subterranean gloom, this time the remnants of the old monkish passageways where they had kept the monastery's treasure and their provisions. The Chapel of the Pyx is always locked. The *pyx* are coins, I believe, and rumour has it that a tenth of all English coins minted is kept here in large wooden trunks. I do not know if this is true (*addendum*: I asked Fidoe and it *is* true) nor why it should be so (*addendum*: Fidoe is also unclear on this) but I believe not even Father has the Pyx key, which is kept by the government itself.

It was very gloomy in the Dark Entry and I smothered a shriek as a figure suddenly erupted from the shadows and advanced on us, duskily, until it reached the critical threshold of light enough to be recognised. (I expect critical thresholds of light are the kind of thing that interest Lindley, but even after all these subsequent horrors I have not yet forgiven him for banishing me from his demonstration, and therefore I avow here that they *do not* and *never shall* interest me.)

'Quintrel!' Lindley said. 'Good Lord, what are you doing here in the dark?'

'Investigating,' the scholar answered evasively, for it was indeed he, a fact announced by a stale smell of tobacco as much as the sight of his grimy neckcloth in the aforesaid *threshold, &c.*

'Investigating? Have you found any new evidence about your friend's death?'

'My friend?' Quintrel looked blank for a moment. 'Oh, him. No, no, there's nothing I can do about *that*. I am returned to my usual business, seeking Apollo.'

'And are these dark passages where you think his temple lies?'

'They are certainly the last vestiges of the original abbey which the Confessor built.'

I looked around at the low vaulted passage with new eyes. It was nearly as dark as Mr Suckling's lair in St Faith's chapel, but the round arches and painted bricks had a homely feel in contrast to the soaring Gothic splendour of the main abbey building, and I thought I would have liked the Confessor's abbey well enough. (For which I expect he is very obliged to me.)

'And about this morning,' Lindley said, perhaps thinking he had shown sufficient interest in Apollo for present purposes, 'can you tell me what happened when you went for the constable?'

'No,' Mr Quintrel said. 'I was not a party to that.'

'But you were there when we found Monsieur Durand,' I said. 'And you left with the others.'

'I left with them but didn't go for the constable. Delingpole was full of bustle so I let him go without me. I loitered about Broad Sanctuary for a while, but he was a devil of a time in returning with the searcher. Just as I began to think I might as well go home, I saw you, Mr Bell, taking Alnutt into the Deanery, and I followed you. The entrance to the Deanery was unchained and the porter was nowhere to be seen. So I came through the cloisters and back down here to the undercroft. When I heard all the commotion of Delingpole returning with the constable, I came into the abbey through the south transept door and joined the party.'

This was certainly proof of two things. First, that Mr Quintrel was the queerest of queer fish; and second, that anyone could do anything in this labyrinth of a building and no one would be any the wiser.

'You and he were both back in the abbey by the time the king left,' I said. 'Mr Alnutt told Father all about the ghost.'

'Yes. And then I saw him again, later in the day.' Mr Quintrel was offhand. 'Coming out of St Faith's with that smirking fellow.'

I looked at Lindley. 'Perhaps Mr Alnutt was taken poorly again, and Suckling was looking after him.'

'I sincerely hope not, for Alnutt's sake,' Lindley said.

'Alnutt is a poor old creature,' Mr Quintrel said. 'And far too taken up with the trinkets of the past, not its gods as I am.'

What I really think of Mr Quintrel I cannot decide, but

in any event he seemed to have nothing else of interest to impart so Lindley and I returned to the abbey where Holy Communion was over, the choir had filed out and the congregation had left.

'Trinkets,' Lindley said thoughtfully, as we passed Blake's empty scaffold. 'I suppose he means all that unseemly gloating over the mummy's paste and beads. Quintrel looks the most dissolute of men, but he clearly thinks himself very spiritual.'

When we came back to the crossing, we found that in our absence the searcher had returned with a couple of assistants and was in murmured conversation with Father (whom they had apparently routed out of his vault) and Mr Suckling (who never needs routing). They intended to move Louis Durand's body to the abbey lock-up during the break before Evensong, they said, a sight I felt no desire to witness. Of course, having missed everything else, Lindley was very eager to see the corpse, and accordingly we parted company.

As Lindley followed the others into the shrine, Blake appeared at my elbow. I realised I hadn't seen him since the meeting in Jerusalem that morning, which now felt like days ago. It turned out that in the interim he had been having some thoughts of his own.

'Those tapestries,' he said to me without preamble. 'The ones round the altar. I just remembered I saw them move.'

'When?'

'Last night, late, before I left the abbey.'

I looked at his face. 'How exactly did they move?'

He frowned, his dreamy eyes remembering, looking through me not at me. 'As if someone were hiding behind them.'

'You had better tell Corbett, the searcher.'

'I was going to. Followed him here. But now—' His eyes grew huge. 'I just saw them move again. In exactly the same way.'

This was unpleasant, regardless of whether the figure behind the curtain proved to be Monsieur Durand's murderer or Edward's horrid ghost. 'Let's go and tell Father,' I said.

But Lindley was just now coming out of the shrine, looking pale and shocked again. Corbett's assistants were carrying out Louis Durand's shrouded body on a kind of bier made of canvas stretched over poles. I could see Father and Mr Suckling behind them, in the doorway to the shrine, evidently arguing.

Blake clutched my arm with his square fingers. 'Look! It moved again! We'd best catch it before it escapes.'

And before I knew what was happening he had hopped over the low iron baluster and crossed the Cosmati-work pavement to where two of the great tapestry hangings meet, suspended on long ropes from the triforium arches above. If a murderer or a ghost was lurking behind them, I thought distractedly as I hurried after him, at least the place was crowded with people to come to our aid. I reached Blake's shoulder just as he pushed back one of the tapestries and we peered beyond it into what turned out to be a shadowy alcove. Behind the curtain and lying at our feet was a body, the folds of its scarlet robe pooling about it. The face was turned up towards the ceiling, its eyes were closed, and a hectic flush stained its cheeks an unnatural vermilion red.

18

THERE WAS A furtive movement behind the next tapestry
along, and before we could gather our wits, Fidoe
stepped out from behind it looking pale. 'Gawd Almighty,
Miss Susan, you nearly frightened me to death.'

The feeling was certainly mutual. My heart was beating
like a bird against my ribs and I clutched hold of Blake's
sleeve to steady myself. 'I thought it was another dead body,'
I said. 'Perhaps even Louis Durand's accomplice.'

Blake squatted down for a closer look at the newly revealed
effigy, and, my heart slowing, I knelt beside him. Unlike most
of the statues in the abbey she had apparently escaped the
defacing attentions of Cromwell and his soldiers, for she was
still painted, even if the paint was patched and faded by time.
She wore what had been a blue skirt, a red tunic and a green
cloak. On her head was a medieval wimple, and her worn flesh-
coloured hands were clasped piously at her breast. I saw now
that she was lying on a low bier, perhaps knee high, which was
fabulously encrusted with gold leaf. Bright, blazing shields of
gold, arches of a duller more tarnished shade, and a line of

small figures below, each as beautifully painted as the effigy lying above, and encrusted with yet more gold leaf. At her feet lay two soulful stone terriers, half-hidden by the hem of her dress. As I have already observed, the abbey is a positive kennel.

'I never knew this was here,' I said, reaching out to lay my living hand on her marble one.

Fidoe shook his head, but now, I noticed, without his customary smile of pleasure at such a find. 'No more did we, Miss Susan. The tapestries were sewn together till yer father went poking about back here the other day.'

'She's magnificent,' I said, running a finger over the gilded arches of her bier. Blake had already got out his pen and paper with an eager look.

Fidoe pulled back the next curtain, whence he had just emerged, to expose another tomb, equally gorgeous, equally gold. A man this time, in knight's garb, with his feet on a medium-sized lion.

'My,' I said. 'What riches! Do we know who they are?'

'Yer father says the man is Longshanks' brother, Edmund Crouchback, and the lady is Crouchback's wife. Aveline de something, he said.'

Still there was none of his usual pleasure in the discovery. As Blake began to sketch, I touched Fidoe's arm. 'Are you quite well, Fidoe? I thought your antiquarian old heart would be delighted to find things like these.'

He shook his head. 'Yer father's had another notion, Miss Susan. Said he fancied a nice wood screen instead of these old things.' He touched the antique tapestry. 'Mahogany again, like the choir stalls. But these here hangings are donkey's ears old and it would be a shocking shame to burn 'em.'

'Burn them!'

'That's what he was thinking.'

'After this morning's business he won't be thinking anything. He will forget all about it.'

Fidoe looked gloomy and didn't answer, so I said, 'I'll talk to him.' And then, hoping to cheer him up, I added, 'But you have far more sway with him than I do.' (His success with Father is patchy, viz. the choir stalls; but it is certainly better than mine.)

At this he brightened a very little. 'Well, I'll do my best.'

'And look at those dogs,' I said encouragingly, pointing to where Blake was now bowed over his paper, oblivious to us. 'Perhaps you should show them to Dame Yates and convince her a gold-leaf dog would be gorgeous enough after all.'

At that, Fidoe lifted his eyes to heaven, which gave me to understand he likes the dame as little as I do. But he looked very tired. The day had been hard on all of us, I thought. It was not Father's vandalism that really troubled him.

'You should go home,' I said. 'It is past seven o'clock and you look weary to death. There's nothing else for you to do here today.' And I began to push him gently towards the north door.

'Terrible to see that dead feller in the shrine, though, weren't it?' he said suddenly as we crossed the paving together, leaving Blake to his new task. 'Gawd Almighty, all that blood.'

'It *was* horrible.'

'And that ghost was a strange thing, Miss Susan. I could hear you all yelling out, from where I was up in the gallery, but *I* couldn't see nothing at all.'

'Perhaps it was hidden from where you were standing,' I said. 'It climbed out of thin air near Edward's tomb, walked up and down, and then climbed back into nothingness again.'

He shook his head. 'I could see everything this side of the shrine. Only thing I couldn't see was them side chapels underneath the gallery where I was standing.'

'The ghost wasn't in there,' I said. 'It was in the ambulatory directly beside the shrine.'

He spread his hands. 'Well, anyways, I didn't see it, and all things considered, I suppose I'm not sorry. Perhaps it only came to them gents on account of being vexed with 'em for prodding and poking it.' (*Obs.*: in actual fact, Edward seemed quite in favour of *prodding* and *poking*, having written a great deal of it into his will.)

'But as I helped take off the lid yesterday, I don't see why it shouldn't be vexed with me, too.' Fidoe looked at me rather earnestly. 'Why do you think I couldn't see it, Miss Susan?'

'I don't know,' I said, 'but just count yourself lucky you were safely up in the gallery and didn't. You were working on the lights, I suppose? I saw the ropes.'

'Not working,' Fidoe said, 'clearing up the mess.'

'Mess?'

'Two o' the lamps had come down in the night and smashed on the paving. Terrible lot of glass everywhere. Someone had roped off the walk by the time I got here, first thing. Must've seen it and thought it best. One of the vergers, I dare say.'

'How had the lamps fallen?'

He shook his head. 'Weak link in the chain, must be. I spent the morning checking all the rest.'

Lindley had appeared at my side in the middle of all this and now, when Fidoe had finally been prevailed upon to go home, he announced he was also leaving. He didn't look particularly eager to go, however, and as we walked back to the crossing (where Blake was still absorbed in his sketch of the new tombs) he tucked my hand under his elbow.

'I promised Tom Ffoulkes to go to the opera tonight,' he said. 'God knows, it's the last thing I wish to do, after seeing that poor dead fellow, but Delingpole told me the king was adamant we should carry on as normal until we can find out what really happened, so I suppose I had better go.'

'Don't tell him anything,' I said. 'He does not strike me as discreet.'

Lindley looked at me sidelong. 'You really think I'd gossip?'

'No,' I said, though rather doubtfully. My own mind was so full of it all I couldn't imagine how he was to get through a whole evening pretending that everything was perfectly normal.

'You don't think me an out and out rogue?'

'No,' I said again. 'No, of course not. *Good God preserve us from the thought.*'

I had managed a tolerable imitation of Cuthbert imitating Lindley and he laughed for the first time all day. (*Hurrah!* I thought. *Give me a nut.* Even in the midst of murder it seems I am incorrigibly frivolous. Or perhaps Fidoe's worried face had made me sad, and I wanted to laugh the feeling away with Lindley, who is ordinarily so willing to be amused.)

'Fidoe's story was interesting, wasn't it?' Lindley said, as we came up to the porter's lodge. 'That he didn't see the ghost at all? If it really was some kind of trick, I do wonder how it was done. Whatever else, it was remarkably clever.'

There was a look in his eye as he said this which made me remember my earlier unease. 'Lindley, it wasn't you, was it? As a joke?'

It would certainly have cleared up one mystery, and I was therefore disappointed when he shook his head vehemently, looking as sober as an old judge. But afterwards I remembered the hideous figure we had seen and, whatever Mr Delingpole might think, I still believed it quite impossible for any living man to have made himself look so unearthly.

But then, oh Lord, as soon as Lindley had sauntered off, Mr Suckling appeared like a horrid spider from the shadowy door to his lair, the Chapel of St Faith, and was upon me before I could escape.

'Miss Bell,' he said, with a happy sigh. 'I am so glad to see you. I have your father's cope waiting for your needle, if you'll oblige me.' He already had a hand on the small of my back and began propelling me inexorably towards the Stygian gloom beyond the old oak door. I looked about in hope of a friendly face, but there was no one in sight.

But when was ever a Dean's daughter ravished in a vestry? All Mr Suckling wanted was for me to mend a seam, I told myself. Even so, when we went inside and the door shut behind us with a hollow click, I felt a misgiving. As usual, it was very dim (I think he has some idea of preserving the bright colours of the ancient robes by keeping them sequestered in gloom). I was on the point of telling him that I couldn't see the hand in front of my face, never mind a needle and thread, when his soupy voice forestalled me. I realised then that he was far too close behind me and exuding a kind of moist eagerness.

'This is a very strange and lamentable affair, is it not, Miss Bell?'

I went swiftly to the table where Father's cope was lying, and got myself behind it, against the dark wooden cupboards – only to discover that I had thereby trapped myself, for at once he followed me and blocked the only passage out again. I picked up the hem of the cope and found the small tear where Father had tripped over it. It was so small a tear I knew it must certainly have been a ruse on the part of the sacrist to get me here alone.

'What do you make of it all, sir?' I answered as brightly as I could, averting my eyes from his greedy gaze. I meant to distract him from whatever charms he might have discovered in my person, but, as I was soon to find out, he had had his own unpleasant reasons for starting the topic himself and was only too eager to continue it.

'Oh, do call me Simon,' he said, prodding the needlebook and reels of thread towards me along the table slowly, with an almost caressing finger. 'You and I should not stand on ceremony, Susan, finding ourselves involved together in such a serious case as murder.'

The sound of my name in his mouth was horrible, especially as he said it in the same fondling way he was poking at the needlebook.

I took a needle from it with a slightly shaking hand. 'We are all *involved*, I suppose.'

'And no one more than your father, who is supposed to be the authority here.'

If he meant to woo me, this seemed a strange way to go about it. 'You can't call this Father's fault. He knew nothing about it.' I tried to thread the needle but it was too dark, and my hands were trembling. I heard the faintest hiss of satisfaction. Lord above, suppose he mistook my trembling for a symptom of love?

'Quite so. A very regrettable lapse on his part; and, as he himself observed, one very damaging to himself if it ever gets out.' He took the needle from my now resistless fingers and held it to the candlelight to thread it for me.

'No more damaging to Father than to the king,' I said. '*He* was the one who permitted the opening in the first place.'

'Ah, yes, it is all the king's fault, I remember you said so before. But His Majesty will hardly like to hear that said and, unjust as it may be, your father is bound to be blamed for any scandal.'

'There need be no scandal if we all keep quiet, as the king bids us.'

He was looking at me with that leer again. But now, if it put me in mind of Caligula at all, it was more in the way of the Emperor's thumb poised to turn up or down against Father, not myself. I saw then that this business with Monsieur Durand had given the sacrist a sudden and unexpected power: the power to ruin Father if he only chose to defy the king and tell the archbishop what had happened. He must think it a personal gift – nay, a personal endorsement – from God Almighty, and the satisfied hiss I had heard in the dark had been that of a predator who had made his prey squirm.

'Of course, we shall be quiet,' he said soothingly. 'Of course, we shall protect the dear dean.' He handed me back the needle and took the opportunity to squeeze in beside me in the gap between the table and the wall. 'Do begin, Susan, and let me watch. The fineness of your stitching fascinates me.'

I bent my head over the tiny seam. I could feel his breath on the back of my neck. He had rested his right palm on the table beside me and at any moment he would plant the other down to my left and have me pinned.

Reader, if anyone was to be *pinned* it was not me. And though it was very bad of me as a dean's daughter, Mr Suckling (God forbid that I ever call him Simon) emitted a yelp of startled pain and fell away from me, sucking the back of his hand.

'Forgive me,' I said, taking the opportunity to slip out of the space between wall and table, towards the door and freedom. 'I hope I didn't hurt you, sir. But the light in here is really far too dim for sewing. If you'll send Father's cope to the Deanery, I'll make sure to finish it there.'

Afterwards, I fled home through the onset of the spring dusk. What with poor dead Louis Durand, the awful ghost, the hungry sacrist and Mrs Bray's story of voices, the cloisters' shadows felt, for the first time, threatening to me. Whoever had killed the Frenchman so brutally, and afterwards stolen Edward's mummy, was still at large. Mr Delingpole maintained he had returned to frighten us in the shape of the ghost. Perhaps it really had been the murderer, and not Fidoe, that Blake had seen moving behind the tapestries the previous night. Then I remembered Mr Alnutt say Longshanks' body was not stolen at all, but on the loose from his tomb, walking the abbey. I remembered the spectre's grotesque shape, and Mr Alnutt's unearthly scream. And then I ran even faster.

19

IT WAS ALL monstrous foolishness, of course. I was the deranged one, while the cloisters were as quiet and peaceful as ever. When I arrived home to the Deanery parlour, I was confronted with a sight much more dangerous to myself personally than anything that had happened that day, however horrible those events had been. Dame Yates was sitting on the sofa, and Father was HOLDING HER HANDS.

She had removed her black crepe bonnet to reveal a large white mob cap beneath it. It looked rather askew, and the frill which hid her face seemed to be trembling strangely. She was weeping, I realised after a moment, and when Father saw me I made a face of consternation and asked him by gestures if I should leave. He shook his head with some imploring violence and turned back to the lady soothingly. 'See, Dame Yates, see, here is my daughter. Susan, my dear, come in, come in. Dame Yates finds herself a trifle indisposed, I'm afraid.'

I perched on a chair where I could better see the dame's

tear-stained face. (It wasn't a very attractive sight – but then neither is my own when I cry, and anyone who thinks a woman's tears captivating must be acquainted with very different kinds of women than I am.) The small fire crackled in the grate while Cuthbert strutted excitedly up and down his perch, his head feathers ruffled as if, like me, he would feign have expelled Dame Yates from the parlour. (Had she called him *hideous* to his face? Could he somehow sense her antipathy?) But I was distracted from further consideration of the matter by the abbey clock striking a lugubrious eight o'clock. I glanced at the window. It was only blue dusk outside, not the full darkness through which Mrs Bray had walked home the previous evening. She had heard the clock chime eight, she had said, but she must have miscounted.

'Dame Yates called in to discuss Sir Joseph's memorial,' Father was explaining. 'In passing, I asked the dame her wishes regarding her own burial when God gathers her to his bosom. I am afraid the question distressed her, for which I am very sorry.'

I thought I could surmise something of the nature of the dame's distress. She would far rather be gathered to Father's bosom and, finding herself alone with him in the parlour, had perhaps hoped for a declaration of love. Instead, she had found he was bent on burying her.

'I shall never seek a grave here in the abbey,' she said, straightening her mob cap with a trembling hand, 'not when Sir Joseph's body lies in Surrey. What is there for me *here*, Dean, after all?'

I thought the question rather pointed, but Father only pressed her hands consolingly, while Cuthbert bristled at the sight, just as I did. (He is a remarkably good judge of character.)

'If needs be, I will lie where I drop,' the dame added, rendered rather bitter now. 'For who cares for an old woman like me? I shall make provision that upon my death I shall be buried in whatever parish I happen to die. I shall have naught but a leaden coffin, to be carried by the yokels of the place to a secluded and forgotten grave.'

'A very Christian, very humble notion,' Father said. (Though I must say I rather pitied these hypothetical yokels, whose views on carrying lead coffins she might not have considered.) 'I congratulate you upon such a resolution, my dear, and may even take the liberty of imitating you.' (This was easy for him to say, for with luck he will remain dean until his death and therefore find himself very conveniently placed for a local burial.)

Poor Dame Yates. I almost began to sympathise with her in the face of his obtuseness. She now looked more vexed than sorrowful, and her tears had dried without anyone noticing. 'But what of my dog, Dean? Have you made provision for my golden dog?'

Father's look of sympathy changed at once to one of weary resignation. 'Yes, yes, my dear lady, be assured that is all in hand.'

'Because, you know, if you will not do it for me, I can take the money myself to a goldsmith.'

'It shall all be done, of course it will. We have merely been a little . . . distracted . . . today.'

Poor Father. It had been such a long and worrying day for him and here was the woman still pestering him almost at bedtime. But such is the nature of a dean's life, even when not beset by unexplained corpses.

'Bring in your dog tomorrow,' Father said, getting to his feet, and raising Dame Yates to hers. 'I shall have the engraver's lad take a very good likeness.'

'An engraver's lad?' Again, Dame Yates looked doubtful.

'A very talented youth – one whom the king himself appointed to make sketches of the opened tomb of Longshanks.'

The dame looked somewhat appeased at this and, after settling her crepe back on her head, allowed herself to be escorted away to her servant and driven home through the dusky streets.

'I just noticed something strange,' I said, as Father returned to his armchair with a weary sigh. 'Remember the canon-treasurer's wife said the clock struck eight after she heard the voices in the dark? But look, it is five and twenty minutes past eight now, and still blue dusk. And besides, your meeting in Jerusalem only began at half past seven. Mrs Bray was certainly with me at the Deanery for more than half an hour.'

'She said she heard the abbey clock, I think?' At my nod Father spread his hands. 'It is very easy to miscount the chimes of a clock, my dear, and whatever time it really was, we were certainly all engaged with Lindley's demonstration at the time and if it was full dark the abbey was certainly locked. The actual hour she heard the bell ring can make little difference.'

He was right, but I was still glad I had told him. God forbid that I should keep something back that might later explain everything.

It was half past ten when Lindley came in. All his efforts to carry on as normal had been in vain since Thomas Ffoulkes had failed to turn up at the opera. 'Probably found a dancing girl to make up for the loss of his married lady,' Lindley said dismissively. So instead, he had gone to the Royal Society, which happened to be meeting tonight, and stayed briefly to watch Mr Delingpole give a paper on the subject of childhood prodigies, and the question of nature *versus* nurture in those interesting cases. I wondered if Mr Delingpole had encountered any precocious fledglings during his songbird studies or had consulted any child geniuses about the North Pole.

'A remarkable man,' Lindley said. 'The best example of a polymath I ever met.'

'What is a polymath?'

'A man who knows everything. From the Greek *polu*: much, and *manthanein*: learn.'

Pollu, polly, pol! Cuthbert said, not unnaturally supposing himself the subject of this conversation, and he spread his grey wings delightedly, revealing the crimson flash of his tail as he revolved on his perch three times, apparently far better pleased with Lindley than Dame Yates. He is probably right in that, too, I admit. Those interesting creases around Lindley's eyes now never fail to strike me when, curiously, a week ago I didn't notice them at all.

'Will I ring for supper?' I asked Lindley as he sat down across from Father by the fire.

'No, no, I have had a chop. There is no need for any fuss on my account.' He looked very much at home – and had evidently been keeping up with all our little dramas, even amid all our larger ones. 'I saw Dame Yates arriving, Uncle, as I crossed Broad Sanctuary on my way to meet Ffoulkes.'

'Father has been trying to bury her in the Abbey and she took it very ill,' I said, curling up on the hearthrug between them.

'Ah. In the newly opened vault in the Lady Chapel, I suppose?' Lindley sounded grave. 'I suspected there was more to your excavations than met the eye, Uncle. And she is, in truth, a very trying woman.'

'You children are cruel,' Father said. 'And tonight, of all nights, to be joking about bodies . . .'

That new seriousness I had liked now returned to Lindley's face, but I was glad it had not banished the mischief entirely. 'You're right, Uncle. And she is a nice old stick, in fact. I helped her down from her carriage and, when I told her I was bound for Drury Lane, she advised me, if I *must* go out, to lay off the wine. But then she said, "You would not conceive the times I have scraped my son up from the paving after a night in town, my dear," and waved her walking stick at me in the most good-natured way, which showed she did not really mean to sermonise.'

Since Father and Lindley went to bed, I have been sitting on the hearthrug writing up this account of the day in my journal – a task which has taken so long the candles are guttering. What a long day it has been! There seems to have been enough incident packed into it to suffice a normal month.

And yet, life in the abbey is always busy, even if its usual events are not particularly momentous. I have remarked before that it is a sort of village, and one where I live squarely in the centre; not separated from the world's various ranks and types as I would be if I were (for an instance) a country lady like Lindley's future wife, nor restricted to the company of one class of mankind, as I would be if I married Mr Delingpole and lived only among lawyers.

Yes, with all its constant bustle and outside visitors like the Antiquities, I like the abbey better than anywhere I have ever lived before (even if Mr Suckling is a constant irritant). And if marriage constitutes a woman's choice of profession, then so, surely, is the choice to eschew it. I will tell Father tomorrow that I am quite decided that I will never leave him. His lack of capital to retire on is a positive blessing, for it requires that we shall always be here in the interesting abbey; and, with me by his side, he need never be so lonely that he must marry merely for companionship. I wonder if that is really what Dame Yates seeks in Father? If so, her judgement is as sound as Cuthbert's, whatever else I may think about her. I ought to say, 'poor' Dame Yates, but I will not risk doing so until I am certain that the solution to her happiness is not to become an obstacle to mine.

20

MONDAY 9 MAY

THE WEATHER WAS dull this morning, and the abbey very gloomy, the two candles on the altar and another dozen in massy candlesticks along the nave the only source of illumination. It will certainly be a spectacle to flood the place with light if Fidoe can do it with his new lamps, but it seems to me that the vastness of the building will swallow up all the petty efforts of mere man to light its cavernous shadows. Nevertheless, Fidoe was back in his eyrie clanging chains, as a kind of fable of indefatigable human ambition against darkness.

Hell might be a fiery place, but Milton imagined its flames gave out no light, and to my eyes poor Louis Durand's murdered body had emanated all the blackness of hell. After the numb shock that had enveloped me on the discovery of the body, my sleep had been troubled by the vision of that horrible wound. I dreamed that instead of those little red stains on my shoes, my skirts and stockings were heavy with blood, so that the wetness slapped about my knees and my feet positively squelched in my shoes as I walked the length of the abbey, towards the dead body which I knew lay in wait for me behind the shrine's marble doors. I had started up in bed more than once, with an urge to wash and wash my feet like Lady Macbeth. (But having no wish to go the same way she did, I resisted the impulse and only wrapped my perfectly clean white toes in my nightgown for safe keeping.)

Blake was absent from his scaffold in the abbey when I came in and, though I looked everywhere, he was nowhere to be seen. I have grown used to his stocky frame perched about the place unnoticed, not to mention the frisson of pleasure occasioned by his admiring glance as I pass him. I had thought, in the night, that I ought to have listened to his poems, since no one else was ever likely to do so, and that I would ask him for a recital when we next met.

Instead, I took a brief turn about the cloisters and then around the College Garden, where a game of cricket was in progress in the school yard, at great risk to the school windows. I remembered Mrs Bray say her husband paced here by the hour, but there was no sign of him this morning. The dull grey sky was as gloomy as the abbey, and an unseasonable chill wind made me shiver and hasten home, back through the quaint Little Cloister where the resident canons live.

Back at the Deanery, Mr Delingpole had unexpectedly arrived and was watching Lindley eat a very late breakfast while he talked to Father. Mr Delingpole's reason for visiting so early was to ask if Blake's drawings had turned up, he said, but I think he was also eager to placate Father, from whose tremulous ire he had escaped yesterday, evidently thinking discretion the better part of valour.

Father was obliged to tell Mr Delingpole that the drawings were still missing. 'Disturbing,' Mr Delingpole said, pensively picking at a loose thread in his waistcoat.

'Disturbing?' Father frowned. He was still fretful and not yet ready to throw his arms about the Antiquity in a show of reciprocated friendship. 'How do you make that out, sir?'

'I mean that if the drawings are gone from your desk, the thief must have been in your study, Dean. And as the thief in question might also be the murderer, that is not a very pleasant idea.'

There can be few things less pleasant, I thought (as I took out my sewing box and sat down at the table with Charles II's hat on my knee) than the idea of assassins creeping about outside one's bedchamber door. But surely Cuthbert would have raised the alarm in such a dreadful event? And whatever could a murderer want with Blake's drawings?

These questions did not seem to strike anyone else as Lindley jumped to his feet and, clutching a piece of fruit loaf in his hand, began pacing about in a manner very distracting to my sewing. 'Mr Alnutt was in your study yesterday, Uncle, do you not remember? I put him there with my own hands. And I left him while I went to fetch him tea and cake. Do you think he could have taken the drawings while I was gone?'

'Alnutt!' Mr Delingpole looked both surprised and disgusted at the suggestion.

'Forgive me. I know he is your friend,' Lindley said, stopping in mid stride. 'I only notice the coincidence of his being there and the subsequent disappearance of the drawings.'

'But why ever would Alnutt take them?' Still, even as he spoke, Mr Delingpole's face was changing and he looked suddenly thoughtful. 'It is true that he has always been the driving force behind the tomb's opening, and he is writing a paper on the subject. It is possible, I suppose, that he might have taken the drawings for that purpose. And, being the man most entitled to have them, it would not really be so reprehensible to take them without asking.'

'Apart from the matter of his rifling through my uncle's private desk to find them.'

At this, Mr Delingpole looked pained, but Father seemed to find this new idea quite cheering. 'I hope you're right, my boy. In that case, the drawings are entirely unrelated to the murder and, to be frank, I'd happily forgive the old man for his rifling, if it solved one of our many mysteries.'

'Unless the two things *are* somehow related,' Lindley said. 'It seems to me a mighty coincidence for two such extraordinary things as a murder and a theft from your desk to happen on the same day.'

I had already decided that it was impossible to imagine Mr Alnutt wielding a round-handled weapon of any kind and it seemed Mr Delingpole agreed with me. 'Nonsense,' he said. 'He is far too old and feeble to have anything to do with the murder. The very idea is absurd.'

'The poor old man was terrified out of his wits by the ghost and shocked to death by what followed,' I added, my needle poised over the battered old hat on my knee. 'You know this is true, Lindley, for you said you found him in a sad state yourself.'

Lindley was determined not to be argued down. 'There

might have been a third accomplice. Quintrel saw him with the sacrist, remember, and we all know that Mr Suckling is a villain, if no one else is.'

The door promptly opened and the sacrist himself came in as if, like the devil, he had been summoned by the speaking of his name. I didn't know if I hoped he had heard Lindley's slur or not heard it. Lindley seemed to be of the same mind, for he cast me an expressive grimace which obliged me to hide a smile, while Cuthbert exclaimed *Good God preserve us!* at the sight of the visitor in what the psalm calls a shout of joy.

'Forgive me, Dean, am I interrupting a private conclave?' Mr Suckling looked very smooth and very inquisitive all at once. 'I did not expect to find a visitor with you so early in the day. I do beg your pardon for intruding.'

Father was still too caught up in all our speculations to ask him what he had come for. 'What is this I hear about your being with Mr Alnutt yesterday, Suckling?' he asked instead, with much deanish authority and without much courtesy. 'I would very much like to know what he said to you.'

Mr Suckling only raised his eyebrows and smiled enquiringly at Father's abrupt manner.

'Mr Quintrel told us that he saw you with Mr Alnutt yesterday afternoon,' I explained. 'The old gentleman had been taken ill earlier, and my cousin had tended to him. Was he taken ill again?'

'He was. Yes, indeed,' Mr Suckling said frankly, and his smile, no longer enquiring, only widened. 'The shock of the mummy's disappearance was almost too much to one whose whole life's work has been the medieval kings, and the finding out of old documents on the subject.' He paused, the incongruous grin lingering about his mouth. 'But I confess I did not know that Mr Lindley Bell was also involved in the affair.'

'I took him to the Deanery and gave him tea, that's all,' Lindley said, perhaps not liking the word *involved* in the present circumstances. Mr Suckling inclined his head politely and only smiled some more.

'But what is it you wanted, Suckling?' Father asked. 'Why are you here?'

There was something dismissive in Father's tone, and Mr Suckling's eyes flitted across us all, seeming to gather that while Mr Delingpole was a welcome confidant here, he himself was not. Lucky for him, he had some unpleasant news for Father. 'Only to tell you that there is an outbreak of mumps among the boys, Dean, and the chanter cannot say which, if any of them, will be fit to sing at the Ascension service on Thursday.'

'Great heavens!' Father started to his feet with such velocity he might have bowled the sacrist over if Lindley hadn't stalled his momentum with an outstretched hand. 'I really begin to think this whole business God's judgement on our doings.'

Mr Suckling was probably pleased to hear Father confirm his own opinion of the matter. 'Though I gather it is all His Majesty's fault, Dean,' he said, casting me a conspiratorial leer. I think Lindley saw it, for he turned his own eyes to me questioningly, and then looked disgusted. I might have lately resolved not to marry anybody, but it still pricked my pride that Lindley thought I had been encouraging the sacrist of all people.

'Perhaps old Alnutt is right,' Father said now, suddenly in something of a passion. 'Perhaps Longshanks' ghost really *is* on the prowl. And having been stolen himself, and his sacred resting place with the Confessor invaded by a Frenchman's corpse, who could blame him?'

At this Mr Suckling looked both piously aghast and profoundly gratified at the opportunity Father's intemperance afforded him to remonstrate. 'My dear Dean, I beg you to remember yourself. Such wild talk is not biblical teaching, and you must know it. Ghosts, if they exist at all, are demons sent from hell, not the departed spirits of the dead. Only papists have any truck with such notions, and a cleric of the Church of England is surely disgraced by such a thought.'

'While a sacrist is disgraced, sir, by venturing a rebuke to his dean,' Father answered sharply, and he and Mr Suckling looked at each other with undisguised dislike.

Mr Delingpole ventured to smooth over the awkwardness with a little joke. 'Well, well,' he said, 'though Mr Alnutt saw only strength and justice in Longshanks' dead face, I myself thought he looked the very picture of an angry old demon, and perhaps he was.'

Lindley laughed. 'The Scots certainly thought him a foreign devil sent from Hades. And I have some Tory friends who feel much the same about His present Majesty and would gladly send *him* packing back to Hanover – or hell – if they could.'

AFTER MR SUCKLING had made his oily farewells and left us, Mr Delingpole looked at Father ruefully. 'I'm very sorry, Dean. You were right to rebuke me yesterday, of course. Our opening of the tomb must have led to all the rest. Tell me, what is your searcher doing to investigate the matter?'

'Very little,' Father said shortly, but in a slightly friendlier way. 'Since the king wants the matter investigated quietly, it is difficult to send the abbey's own constable out to ask questions without the connection to ourselves being obviously made.'

Mr Delingpole nodded. 'I see the difficulty. Well then, as some recompense, will you let me do a little of the asking? If I were to investigate the matter in my professional capacity I would, as always, look to the money, and therefore I suppose our strongest suspicion must be that Durand was in league with the artefact trade. I am acquainted with some of the dealers in antiquities from my work for the Society. Perhaps I could ask them.'

Father's birdlike eyes had brightened. 'By all means, Delingpole, I would be very grateful. But what will you ask them? Nothing too direct, I hope?'

'No, no. That would, as you say, only raise unwanted curiosity. I shall talk to them about mummies in general, perhaps, and if such things are ever to be had on the open market.'

'Yes, yes.' Father nodded. 'That is a good notion, and I'm obliged to you after all, Delingpole, whatever I might have said in anger yesterday.'

He shook hands with Mr Delingpole, who then took his leave.

I laid down Charles II's hat and went with him back

into the abbey. Yesterday, before my resolution to forget all thoughts of marriage, I might have been discouraged by his silent disregard of me as we walked through the cloisters. But in my new, detached state of mind, I could see he was still reflecting on everything that had been said in the Deanery parlour, and the horrible suspicions that Lindley had managed to raise against poor old Mr Alnutt. As I have previously noted, suspicion is an intoxicant and some men, like Mr Suckling and Mr Quintrel, invite it by their mere manner. In contrast, reliability and good sense emanate from Mr Delingpole like the pleasant smell of pipe tobacco and, in fact, it was a kind of companionable silence we walked in through the quiet cloisters, only disturbed by the swallows building their nests in the vaulted eaves.

As we came into the abbey, Ben Fidoe was striding purposefully across the paving towards the small oak door beside Spenser's memorial which leads to the spiral staircase up to the triforium.

'What is that man's name again?' Delingpole asked me, and when I told him he hurried after Fidoe, calling out to him to stop. Fidoe turned back to us, rather weighed down by two large parcels and a hessian sack. 'My good man, are you going up to the triforium now? Can I come with you?'

Yes, if I had been looking for symptoms of love in the Antiquity I should have been disappointed, for his steady eye had brightened at the sight of Fidoe far more than at the sight of me. Fidoe put down his packages and looked doubtful.

'The dean told me the place is a treasure trove of abandoned things,' Delingpole explained eagerly. 'And, as a scholar of antiquity, the idea whets my appetite, I do confess.'

'Ain't nothing up there you'd want, sir. Only funny old shoes and scribbled papers.'

'Scribbled papers? Old shoes?' Mr Delingpole looked as if he might swoon with joy. 'My dear fellow, such things are priceless to a man like me. Will you show me? May I follow you up? I shall not be in the way, I promise you.'

'Did the dean say it was all right?'

'Well . . .' Mr Delingpole seemed constrained (perhaps by my presence) to be entirely frank. 'Well no, not exactly. But he certainly did not forbid it.'

Even this was stretching the truth a little. 'Father said you're the only man allowed up there, Fidoe,' I said, probably to Mr Delingpole's chagrin. But if he was to plummet through the ceiling and smash off the pavement, &c., it was not going to be my fault. (Besides, despite my resolutions viz. marriage, his immunity to my charms as opposed to those of old shoes was somewhat vexing.)

Fidoe shook his head. ''Fraid I can't help you, then, sir. You'll have to ask the dean about it. If he's happy, then I'm happy.'

He shouldered his burdens for the short distance to the little oak door, put them down to unlock it, then picked them up again and went inside, closing the door behind him. Mr Delingpole watched him go as if he were itching to follow, but instead he only sighed and smiled at me as we resumed our walk.

Blake had reappeared while I had been at the Deanery and was back in his scaffolding. He was now a good six feet higher, so that he could draw Sir Isaac Newton's thoughtful expression. The great man was leaning on a pile of books, apparently unaware that he was about to be knocked unconscious by the *perpendicular descent* of a large celestial sphere above his head.

Mr Delingpole paused by the scaffold and touched Blake's dangling foot to get his attention. 'I'm afraid your drawings have gone missing,' he told him. 'It may be that one of the society members has taken them without mentioning the matter to anyone, though the circumstances are rather strange.'

'I can draw them again from memory, if you like.'

Mr Delingpole looked sad. 'Well, well, it may come to that, though it is at odds with all our best practices.'

He walked on down the nave towards the west door and I followed him. 'You have not said anything about the ghost today,' I said. 'Have you forgotten it already?'

He smiled at me sidelong. 'I have not, any more than you have, I am sure. But until I know what in heaven to make of it, I suppose there's no point in speculating.'

Perhaps there was no point, but after a moment he added, 'I still believe that, whatever else, it must surely be connected with the dead man, and in that case his accomplice was inside the abbey with us the next morning when the ghost walked.'

A shrill yapping from the direction of the west door distracted us from this unpleasant idea, echoing around the place even to the very rafters. Dame Yates's square, tortoise figure was approaching up the nave at a march, with a very small dog dancing like a fish at the end of a leash behind her.

21

By the time the small terrier had cocked its leg against half a dozen members of parliament and defecated on Ben Jonson's head (he is buried upright, poor man, for want of money to pay for a larger plot), Father had been called once more from the Deanery. He appeared on the scene with Fidoe (summoned down the spiral stairs again) and also with Blake in tow behind them, clutching his drawing materials.

'Admiral!' Dame Yates kept crying out at intervals, which seemed puzzling until I remembered that this was the animal's name (which it resolutely ignored nonetheless). Blake squatted down, putting himself to the task of calming the little creature sufficient to take its likeness at all.

I don't know what Admiral's home life is like, but he seemed deliriously happy to escape it, and delighted by every novelty, even if he had a tendency to snap in his excitement. He is a terrier of quite the usual white and tan type and might look well enough curled up at the feet of his master, like the painted lady's two dogs. But to depict him standing guard atop the monument, as Dame Yates had proposed, would present Blake with a ticklish task, I thought, teetering on a very narrow point between the mundane and the ludicrous.

Mr Delingpole took pleasure in the commotion until Admiral bit his ankle, upon which he remembered his errand to the antiquarian dealers and departed. Meanwhile, Dame Yates had resigned the dog entirely to Blake and its droppings to the vergers (with a kind of cheerful effrontery that was rather remarkable in an old lady). She had taken Father's arm again, and they ambled away together, up the north aisle, to look at her memorial and no doubt give the mason more of her detailed criticism. Fidoe went with them, so I stayed behind with Blake and the dog. Someone would need to hold the leash while he drew, and I didn't see why it shouldn't be me.

I quite like dogs, though I do not believe them so intelligent as parrots. Their conversation is more limited, in general, though I must grant their eyes and ears are more expressive. At any rate, I am not afraid of being bitten. (*Obs:* there is nothing so efficacious as parrots to inure one to painful nips.) I knelt down on the floor, endeavouring to impart the same calm to the animal as I did to Father when similarly roused.

Dame Yates's departure seemed to soothe the poor creature. Gradually his panting subsided and he grew sufficiently tranquil to look about himself, sniff at my hand and then Blake's, and afterwards to sit down, trembling, on his haunches while I stroked his head and made peaceable noises.

Blake was drawing already, swiftly, laughing to himself. He turned the page to show me the dog very fierce on two legs, pawing the air. '*Canis familiaris rampant*,' he said. Then, after a moment, he showed me another sketch, the dog sidelong on three legs this time and waving a cheerful paw. '*Canis passant guardant.*'

'All very heraldic,' I said, 'but it's no good, you know.'

'As I intend to show her.' After a moment's further scribbling he turned the page again, this time to show me poor Admiral leaping from the page with a dreadful snarl. The boy wasn't taking his ticklish task very seriously after all.

'Draw him sleeping like the painted Lady Aveline's terriers,' I said.

'Or like her husband's tomb, with the sleeping lion under his feet,' Blake said. 'For are not all small dogs lionhearted?'

I coaxed Admiral to lie down, whereupon he curled into a ball and rested his nose on his tail. Poor thing, he was so exhausted by the excitement that he actually went to sleep while Blake's pen scratched over the paper, his dreamy eyes moving between page and subject just as they had done with Edward I's dead body.

'Where were you this morning?' I asked. 'I looked for you.'

'At breakfast.' He glanced up, as if weighing an admission. 'I was here all night and was hungry.'

'All night?'

'I often am.'

'You hide yourself from the vergers before they lock the doors?'

'Or forget to leave. The light in the abbey is so dim it is often hard to tell the time. Have *you* ever stayed in the abbey alone at night?'

'No,' I said. 'And after the ghost and the murder I don't ever wish to.'

He looked earnest. 'All sorts of creatures walk then.'

'Creatures?'

'The abbey cats hunting mice under the choir stalls. Bats chasing moths in the rafters. Angels walking in conversation.'

'Conversation? About what?'

He dropped his eyes to his paper and began drawing again. 'I cannot tell you. It is quite between me and them.'

I wasn't sure if he was joking or not. But I thought the idea of angels walking up and down the aisles almost as disagreeable as Edward's ghost. Then I remembered St Michael's flaming sword and reflected that an angel might be quite as capable of smiting someone down as a ghost. But such a conveniently supernatural murderer is, I suppose, too much to hope for.

'Were you not fearfully cold?' I asked after a moment.

'Frozen,' Blake said frankly, and then added, '*He withers all in silence, and in his hand unclothes the earth and freezes up frail life.*'

'I beg your pardon?'

'Another poem. Edward's ghost made me think of it. *He hath rear'd his sceptre o'er the world!*'

'Who has?'

'Winter. *The direful monster whose skin clings to his strong bones.*'

That did sound rather like the mummy. And the poetry wasn't as bad as I had feared, though I hadn't detected any rhyme or metre.

'But what do you do all night?' I asked. 'Apart from eavesdropping on angels?'

'I sleep when I can. I listen to the building breathe. Then comes first light and the roosting birds wake up, while the bats go home to rest. The cats slink off and at length the vergers come in and the new day begins.'

'It was very rash of you to stay behind last night of all nights. If you had been discovered, they might have thought you the murderer returned.'

He dipped his pen in his ink pot. 'I wanted to see the ghost again. If he was to walk, I thought it would be then. But I only saw that old man.'

'Old man?' I was still thinking with a shiver about the night-time abbey and the ghost.

'Mr Alnutt, the antiquary.'

I looked at Blake sharply. 'You saw Mr Alnutt, in here? Last night?'

He nodded, and I remembered the chanter telling the king that he had seen Mr Alnutt at the early Eucharist Service yesterday.

'What was he doing?' I asked.

'I saw him once by the quire, shortly before midnight. And then again by the altar at dawn.'

'Did you not ask him what he was doing here?'

'I said nothing. I was trespassing myself.'

This was, of course, true. But if Mr Alnutt had trespassed last night, might he not have done so before? Was it possible, after all, that he had been in the abbey when the murder happened?

'I wonder how he got in,' I said, but Blake didn't answer, absorbed by his drawing again. I should tell Lindley, I thought. Blake is very striking, with his soulful gaze, and it is gratifying that the gaze rests so often on me, but he is not a person to *discuss* things with. He is somehow always a little removed, lost in his own thoughts and fancies. By contrast,

Lindley listens carefully and makes remarks, even though he does not ever look at me as Blake does. If only one could fix two men together! (Or, at least, the desirable parts: viz. the ears and admiration of one with the practical good sense of the other. And if Lindley would only live up to his romantic name and gaze at me the same way Blake does, I really think I could overlook his ears.)

Dame Yates and Father were walking back towards us now, still arm in arm, and looking rather more companionable than I liked. Admiral was fast asleep, curled up on my skirts where I sat on the flagged floor.

'This is how you should have him, ma'am.' I gestured to the sleeping dog when they came up. 'Slumbering for all eternity.'

'Dear little thing,' the dame hooted, and at that poor Admiral woke with a start and began immediately to yap exactly where he had left off before her departure. Perhaps he enjoys it. His tail was certainly a blur of cheerful wagging.

Blake handed Dame Yates his sheaf of drawings. She looked through them a moment and then cackled in a manner highly unlike a respectable Dame. 'Splendid!' she said, shaking a new picture at Father and me, entitled *Canis Leonine Rampant* in which Blake had given the rearing Admiral a lion's mane and tail. 'This is the very thing, Dean. But if he is to be a lion, I must have him much larger and more splendid than ever.'

22

As the day wore on, Mr Delingpole did not return from his researches and there was no news from the king. With Louis Durand's body gone from the shrine and the daily round of services re-established, the events of past days began to seem dreamlike, and though I thought Father ought to be investigating, I still had no more idea than he did where he should begin.

He had done one thing: the vergers had been tasked with making a thorough search of the shrine for any trace the murderous thief might have left behind. They had found some wooden chocks, along with a rusty old iron rod and one of the workmen's wooden scaffold poles rolled away to the east of the Confessor's tomb where we had not seen them the previous day.

Pressed to speculate upon the matter, Fidoe declared it likely that the two men had picked them up from the workmen's pile of building materials and used them to lever open the weighty outer lid of Longshanks' tomb and the marble sarcophagus lid within. They had plainly succeeded, but I thought it strange they had not brought tools of their own for the job, the whole affair having been surely premeditated.

At any rate, this was all we learned, and Lindley, Father and I ate our dinner as if nothing at all strange had happened. Afterwards, I darned Charles II's hat, its extravagant feathers tickling my cheek, while Father dozed by the fire, Lindley read his book and Cuthbert copied the chinking call of a sparrow, which was pottering about the Deanery yard outside the window.

'The question,' I said, 'is how Louis Durand got into the abbey at all. Did he come after sunset, in which case he must have been admitted by a member of the abbey? That is the worst possible supposition. Or did he hide himself beforehand as you thought, Lindley? And how can we find out?'

Lindley lifted his eyes to mine abstractedly, but he only grunted a reply, not really listening.

'He was certainly not alone,' I went on, brushing the troublesome ostrich feathers aside. 'We know that much from the fact that someone killed him and afterwards took the mummy. But was it a quarrel between friends or a rival thief who killed him? I asked Fidoe this afternoon if one man alone could have lifted those coffin lids with the levers, but he only pursed his mouth. He said it might be possible, but how one man could hold up the lid, and steal the corpse inside, without having four arms or a useful grasping tail like a monkey, he couldn't imagine.'

Lindley had stopped reading now and finally turned his own mind to the problem. 'In that case, the murderer was most likely a friend turned foe, who had come there with Durand and only afterwards killed him,' he said. 'But that scarcely gets us any further, since even Quintrel hardly knew Durand and can tell us nothing useful about him or his associates.'

'Mrs Bray's testimony as to the voices is the only real clue,' I said. 'I suppose the fact she thought the second, English voice was familiar tends to support the worst case: that it was indeed someone from the abbey.'

Lindley closed his book, while Father stirred in his sleep at the sound of our voices. My cousin glanced at him and then came to sit beside me at the table so as not to disturb him more. 'It was lucky she heard them at all. It was very fortunate she was at the Deanery that evening, and even more that she left early.'

'If you had permitted ladies at your demonstration, she would not have done,' I said. 'So, though I thought it unamiable in you to keep us out, I suppose it served a purpose.'

'I did not keep you out,' Lindley objected. 'Your father said you had arranged to entertain the females separately.'

'Only because he bid me do it, just as he bid me leave the tomb opening and go to make sandwiches in Jerusalem.'

'But I never thought you would care to come. You are always very disobliging about my interests.'

'How can I be disobliging when I don't know anything about them?'

He frowned at me. 'Of course I would have been glad if you had come. But you were in such a bad humour when you brought me my supper before the demonstration it did not cross my mind you wanted to.'

'I thought you were hammering nails into the walls.'

'Hammering nails?'

'To hang that picture over the fire.' I hesitated, probably now looking positively consumed by curiosity. 'Only, when I looked in the next day, I could see no marks of nails at all.'

He stared at me a minute and then grinned. 'You thought I had hung a picture?'

'How else was it there?'

'Wait five minutes and I'll show you.'

IN FACT IT was ten minutes before Lindley reappeared with a large lantern-shaped wooden box. I had finished darning another moth hole in Charles II's hat, and I laid it aside, as Lindley set the strange machine down upon the table with a clatter that woke Father. The box had a tube projecting from one side, a small door secured by a brass clip on another, and a chimney on the top.

As Father rubbed his eyes, Lindley undid the clip and opened the door, releasing the same fishy smell of whale oil I had noticed in Jerusalem. He beckoned me closer and I went to his elbow to peer inside. There was a wick, which told me the large box was certainly intended as a lamp of some kind. But what use was a lamp with no glass? All the light would remain shut away inside the box.

'It is a magic lantern,' Lindley said. 'When I light the wick and close the door, the lamplight within is projected out through the circular opening at the end of this protruding tube.'

He took a taper from the candle and lit the wick inside the

box. At once, a dim circle of light appeared on the opposite wall of the room. Lindley blew out the candles and put the wooden summer screen in front of the fire. As the room darkened, the glowing disk grew brighter.

I looked at the projected light on the wall and then at the circle at the end of the lantern's jutting tube. 'This is very strange,' I said. 'The tube is scarcely four inches across, yet the circle it throws out is several times larger.'

'Very true. See, you are a scientist after all, cousin, for you ask the right questions.'

I wasn't sure whether to be flattered or to poke him with my sewing needle as I had done the sacrist. Nevertheless, I was interested. 'But what is it that makes the circle bigger?'

Lindley opened the lantern again. Against the back of the box, furthest from the tube, was a mirror, for when I peered in I could see the reflection of my own nose and the side of my cheek. My reflection seemed distorted, but it was far too awkwardly placed inside the machine to get a proper look without singeing my eyebrows as I had once wished Lindley might.

'The mirror is concave and concentrates the light of the flame on to two lenses in the projecting tube,' Lindley said. 'One condenses the light, the other magnifies it.'

'I see. A kind of *refraction*, I suppose.'

Lindley turned to stare at me, his mouth hanging ajar.

'I read about it once, in a book,' I said, with tremendous nonchalance. 'But what is the machine for?'

Lindley stirred himself from the admiration of my hitherto unsuspected intellects and opened the sliding lid of a small wooden case he had brought down with the machine. He took out a piece of painted glass about the size of my palm and handed it to me. When I held it to the light, I saw it was a picture of that same painting I had seen hanging on the wall of the Jerusalem Chamber the night of Lindley's demonstration. The picture with the heavy gilt frame I had reproached Lindley for hanging there, but which subsequently appeared to have left no mark of nails at all. Lindley took it back from me with careful fingers. There was a slot, I now saw, between the large cavity which held the lighted wick and the projecting tube. He slotted in the glass and closed the door of the lantern so that the room was darkened once more. And there was the painting, on our wall, just as if hung there on a nail.

'Well?' Lindley said, apparently impatient for my admiration.

'Ingenious,' I said, with another, less successful effort at nonchalance, for I was really entranced by the picture's bright colours, which reminded me of the stained-glass windows in the abbey.

'I think you had better put it out,' Father said fretfully, poking at the wooden screen Lindley had placed before the fire, which was now adding a pleasant, toasted smell to that of the fishy whale oil. 'You will burn the house down in another minute.'

'Just one more, sir,' Lindley said. He took out the painted slide and slotted in another. Monochrome this time, it showed a greyish sphere pitted with black marks. It was considerably less pretty, but there was something impressive, even melancholy, about it all the same.

'The moon, as seen through a large telescope,' Lindley

said, watching my face. 'They have mapped its mountains and seas.' He pointed to what I saw now was a scribble of names. I went closer to read them. *Mare Tranquillitatis*. *Terra Fertilita*. *Peninsula Deliriorum*. It was a strange world, both very like and very unlike our own, and its strangeness made me feel rather dizzy, just as the ghost had done. It, too, had brought the feeling of another world with it and had made even the pillars and statues of the north ambulatory seem altered from those I knew so well.

'It's beautiful,' I said, turning my face to Lindley's. He had come up to look at the picture beside me, and he smiled at me, his face close to mine. Our heads cast a shadow on the opposite wall, and by some trick of perspective our silhouettes seemed to be kissing.

23

TUESDAY 10 MAY

IT WAS TEN o'clock, and we were all at breakfast, when His Majesty came striding into the Deanery parlour at a brisk march which carried him clean across to the fireplace before he realised he was in a room and not merely a corridor.

Mr Delingpole had followed him in (muttering something about an equerry stationed at the Deanery door to forestall assassins) while the king stood with his hands under the tails of his coat, warming his legs at the fire. His Majesty looked about attentively at all our little possessions, while we hurried to our feet and made the required obeisances. (I wonder if he ever thinks it strange that all the world must be seized with a kind of St Vitus's dance at his first appearance?)

'Yes, yes, a very pleasant room, if rather small,' he said. 'But warm, by God! I am so infernally used to that barrack of a building, Buckingham House, where I am always froze as stiff as an icicle, what, what?'

'Do sit down, Your Majesty,' I said, proffering my own

chair. He waved a hand and instead wandered over to look at Cuthbert. They examined each other frankly for a moment and then Cuthbert scratched his head, perhaps abashed by the royal stare. *Bad bird, bad bird, dong, dong, dong.*

'Capital!' His Majesty said, clapping his hands. 'Capital, by Jove.' He thrust his face closer to Cuthbert's. 'Can you say, *God save the king*, bird? What, what?'

'I'm afraid we have never thought to teach him that,' I said. 'But, Your Majesty, do be careful. If you put your face so close he may nip.'

His Majesty seemed to take this as a challenge and thrust his face even closer. 'God save the king, what, what! God save the king! God save the king!'

Cuthbert regarded him rather coolly, while Mr Delingpole took the opportunity of the king's drawing breath to speak to Father and Lindley.

'I am come with my report from the antiquity dealers,' he said. 'There is a fellow in St Paul's Churchyard, and another in Covent Garden. Between them I think they know every other man engaged in the London trade. I asked them if they had heard any strange stories among themselves these past days, at which they looked quite blank. So I then asked them straight out about the mummy. Or, at least, as you might say, the *possibility* of a mummy.'

'Oh dear,' Father said reflexively.

'What did they say?' Lindley asked. 'Did they know anything?'

God save the king, what, what?

I had never known the bird so quickly learn a phrase or enunciate it for the first time with such perfect clarity.

'That is my voice!' the king exclaimed, unaffectedly gratified. I suppose he is used to the flattery of courtiers, so the disinterested friendship of animals, who have no idea of kings and commoners, must be particularly sweet. (I have heard that Buckingham House is as much a kennel as the abbey.) 'My own voice, what, what! What a remarkable animal.'

God save the king! What, what? What, what?

Mr Delingpole was not to be upstaged by Cuthbert or the king and turned back to us under their cheerful noise. 'I'm afraid I drew a blank, Dean. That is, perhaps I am glad to have drawn a blank. If we had found the mummy and, through it, the culprit, I would have been very glad. But I can't say I'm sorry to find there is as yet no sign, and Longshanks has not been reduced to the position of a mere doll to be bought and sold. Nevertheless, we are no further forward for my investigations.'

'No,' the king said rather severely, 'no, I fear you ain't, though I expressly required you to find it all out, Dean, before the press could sniff out the story.'

'I am very sorry,' Father said humbly.

The king looked at us all with a rather dissatisfied frown before taking out his pocket watch and comparing it to our clock on the mantelpiece. (This reminded me, with a pang, of my present to Father, which I had last seen wrapped up again in his desk.)

'Well, well, I had best be getting back,' His Majesty said. 'Princess Elizabeth's fourth birthday is almost upon us, and I have promised her a gift, but damned if I know what it shall be. I am to meet the queen to consult on it.' His eyes softened. 'Little scrap. Daughters are a man's delight, ain't they, Dean, what, what?' He moved to the door. 'Let me hear a good report next time we meet, eh?'

I suppose it might have been the princess's birthday, but *I* fancy he was equally eager to tell his wife and children about his success with Cuthbert. After he was gone I took the bird on my shoulder and let him nibble my hair. As the others resumed their discussions he continued murmuring *what, what?* into my ear at intervals, in His Majesty's voice, which I must say was rather disconcerting.

'But in this case, we must look inwards to the abbey again,' Mr Delingpole was saying. 'If the canon's wife heard Durand in conversation with another man, that was likely his fellow thief and subsequent murderer. Or there might have been three men, of whom only two spoke, for I am afraid the king was right and we must consider how they got inside. What time is the abbey locked, Dean?'

'At sunset, about half an hour before full dark.'

'Durand might have hidden himself in the abbey before the doors were locked,' Lindley said. 'My cousin and I both think it possible.'

'Very well. But supposing for a moment that he did not do so, but was admitted later by someone from the abbey, could the thing be done? Where are the keys kept after the doors are closed for the night?'

'The doors to the abbey from the cloisters are always open, but the vergers lock the north and west doors to the street,' Father answered, 'and the porter remains at his post all night by the entrance to the cloisters and the Deanery.' He hated the suggestion of inside help and shifted uneasily in his chair. 'The door keys are very large and are placed in an oak chest which is then taken to the canon-steward's house.'

'Why to him?'

'Merely by long tradition, I imagine. In monastic times, the steward would have been charged with admitting visitors and pilgrims and seeing them fed and furnished with lodgings, if necessary.'

'And these are the only keys?'

'No,' Father said. 'I also have a set, though they are mainly symbolic of my absolute rule here. I keep the key to the Confessor's shrine in my pocket, but the rest are never used.'

'And where do you keep them?'

'In my study.'

'Will you be so good as to show me?'

In an exact repetition of Sunday, Father obligingly got up and led Mr Delingpole off to his study. And in an exact repetition of Sunday, they came back shortly afterwards, to announce that the keys, like Blake's drawings, were missing.

Father looked very pale again, and I fetched him another sherry. (If this goes on, he shall soon be a dipsomaniac.) As I did so, I reluctantly confessed what Blake had told me yesterday – that he had seen Mr Alnutt in the abbey overnight, wandering between the quire and the altar. 'I did not like to say so before the king,' I said. But as with the chimes of the abbey clock (viz. the number thereof) I felt unable to hold back what I had learned, and I was glad to find that they were sufficiently preoccupied with astonishment at the old man's nocturnal wanderings to disregard Blake's own trespassing entirely.

'Then we must call Alnutt in, I fear,' Mr Delingpole said. 'Better to confront him directly and see what he says about all this. At least it will be doing something, and His Majesty cannot then call us dilatory in our efforts.'

24

MR DELINGPOLE DEPARTED to fetch the old man and the rest of us sat quietly in the parlour for the hour or so it took to produce Mr Alnutt from his rooms in Bloomsbury. Lindley read his book on coalmines and Father dozed in his chair, every now and then twitching and uttering little wordless exclamations of dismay.

Holy Communion was being taken in the abbey, for I could hear boys' voices (rather sparse, which I supposed must be ascribed to the mumps) through the open parlour window singing the *Agnus Dei*. The scent of gillyflowers wafted through, while the climbing rose that grows out of the paving outside the window had one pink bloom bursting from its bud like crinkled tissue. Cuthbert, apparently well pleased with his royal success, was quietly turning head over heels on his perch.

Despite Lindley being so recent an addition to our family party we were really very companionable. It seemed odd to think that until these past few weeks he had been as much a stranger to me as any other gentleman, and it struck me now how naturally he had fitted himself to our little ways.

Perhaps he felt my gaze on him for he looked up and smiled and reached out a hand to take Charles II's hat from me. He put it on his head and struck a foolish pose, just as he had done when wearing the crown in Bishop Islip's chapel. 'It would suit your friend Thomas Ffoulkes rather better,' I said as he handed it back to me.

'And I imagine he would very much fancy to wear it.'

About one o'clock, the Antiquities came in. We could hear Mr Alnutt's piping tones and Mr Delingpole's deeper ones as the maid led them to us through the hall. Lindley cast me a look that made me think he also considered himself a pigeon on this occasion and meant to keep his mouth closed, in case Father should remember to banish us both from what really should have been a private interrogation, if only for Mr Alnutt's sake.

'Mr Delingpole said you had some questions for me, Dean,' Mr Alnutt quavered, perching on the edge of a chair in a very old-fashioned way, his old back ramrod straight.

'Yes, indeed, Mr Alnutt, I'm afraid we do,' Father said. He looked awkward, however, and cast an appealing glance at Mr Delingpole, who took charge at once and with the utmost tact. (Mr D. is a lawyer, of course, and fortunately must be well used to asking probing questions without frightening the subject to death.)

Also like a lawyer, he seemed to have come to an understanding with the witness out of court, so to speak. 'Mr Alnutt and I have discussed the matter on our way here, Dean. I took the liberty of asking him about the drawings and the keys missing from your desk.'

Even though the old man had been forewarned, it really

was awful to witness such a dreadful accusation being put to him: that a worthy old gentleman like himself could be a thief.

'And I told Delingpole that I had certainly not taken the engraver's sketches,' Mr Alnutt said with rather more energy than previously. 'I never even saw them, Dean. I gather, from what Delingpole says, that they were in your desk. How should I ever have seen them there?'

By opening the desk and looking, was the unspoken answer to that. Lindley shifted ever so slightly in his seat (he has not learned the art of perfect stillness common to a pigeon) and Father glanced at him. I suppose Lindley was torn, as I was, between disliking the whole inquisition and yet being dissatisfied with the witness's answer. It was too easy for Mr Alnutt to say he had not taken the drawings, after all.

'And the other thing?' Father asked. 'The abbey keys are always displayed on the mantelpiece in my study. Forgive me, sir, but you might have seen *them*.'

'By no means.' Mr Alnutt was trembling again as he had done before when very moved. 'Why should you think so, Dean? It is very hard to be suspected in this way.'

'Because the keys are missing, and you were alone with them, sir.'

'I am sure a dozen others must come in and out all day. Your housemaids. Your canons. Though heaven forfend I blame anyone.'

I could see Father really disliked the interrogation but felt obliged to continue. 'And the fact is, sir, that you were seen in the abbey two nights ago when the doors were locked.'

'Ah!'

Mr Alnutt sat back in his chair, as if the ramrod in his spine had evaporated of a sudden. 'Ah, yes, Dean, *that* is certainly a fault, I own.'

'You admit to it? You took the keys and let yourself inside?'

'I admit to the trespass, but not the keys.' Mr Alnutt slowly straightened again. 'I saw the engraver's lad slip into a side chapel when the vergers began to call out that the abbey was closing. I perceived he meant to remain there unseen. And so I copied him.'

'Good heavens,' Father said faintly. 'Whatever for?'

What, what? Cuthbert put in and Mr Alnutt started, looking about nervously as if he expected to see the king burst out of a cupboard.

'To see Longshanks' ghost,' he said, looking appealingly at Mr Delingpole. 'I felt sure that if the spectre were to walk again, the depths of night would be the best time to see it.'

This was so like Blake's words I thought it a shame they had both been disappointed, and equally a shame that they had not regaled the long hours of the night away companionably together.

'And did you see the ghost?' Lindley asked, daring to be remembered again now the story was all told.

'To my infinite regret, no.' Mr Alnutt shook his head. 'Though I saw a figure in the shadows betimes and I did wonder . . . But I suppose it was just the boy.'

'So our two lesser mysteries remain stubbornly unsolved,' Mr Delingpole said. 'The drawings and the keys are still unaccounted for.'

'But one thing is clear,' Lindley observed. 'The place is such a labyrinth there are any number of hiding places.

Durand could easily have done as Mr Alnutt did and hid himself away before the doors were locked the night he died.'

'But then there is the other man. The man that killed him.' Mr Delingpole looked dissatisfied. 'If he hid himself with Durand in this way, and no one from the abbey let them in after all, then we are no further forward.'

Lindley turned back to Mr Alnutt. 'Quintrel saw you with Suckling on the day of the tomb's first opening and then again the following day. Can you tell us what you spoke about with the sacrist?'

What, what? What, what? Cuthbert echoed and Mr Alnutt gave another little start.

'Certainly, I can. The sacrist was captivated by the sight of the mummy and its grave goods. He quizzed me at length about the nature of Longshanks' funerary accoutrements and their relation to the real crown jewels. He was also highly interested by Quintrel's story of Apollo. He walked me round the cloisters until I was quite worn out, asking all manner of questions about it.'

'Questions?'

'Whether I believed in Apollo myself, whether I believed in the old sources I had quoted.'

'And the next day?' Lindley asked. 'Did he talk to you again?'

'He did. He was astonished by my account of Longshanks' ghost and wanted to know exactly how it had looked and moved.'

In this he seemed to have been like Lindley, who had quizzed us in just the same way. But the sacrist's questions about the funerary jewels made me remember the disarray of the crowns and sceptres in the ragged regiment's cupboard, which I had ascribed to unruly visitors. Now, I wondered whether Mr Suckling had been there before us that day, examining them with a new interest in the light of all he had learned. But, whatever his other faults, he was very attached to the abbey's treasures and surely would not have left them in such a dreadful mess.

'The sacrist also asked how one became a member of our society,' Mr Alnutt added. 'I am afraid, Dean, that I was a little disingenuous in my reply. I confess, I do not find the sacrist's manner very congenial, and found myself unaccountably averse to the prospect of enjoying his company at our meetings. In short, I told him a positive untruth. I pretended to him that it was customary to show evidence of some relevant antiquarian research as you have done, with your excavations. He was extremely disappointed that he might not join at once, and indeed looked rather vexed, as if he did not quite believe me. In the end, he thanked me rather ungraciously and said he would put his mind to it. To which I replied very little, and only made my escape as quickly as I could. Forgive me, Dean, if he is an especial friend of yours.'

Lindley snorted, and I thought it might surprise Mr Alnutt to know how little esteemed the sacrist was by any of us. I suppose I have always assumed Mr Suckling is oblivious to his own nastiness and merely sees the continual cold-shoulder of the world as the natural state of affairs, which he has experienced since his oleaginous boyhood. But now Mr Alnutt's story made me wonder. Did the sacrist's bad-tempered doubt that Alnutt was telling him the truth suggest otherwise? Does he know we dislike him? And does he, in fact, resent it? I now remembered seeing him arguing with Father in the Confessor's shrine while they took Monsieur Durand's body away. Perhaps, unknown to me, he is often as bad-tempered with Father as he was with Mr Alnutt.

'But returning to the murder and the theft,' Father was now saying sadly. 'Do you truly believe the antiquaries entirely innocent of any involvement? The mummy might have been a temptation, might it not? I wish you would tell me frankly what you think.'

'Frankly, Dean, such a thing would go directly against our principles.'

'And you are certain that Mr Quintrel, for instance, respects those principles as you do?'

Mr Alnutt hesitated, just for a moment, before rallying again. 'In this regard, I am. Mr Quintrel has his peculiarities, of course.' He hesitated again. 'He has stolen ideas from other men. But *he* would never steal so valuable an object as Edward's body. Of that I am quite certain.'

'*He*? You think, then, that someone else might?'

Mr Alnutt looked surprised. 'The young Frenchman, of course. And I have had some thoughts, Dean – some passing fancies – though I scarcely like to share them without far more research into the sources than I have had the time to conduct . . .'

He paused. Father cocked his head.

Mr Delingpole smiled his usual, genial smile. 'If you think you know something of use, Alnutt, why not venture a guess among friends?'

'I cannot say if it is of use or no. But it might go some way to explain . . .' He paused again.

Lindley got up and began to pace energetically, as if he thought that by doing so he might hurry the old man into spitting out his ideas. It seemed to work. Mr Alnutt left off gazing at his hands and looked up with a new if feeble energy.

'Since our examination of the mummy on Saturday I have been looking into the matter of the Confessor's crown jewels. If you remember, I expressed surprise that Longshanks was buried in a crown unlike the one the Confessor wore and which he himself had also worn at his coronation. Delingpole suggested they had run out of money.' He began to laugh an old man's coughing laugh. 'Run out of money! No, no, that was absurd. If you remember, I advanced the idea that the crown the mummy wore was a memorial of Longshanks' conquest of Wales and defeat of Llewellyn. Since Saturday I have returned to my books and find that Llewellyn's crown was certainly brought by Edward here, to this very abbey, and laid in triumph before the Confessor's shrine.'

'Dear, dear,' Father said again, probably at the idea of such martial swaggering.

'You will understand, Dean, from your own copious collection, that gilt objects are usually silver or copper in composition. But Mr Delingpole particularly remarked that the crown we found in Edward's tomb was made of iron, overlaid with a gold plating that had failed with age, the rust showing through and thereby betraying its ferrous nature.

'Returning to my books I was gratified to learn that Llewellyn's crown was also iron and that, before Longshanks presented it at the Confessor's shrine, he plated it with gold, to make it a finer gift.'

We all looked at him.

'I remarked on Saturday that the Welsh crown was known to have been among the jewels melted down at Cromwell's command during the late regrettable rebellion. At least so the sources say. But then I went to Mildmay's catalogue of the items sent for destruction, and there was no mention of the Welsh crown. No mention of Llewellyn's crown at all.'

'Good God,' Mr Delingpole said with dawning understanding.

'It is possible – possible only, I say – that the Welsh prince's crown escaped destruction. Ordinarily one would ask, *Then where is it?* And ordinarily one would answer, *Nowhere. And therefore it must indeed have been destroyed.* But . . .'

'Instead, it might have been in Longshanks' tomb all along.' Mr Delingpole was now deeply moved. 'They might have hidden it there against Cromwell.'

'They might. But who were *they*? And why choose to hide Llewellyn's crown instead of the Confessor's?' Mr Alnutt shook his head. 'Lord knows, they should have hidden that if they were to have hidden anything.'

'Perhaps because the Welsh crown was of less importance to Cromwell's men,' Mr Delingpole said thoughtfully. 'Less famous, and also of less monetary value, being only gold plated. Mildmay would have noticed the disappearance of the Confessor's crown, I dare say.'

Mr Alnutt shook his head and made to stand up. Lindley hastened to help him.

'I do not say I am right,' he quavered, once upright, 'but I do not say I am wrong.'

'It is a help, Alnutt,' Mr Delingpole said, standing also. 'I am sure it is a help, though at present I can't see how.'

'Your dead man might have been a Welshman, I thought, Delingpole.'

'If only he had not been French.'

My mind went back to that first day, when we stood around Edward's tomb. 'But you did say he had a strange accent, Mr Delingpole. You remarked upon it. And for a Frenchman he was remarkably knowledgeable about Edward's wars with the Scots.'

'That's true.'

I grew bolder, my ideas enlarging. 'And whatever would a Frenchman want with the Holy Grail? That is surely an absurdity, when Arthur has always been *our* king.'

Mr Alnutt had turned to go, but now revolved around to face me.

'My dear young lady,' he said gravely, '*grail* or *graal* is itself a French word, and almost all the original sources are French. The first writer to mention the *graal* was Chrétien de Troyes in the twelfth century. For him the grail was a magical dish that could feed a multitude, rather like – forgive me, Dean – Christ's miraculous loaves and fishes.

'Manessier expanded on de Troyes' work, and in his writings the grail became a cup, belonging to Joseph of Arimathea, who caught drops of blood from the spear wound in Christ's dying side within it. Robert de Boron—'

'I am sure we are grateful to you for the lecture, Alnutt, but let us keep our attention fixed on Durand,' Mr Delingpole broke in dampeningly. 'Miss Bell is right to remember Durand's curious accent, but nevertheless Quintrel certainly met him in Calais.'

He frowned and tapped his hat against his knee before jamming it on his head with sudden decision. 'I tell you what I shall do. I shall go to the king. I don't suppose he will see me himself, and to be frank I don't much want him to, since they are so very formal at Buckingham House. Even if he agrees to meet me I shall be standing with my back to the wall for an hour before he deigns to come in, and I shall have to leave backwards, bowing like a fool. I shall ask instead for his equerry Desaguliers, who was here with him before, and pass on the message that way.

'It is beyond any of us to find out much about who Louis Durand really was,' Delingpole added, 'or where he really came from. But I suppose the Bow Street Runners might have more luck. I shall ask Desaguliers to persuade the king of that, however much he desires to keep the thing quiet. The Runners need not know why the boy is wanted, or that he is dead here, poor soul, in the abbey lock-up with a hole in his throat.'

'I'll come with you,' Lindley said, rising to fetch his own coat and hat.

'And if the dean likes to accompany me I can show him my sources on Llewellyn,' Mr Alnutt said, with so much wistful hope that Father could do nothing else than say he should be delighted – that he was particularly interested by the whole story of the Confessor's lost jewels – and go with him.

*

$\mathcal{A}$ND SO, SINCE THEN, this afternoon has dragged. Father has not yet returned and neither has Lindley. I have turned down the maid's offer of dinner at the usual hour and instead am eating bread and butter while I write my journal. I have drunk two whole pots of tea and now feel somewhat waterlogged. It is very lonely, and Cuthbert is no comfort, being still preoccupied with the king's visit. All he will ever answer to my conversational overtures is *What, what,* along with repeated admonitions to *save the king,* in which, as I am not God, I am utterly unable to oblige him.

25

WEDNESDAY 11 MAY

IT IS EVENING as I write this, finding my hand at last able to hold a pen. Though it is only the palm of my right hand that is scorched, and my fingertips remain mercifully unscathed, I have been seized by a trembling that has only now subsided. Even so, I am afraid this entry will be somewhat muddled, since the events subsequent to that moment's peace with Cuthbert in the parlour, yesterday afternoon, have been so various and so surprising that it will only be in the writing of it all down that I will make any sense of it – if there is, indeed, any sense to be made at all.

FEELING STILL VERY lonely and dissatisfied with Cuthbert, I decided to go to Evensong, hoping I might meet Blake and have some conversation. (I would say, some *sensible* conversation, but that certainly depends on his mood.) As I came into the nave the service had begun.

The chanter was asking God to open His lips and the choir were answering that their mouths should shew forth His praise as I perched on the base of a monument, rather than announce my tardiness by walking around the quire to my usual seat under the eyes of the assembled canons. Mr Lamb was now begging God to make speed to save us. Under my breath I joined the choir in enjoining Him to *make haste to help us*, although I must say the idea of God hurrying along to help always makes me think of a hot and harried waggoner trying to right a greengrocer's stall overturned by his unruly set of oxen.

Mr Slater the canon-steward read the first lesson, and then the choir was off into the *Magnificat*, which I have always particularly liked, being, for a change, the words of the young woman who found herself unexpectedly required to bring forth the saviour of mankind. *He hath regarded the lowliness of his handmaiden* – and thereby remembered she is not a pigeon. (Though one would hope that God, at least, would be able to keep such things straight in His mind.)

It was all very grand and very soothing but didn't dispel the feeling that I had been abandoned in favour of outdoor excitements. There was no sign of Blake, or Father, or Lindley as the service ended and the choir processed out. The canons bowed to each other and walked away, hands folded in their long sleeves. The small congregation departed and I returned to the Deanery.

Dusk was now falling. Time, indeed, for a pigeon to go to roost, but just now I was tired of pigeonhood. Until today I had done pretty well at perching unseen on all the extraordinary events of recent days. But now the investigation had moved out of doors and into the world beyond where I could not follow.

I often forget that the abbey is not the world. Father is so busy he neglects to take me out into the town. I never go to Vauxhall or Ranelagh any more than the Miss Turnbulls, the canon-almoner's daughters do. I never go shopping, for the dressmaker comes to the Deanery. If I had a mother living I suppose we should visit about the town, but Father does not do so. We never go to the theatre or the opera, it being against Father's dignity. No, the abbey is the world, and a huge world it seems to me as I go freely about its passages and gardens and vast interior.

But yesterday my luck had finally run out, and I had remembered the other world. The world where Blake goes at the end of his working day. Where Mr Delingpole keeps his chambers. A vaster world even than the vast abbey, and the preserve of others than myself. Gentlemen may go there. And the poor of both sexes live out their lives beneath its vast dome of sky. But respectable ladies must always keep to their coop.

Father came in just as I was donning my bonnet and shawl again in a rather rebellious spirit. I had driven myself antic, imagining Mr Delingpole and Lindley at Buckingham House, consulting with the equerry, and Father himself in some splendid library frequented by the Antiquities.

'Where are you going, my dear? It is almost dark.'

Whatever would he say if I told him I was going to venture out past the porter into Broad Sanctuary and disappear into the London streets? Of course, I was not going to do so. It was beyond either of our imaginations that I even could.

'I am going to call on Mrs Bray,' I said instead. 'I thought I might ask her more about her strange voices.'

'Mrs Bray will hardly like a visitor at a quarter after nine in the evening.'

'If she has another headache she can always turn me away,' I said. 'But I want to quiz her about it all again.' And I wanted to be out in the fresh air, even if the sky above me was always shut off by the cloister roof.

'Young ladies need not trouble themselves with such matters, you know, my dear.' Father sat down by the fire and looked at me plaintively. 'I do not like to see you so discomposed, Susan. You should not have looked at that poor man's dead body, my dear, you really should not have done.'

I disregarded him and only wrapped my shawl about me more tightly.

'And I shall not like to be left all alone,' he said. 'If you stayed we might play a game of cribbage to distract our minds from our troubles.'

'I'll play with pleasure when I come back. I don't suppose I shall be gone above half an hour.'

It was dropping dark when I stepped out of the Deanery garden into the cloisters. The shadows were already very inky and there was no moon. Walking through the Dark Entry to the Little Cloister was therefore rather disagreeable in the light of murderers, ghosts, &c. But I survived the passage by taking it at a run and came out, a little breathless, into the ancient square with its low roofed walks, far more private and sequestered even than the cloisters between the Deanery and the abbey. In the centre of the Little Cloister is a lawn, and at the centre of the lawn is an old trickling fountain, with a mossy stone basin filled with quiet water. I could hear its gentle gurgle as I walked past it to the canon-treasurer's house.

Contrary to Father's predictions, the Brays were perfectly pleased to have an interruption to their quiet evening. The two young daughters were abed, they said, though I had heard pattering footsteps and stifled laughter from the upstairs landing when I passed through the hall.

Mr and Mrs Bray sat me down and gave me wine. Mr Bray had a half tumbler of brandy in his hand and swallowed it down in order to refill his glass along with mine. I wondered if the brandy helped the irritability which, I remembered Mrs Bray had said, often drove him to pacing the College Garden.

They were quite ready to discuss the whole matter anew, being, of course, just as caught up in speculation as we had been at the Deanery. There was a verger they disliked and seemed very eager to identify as the second voice Mrs Bray had heard in the dark. 'Make no mistake, Miss Bell,' the canon-treasurer said, 'he is the one. We have too many vergers, tell your father, and might easily turn half of them off without any inconvenience to the running of the abbey.'

I asked Mrs Bray what had made her think the second voice belonged to the verger in question. She paused, and I remembered then that she had hesitated similarly when questioned before, by the king in Jerusalem. 'You recognised his voice?' I suggested. 'He had some strong accent? Some notable way of speaking that made you think you knew him?'

'No, nothing of that sort.' She hesitated again. Mr Bray

had already returned to the decanter, and she bent towards me speaking low. 'I do not say it was the verger at all, Miss Bell. It is only my husband that thinks so. All I can say is that I knew the voice. It was a voice familiar to me, though by no means that of an intimate acquaintance.'

'A voice familiar from the abbey?'

She nodded. 'I think so, but not a canon or a minor canon. Not someone I speak to regularly. And of course not, for weren't they all in Jerusalem with your cousin?'

'And you can't remember what the voices actually said?'

She sat back in her chair. 'Hardly. Though I have been racking my brains about it, as you may imagine, Miss Bell. I'd be very glad to be of more help if I could.'

She had said she *hardly* knew what they had said, not that she didn't know at all. 'What did the first voice say that made you think him a foreigner? Dear Mrs Bray, do tell me what you heard. Anything will be useful to Father's investigation, you know, and there is no shame at all in being wrong. You heard one of them speak a foreign word?'

'*Bonjour*,' she said. 'I think I heard him say *bonjour*. But it was dark, Miss Bell. That is what makes me doubt myself. Even from my schoolroom French I think he should have said *bonsoir*.'

'Perhaps it was his English accomplice speaking,' I suggested, 'greeting him in faulty French.'

She brightened. 'That is certainly possible.'

'And what did the Englishman say in reply? The voice you thought you knew?'

'He exclaimed something. I think he said, *Good God preserve us*!'

I sat back.

'Where exactly were you when you heard these voices, Mrs Bray?'

'Scarcely out of the Deanery Court.'

'And was it then that you heard the clock chime eight?'

'Just then. Almost as soon as the words were out of the men's mouths.'

Bonjour. Good God preserve us. Dong, dong. I put down my glass of wine, half finished, and rose to my feet.

I didn't know how I felt. I had wanted to do something – discover something, just as the men were doing out there in the great world. I had now shown I was as well equipped as anyone – perhaps even better equipped – to coax answers from the unworldly residents of the small abbey universe. Whether I liked those answers, when once they were given, was quite another matter.

'Father will be tremendously pleased to hear what you have said, Mrs Bray. I'm so grateful and shall be sure to pass it on directly.'

The canon-treasurer wished me goodnight from the depths of his armchair and his brandy. As I crossed the hall I heard the patter of feet again upstairs. What we think we know and what is really true so often differ. We had based all our surmises thus far on Mrs Bray's testimony that she had heard strange voices in the cloisters while the senior members of the Chapter were watching Lindley's demonstration in Jerusalem. From what she had heard, we had dismissed all the members of the Chapter, Mr Delingpole and Lindley from any shadow of suspicion. Father had been pleased, and it had certainly reduced our list of suspects to only the whole world outside the abbey, be they Welsh or French or just plain English.

But the voices Mrs Bray had heard had not been intruders come to rob or kill anyone at all. I had left the parlour window open that evening while I entertained the ladies in the formal drawing room. Left alone, Cuthbert had doubtless been chattering quietly to himself, and dinging away at the abbey bell in his loneliness. *Bonjour. Good God preserve us! Dong, dong, dong* . . .

And this being so, Louis Durand could have entered the abbey at quite another time entirely. And, consequently, any member of the abbey clergy, my cousin, or even Mr Delingpole himself, could have been his accomplice, after all.

26

I WALKED BACK SWIFTLY through the Little Cloister towards home. The darkness that had made me think of ghosts when I fled from Mr Suckling in his sacristy, or of unknown murderers earlier tonight in the Dark Entry, was suddenly freighted in my mind with real danger. I was here alone, locked in the abbey precincts with all the clergy whom I had always implicitly trusted to be what they seemed, whether good or bad.

There was no moon, but I now noticed that the darkness ahead was dimly illuminated, though not by a common lantern or candle or rushlight, or anything else I knew of. Not by the warm light of a drawing room either, spilling its lamplight across the paving. No. The houses were all dark as if they had turned their backs on me, and the light I could see ahead in the darkness was like nothing I had ever seen before. An uncanny, pale blue. I paused, afraid. The light was in the Dark Entry, I could see that much now, and to get home I must pass it.

It was no natural light, I thought, after I had watched the

pulsing blue shimmer a moment more. It was other-worldly and, if it presaged anything, it presaged another appearance of Longshanks' ghost. If I had only been Mr Alnutt I should have run towards it at once. The light was now advancing. At any moment it would appear from the dark mouth of the entry. Reader, I was not Mr Alnutt, and I fell back, with a vague thought to return to the Brays' door and hammer for admittance.

But then the thing emerged into the Little Cloister and I forgot to run. It was not Edward's ghost. It was not that strange, bulging, monstrous shape. Instead, it had the body of a human man, dressed in a long robe that might have been a cassock or a cloak – or even a linen winding sheet, for all I could make out in the dimness. But it wore no crown this time; I could see that much, for the outline of its shrouded head was illuminated by the strange light that emanated from a rod – or was it a sword? – that the figure held aloft in its right hand. Instead of a crown, strange fluttering forms shimmered around its head, dancing in the air like butterflies, glowing like fireflies – only with this eerie blue instead of a friendly yellow light.

The figure was striding purposefully towards me and as I came to my senses and fell back again, I saw another shadowy form following behind it, face lit by the strange blue glow. Shambling along, looking as if he were half-dreaming, was Mr Quintrel. The rapt expression on his face was almost as strange as the light itself. For hadn't Mr Quintrel been ever the most cynical of men?

The dark figure with its shimmering rod strode to the centre of the little lawn and touched the shining blue brand to the water in the mossy fountain. At once the water took fire, flames licking up brightly from the basin into the dark evening air. Then, after only a moment and just as suddenly, the light of the rod was extinguished and the flames in the mossy tank died. I had been staring so hard at the strange gleaming butterflies about the figure's head that in the following pitch darkness they still danced in front of my eyes. I did not hear the figure's retreating footsteps. Perhaps the soft grass under its feet made no sound. Or, perhaps, if it were really a spirit, there were no footsteps to be heard at all.

I blinked, trying to dispel the fluttering shapes still dancing on the inside of my eyelids. Mr Quintrel was now near to me, murmuring some prayer in Latin, a prayer I did not understand, though I heard the words Phoebus Apollo on his tongue.

I opened my eyes again and something glimmered at my feet. This time it was not the after-effects of the vision, but something real. I bent to retrieve it, but couldn't see what it was, until an honest-to-goodness everyday yellow lantern came hastening suddenly through the Dark Entry into the square, dispelling the memory of the eerie light and making everything seem homely again.

Inexplicably, it was Mr Delingpole, and Father was behind him. 'What have you got there?' Mr Delingpole asked me abruptly as he came up. I remembered the glowing thing I had just picked up from the paving and tried to hand it to him, but whatever it was seemed inclined to dance up out of my fingers in the light evening breeze. Delingpole snatched his hand around it, as if it were a moth, and then held it to the lantern to look. 'Gold,' he said. At this Quintrel came over to see and with a glad cry fell to his knees again to find more of the fluttering scraps.

'What in heaven are you doing, Quintrel?' Delingpole was irritable. We must certainly have looked very strange – his fellow scholar on his hands and knees, scrabbling up gold fragments from the floor, and my own face white with shock. I suppose Mr Delingpole had now realised he had missed some new, extraordinary spectacle and was probably feeling naturally aggrieved.

'I saw Apollo, Delingpole,' Quintrel said eagerly, looking up from his knees. 'He sent for me. He led me here. These are his sunbeams.'

'Fudge,' Mr Delingpole said rudely. 'Quintrel, get up and be sensible. Miss Bell, what did you see? Tell me something rational.'

Between us, we tried to tell him, but we had both seen something different. Mr Quintrel had seen a god, holding aloft Apollo's golden spear. To my eyes the figure had been black as hell and I had fancied the rod might be a sword.

'Very unsatisfactory,' Mr Delingpole said. 'If only your cousin had been here, Miss Bell, we might have had some sense. Or if only I had been a moment sooner, for neither of you thought to catch the fellow and find out the truth once and for all. Well, well, and what then?'

'He set the fountain afire,' I said. 'He made the water burn.'

'Nonsense.'

'And then he vanished. The light went out all at once – the sword, the burning water – and he was gone.'

Mr Delingpole harrumphed again. 'Upon which you both stood gawking here.' He looked at Mr Quintrel. 'You got a message summoning you to the abbey, I suppose, as I did?'

Mr Quintrel was still dazed, his face beatific in the lantern light.

'Well, well. Let us look at this burning water of yours.' Mr Delingpole carried his lantern across the lawn to the old stone fountain, gold sunbeams dancing around his ankles in the grass. I followed him, with Father close behind me. Mr Quintrel remained behind, still trying to snatch the sunbeams from the grass with his cupped palms as Mr Delingpole had done.

Mr Delingpole's down-to-earth voice now reached us from the fountain. 'Well, the water is as dead and wet as any self-respecting water should be—' He broke off. 'But what's this?'

When Father and I came up to where he was standing, we saw there was a strange, large jar atop the fountain, and the sword (or rod) that the figure had carried had been slotted into its wide mouth. 'That is what he was carrying,' I said. 'That is his sword.' I reached up and laid my left hand on the side of the jar to steady myself. Whether Mr Delingpole and Father could see what I was doing by the lantern light I don't know. At any rate, they didn't stop me. I stood on tiptoe and reached up with my right hand to draw the strange rod out of the jar.

The moment I took hold of it, I was seized with a cramping spasm in all my body. I felt stretched as long as a ribbon, and then squeezed as tight as a ball. I could smell burning flesh, and fire tingled in every part of me before I fainted dead away.

27

I CAME TO MY senses again quite quickly, to find myself
no longer by the fountain but by the cloister walk. I
supposed I had been carried there by my father and Mr
Delingpole, but I have since found out that was not so.
However, that explanation must wait, for I mean to tell what
happened all in order.

They helped me back to the Deanery (and though I found
I could walk, I felt as bruised as if I had been run down by
a horse and cart). Mr Quintrel trailed after us and, after
Father had sent for a doctor and bidden the maid put me
to bed, the gentlemen convened once more in the parlour.
(I had the gist of what follows from Mr Delingpole this
morning.)

Mr Quintrel was still in a daze, not helped, I suppose,
by the added shock of my own peculiar accident. He was
mumbling about sun rays and golden chariots, Mr Delingpole
told me, and they were obliged to ply him with brandy to
bring him to any semblance of sense. After that they went
over the events of the evening. It seems that a boy came to

Mr Quintrel's rooms about seven o'clock, advising him to come to the undercroft at the abbey at once, for something to be seen there would interest him greatly.

Mr Quintrel came accordingly and secreted himself from the vergers down in his usual haunt in the undercroft until the glowing vision appeared to him and led him through the Dark Entry and into the Little Cloister where I was standing.

Meanwhile, Mr Delingpole had returned from Buckingham House to his chambers in Middle Temple to find a verbal message to the same effect had been left there by the same boy. He turned about and came straight back to the abbey, but by now it was well past sunset and the doors were locked. He roused Father from the Deanery, and they both came hurrying to the Little Cloister with the results I have already described.

The message being a verbal one, they had no means of discovering who had sent it, and the boy had melted back into the streets quite beyond their questioning.

Mr Quintrel fully believed the vision had been his longed-for Apollo, and that he had been granted a great favour. He maintained the messenger had been a heavenly one (likely winged Mercury, though he had not examined the boy's heels for feathers). He still had a handful of sunbeams, too, which when examined transpired to be flakes of gold leaf. How they had been suspended floating about the figure's head was a mystery. But Mr Delingpole and Lindley have been into the abbey this morning and discovered a scraping knife at work about the newly revealed golden tombs of Edmund Crouchback and his wife Aveline. This proves conclusively (and I dare say to Mr Quintrel's disappointment when he hears of it) that the vision was perpetrated by a human hand, and one that knew the abbey well enough to avail itself of our new-found treasures.

After my injury, no one dared touch the jar atop the fountain in the Little Cloister until Lindley came in about half past eleven o'clock. Father and Mr Delingpole were still sitting over the fire, talking, and drinking themselves into tranquillity. When they told Lindley the circumstances of my accident he turned very white, Mr Delingpole said. Lindley ran up to his bedchamber and returned looking even worse. Some of his equipment had been stolen and, when they three hastened back to the Little Cloister, there it all was: the rod I had thought a sword, the jar and the lathe-like machine with the glass globe I had glimpsed in Jerusalem the night of his demonstration. They carried it all home (Lindley picked up the jar without fear, remarking that it had been *discharged* with my mishap, but of that more hereafter).

L INDLEY CAME TO see me the moment I was awake this morning and sat on my bed, quite as pale as Mr Delingpole had said he was, while Father fussed about the room picking things up and putting them down by turns. Lindley asked me, with some abruptness, if I was quite well, but he seemed preoccupied, a fact accounted for when Father remarked that the doctor had been mystified by my injuries when he came the previous evening and had only prescribed a salve for my hand and gone away.

'Of course he was mystified,' Lindley said, still strangely

abrupt. 'It was a matter entirely beyond his ken, but well within mine, unfortunately. Susan, if you are recovered enough to come down to the parlour, I will show you all about it. Delingpole is there, waiting for us, equally eager for an explanation.'

Bonjour, Mrs Bell! Cuthbert cried upon my entrance a half-hour later, when I had dressed myself and washed my face and trembling hands. *Good God preserve us!* And thus, in a nutshell, he reminded me of what I had learned from Mrs Bray last night and not yet had the chance to tell.

They sat me down in Father's armchair close to the fire. Lindley had brought his equipment into the parlour and very strange (I admit even beautiful) it was. The large glass jar was sitting upon the table, half-filled with water. The rod I had seen last night was inserted through the mouth, along with a chain clamped at one end to the inside of the jar and in some way attached at the other to the lathe-like machine.

'I am very sorry to say my cousin has suffered an electric shock,' Lindley said. 'You recall, Uncle – Delingpole – that I demonstrated this equipment the other night in Jerusalem. To my utmost regret I didn't stress the great danger attendant upon its use, hardly thinking such a warning could be necessary to an audience of clergymen who were never likely to use the machines themselves.'

He went to the lathe. A polished wooden frame supported a pole, which could be turned very quickly by means of a large flywheel powered by a wooden handle. Halfway along the pole was suspended the glass sphere. Lindley took the rod from the jar and, turning the glass sphere very quickly until it was only a blur of movement, he touched the rod to the glass. Scarcely a moment later he stopped turning the handle and held out the rod towards us.

'If it were dark, as it was last night, you would see a blue glow about the spinning sphere and a blue flame projecting from the tip of this brass rod,' he said. He then touched the rod to a bowl on the table containing the shreds of gold leaf gathered up from the lawns of the Little Cloister. As the rod hovered close to them, they rose into the air and attached themselves to the rod. Being so very light, some danced away as Lindley raised it, then returned as if magnetised, others fell gracefully to the floor like butterflies. In an outdoor breeze they would have danced in the air just as we had seen last night.

'Electricity has been known since ancient times,' Lindley explained. 'The word itself is Greek – *elektron* – their word for amber, which they learned could create effects rather like this if they rubbed it briskly enough with a cloth. Today, this spinning globe acts in some wise like a cloth, rubbing at this brass rod, but much more vigorously than any human hand could do it. A much larger charge of electricity builds up than the Greeks ever knew, which results in the blue flame and makes Quintrel's dancing sunbeams.' He smiled at the quaint idea, despite his sober mood. Then he held out the rod to a glass bowl of water on the table. At once it burst into flame, just as the fountain had done last night. 'There is brandy floating on the surface of the water,' he said, 'which is ignited by the blue spark. The effect is momentary, but spectacular, and much beloved of theatrical electricians.'

'And the jar?' I asked.

Lindley frowned. 'Thus far, these effects I have shown you

are harmless amusements. But the Leyden jar is more serious. I made it spark at the demonstration, you will remember, sirs, but in fact more than one man has been seriously injured by the device and one or two have even died. Thank God, last night's culprit didn't charge the jar to its full capacity. He probably did not understand the mechanism. But if he had, my cousin might not be here this morning.'

He picked up the jar and cradled it in the crook of his elbow as he cranked the handle and span the globe again, gesturing to the chain which ran from the lathe to the jar. We all looked at the jar, but it sat there quietly in his embrace apparently unchanged and quite innocuous. At length, Lindley desisted from his spinning, set down the jar, and then picked up a smaller, bent iron rod from the table, holding it with a pair of wooden tongs. Going to the jar he touched one end of the bent metal to the glass side and then gingerly touched the other to the rod protruding from the mouth. There was a loud crack, and a blue spark flew like a miniature lightning bolt from the rod's end. We all cried out and Lindley carefully put down the bent rod again.

'Electricity is what we call a charge, both positive and negative,' he said, looking around at us (I am afraid to say, he was now rather in his element despite my accident). 'The one seeking always to cancel out the other. Here, in this jar, the positive is now within and the negative without, the glass acting as what we call an insulator, keeping them apart. Simultaneously touching the exterior of the jar and the rod in the neck, which connects to the positively charged water, this bent metal became a bridge through which the positive and negative forces could meet.'

He picked up the jar again in his two hands and smiled as he saw us flinch. 'This is quite safe since I am only touching the jar's exterior. But when my cousin touched both the glass and the rod at once, her body became an open door, just like the bent metal, through which the positive and negative charges met. The shock of it threw her clean across the lawn, as you described, Uncle.' (And at this I was astonished. What kind of force could lift a human body and throw it twelve feet through the air? Whatever it was, it had been stronger than a lion and it certainly accounted for all my bruises.)

'Then, the positive and negative forces being resolved and discharged,' Lindley ended, 'the jar was quite safe again.' He set the jar back on the table and sat down.

'Very well then,' Mr Delingpole said after a reflective pause. 'You have explained the means by which last night's illusion was created. The question now is who did it and why?'

'The obvious answer would be someone who saw me demonstrate the equipment in Jerusalem, and therefore knew both that I had it here to be stolen and how to use it, at least in a rudimentary way. *Why* they should do so is a mystery to me.'

Mr Delingpole frowned. 'But if the creation of the illusions – both this one and the ghost – are connected in some way to the theft of Edward's mummy and the death of Louis Durand, we know it cannot have been anyone in that room. The intruders' voices were heard in the cloisters while we were all in Jerusalem.'

How many times had Mr Delingpole, and Father, and the king, and Lindley said so! I hesitated a moment, hardly daring to dispel the one fact they thought they knew. But there was no choice.

After I told them what Mrs Bray had told me, we all sat and looked mournfully at Cuthbert peacefully preening under his wing. 'I don't like to say so,' I said, 'but you know, whoever made this trick and called Mr Quintrel to see it must also have known about his special interest in Apollo.'

'Then you suspect one of we antiquaries?' Mr Delingpole frowned at me.

'I don't see how I can, sir. I saw Mr Quintrel with last night's vision, and you and Father came so soon afterwards that unless you are in league together to make mischief you could not be Apollo either. The figure was certainly too strong and tall to have been Mr Alnutt. And poor Louis Durand did not attend the demonstration and, moreover, he is dead.'

'Very well then,' Mr Delingpole said with sudden resolution, 'we begin again. We go back to first principles. But this time we must unfortunately include the abbey clergy in our list of suspects. Now Mrs Bray's evidence is discredited we are obliged to do so.'

Father gave a little moan.

'Don't despair, Dean,' Mr Delingpole said. 'We will not leave you to investigate alone. I bear the heavy responsibility of starting the whole trouble by applying to His Majesty for the opening of the tomb in the first place. Your nephew is a clever man whose first duty must surely be to protect the abbey's reputation for your whole family's sake. And you have a daughter in Miss Bell who is remarkably astute for a member of her sex.' (*Obs.*: he once told me female songbirds

230

were slower to learn than male ones. I dare say there must be an exception to every rule and I suppose I ought to be gratified to learn that I am it.) 'Between us, we will get to the bottom of it, Dean. I firmly believe we will. I have been to Buckingham House and talked to the equerry. He undertakes to find out more about our mysterious Louis Durand, and information on that head can only help us.'

28

IT WAS HARDLY to be expected that Father would be
left long to brood over this troubling development. Mr
Delingpole and Lindley had only been gone a half-hour
when news came that Dame Yates had reappeared in the
apse, demanding yet another discussion of her statue.

'Don't go,' I said. 'Tell her you are busy. It is nothing but
the truth, for I am poorly and you must look after me, you
know.'

I was smiling, but he had already got wearily to his feet.

'Father,' I said, 'don't let the dreadful woman bully you.'

'Bully me?' He paused, with his hand on the doorknob.
'What do you mean by that, my dear?'

I hesitated. 'Can you not see that she has designs on you?'

'Designs!' Father looked displeased. 'Indeed she does. She
has designs of her husband's memorial, which I am obliged
to see executed.'

'Why must it always be you? Why can't her architect do it?'

'Because it is I who draws the banker's drafts for payment.
There will be no dog statue unless I arrange it.'

'Then draw them swiftly, for heaven's sake, and let us be rid of her.'

He frowned at me again. 'Your dislike of the lady is excessive, Susan. What has that poor bereaved creature ever done to you?'

'Nothing as yet. It is what she means to do that troubles me.'

He was still frowning. 'You think there is some special understanding between Dame Yates and myself?'

It alarmed me that he did not laugh out loud at the ludicrous supposition. 'I don't know. I hope not. I only know she wouldn't make you happy, Father.'

'Happy!' Yet again my words seemed to startle him. 'Are you so foolish as to look for happiness in this life?'

This was very odd. 'We have, Father,' I said. 'We always have.'

'Then we have been fools.'

The news of Mrs Bray's mistake seemed to have crushed him entirely. I half rose from my chair, concerned at the bitterness of his tone. 'Shall I come with you? Do you need me? I am quite well enough for that—'

'No.' He was actually displeased with me. 'No, I would not wish my *courting* to grieve you.' But then he seemed to remember my accident and his face softened. 'Stay here, my dear. Rest yourself. You are not well enough to be troubled with all this business. See where your efforts last night got you. Got all of us. It is really too bad.'

He went out and I found I was trembling. I had rarely argued with Father before, and even now I thought he was wrong. The king had taxed us to solve the mystery and how could we do so when all our investigations had been based on a mistake? And could he really mean it when he spoke of *courting*? In my own mind it had always been half a joke, but what in heaven would I do if I really were saddled with Dame Yates as a stepmother? I would have to marry someone – anyone – after all, and get away at once.

And, again, as if summoned by the thought, Mr Suckling now knocked at the parlour door and came in, carrying Father's torn cope draped across his arms.

'Oh, Mr Suckling. Good morning,' I said, feeling even more uneasy, if that were possible. 'Do put the cope there on the table.' At least that precluded any possibility of offering him tea and prolonging his visit more than was absolutely necessary.

But Mr Suckling, having done as he was bid, sat himself down in a chair as he was *not* bid, and looked at me. Cuthbert seemed to catch the infection of my anxiety. *Bad bird, bad bird, what, what?* He rang his bell six times in his agitation and ended with an inconsequential *God save the king!* I went to quieten him and he climbed on my shoulder and pecked at my ear fretfully.

Mr Suckling watched all this with his usual, cryptic smile. 'My dear Susan, what is this about an accident? Rumour has it that you suffered some kind of injury last night.'

I displayed my wound. 'Only a scorched hand, sir.'

'Dear me. From this new apparition I hear tell of?'

Of course, the story would be all over the abbey by now, and there was hardly any point in denying it. 'I'm afraid it was. Another trick – like the ghost, Mr Delingpole thinks – and certainly a trick this time, since it was done with my cousin's apparatus. He showed us this morning how the effect was achieved.'

'It was done with your *cousin's* apparatus?'

I remembered Mr Suckling had raised his eyebrows and spoken meaningfully in just this way when Lindley admitted to giving Mr Alnutt tea on Sunday. *I did not know that Mr Lindley Bell was also involved in the affair.*

'Some of Lindley's scientific things were stolen and used,' I admitted. 'And he said this new trick copied things he had demonstrated in Jerusalem on Saturday.' Now I remembered the destruction of Mrs Bray's alibi for all the Chapter. 'Tricks made by his electricity machine, which I believe you yourself witnessed.'

Mr Suckling did not look at all abashed at the question. 'Ah, yes, the dancing feathers, I remember. Your cousin wafted them about the room with a stick until the canon-treasurer began to sneeze. But to return to more serious matters, has this latest atrocity helped the dean to any new insights? I imagine he is eager to do as His Majesty bids and find it all out.'

'I believe there have been some new speculations,' I said cautiously.

'Ah.' He sat back. 'Rather a dangerous activity.'

'What is dangerous?'

'Speculation, Miss Bell. It can lead in so many unexpected directions. Ones even unfortunate to your father, I fear.'

My fingers were still tingling from last night's shock, and my palm hurt. 'Mr Suckling, if you mean this latest accident could be used to replace Father with the archbishop's favourite, only *you* will think so.'

He smiled again. Not a leer this time, more a sad smile of pity. 'Oh, your father is certainly a very well-loved man in the abbey, Miss Bell. I see it more and more with every passing week. The vergers, the gardeners, the canons and the chanter all much esteem him and look upon his little acts of destruction and upheaval to the old fabric with a remarkably tolerant eye.'

'And His Majesty is highly pleased with him.'

But Mr Suckling, far from being rebuffed by my irritation, got suddenly to his feet and came over to where I was sitting. I recoiled. I suppose I thought the moment of his proposal had finally come and I wished I still had a pin about me. But he was not leering. Indeed, now there was no smile on his face and I thought abstractedly that a fierce intelligence shone in his eyes.

'Susan, I confess I have come here on a pretext.'

'Oh?' I said faintly.

'The cope was but an excuse. I saw your father engaged with that awful woman and her memorial. I took the opportunity to find you alone.'

'Mr Suckling,' I said, 'I am very honoured, but—'

'I have a number of troubling suspicions and I feel I can only confide in you.'

Cuthbert must have seen my face. *Bad bird, bad bird,* he said with some agitation and then made a loud and highly improper sound more suitable to the privy than the parlour.

'I do not want your confidences, Mr Suckling.'

'Nevertheless, I must share them. I cannot speak to anyone else, for your father's sake.'

I was angry now. 'How many times must I tell you that *he* has done nothing wrong?'

'Perhaps he has not. I hope he has not. But I fear family feeling may have—' He broke off. 'You say your cousin demonstrated how last night's trick was done? I would not upset you for the world, but I have been wondering . . . fearing . . .' He hesitated. 'Did he take pleasure in showing you all how it was done?'

'Pleasure? Hardly that . . .'

But Lindley *had* been pleased. I had noticed his ears grow pink when he turned the flywheel of the spinning globe.

'Susan, are you able to walk? Could you climb a stair? May I show you what I have found?'

29

WE WERE CLIMBING the spiral stairs to the triforium gallery where only Fidoe was permitted to go and which Mr Delingpole had so longed to see. It was a remarkably long climb up to that lofty space fifty feet above us. If I had foreseen the turning stair going on and on, and judged my own strength aright, I might have refused to go. But it was too late now. There were rope handrails to either side and I held on to the left one with my good hand. The steps were very narrow and very steep. Mr Suckling was directly behind me, so I knew I could not fall, but I disliked his presence even so. As ever, he was just a little too close.

And then, all of a sudden, the stairs ended and we stepped out into a lofty space. I had always imagined there would be only a narrow bridge of boards running around a cramped dark attic, but instead the space was vast and light. The only obstructions were the roof beams, huge oak timbers criss-crossing the place from floor to high ceiling. On the outer wall, grand blossom-shaped windows looked down over the cloisters and the College Garden, their mullions beautifully glazed and carved, though there was no one at all to see them. On the inner wall, which looked down into the abbey, were the run of arches I had only ever seen from below, craning my neck to look at them. In the arches to the left of the stairs, at the corner where the gallery turned to run above the high altar, I could see the chains and lamps Fidoe had been installing.

'Be careful,' Mr Suckling said. He had turned the other way, towards the great rose window at the south transept. 'Whatever else may be lies, the floor *is* treacherous.'

That stopped me in my tracks and I peered down at the boards under my feet, wondering if they were rotten. The idea of smashing off the pavement no longer seemed at all amusing. After a moment Mr Suckling came back and took my hand, hurrying me along.

When I peered down through the arches into the body of the abbey below it was all strange – as strange as it had looked when the ghost walked. Familiar things were changed, seen from this different angle, and everything below us looked foreshortened. I glanced across at the opposite gallery which ran along the other arm of the cross. 'Look,' I said, tugging at Mr Suckling to stop. 'There is someone there.'

There was indeed a solitary figure to be seen, its back turned to us, looking out of another blossom-shaped window down on to the huddled fortress of Parliament below.

After a moment I said, 'It's all right, it can only be Fidoe.'

Mr Suckling hushed me. 'Keep still, Susan, lest he sees us.'

I didn't know why we should. Why it would not do for Fidoe to see us – except, I supposed, that he was so very possessive of the place. And then, fleetingly, I wondered how the sacrist had got up here at all when the door was always locked. But I was still not quite myself, weak and trembling from the climb, and I kept very still, watching the distant figure across on the other side of the vast abbey. Mr Suckling's grasp on my hand tightened, and I pulled it away. He took it back.

We stayed there for some minutes more. The distant figure was still motionless. Strangely motionless. As if turned to stone.

'What can it be?' I said. 'Is it . . . ?'

And then Mr Suckling began softly to laugh. It was not a sound I had heard before and I was unsurprised to find out it was quite as discomfiting as the rest of him.

'It is only a statue,' he said.

It *was* a statue. Of course I knew there were always works going on in the abbey; always memorials and effigies being moved to make room for new ones. Whoever this unfortunate creature might be, it had been considered lowly enough to be stored away altogether. I was obscurely glad they had at least given it a view out of the window. Nonetheless, its lonely, silent vigil made me shiver.

'This way, Susan.'

It was not far until the wide expanse of the triforium ended above Poets' Corner. Across the paved floor and the statues below, I could see the gallery resume its course westwards, above the nave. Mr Suckling had led me to where a narrow bridge (about three feet wide) joined one gallery to the other. It was really no more than a shelf, running along the front of the stained-glass panels below the rose window.

'You cannot mean us to cross here,' I said, drawing back.

Mr Suckling's smile was implacable. 'It is quite safe, Susan. You see, there is a railing. You will not fall.'

There was a railing – a single metal bar at waist height. If one tripped, one would infallibly slip beneath it to one's death. And even if one kept tight hold of the railing, when had it last been checked? What if it fell away under one's grasp, and one was left, flattened helplessly to the wall, with only a step between oneself and the fifty-foot drop?

'I have crossed it twice this morning,' the sacrist said. 'It is quite safe. And there is something on the other side you must see, for your father's sake.'

I was still peering across the void, uncertain and afraid, when he took me in hand. Before I knew it he had grasped hold of me again, even more firmly, and was dragging me onto the narrow shelf. I was too shocked and too afraid to scream, and he went so fast I could not even reach for the handrail. I believe I closed my eyes, for I have no recollection of that terrible fall to the ground at my right hand.

And then we were across, and ahead was what seemed to be another window. But this, unlike the blossom windows of the triforium, was roughly hewn at all odd angles like a jagged door. The jagged door was open, and that same strange golden shimmer was returned, as if this door also led to that other unearthly world from where Edward Longshanks' ghost had emerged in the north ambulatory. Mr Suckling still had hold of my hand and was pulling me after him towards that eerie light. I resisted, for I thought I had glimpsed something stirring in the shimmering depths. I opened my mouth in a silent scream as we came closer. There were two spectral forms now. One all long tendrils

242

like Edward's ghost. The other a shrunken shape at its feet, the very image of a demon imp.

Mr Suckling was still pulling me towards them. They were advancing at the same pace towards us. The air bulged around them. The taller figure was a headless, long red streak like a lick of flame. The shorter flared out as if dressed in a wide court crinoline. I put my hand to my mouth and the short figure copied me. Mr Suckling stopped and turned, and so did the tall, tendril ghost, exactly at the same moment.

It was a broken mirror, leaning against a pillar. Mr Suckling dropped my hand and I stepped closer to its many shattered surfaces. In one I was the imp. In another a long strip of dark blue, the colour of my gown. In a third, my normal self.

Mr Suckling watched me and said nothing. Perhaps he was waiting for me to draw the same conclusions he had drawn as I stepped back and then walked towards the mirror again. Its strange, bent surface made everything about me seem to bulge and shrink as I moved. The glass was pitted, so that everything shimmered, and the cheap mirror backing made the reflection a golden brown.

'I have seen such a thing before,' Mr Suckling said. 'At your cousin's demonstration on Saturday night he brought a curious mirror like this to show us. It was convex and made everything short and fat like your father, or like yourself in that smaller shard there. This other pane is concave, as you can see, and has the contrary effect.'

I nodded.

'Your cousin said he had other such mirrors,' the sacrist went on. 'Other mirrors that gave different but equally remarkable effects. He said they were too big to conveniently carry to Jerusalem. From everything I have heard about it, from quizzing Mr Alnutt, I believe this mirror is how your strange ghost was conjured.'

I was very much afraid that I thought so, too.

'Of course I was not there, but Mr Alnutt described the whole thing to me,' Mr Suckling said. 'He remarked that everything looked eerie and changed.'

I nodded wordlessly, still taking in the strange unearthly light the mirror cast on everything.

'Even an ordinary mirror would do so, would it not? Merely by reversing the familiar world we know.' He gestured to the broken mirror, and I saw that even in the shard where we were reflected without distortion, Mr Suckling did indeed look strange. (I looked just as I expected, but of course I only ever see myself reflected back to front.)

'See how the light falls differently in the mirror? See how even the familiar is unfamiliar? And then the glass is so pitted and distorted that everything shimmers and moves.'

Mr Suckling eyed the mirror thoughtfully, then went to one side of it. Experimentally, he put out a foot before the concave distorting pane and its grotesque, stretched reflection appeared in the glass. He put out a hand and it followed the foot, just as we had seen the spectre's figure emerge from thin air by Longshanks' tomb.

'It would all depend on the angle of the glass,' he said. 'The mirror had to be angled so that you would only see the reflection and not the man making it. A very clever trick, and a complicated one too. The work of a cunning man who had taken his time to create it.'

'But what is it doing up here?' I asked.

'Someone has hidden it.'

'But Fidoe would see it and tell Father.'

'Fidoe has seen it. How can he not have done?' Mr Suckling looked at me meaningfully. 'Why do you imagine he has said nothing? Why do you imagine he has not told your father?'

'You think Father *does* know?'

'He would be bound to protect his nephew, would he not?'

I looked deeper into the mirror. My mouth was open, and my face looked like some death's head. The fractured surface reflected so many pictures it made me dizzy and that was not a pleasant feeling up here in the roof. I was silent for a long minute. Each one of my faces looked pale. Had I not once thought . . . ? Had I not even asked him . . . ?

'If it was Lindley it was merely a joke,' I said. 'A stupid joke.'

'Then why not say so? Why go to this trouble to hide the evidence?' He shifted, so that his face joined mine in the shattered mirror. His expression alarming as always, but now twofold – threefold – twentyfold. His spoon face bulged and shrank as he talked and I watched it, mesmerised. 'Where was your cousin when Longshanks walked? Where was he last night when Apollo walked?' He didn't wait for me to finish. 'Missing. He is always missing, Susan. And does not your esteemed Mr Delingpole say the ghost and the murder are connected?'

He reached out and took my hand again, but this time my thoughts were so busy I hardly noticed. 'Susan, this is his mirror, and he is a clever man. If it is discovered that your cousin is involved with this mystery . . .' He hesitated. 'And

245

if it is discovered your father has protected him by having Fidoe hide this evidence here . . . We must decide together what we are to do.'

Finally he had succeeded in pinning me, not by his hands, but by the force of his insinuations. 'You can certainly ruin Father *now*,' I said. 'And I know full well you have always wanted to.'

He hissed softly, as he had done that day in the sacristy. 'Ruin him! Indeed no, that is the last thing I desire to do, Susan.' He began to lead me away from the mirror back towards the horrible narrow shelf to the other side. 'I told you, I have seen how well beloved he is in the abbey – and I see now that, if this mystery is solved to the king's satisfaction, he might well rise even higher in the Church. Perhaps even to the rank of archbishop himself. I brought you here that we might discuss between ourselves how best to protect him.'

'Protect him!' I said. 'I told you before, we only need to keep silent as the king commands.'

We had stepped onto the narrow ledge, Mr Suckling still grasping me with one hand. The other he now placed at my back and turned me so that I was in his loose embrace, my back to the giddy drop.

'Then silence is what he shall have, the dear man,' he said. 'I only wish I might call him *father*, too, as you do, and share all his troubles and triumphs to the end.' His grip tightened. 'What do you say, my dear Susan? Would that not be the safest and most certain way to protect him? To protect you both?'

It was hard to think straight with that drop at my back. I dared not push him off lest I overbalanced both of us. My hand reached out blindly for the metal banister, and when my fingers closed around it, it moved ever so slightly, just as I had feared it would.

'Mr Suckling, it is no use your asking me. It is no use your pestering me. I would as lief marry Dame Yates's dog as you.'

God knows why he didn't push me ever so gently backwards over the void. Instead, his eyes only widened at my insulting words and his hands dropped from my waist. I darted from him, across the horrid chasm, and then, despite all the weakening after-effects of my electric shock, I scrambled back down the spiral staircase without stopping.

I remembered the sacrist's sudden frankness. The intelligence in his eye when he forgot to smile, and then the hideous transformations as his face rippled between the broken surfaces of the mirror. The mirror that had certainly been used to create the illusion of the ghost, and which, unless Mr Suckling was lying, belonged to Lindley – as did the Leyden jar that had almost killed me.

30

I WAS BACK IN the parlour. The clock on the mantelpiece said a minute to two o'clock, and a moment later the abbey bell (the real bell this time) confirmed that our clock was reading true.

Father was away somewhere as usual, and I abstractedly took up Charles II's hat and went to sit in the window that looks out over the Deanery yard. It is that particular week in May when everything grows all of a sudden while one's back is turned. The climbing rose around the window was bursting into shoot, while bindweed twined through it from a crack in the paving, with thick, juicy, vigorous stems.

I ran the hat's plume of ostrich feathers absently through my fingers while I thought about what Mr Suckling had told me. I desired to disagree with him – to prove his accusations against Lindley wrong – but I didn't know how to do it. I had not seen any such strange mirror as the sacrist had described when I peered over Lindley's shoulder into Jerusalem the night of the demonstration, but that meant little, since I had snatched only the merest glimpse of the apparatus then. If

I had been invited to the meeting (as I really ought to have been), and if the sacrist was telling me the truth, I might have seen it just as he described.

But if Lindley was behind the ghost illusion why did he not say so when I asked him outright? Why did he let Mr Delingpole go on supposing that the murderer was the same man that made the ghost? What had possessed him to make Apollo walk last night and almost kill me? And why had he not hidden the evidence of his own involvement as he had done with the mirror? Why had he been idiot enough to leave his apparatus lying there, in the Little Cloister fountain, for everyone to see and draw conclusions from?

That was an argument in favour of my cousin certainly. Even I did not think him fool enough to have incriminated himself in that way. Then again, if he had not made the ghost walk himself, still he of all people should have guessed how it was done, just as he had guessed the details of the Apollo trick with such perfect accuracy. Had he not quizzed us all endlessly about the ghost? If the trick had been done with distorting mirrors, as Mr Suckling claimed, then Lindley could hardly have failed to make the connection, if he was really as clever as Mr Suckling thought him. Indeed, I remembered with a sinking feeling, there had even been a concave mirror in his magic lantern.

Not for the first time, I found myself hoping Lindley was not as clever as he liked to think. In the past, I had hoped so in order to puncture his self-conceit. Now I hoped so because, otherwise – if Mr Delingpole was right to link the apparitions to the murder – he might also be involved in things far more terrible than the mere conjuring of a ghost and a god. Moreover, if Father was protecting him, as Mr Suckling supposed, even worse might follow.

I picked up my needle and commenced darning the hat. Another memory had returned upon me – Lindley shoving William II's crown on his head when I showed him the ragged regiment in their cupboard. The ghost had worn a crown. Had it been the one buried with Longshanks, as I had assumed, or another one entirely? Had it been plain, like Llewellyn's, or jewelled like the Confessor's? I couldn't remember. The mirror had distorted everything and I had been too frightened to notice much.

No, I told myself, Lindley is not clever and is certainly not involved. The only concave mirror he possessed was that small one in the magic lantern; scarcely more than six inches across and fixed firmly in place. He owned no other and the sacrist was a liar.

The light from the garden was very good and Cuthbert was peaceful, preening his red tail and cracking nuts. But my fingers were still trembling and my palm was really too sore for sewing. I laid my needle down.

Mr Suckling had been right about one thing. Lindley had always been missing when any extraordinary thing took place. He had been there at the tomb's first opening, that was true, but he had not seen the ghost walk. He had not seen the tomb reopened or Durand's dead body found. And last night he had gone out with Mr Delingpole long before Apollo cast his sunbeams on Mr Quintrel.

He himself had been in Father's study on Sunday, while we were in Jerusalem with the king, for he had taken Mr Alnutt there. And if Mr Alnutt had not taken the drawings or the keys, then Lindley could have done. And if he had the keys, then, apart from the Confessor's shrine, he had access to everything in the abbey. How else had he taken the mirror to the triforium? He could have come and gone without the porter's knowledge. He could easily have let Louis Durand inside, the night of the murder.

I laid my head against the windowpane and closed my eyes.

I have a number of troubling suspicions and I feel I can only confide in you.

Was it really possible that it was my cousin who had hurt me last night? He had looked pale, it was true, but I remembered his strange, distracted abruptness as he asked me how I felt. *The culprit didn't charge the jar to its full capacity. He probably did not understand the mechanism. But if he had, my cousin might not be here this morning.* On the whole he had been remarkably cool about my narrow escape and afterwards, as Mr Suckling had guessed, positively excited by the whole affair and eager to explain it to us.

My head ached, my nerves jangled and my burnt palm itched.

I cannot speak to anyone else, for your father's sake, Mr Suckling had said. And who, then, was *I* to speak to? With whom could I share all these horrible accusations and the thoughts they had raised? If Fidoe knew that mirror was in the triforium, and Father knew it too, then they must be protecting Lindley just as the sacrist thought. If so, I could not tell Mr Delingpole or the searcher or the king without getting Father and Fidoe into terrible trouble. And as for Lindley – if I said anything, he might find himself strung up for Louis Durand's murder.

But could any of it be true? When Father blinks his beady eyes at me I know exactly what it means. I have always known his absence of mind and loved him for it. It is quite impossible that he should know what Lindley has done and keep it secret from me. It is impossible, I thought, that he has seen the broken mirror. How could my portly little father ever cross that horrid ledge to the gallery above the nave? Probably even Fidoe avoids it. And even if Father *has* seen the mirror (and I have not heard him say he has been up in the triforium at all since Saturday) he would hardly associate it with the ghost, especially since he did not see the spectre's weird, elongated form himself.

He might have supposed it merely another piece of rubbish stored away up there like so much else. And Fidoe? He might have noticed its arrival, but anyone could have sent the mirror up to be stored, just like the poor abandoned statue, and Fidoe might be entirely ignorant of its nature. After all, he did not see the ghost walk either. (And now I understand why he didn't. The mirror was angled towards us on the ground and its reflection therefore was invisible to him in the triforium.)

I could not so easily acquit Lindley in my mind. I waited for him all afternoon, but he did not appear. I wanted to see him – yet I was afraid to meet his eye. I didn't know what I could possibly say to him, and the longer he was missing and the longer I thought about it, the more Mr Suckling's insidious accusations rattled around my brain.

Abandoning any pretence at needlework I went out for some air in the cloisters, and spent a long time with the strange, smudged monks worn away almost to nothing in the paving. I wondered what they would have thought of the walking spectre. A demon from hell or the soul of the departed king? Perhaps neither. Instead, they would have called it a miracle and advertised it far and wide to bring still more pilgrims to the Confessor's shrine.

How much easier it would be to decide the spectre was a real ghost, than trouble ourselves with questioning and measuring and looking for rational answers. But, alas, I am a daughter of the Anglican eighteenth century. I cannot think of ghosts as souls lost in limbo as the Catholics do, for we have abolished purgatory altogether and there is nowhere for Protestant spirits to linger between here and heaven – unless in the abbey, which is, in many ways, more a mausoleum to the famous dead than a living church.

I have a number of troubling suspicions and I feel I can only confide in you.

Lindley could not possibly be involved.

I cannot speak to anyone else, for your father's sake.

Mr Suckling had persuaded me that I, too, was helpless. That I could not ask Father for fear of what he might tell me. That he, himself, could be my only confidant. (And that to save my family, I must marry him, for which horrible threat I had repaid him by more or less calling him a dog.)

But supposing Father was ignorant of Lindley's delin-quency, as he must be, then surely I could tell him everything and seek his counsel? Yes, I thought, I could certainly do that. But the next question was: *should I?* Mr Delingpole was convinced that the ghost and Apollo and the murder were all part of one scheme. Was I, therefore, ready to bring such dreadful suspicions down on Lindley's head? If Father was not protecting my cousin, I myself could do so. But no, I thought. If Lindley is guilty, I must tell Father, if no one else, and confer with him as to what should be done.

If he is guilty. But how am I to tell?

I had thought that since Lindley owned one distorting mirror in his magic lantern, he would have surely guessed how the ghost trick was done. And Mr Suckling had said he had seen another, larger, mirror in Lindley's possession at the demonstration. Should I ask Father if he remembered seeing such a thing? But then I imagined asking him and, knowing Father, his answering blank look.

Then should I instead ask Mr Delingpole? But he might thereby guess the direction of my thoughts. *He* was certainly clever enough to do so.

No, I needed to find out for myself before I spoke to anyone else. Lindley and Father were both out, and the maids would not set the fires in our bedchambers for another hour. I would slip upstairs to Lindley's room now, I told myself, and prove to my own satisfaction whether he owned any such curious mirror or not.

31

THE READER NEED not purse her lips, nor shake her head. The reader need not heave a sigh of patriarchal disappointment, nor get out his book of sermons. I am perfectly aware of the impropriety of an unmarried young lady entering a gentleman's bedchamber regardless of whether he is in it or not. But if the reader, be it *he* or *she*, cannot see that there was no impropriety in my thoughts just then, they had better close this account at once and be done with me.

I tapped gently at Lindley's chamber door just in case he might have returned without my knowing from wherever he had got himself to. He might be out in town. He might be with his strange friend Tom Ffoulkes. He might merely be walking in the College Garden, like the canon-treasurer. Wherever he was, he might come running up the stairs to his room at any moment and discover me there.

But surely I was not afraid of him. Apart from the possible embarrassment (*vide* impropriety *&c.* above) I told myself I was not afraid of him barging in. Nevertheless, dratted Mr

Suckling would not be quiet. *Whatever else is lies, the floor is treacherous*, he had said in the triforium. And that was how I felt now. My heart beat faster when, receiving no answer to my knock, I turned the doorknob and went into Lindley's silent and empty room.

It is the best guest chamber and a very pleasant one, overlooking the garden. In the late afternoon it was very bright, so that the dust danced in the sunbeams falling through the window as I skirted the bed to where the large trunk he had brought back with him from Europe squatted, its lid closed.

Perhaps it would be locked and my fears need not be confirmed, but only remain a nagging thought at the back of my mind. That would be best, after all. It would certainly have been best if Pandora had left the Box alone.

The trunk was not locked.

It opened under my fingers and I pushed the heavy lid up to rest against the wall before looking inside. It was not, at first sight, a swarm of demons. Having always thought Lindley such a boy, I think I expected his belongings to be all of a jumble, but the contents of the trunk were very neatly arranged and labelled. He must have been wearing his new sensible look when he packed these things away.

The electricity machine had been dismantled to fit back in the trunk – I recognised the beautiful glass sphere that had spun under Lindley's hand this morning. (The Leyden jar with the protruding rod still in its mouth was sitting on Lindley's dressing table.) In the trunk, beside the sphere, was the box of lantern slides Lindley had brought to the parlour, and when I opened it I saw it contained dozens more of those painted glass pieces for the magic lantern. There was such a variety of pictures of animals and people, angels and devils, that I would have liked to study each in turn, only I had not now the time.

Another box read 'lenses'. When I opened this, there were more glass rectangles. (*Query*: how on earth did Lindley get all this home by sea and potholed roads without smashing it?) These were different from the lantern slides, and different one to another, the glass this time made of varying thicknesses and bowed in diverse ways, so that when one looked through it, everything was distorted, magnified or foreshortened by turns. *Refraction*. Of course, I knew what these were well enough, having looked so often through Father's reading glasses and laughed at the effect. (*Another query*: does Lindley mean to eschew his country estate and set up as an optician? He certainly has a sufficiency of lenses for the venture and it would be a far preferable ambition than turning murderer.)

And now, with a lurch at my heart, I saw what I had hoped not to find. A round mirror, perhaps a foot in diameter, tucked against the side of the trunk, reflecting back the light from the window, so that at a casual glance one might have thought there was another, identical trunk opening out the other way (just as those in reduced circumstances sometimes put a large mirror on their wall to create an illusion of more space.)

This mirror was held safely in place by all the adjacent objects, which I now lifted out one by one, setting them down carefully on the floor beside me. One of these was another piece of glass, but triangular in shape this time; perhaps six inches long and two inches wide. When I lifted the long end to my eye and looked through it, the world arched. The window was a vivid rainbow, and there were more rainbows wherever the light fell. The edge of the dressing table. The counterpane on the bed. It was suddenly a room full of colour so beautiful it made me gasp. Was this the thing Blake had scornfully described to me: the glass that could capture the rainbow? Surely he couldn't call this beautiful effect a shameful example of man's overweening scientific pride. It was called a *prism*, I now remembered, and perhaps Blake had never seen one. My fingers itched to slip it into my pocket to show him later, but I resisted such criminal larceny and instead turned the prism to put the short end to my eye. The world fractured, like the reflection in the broken mirror in the triforium, some images reversed and some turned upside down.

I put the prism reluctantly to one side and, clearing away all the other impediments, finally lifted the mirror from the trunk. One look showed me what Mr Suckling had said was true. It made everything *short and fat like your father*. The surface of the glass bulged out, like Father's belly indeed, and within its depths my face was reflected back at me, rather small, and quite unrecognisable. I was an imp again, as I had been in the triforium mirror. My slim face was as round as the moon Lindley had shown me through the magic lantern, my freckles huge like the *mare tranquillitatis*, and my eyes like the deep black craters of the *Peninsula Deliriorum*. I opened my mouth and the whole picture swelled and bulged in just the same grotesque way as the ghost had done.

I thrust the mirror away from me, disgusted, but then

couldn't resist taking another look. It was at that moment I heard footsteps downstairs in the hall. At once I began to thrust everything back into the trunk pell-mell. But as I closed the lid and hurriedly crossed the room I heard the same footsteps outside on the landing, and before I could grasp the doorknob it turned of its own accord and Lindley came in.

'Susan!' he said, glancing around the room as if he thought – quite naturally – that I could not possibly be in there alone. 'What in heaven are you doing here?'

'Looking for Father,' I replied, attempting a nonchalance I certainly didn't feel. 'Have you seen him, Lindley?' (This was hardly very convincing. Why in heaven would Father be in Lindley's room? In any case, I would surely have knocked at the door and, receiving no answer, merely gone away again.)

Lindley still looked puzzled but seemed willing to take my words at face value. 'Not lately,' he said, taking off his hat and pitching it accurately onto the bedpost. 'I last saw him about noon, in the nave, arm in arm with Dame Yates. They looked very comfortable together.'

He was so like his usual self that my suspicions seemed absurd. I was frowning – an expression he seemed to think was conjured by the idea of Dame Yates, not himself. He smiled at me.

'She is probably a kind woman, you know, Susan.'

'That is easy for you to say,' I said, aiming at an everyday tone that might distract him from more questions about my perplexing presence in his room. 'The thought of growing old in her company is very dismal.'

'You won't do that,' he said, looking at me in a way I

didn't quite recognise. I almost thought he looked, at last, as sentimental as his name. '*That* will hardly happen.'

'Forgive me, as a spinster aunt that is exactly what will happen.'

He took a step closer. His voice was no longer teasing. 'But as you once informed me, you have no brothers and sisters, and therefore can never be an aunt. Or, at least, not a spinster one. If you marry, your husband may have brothers and sisters, I suppose.' He hesitated. Took another step closer. 'As I do, as a matter of fact.'

I am very much afraid I was gawping at him, perplexed by his new tone – by this apparently whole new Lindley. He reached out and took my right hand. 'Does it still pain you, dearest?'

'A little.'

He stroked my palm gently and then moved his fingers to my hair. 'I am so sorry. I can't help but feel it was my fault.'

Trying to answer, I found my throat was dry and I was obliged to swallow. '*Was* it your fault, Lindley?'

But he wasn't listening. He had now got his hands about my waist somehow and was drawing me to him. Reader, I beg you to understand that I did not raise my mouth to be kissed. At least, I am sure I did not. That is, I think I did not. It seemed inevitable that our lips would meet, just as those of our silhouettes had done in the light of the magic lantern.

He wasn't hot and moist like Mr Suckling. His lips were as light and warm as Mr Quintrel's sunbeams. I think I closed my eyes.

And now the reader may shake her head if she wishes. The reader had better get out his book of sermons at once. I am perfectly aware of the impropriety of an unmarried lady kissing a gentleman in his bedchamber. I dare say the thing has never before been done. And so it was lucky that there were just then voices in the hall below.

It was Father greeting the footman. Then he was clattering about in a state of high excitement, going from room to room in search of me.

'Susan!' he was calling. 'Susan, my dear! Fidoe has just found Longshanks!'

32

AN INTERESTED AUDIENCE had gathered in the Lady Chapel where the mummified corpse of Edward Longshanks had been laid out on the paving. He was still dressed in his red satin tunic. His legs were still wrapped in the cloth of gold, and he still miraculously held his dove-topped rod in one hand and his sceptre in the other. All in all, he seemed quite unscathed, except that the famous Welsh crown was indubitably missing.

Nevertheless, he had given Fidoe an exceedingly nasty turn. 'We opened up this vault last Friday, you know,' he was telling everybody, in a state of nervous self-importance. 'This vault 'ere, under Elizabeth's monument. If you poke your head down the hole, you can see the coffins one atop the other. The top one has rags of red velvet still on it, and there's a carving of a Tudor rose. 1603 it says, with the initials E.R..

'There was a hole into another passage, closed up with loose rubble, what we meant to look at next, afore all this trouble happened in the abbey and the dean became far too busy. Well, I had a spare half-hour and thought I'd just have a look. Bless me, if the hole hadn't been opened without us, and then the stones shoved back in, rough-like, all ways. I pulled 'em out and saw it led into another smaller tomb. When I looked through, with my lantern just now . . . Well. Dear me.'

He had come face to face with Longshanks, shoved sideways into the narrow space. At Fidoe's cries, the other workmen had come hastening, and helped him pull out the poor king.

'If I hadn't've found him, he might have lain there till Judgement Day,' Fidoe was saying. 'Gawd Almighty. Lost for ever, like old King James.' (Not that a resting place beside the great Queen Elizabeth would have been so disgraceful, *I* think.)

Blake had now appeared among us and squatted by the body, examining it from head to toe – I suppose, having drawn it all with such care on Saturday, he was better placed than the rest of us to make sure it was essentially unharmed.

'We should return him to his tomb at once,' Father was saying. 'It is quite ready for him, you know.'

'But the king will wish to see it,' Lindley objected. 'And so will all the antiquaries. Why don't we lay him out in the Confessor's shrine until we have properly examined him? He will be quite safe and out of sight in there, Uncle.'

I looked at Lindley, wondering again what he was thinking. If he had had anything to do with the mummy's theft surely he would be as eager as Father to hide the body away again. Or, perhaps, he feared that would attract suspicion and therefore affected his usual cheerful curiosity. He had kissed me alone in his bedchamber. And I had liked it. I will not deny I had liked it. But it had been very wicked of him. And if he was capable of such ungentlemanly licence as *that*, what else might he be capable of? He watched the workmen carry the mummy carefully to the shrine and his face told me nothing.

'Alnutt was right,' was all he said to Father. 'He always believed Edward hadn't left the abbey.'

'But what does it mean?' I asked. 'Why was his body there, stuffed in that hole?'

'The thief only wanted the crown.' Lindley was thinking aloud. 'He couldn't put the mummy back in the tomb as it was closed, and having killed his accomplice he couldn't open it again.'

This seemed poor reasoning. 'Then why not just leave the mummy lying where it was? Why take it from the coffin at all? And why go to the trouble of opening this passage in Elizabeth's vault to hide it in?'

'It *is* odd,' Lindley conceded. 'Whoever did it clearly knew about the vault, and therefore must know the abbey like the back of their hand. I am afraid we come back to the probability of an inside accomplice, Uncle.'

I had forgotten our interested audience, but at Lindley's words there was a general murmur of dismay. I looked at them all: canons and minor canons (the canon-treasurer looking very grey, the chanter very faint and Mr Suckling for once strangely inscrutable). The vergers were plainly vexed that they had not found the king's body for all their endless polishing of nooks and crannies; and the workmen, who had just rejoined us, were frowning.

'Blessed if they don't mean to blame us again,' the one

who had spoken up in Jerusalem said to his fellows. 'But ain't it always the way? Poor folks always come off worst.'

Father glanced up irritably. 'Benson, that's enough. You forget it is the Church you serve. *We* are hardly likely to blame a poor man merely because it is easy to do so. You are valued here, and Fidoe is quite as trusted as the sacrist.'

'God bless your reverence,' one of the other workmen said, and though I thought Father was preaching what *ought* to be, rather than what *was*, I still felt very proud of his Christian disregard for rank. As for trusting Fidoe as much as Mr Suckling! I knew for a fact that everyone trusted him a good deal more. I stole a glance at the sacrist and his lips were compressed into an uncharacteristic frown that made me remember the *bad temper* Mr Alnutt had spoken of but which I had never seen.

Father sighed. 'My dear brethren, my dear, dear, friends. All this is very troubling, I know. But let us look on the bright side. Here is the king, quite safe and sound, and I promise no man will be falsely accused of what remains to be discovered. That is: who is behind these foolish supernatural events we have witnessed, and who killed Monsieur Durand.'

'Foolish!' Mr Lamb said. 'Do you call them merely foolish, Dean? The word about the abbey is that even you yourself think the spectres real.'

Father's petulant grumbling had got out – presumably by way of Mr Suckling. Father waved a deprecating hand. 'I did say so once, Chanter, in a fit of vexation. But I am now quite persuaded that they were only tricks perpetrated by our mysterious murderer, just as Mr Delingpole and my nephew think.'

'*You* may be persuaded, Dean, but not all of us are.' Mr Lamb was stubborn. 'The Chapter is very troubled. We have talked about it among ourselves and we are very troubled indeed.'

Father waved his hand again, this time as if to say, *Naturally*.

'Of course, as churchmen it pains us to say so. But we do fear the hand of the Devil in all this.' (*Obs.*: is it not curious to believe God might meddle in human affairs, but be squeamish about the Devil?) 'We think something must be done about it,' the chanter went on, 'and as soon as may be.'

'Of course something must be done,' Father said wearily. He looked suddenly so ill that for a moment I really feared we would have to resign ourselves to Dame Yates as his only escape from all these endless troubles. 'But what do you suggest?'

Mr Lamb was prompt. He had been waiting for an opening and was not going to miss his chance. 'Casting out the demons from this place, Dean. That is what we think. And the grave to be permanently sealed.'

Casting out demons! Whoever heard of such a thing happening in an Anglican church! Father, like the rest of us, looked shocked. 'Those are strong words, Chanter.'

'Strong measures to defeat strong devilry, Dean.' (Behind him, the other canons present were nodding their heads. How shallow the current of Protestant scepticism turns out to be!)

Father wilted under the force of their collective stare. 'Oh, very well. You are right, I dare say. There is, at least, nothing to be lost by the measure. Can you rustle up the form of an exorcism for us, Chanter? I am afraid I am unfamiliar with the rite.'

Mr Lamb looked palely excited at the idea and a tremor ran through the assembled company.

'But I do not know what you mean by permanently sealing the tomb, Chanter,' Father said. 'Though I dare say you have a plan for that, too.'

If there was any sarcasm in Father's voice, Mr Lamb didn't notice. 'Pitch was what we thought, Dean. Pitch poured in, up to the brim of the casket, and the lid pressed down upon it until it sets fast. That, along with the exorcism, will surely stop any further ghost from walking.'

Father frowned, then waved his hand for a third time, now in dismissal. 'I shall think upon that, Chanter, but in the meantime, by all means prepare for an exorcism. It, at least, can do no harm.'

As the chanter and the canons departed, trembling with eagerness, Lindley looked at Father. 'From what we now know, I do not think an exorcism will help you much, sir.'

'Probably not,' Father answered. 'But it will please the chanter, and whether these mysteries have been carried out by a spirit or a man, it is certainly the Devil behind it all. I cannot be a Christian clergyman and disbelieve in *him*. And therefore, some good may be done by the ritual, whatever your doubts.' He sighed. 'And Lamb's other idea is probably a good one, too. With pitch poured up to the brim, there will, at least, be no more interest in the dratted tomb. I will put Fidoe on to it. We will do it between us just as soon as the pitch can be procured.'

*

'AND FINALLY, WE SEE the wax bands revealed,' Mr Delingpole said with a happy sigh. It was later the same evening, the joyful news of Fidoe's remarkable discovery having gone out to all the Antiquities. They had flown like homing swallows to the abbey and we were now finally examining the mummy's nether regions, stripped of their gold cloth. My former mixed feelings were assuaged by the discovery that the mummy was entirely bound in bandages so that its (and my) modesty was assured. 'Beneath these, I imagine the flesh will be leathery like the face and arms, but perhaps not so dark a brown, having been protected from the air.'

'Never mind imagining,' Mr Quintrel said. 'Peel one off and see.'

'Mr Delingpole, I forbid it,' Father said. 'The poor creature has been meddled with enough and I will permit no more.'

Mr Delingpole sighed. 'Very well, Dean. Blake, have you seen enough?'

'Yes, sir. I have drawn it all again.'

Mr Delingpole replaced the fragile gold cloth and straightened the scarlet tunic before laying the crimson cloth across the dead king's features. The sacrist placed the sceptre topped by its plain gold cross back in the mummy's right hand, and Mr Delingpole wistfully examined the lovely green enamel dove atop the rod for the last time, before placing it back in Edward's left.

This time Father recited the Lord's Prayer to its conclusion, and then gestured to the workmen to replace the lid of the inner sarcophagus. This done, they prepared themselves to lift the lid of the outer tomb and we left them to carry on with it, under Mr Suckling's oily directions.

By the time Father had walked down the nave with Lindley and the Antiquities, exchanging urbane pleasantries as I suppose they would have done last Saturday if everything had not turned out so peculiar, Blake was back at his own work. The ancient altar tapestries had been pulled aside and he was on his knees before the painted effigy of Aveline.

I could see the knife marks on the wooden frieze of her bier, and a loose fragment of gold leaf still clung to the wood from Apollo's meddling. I blew gently and it hovered in the air for a moment before coming down to settle softly on the toe of Blake's boot, lighter and more fragile than a petal.

He had brought out his paints and was making a miniature copy of his main pen and ink sketch, painting in the bright reds and blues of the lady's dress. 'You are done with the objectionable cherubs?' I said to him, leaning over his shoulder to look at the new drawing, but he seemed abstracted and only grunted an answer. He glanced at me as if for the first time I was an obstruction to his work, dried the paint off his brush with a rag, and began to pack away his things.

'What is it? What's the matter?'

He looked at me properly then and, a shade reluctantly, the old sweet smile returned. He didn't answer my question however, only said, 'I heard there was another vision. I heard you were hurt.'

'Yes, there was another trick. I touched something I shouldn't have, and it burned me. It was all done with electricity, my cousin said.'

'A rational man is a fiend in a cloud,' he remarked, taking the hand I showed him and examining the scorch on my palm. At least, I think that's what he said, for I didn't entirely take his meaning. 'And what the hand draws, the mind remembers.'

'Is this another poem?'

'No.'

'Blake, what is it? You are really acting very odd. Tell me what you are thinking.'

'Those men from the society are fools.' Absent-mindedly he got out his things again and dipped his brush in the paint before carefully filling in another fold of the lady's dress. 'Unobservant fools. *They* did not see it.'

'Since I haven't the faintest idea what you're talking about, it seems I didn't either,' I said. 'But if you saw something about the mummy that we did not, I am hardly surprised. No one looked as closely at the body as you did. What was it you saw?'

'It was different.'

I wondered if the conversation of angels would prove as maddening. 'What was different?'

'The sceptre in his right hand.'

'How was it different?'

'It was a different sceptre.'

33

ONLY BLAKE HAD noticed the change, but when I look back at my journal, and the account of the tomb's first opening, I see he is right. There I described the sceptre as topped by three small trefoils, while the one we had just seen had only a plain gilded cross.

If the sceptre had been swapped, I was suddenly very sure where the new, plain one had come from. Blake followed me to the ragged regiment's cupboard and watched me pull out the effigies again one by one. It was as I had suddenly guessed: Queen Mary II's sceptre, with its plain gold cross, unadorned by the added decorations on Elizabeth's, was entirely missing.

'They stole Longshanks' sceptre as well as his crown,' I said. 'Then they took Mary's sceptre from this cupboard and swapped it for the original. Perhaps they also hoped to find a crown like his here, too, but see, there is nothing at all like it among the regiment. All the ragged royals wear wired coronets with a cross at the top – just as Mr Alnutt described the Confessor's crown.' And then I realised, Elizabeth's crown was now missing too. I had already wondered if whoever was behind the ghost had rifled through this cupboard in search of a crown. It seemed I was right. And if the same thief had taken Mary's sceptre, it seemed incontrovertible that the thief and ghost – and therefore the murderer – were all one and the same, as Mr Delingpole had always thought.

I closed the cupboard and sat down between the watchful figures of Christopher and Alice Hatton on their tomb. 'If Mr Alnutt is right, and the crown is a really ancient thing, I can see it would be valuable. But why swap the sceptre? Unless Longshanks' sceptre was *also* valuable.' I looked at Blake, the germ of an idea forming. 'Mr Alnutt guessed the royalists had hidden the Welsh crown in Longshanks' tomb before Cromwell could destroy it. Suppose they hid a sceptre, too?' I shook my head. 'But surely we would have seen it was real, just as we saw the crown was?'

Blake demurred. 'Remember, we were hurried out just as your father made to take it from the mummy's hand.'

I remembered the king's dead fingers slacken as Father took hold of the gleaming sceptre. And, good heavens, Louis Durand himself had gone to help Father lift it from the mummy's grasp. But then we were rushed away by Fidoe's anxious cries that the roof was falling.

'The thieves came for the jewels,' I said meditatively. 'They hoped to swap the sceptre and crown for our abbey replicas and replace the mummy so that no one would ever know. But there was no suitable crown among our things, so instead they hid the mummy in the vault. Then one of them killed the other and left.'

But Lindley had said that the mummy's presence in the

vault meant that the accomplice knew the abbey like the back of his hand. Then why would he not already know that there was no suitable crown among our ragged regiment to stand in for the stolen one? I shook my head. Some of it was right, but not all of it.

'Mr Alnutt said he'd consulted a register of the items destroyed by Cromwell,' I said. 'He discovered Llewellyn's crown wasn't on it and guessed it had been hidden with Longshanks. But surely he would have noticed if the Confessor's sceptre was also missing from the list?'

'Perhaps there was more than one,' Blake said, coming to sit beside me so that I had to squeeze up against Alice Hatton's wimpled shoulder.

'More than one?'

'Didn't Delingpole say there weren't two sceptres alike in the abbey? And look here.' He gesticulated to the ragged regiment laid out before us with all their various ornaments. 'Perhaps the Confessor had many sceptres, each one different from the next.'

'So Cromwell may have destroyed one of the Confessor's sceptres, while another survived in Longshanks' tomb,' I said, now fired with investigative zeal. I got to my feet and bundled all the wooden royals back into the cupboard. 'I must go to the library and find a book that will tell me all about it.'

WHEN I CLIMBED the stairs into the musty chamber, its rows of books mere dark smudges by the feeble light of my candle, I saw with a shock of surprise that another reader had been there before me. A chair had been moved and a couple of books lay on the reading desk. The circumstance was so stunning in its rarity that I paused to look. The spine of the larger book announced it to be the fourth volume of a *History of the Rebellion and Civil Wars in England* by the Earl of Clarendon. I set down my candle and scanned the open page. A word leapt out at me and made me gasp.

Sceptre.

The rest of the sentence was meaningless, at least to me. Something about a cardinal who held the sceptre for a French dauphin and worshipped Cromwell. I didn't think it could have meant anything to my unknown fellow reader either. But perhaps it showed they had been searching for the mention of *sceptres*. Had the unknown reader also been thinking about Llewellyn's hidden crown? Had they been looking for evidence that both crown and sceptre had been hidden in Longshanks' tomb in Cromwell's time, just as I had come here to do?

The thought made me shiver, made me feel again that fear of being locked in with an unknown murderer. My solitary candle left the corners of the library in deep shadow, but there was no sound. No breath. No creak. The place felt empty, if no less ominous for that, to my heightened senses.

My unknown fellow reader must also, like me, suppose himself the only visitor to the library, else he would not have left the books lying out to be seen. I closed the *History*, out of reverence to the volume's fragile old spine, and turned my attention to the other book on the desk. It was an ancient edition of the *Book of Common Prayer* printed in strange, old-fashioned script. When I picked it up, a folded piece of paper fell from among its pages. A letter, dated yesterday noon, from Covent Garden.

My dear sir, the letter read. *As requested: Quantitas: twenty-four troy pounds one ounce; faciam: 2 x 2 x 6. Please let me know if you wish to proceed on this basis. I am, etc, etc* . . . An illegible signature.

Then, from somewhere out in the body of the abbey, I heard a dull thud like the closing of a door. I went up the steps to the Muniments Gallery, my own little perch in the rafters. It was always peaceful up here, among all the abbey records in their cupboards and drawers and boxes. Vast wooden trunks took up half the space, trunks which in olden times contained the abbey's cash money, received from its vast land holdings around the kingdom, and which kept the whole abbey vessel and its crew of clergymen afloat.

It was now very quiet. There was no intruder here save myself, and the cupboards were closed and locked as always, the abbey documents safely shut away.

But as I drew near to the archway, looking down on to Poets' Corner, I saw a light above me, in the triforium gallery. No, not there exactly. It was coming instead from the narrow ledge which I had crossed in fear and trembling with Mr Suckling that morning.

A cold blue light. Very strange and very dim.

Electricity.

34

THOUGH IT IS thought bad taste in a Church of England clergyman to make much of devils and hell, it is considered equally vulgar to make more of God than is absolutely necessary to the profession. The chanter cares most for his music, Mr Suckling for his silver and gold, the vergers for their polished woodwork and the canons for their books and ledgers. The canon-treasurer thinks more about the abbey's money, and the canon-steward about the wax chandler's bill, than either of them do about their relationship with the Almighty, I am sure.

It is partly human nature and partly the grandeur of the abbey that does it. The place is so very busy, so very thronged with life and statues, that God is often hard to find. By contrast, a small country church is a place of peace the moment you enter. Perhaps there is only a vicar and a churchwarden, off ministering to their flock, so that in the muffled emptiness of the deserted building Christ can meet your eye as he looks down from his cross at the altar.

I felt someone was looking at me now, here in the darkness

of the night-time abbey where I had never before ventured. Perhaps it was the bats or the cats Blake had spoken of. I hoped so, for I did not think it was God. I felt suddenly sure that He was gone from the abbey entirely and a dreadful emptiness had taken His place; an emptiness that pressed upon me, just as the columns and arches had bulged in the strange reflecting mirror. It was a tangible absence, if such a thing can possibly be. Perhaps the dull thud that had drawn me up here to look had been God leaving the abbey and closing the door behind Him.

But, then, somewhere in the periphery of my vision: somewhere here, inside the shadowed building, I was conscious of something new. Some shape far below me on the paved floor that should not be there. Another meaning to that dull thud then presented itself horribly to my mind and I raised my candle in a hopeless attempt to see, before turning swiftly and hastening down by its feeble light into the vast blackness of the church below.

That sense of dreadful emptiness – of tangible absence – was concentrated here. A foot, protruding from a shapeless heap of clothes. An upturned face, the neck bent at a peculiar angle. The body had fallen from the narrow ledge above, to land in Poets' Corner at the foot of Shakespeare's statue, which held out a scroll with his prophetic words upon it, carved in stone.

The Cloud capt Tow'rs,
The Gorgeous Palaces,
The Solemn Temples,
The Great Globe itself,

Yea all which it Inherit,
Shall Dissolve;
And like the baseless Fabrick of a Vision
Leave not a wreck behind.

Mr Suckling, the man I had loathed, the man who had fascinated me nonetheless with his sharp intelligence, was still here in body, lying at my feet, but he was also irretrievably gone; departed to whatever mysterious place we all of us will go in the end.

35

I HAD DISLIKED THE sacrist about as much as a woman can do, but as I looked down on his broken body I could not believe his unctuous smile was stilled for ever, or that I would hear his damp voice no more. It is a fallacy to think one may not grieve for an enemy. I had not wept for Louis Durand – had only stared at his awful wound and his blood on my shoes with a kind of numb disbelief – but as they carried the sacrist's body away, sobs overcame me. The awfulness of death was upon me, and its eternal triumph. For it takes everyone – it has already taken many I have loved – and it will take all of them from me, or me from them, in the end.

Father and Lindley and the vergers scouted about with lanterns, but it seemed there was no other explanation than that the sacrist had fallen from the narrow walkway far above, over which we had inched together that morning. What Mr Suckling had been doing up there was of course of no interest to Corbett, the searcher.

'Nothing amiss besides a score of broken bones,' he'd

said, rising from a brief examination of the ruined body. 'Dangerous place to be venturing though, Dean. Can't say *I'd* fancy it. I'll call the undertaker and I suppose you had better make sure to keep folks off that walkway, it being such a bloody liability.'

'But how did he get up there?' Lindley asked, and even through my tears I remembered wondering the same thing myself, when the sacrist had taken me up there that morning – when he had held my hand with his own moist, living one, as he would now do no more.

'The door is open but there is no key in the lock,' Lindley called out from the corner. 'But it surely must have been Suckling that took your keys, Uncle. How else did he let himself in to the triforium? That is one mystery solved at least.'

I remembered what Mr Alnutt had said when Father accused him of the theft. *I am sure a dozen others must come in and out all day. Your housemaids. All your canons.* Not for the first time, the learned old gentleman had proved to be right.

We all followed Lindley through the door, up the endless spiral staircase to the triforium. As we stepped out into the wide space of the gallery I glanced instinctively across the void of the transept to where the funny old statue stood at his window and the broken mirror bulged and shimmered. But there was no danger of that secret being discovered now, since the illumination from our lanterns cast pools of light scarcely six feet across.

As we approached the horrible ledge, the cause of the sacrist's fall seemed clear. The metal handrail that had moved under my hand that morning was now hanging vertically by one end, the other having come loose from the masonry. It seemed it had given way entirely under Mr Suckling's grasp and he had fallen to his death. If the dangling bar were to fall after him, it would infallibly impale anyone below it like a spear, and I hoped Fidoe would do something about it before some such dreadful accident really happened.

'What's this?' Fidoe's voice came from the shadows beyond the pool of lantern light. 'Mr Bell, sir, bring that lantern, will you? Searcher, you'd better have a look at this.'

We now saw that in the light of Lindley's lantern everything sparkled. There was broken glass everywhere and Fidoe, leaning out to peer through the arch to the floor below in a manner calculated to give us all heart failure, reported that he could see the glimmer of glass below. I dare say it had crunched under our feet as we hurried to the sacrist's dead body, but none of us had noticed.

'A rum go, here,' the searcher said, from the horrible narrow ledge onto which he had ventured by a step or so. 'Can't say I can make head nor tail of it.'

'It is my apparatus again,' Lindley said. 'Look, my generator is here, tucked in this corner.'

It was indeed. The glass globe I had last seen packed away in his trunk that afternoon was back on the lathe-like pole, with the flywheel and chain all reassembled. The chain that had connected the machine to the Leyden jar, when Lindley had demonstrated its use to us, was dangling loose into the void.

Lindley touched the searcher's shoulder and the constable fell back to let him peer out across the ledge. 'Good God, what the devil was Suckling up to?'

Lindley's voice had taken on its familiar tone of eager curiosity and excitement, and, before I knew it, he was out on the ledge himself. After a step or two he prudently dropped to his hands and knees, but even so I shut my eyes.

'There are more things out here.' His voice came back to us from somewhere about the middle of the void. It was perhaps lucky for him that it was dark and he could not see the fall to his right-hand side, though he must surely be able to feel its dreadful yawning emptiness. 'I have got them. I am coming back.'

We could hear him shuffling backwards, whatever it was that he had found plinking tinnily off the stone ledge as he came. The searcher held out his lantern as far as he dared, and into the pool of light came my cousin, cautiously inching back to safety. When he regained the wooden floorboards – however rotten they might be – he sat up on his haunches and pushed the hair out of his eyes with a relieved smile.

The smile faded, however, as he examined the first of his findings by the searcher's lamp. It was the rod from the Leyden jar.

'And all the broken glass must therefore be the remains of the jar itself,' he said grimly, holding up the rod to show me and Father. 'And there was something else too . . .' He fumbled under his coat and produced the final piece of the jigsaw, which he had apparently taken hold of blindly in the dark and shoved under his arm before retreating along the ledge.

'Llewellyn's crown,' he said, in such a tone of astonishment all my former doubts about him were dispelled in an instant. 'Good God. Uncle – Searcher – I suppose we have finally found our thief.'

*

'WELL, WELL, WHAT, WHAT?' His Majesty said as he came into the Deanery parlour, apparently quite content to be routed out of his palace at midnight. Father had sent word as soon as the sacrist's body had been dealt with, and His Majesty had not been able to resist the promise of new excitement. His equerry stood in the door as usual, his hand on his sword.

'So I hear the whole affair is solved, what, what? Thank God, thank God. I congratulate you, Mr Dean, on a successful outcome.'

'Thank you, Your Majesty.' Father looked relieved, though rather pale. 'Yes, I think we can safely say that the sacrist was the culprit we sought. It now seems clear that he and Louis Durand met over Edward's body, both in pursuit of the grave goods we had seen that morning at the opening of the tomb. Durand had been quite open about his interest in artefacts – though he spoke only about the Holy Grail – and we have since learned from Mr Alnutt that Suckling was very taken by the sight of the mummy and afterwards quizzed him about the crown jewels at some length. When the sacrist died, I am afraid to say he had the missing crown in his possession. It seems he was the victor in the tussle with Durand and carried away the mummy for himself.'

'A rum carry-on for a clergyman,' the king said, 'but all's well that ends well, what, what? Do we know what the rascal was doing up on that platform tonight?'

'It seems he had also been behind the ghost, and the god,' Father said. 'The housemaid confesses she saw him in the Deanery earlier in the evening but thought nothing of it. He had been using the triforium gallery for his own purposes.

289

We have found a mirror up there, which my nephew says was likely used to make the ghost walk, and the same electrical equipment he had used to summon the god Apollo. There was a deal of broken glass, and some other things my nephew recognised as his own. We believe Suckling meant to dazzle us all with a new trick from on that high ledge, using the stolen crown.'

'The *beatification*,' Lindley put in. He had sat himself down in Father's armchair and, after all the excitement, now looked rather sick. 'I also described it at the demonstration. The trick involves a crown, electrified by the generator, and a man seated on an insulated chair. The effect is to make the sitting figure appear to wear a halo of light. Unfortunately for Suckling it seems he had misremembered my account and attached the crown to the Leyden jar, not the generator. Perhaps he meant to use the jar's greater power to create a more dazzling effect than the generator alone might produce. But, unknown to him, I had recharged the jar this morning to show how the god trick was done, and when he touched the rod the shock threw him backwards, just as it had my cousin. Being on that ledge, however, the force threw him to his death. I have looked at his corpse, Your Majesty. His palm is black, just as my cousin's was last night.' He looked up, earnestly, at the king. 'Suckling thought the jar had discharged itself on Susan in the Little Cloister. He thought it was safe to touch. And, by recharging it, it was therefore I that killed him.'

'Fiddlesticks,' said the king. 'It was your equipment for you to do with as you liked, what, what? *He* was the one who stole it. We cannot blame anyone but him for what happened.'

But it seemed the whole extraordinary story had dumbfounded even the king. 'Curious, however, very curious,' was all he said, wandering over to where Cuthbert was asleep in his cage and tapping on the bars, eliciting a sleepy *what, what?* from the bird. 'What the devil was Suckling's purpose with those tricks? It seems a strange thing to raise so much fear and suspicion about the abbey when it might have been wiser to let the thing settle and his crimes be forgot.'

'I suppose he first hoped to frighten Your Majesty away,' Father said.

'Fiddlesticks,' said the king again.

'And then, when that failed and Durand's body was discovered,' I said, 'perhaps he feared we would remember Mr Alnutt's report of his own unusual interest in the grave goods.'

'Just what I think,' Lindley agreed, evidently restored by the king's exoneration, which, frankly, was the next best thing to a pardon by God himself. 'We always knew the man was a villain, and his whole life was chalices and vases. I can easily imagine he saw the grave goods as a most desirable addition to his collection. I can also easily imagine he helped Durand steal them and then coolly killed him. The equerry said the wound was made by a point with a round haft. Who knows? Perhaps he skewered him with the rod or sceptre from the tomb.'

The king looked delighted at this deductive flight of reasoning, but Father shuddered. 'What a dreadful idea. The sacrist was an objectionable man, but a murderer ...' He shook his head. 'I still cannot think it possible.'

I would have agreed with him if it had not been for my

encounter with the sacrist in the triforium earlier. 'He told me Lindley had done it all. I expect he wanted to pin the blame on him by stealing his things and using them.'

'That is very uncivil,' Lindley said, going rather red. 'I hope you told him he was mistaken.'

I hesitated.

'Susan! For God's sake. What did he say to you?'

'He took me up to the triforium this afternoon,' I said in a rush. 'He took me across that horrible ledge.'

'Good Lord,' Father said weakly, and sat down. Even His Majesty looked grave and harrumphed something about *young ladies* and *never in his life had he heard* . . .

'You did not tell us!' Lindley said. 'Why did you not tell us?'

'There was never time.'

Lindley had evidently now remembered our later meeting in his bedchamber and deduced my real reason for poking about in there. 'And you believed him? Cousin, do not tell me you believed him?'

'He showed me the broken mirror. He said you had one just like it.'

'And did he ascribe any motive for my actions?' Lindley now sounded vexed.

'No. But he has always disliked Father, you know he has, and I suppose he wanted to hurt us all as well as deflect suspicion from himself.'

'Curious,' the king said again. 'What did you ever do to him, Dean? You are rather a jolly little creature to be amassing such enemies, ain't you?'

Father shook his head. 'The sacrist had an unfortunate

manner, God rest his soul, and I could never warm to him for all he tried to make himself indispensable to me from the first day I arrived. And there were other things . . .'

What, what, God save the king, what, what? Cuthbert had woken up and was displaying his beautiful red tail feathers as he hopped about the bars of his cage.

'Ha! There is your remarkable bird awake,' the king said. 'Hey, bird, you remember me, what, what?'

What, what, what, what, God save the king! Cuthbert replied obligingly.

His Majesty looked suddenly thoughtful. 'I say, Dean, will you have the bird brought to the Ascension service tomorrow evening? I should very much like to show him to my children.'

'Certainly, Your Majesty.'

The abbey clock struck one as the king finally left us, and Father reached out a hand to me, pale again. 'I am getting too old, Susan,' he said. 'My dear, I wish more than anything that I could find us some quiet nook where we might retire away from all this trouble.'

'Nonsense!' I said, Dame Yates being the only person who could grant this wish. 'It is all over, Father. In the morning you can turn your mind back to common things and it will be just as if all this never happened. The king will mightily admire your effect with the lights tomorrow, and then there is only Pentecost before we can settle down into ordinary time.'

Ordinary time: all the peaceful months of the summer until All Saints and Advent will begin the annual retelling of Christ's life and death for the seventeen hundred and seventy-fourth time. And a deeper peace than we might ever have hoped for, in fact, without Mr Suckling in the abbey as a constant irritant to our happiness. I hope the Almighty will forgive me for thinking so and take my earlier tears as homage enough to the poor dead villain.

36

'AND YOU WILL THINK better of this nonsense about pitch?' Mr Delingpole asked Father. He had arrived shortly after breakfast, on receipt of a message from Lindley concerning the discoveries of the night. 'There is surely no longer any need for that, or a ridiculous exorcism. Even your very sensitive chanter must see that by now.'

'One might hope so. But I am afraid Mr Lamb was not made for this earthly sphere, Delingpole.'

It was remarkable how much Father had recovered now that the matter was solved. Having found himself helpless to *find it all out* as the king had bade him, the weight had been intolerable upon his shoulders. Now the danger and mystery was over, and himself back in kingly favour, his old genial common sense had come back upon him. 'To be frank, they none of them are much of an aid. It turns out that Mr Suckling was a murderous thief, while the canon-steward is more taken up with his womenfolk than his duties

295

in the abbey, and the canon-treasurer is always fretting about money.'

'Speaking of money,' Mr Delingpole said, 'I suppose the sacrist's stipend was a modest one? I cannot see any other explanation for such extraordinary actions.'

'I remember you saying, at the very beginning, that you would look to the money were it a case in court,' Father said. 'And, of course, you lawyers will always say so. The sacrist's stipend is certainly very small – scarcely more than twelve pounds per annum, but Suckling came of good family and expected preferment with the archbishop. Whatever motivated him, I do not think it was money.'

'Twelve pounds!' Delingpole looked astonished. 'I could scarcely clothe myself for such a sum.'

'But, recall, he had board and lodgings in the Little Cloister all found, along with his vestments gratis. We lead simple lives, Delingpole, and I dare say you would think my own stipend a trifle among other men of my standing.'

'Well,' Mr Delingpole said, 'I shall certainly ask questions as to his finances.'

'I wish you would not,' Father said. 'Above all things, I would have everything forgot and ordinary life restored.'

I walked with Mr Delingpole back through the abbey as I had done before. His own value as a possible husband had lessened to my mind since finding myself *remarkably astute for a member of my sex*. He might be kind and full to the brim of common sense, but I think even Mr Suckling thought more of me than that.

After we parted, I loitered in the fresh air of the cloisters, thinking it all over. What a mystery the sacrist had been, alive and dead, not least for his apparent partiality towards me when he was so much the archbishop's man. I still cannot see the advantage to him in marriage to me, except to vex Father even more than common, which would have been a very permanent act of mischief to his own happiness, too.

I was halfway along the East Cloister, just outside the library door, when ahead of me the tortoise figure of Dame Yates emerged from the south transept door and stood blinking her little reptile eyes in the bright sunlight. Without a moment's hesitation I opened the library door and stepped inside before she could turn her head and see me.

The prayer book still lay on the reading desk and I picked up the letter from someone in Covent Garden, which had fallen from it last night. In the hurry of Mr Suckling's death I had forgotten all about it. Now, it seemed to make a degree more sense. He had quizzed Alnutt about the crown jewels and then killed Louis Durand to take possession of them. He had a stipend scarcely more than twice the annual wage of the butler, who also had his board, lodgings and suits of clothes provided.

As requested: Quantitas: twenty-four troy pounds one ounce; faciam: 2 x 2 x 6. Please let me know if you wish to proceed on this basis. I am, etc., etc. . . . .

The words were scrawled on what I now in daylight saw was a large piece of laid paper of a type I had seen before, folded in half and half again. I unfolded it, turned it over, and dropped it in sheer surprise. Sketched upon it were Blake's first drawings of Longshanks' open tomb from last Saturday. The drawings stolen from Father's desk, and which I had turned the Deanery upside down in search of.

Along with this letter I had also forgotten the swapped sceptre in all the manifold shocks of the past hours. I had not even told Father or Lindley about our discovery in the ragged regiment's cupboard. But Blake had certainly been right: the sceptre we had seen yesterday was not the same as this one he had drawn on Saturday. The sceptre in the drawing was surmounted by a cross made of three small trefoils, just as he had said. The reason why the thief had taken the drawings from Father's desk was therefore clear enough. If the sceptre had been swapped, then the culprit would want no record of the change.

Twenty-four troy pounds, one ounce, the scrawled message said on the reverse. It seemed clear the sceptre and drawings had been shown to this person in Covent Garden, and they had returned the drawings with their verdict. Was it the sceptre's weight? Was this some part of a negotiation to sell it? I turned over the paper again to look at the hasty words. There was no sum mentioned, unless the mysterious figures 2 2 6 were meant to signify two pounds, two shillings and sixpence.

Fudge, as Mr Delingpole would say.

How much would a pound of gold fetch? Dame Yates had said something about it once. Four guineas an ounce, she had said was the price of gold. Whatever a *troy* pound might be, twenty-four of them must equal very many ounces. And then there was the sceptre's historic value, which must, surely, be many times more. Might the figures signify two thousand, two hundred and sixty?

But why write it so curiously? Perhaps it was meant to be cryptic and secret, the writer knowing the sceptre was stolen property and wishing to disguise their interest. Still, the letter told me one thing. Though there was no addressee on the paper, and no indication of the sender beside the illegible signature, it did say *Covent Garden* – where Mr Delingpole had certainly ventured, to find out dealers in antiquities.

Might Mr Delingpole be able to find out the writer of this letter? So much would be explained if the sacrist's intentions could be known. Whatever else, I should show the letter and the long-sought-for drawings to Father and tell him what Blake and I had learned about the sceptre yesterday.

I refolded the paper and slipped it in my pocket. I was turning to go, when, from the direction of the Muniments Gallery, I heard voices. When I reached that little eyrie and peered down into the abbey unseen, they turned out to belong to two figures hurrying across Poets' Corner in friendly conclave. One of them was Father. The other was the verger, Henry Ede.

'I'm sorry to trouble you, Ede,' Father was saying. They had paused by the statue of Shakespeare where Mr Suckling's dead body had lain. 'Today I'm afraid you shall have to be sacrist, too. You'll find the things in the dark vestry. If you'll bring them up to St Faith's and polish them I'd be much obliged.'

'I don't have a key to the crypt, Dean.'

'No, of course not. There are only two: the one I hold on my keyring and Mr Suckling's own. He won't be needing it now.' Father fished in his pocket and pressed something into Ede's hand. 'I hope you're not afraid of ghosts like the chanter. It's a dreadfully dismal spot.'

Ede laughed, in a way that made me think he had little time for ghosts and still less for Mr Lamb, and then they parted. I was about to call out to Father and warn him that the dame was somewhere about, but what Ede did next made me forget all that. The verger went to the little doorway beside Edmund Spenser's plaque in the corner, used the key Father had just given him to open it, and went inside.

It was the same door that led to the triforium. But whereas I had always seen Fidoe re-emerge between the triforium arches above, Ede did not reappear at all.

I thought back to my visit with Suckling to view the broken mirror, and then our hurried visit yesterday, in the dark, after the sacrist's death. I had been half-dazed on both occasions, but now I remembered that when we went in through that first, small door, there had been steps leading down, as well as up to the triforium. Did this downwards staircase lead to the dark vestry, where the abbey kept its most precious things?

Suckling's key, Father had said, handing it to the verger without any ceremony. I had wondered how Suckling had reached the triforium – had thought he must have stolen Father's keys to do so – and Lindley had made the same guess when we found the sacrist's broken body. Perhaps no one else had been listening, for no one had corrected him or explained that Mr Suckling had a key to this door of his own. Where, then, were Father's missing keys? That mystery remained unsolved after all.

Still musing on all this, I hurried back down the stairs to the library and then out into the East Cloister, where I found Dame Yates sitting in one of its sunlit arches, peacefully waiting for me.

37

'AH, THERE YOU ARE, Miss Bell!' she said, getting to her feet with remarkable agility for a tortoise. 'I called after you earlier, but I think you did not hear me. Good afternoon, my dear.' Curiously, there was something almost furtive in her manner. Her hoot was positively soft and she glanced up and down the cloister as if she feared to see an approaching figure.

'If you are looking for Father he is in the south transept,' I said. 'I have just seen him.'

'No.' She held out a detaining hand, for I had turned in that direction expecting her to follow me. 'No, my dear, I have also just seen him. It is you I want now, Miss Bell. Will you give me a moment?'

Lord above, I thought, amid everything else, Father has finally offered and she has accepted. But I followed her around the corner into the South Cloister where she paused by my favourite smudged monk in the paving.

'Dear creature,' she said. 'I have always adored him.'

This was ghastly and not at all the sort of thing anyone

should say to their middle-aged lover's grown-up daughter.

'You mean Father?'

At this, she cackled a laugh as she had done at Blake's drawings. 'Oh, no. Dear me, no. I meant this dear, weathered gentleman in the paving here. Do you not like him? I always bid him a good day when I pass and wonder what he would think of all our modern ways.' She sat down in one of the cloister arches again and this time patted the stone sill for me to sit beside her.

'Miss Bell,' she said, as I obeyed, 'we do not know each other very well, and I know it is an imposition – a great imposition – to ask you for your help. But as you do not wish to have me as your stepmother, I hope you might be willing to do me a good turn.'

There was something rather soothing about her large figure after all, I thought, as I settled beside her. But perhaps I only thought so now we had discovered a shared affection for the old monk. Not to mention that it seemed she had been sizing me up, just as I had done her, and had so accurately read my feelings.

'I can't think how I can help you,' I said, but a little less stiffly than usual.

She stretched her wrinkled neck and blinked at me sidelong. 'My dear, you don't know it, but I'm afraid your father has become something of a pest.'

'A pest?' I repeated. 'Father?'

'Oh, the dean is very good, and very holy, and very kind – *very* kind, in fact, the dear little man. But I am afraid I shall be obliged to take my monument elsewhere if he will not desist from proposing marriage to me.'

'Marriage!' (I was turning into something of an echo. A deep old coalmine, perhaps.)

'He has asked me to marry him positively a half-dozen times this past fortnight and will never believe me when I decline him. I am hoping that if I send my final *no* by you, he will be obliged to see I am in earnest.'

'I hardly think—'

'Oh, Miss Bell, I know it is a frightful thing to ask of you. But I can't suppose it will break his spirit. I can't suppose his heart is really involved.'

Looking at her, I couldn't suppose it either. Except – except – I saw now that there was a twinkle of humour in her little tortoise eye. I began to wonder if there was more to her than I had thought.

She stretched her old mouth into a thin, lipless line. 'I believe he only asks me because he is so ashamed of the dreadful business with the monument.'

'Dreadful business?' I repeated again.

'Have you not noticed how shoddy it is, my dear? The stone is so poor the mason cannot carve it, for all his skill. The abbey has bought the cheapest materials it can find. And your father hints – no, that is too strong a word – he *does not deny*, when I ask him, that some of my money, at least, has gone astray.'

'Gone astray!' (I was really deep down the coal hole now.)

She looked at me, her mouth still a grave straight line. 'I see you don't know anything about it.'

'Nothing, ma'am, nothing at all,' I said, perplexed.

'Ah, poor child, why should you? Well, without seeking to alarm you, my dear, I fear the abbey finances may be a little . . .'

303

She hesitated. 'A little *rocky*.'

The canon-treasurer is always fretting about money. Father's words to Mr Delingpole that morning came back to me unbidden, along with an image of the canon-treasurer nursing his third glass of brandy and pacing the College Garden until he sneezed.

'And so, my dear,' the dame was going on, 'I rather think your father wishes to make amends and imagines the offer of his hand might do it. But, as I think I have always made plain to you both, the memory of Sir Joseph is sacred to me, and a marriage to your father the very last thing I would wish for.'

At this, despite everything, I think I must have looked a little affronted.

'Oh, not for his own sake,' she added hastily. 'Your father is a dear little creature, truly he is, and quite as lovable as Admiral in his own way. But I like my widow freedom, and to be frank, my dear, I have such a horror of birds in general and your parrot in particular. I was no sooner in your parlour t'other evening than it flew at me from its perch and knocked my cap quite for six. I was so frightened I began to cry, and your vexing father chose that very moment to propose to me for the seventh time.'

I wondered briefly what had set Cuthbert so much against her. He is a creature much used to being loved, and perhaps her fear had communicated itself to him and made him anxious. God forfend that he ever finds himself without us, in the company of perplexing strangers.

But all this was by the by. I stood up and began to pace about, I imagine very much in the manner of the fretful canon-treasurer. I remembered thinking that he and his wife were deceived in their little girls, supposing them abed when they were really playing. But that harmless mistake was nothing to this. Father wanted Dame Yates and not the other way about! And the abbey finances were *rocky*!!

'I wish you would tell him I am in earnest in my refusal,' she said again, watching me perambulate up and down before her. 'I hope he will believe it from your lips more than mine.'

'I will try,' I said, stopping to look at her, somewhat shamefaced. 'But I'm afraid he may suspect my motives, as I have always been so . . .'

'Discouraging?' She actually twinkled at me. 'My dear Miss Bell, I am not offended in the slightest degree. In your shoes I should certainly not wish for a stepmother either.'

I stared at her, astonished again to see that mischief in her tortoise eye, and I began to think that, if it were not for poor Cuthbert, she might have been the very best stepmother I could ever have hoped for, after all.

38

THE CANON-TREASURER'S DRINKING. His wife grumbling about his endless pacing up and down the College Garden. The abbey finances were *rocky*. Back in the parlour, where only Cuthbert waited to greet me with a kingly *what, what?*, I took the sheet of Blake's drawings from my pocket, unfolded it, and studied the cryptic message scrawled on the reverse anew.

I had been going to give it to Father and tell him about the missing sceptre, as proof that the sacrist had wanted money after all. But now I felt muddled. Out of the blue sky, this knowledge had come upon me like a swooping gull, that money was indeed wanted. Yet not, it seemed, by Mr Suckling, but by the abbey.

And yet the sacrist's body had been found with the stolen crown and, surely, if there had been anything amiss with the abbey's finances, Mr Suckling would have known about it. Lindley had called him a spy and, whether the sacrist really reported to the archbishop or not, he had certainly always been watching, always prying. Surely if there had been any special trouble he would have found it out. Surely he would have told me, being always so very eager to find fault with Father's management of the abbey. And now, after everything that had passed between myself and Mr Suckling these past days, I would have had no compunction in asking him all about it.

But there was to be no asking him anything, ever again. He was dead, and the horrible finality of it struck me anew.

Here's the Dean! Cuthbert cried out joyfully. Father was coming in, looking better than he had done for days. He fed Cuthbert a nut from his pocket before stroking the bird's grey feathers with the back of his finger. There was the old, contented smile on his face that had been banished through all the troubles of the past week. He, along with everyone else, believed the matter settled. I put Blake's drawing back in my pocket, irresolute. Could I really inflict such misery on him as to make him reopen the whole mystery?

'I saw Dame Yates just now,' I said instead, taking up my sewing as if I were just as tranquil as he seemed to be. In my haste to poke about in Lindley's room yesterday I had left Charles II's hat lying in the sun, and I feared now that the brim had faded.

'Ah?' Father rang the bell for tea and pottered to the table where I was sitting.

'She is a much nicer woman than I ever took her for. I'm sorry if I teased you about it, Father.'

'You young folk suppose everybody must be to your own taste and act and think as you do. But I am glad you find she improves on closer acquaintance.'

'She does. And I now think I should not be sorry if you married her after all.'

He smiled faintly. 'I am obliged to you for that, my dear.'

'But . . .' I had knotted my thread and now put the needle through the hat and pulled it until the thread tightened. 'I am afraid she had a very decided message for you, which she asked me to pass on in the hope you will believe it from my lips more than hers. She says she is quite determined she shall not marry again.'

Father bowed his head. 'So she has already told me.'

'But she fears you did not believe her. Meant to ask her again ...' I hesitated. '*Yet* again. She hoped that if I told you she was resolved against it, you might finally be convinced. I told her I doubted it, since I had vexed you so much about the matter you would hardly believe me, at which she only laughed. Yes. I did like her a good deal.'

There was a pause while he mildly watched me sewing.

'Father,' I said, my mind returning to what the dame had said (viz. rocky, *&c.*), 'has there been anything wrong? Anything you should tell me?'

He blinked his little eyes at me as usual. 'Wrong? There has been a good deal wrong, my dear, but now it is all right again, I hope.'

There: another moth hole darned. I bit my thread. 'And everything is all right – about the abbey, you know?'

He blinked again. 'Well, we shall certainly need a new sacrist. But there is no hurry for that, and his salary will be a small saving in the meantime.'

'Is the abbey in need of a small saving?'

He smiled. 'The abbey swallows up everything it receives, my dear, like a great whale. It has swallowed me up this week and spat me out again just like poor old Jonah. But like

Jonah, I have survived and so has the abbey's reputation, thanks to God.'

There was a weariness somewhere in his tone that worried me, but it was clear he didn't want to tell me more and, if I persisted, would only deflect further questions in his gentle way. Who then could I ask? Who else might know? The canon-treasurer above all, of course, but I could hardly ask him either, the financial affairs of the abbey being in no wise communicable by a great man such as he to a pigeon like myself.

I thought of going back to the Muniments Gallery and digging out the abbey account books from their cupboard. But the cupboard would be locked, I was pretty sure, and only Father and the canon-treasurer would have the key. Besides, if the finances were *rocky* and the canon-treasurer was anxious, how likely was an admission of such a thing in pen and ink on paper? It was probably a deadly secret locked away in his bosom, to be shared only with Father and his Maker. And, perhaps, I thought then – being a confidante likely to be far more nagging than the Almighty – his wife?

THE MISS TURNBULLS, the canon-almoner's unmarried daughters, were taking a turn around the Little Cloister as I came through, and we all bobbed a greeting to each other. They are not in the habit of haunting the abbey as I am, for I think they prefer to go to St James's Park each morning accompanied by a servant to observe the fashionable world. But that is an amusement that can only be accomplished once a day without looking eccentric, and by afternoon their only entertainment is perambulating the mossy old fountain. It being silent as the grave in the old square and the sun having gone behind a cloud, it seemed a dismal amusement to me. But then I remembered Father saying I wanted everyone to suit my own way of thinking, and I resolved to allow the Miss Turnbulls to choose the ennui of the Little Cloister if they liked it.

Mrs Bray was at home and the canon-treasurer was out: the exact circumstance I had most wished for.

'Miss Bell,' she said. 'How very good of you to call.' Her hair was pulled about and her gown was torn. There was a hullaballoo coming from the next room involving screams of childish mirth and a good deal of ominous banging.

'I am arrived in the middle of playtime,' I said. 'Shall I come back later?'

'Dear me, no. It is always playtime in this house, Miss Bell, and some rational adult conversation a very welcome distraction.'

A small girl thumped into the room, throwing the door wide open so it smashed off the neighbouring pianoforte. She looked at me, brought up short, then laughed breathlessly and ran out again.

'How is Mr Bray? How is his hay fever?' I asked as we sat down at the tea table.

'Very bad, Miss Bell, I am afraid to say.'

'Is he still pacing the College Garden?'

She looked at me, arrested in the act of ringing for the maid, and laughed. 'How remarkable that you should remember that! Dear me, I cannot retain a single thing anyone tells me for more than half a day.'

Now two small girls were peering in at us around the open door.

'You have your hands full,' I said, 'while mine are very empty.'

'Do not wish your peace away,' she said, catching sight of the children and signalling them energetically to be gone. 'A time will come when you may not call your life your own.' She stood up to examine her reflection in the mirror and tutted as she tucked the disordered hair back into her bun.

'There is no reason to suppose so in my case,' I said. 'I am more than three and twenty and still unmarried.'

'But you will have your cousin, will you not? Everyone supposes so. And I know your father is particularly eager for the match.'

'I think he is,' I said, rather astonished to discover myself the subject of general gossip about the abbey (which is very foolish since I gossip about everyone else in this journal). 'I did not know he had told anyone about it.'

'Oh, he and Mr Bray have many confidential conversations, Miss Bell. Naturally they do, since between them they must keep the abbey afloat and manage all its affairs.'

I didn't much like the idea of Father talking to the canon-treasurer about my marriage, but this was too good an opening for my present enquiries to pass up.

'Speaking of abbey affairs,' I said. 'I have been thinking about Dame Yates and her memorial. Do you think it has cost a very great deal of money?'

Mrs Bray nodded to the maid as she brought in a pot of tea and set it on the table between us. 'Oh dear, yes. Several thousand pounds, I should think.'

'As much as that!' I put on a wistful look. 'I have been thinking of suggesting Father erect a memorial to my mother. But of course he is far too busy. Do you think the canon-treasurer would manage the whole affair for us if we asked him?'

Mrs Bray looked up at me kindly from pouring the tea. 'I'm afraid he wouldn't, Miss Bell. That is not how the thing is ever done.'

'Is it not?' This time my frown was genuine. 'Forgive me, Mrs Bray, I thought Dame Yates said the abbey paid for all the works on her behalf.'

'Oh, no, by no means. When a family desires a monument be erected to a loved one, the abbey sells them the plot – you remember poor Ben Jonson, my dear, and his little square foot of ground, so that he had to be buried upright?

'Thereafter it is the family's business entirely to employ the architects and pay for the monument out of their own pockets. Dame Yates will have paid the receiver general a fee for the plot, a sum usually divided between your father and the canons, but that is the only money the abbey will have seen from the works, and we certainly do not direct the workmen.'

'I see,' I said, though in fact I felt rather foggy. 'So if Father wanted a memorial to Mother, he would see to it all himself?'

'Yes, my dear. And pay the abbey a sum for the privilege, according to the size of the memorial and its place in the abbey.'

'That is all very peculiar,' I said (perhaps too frankly). 'I am sure Father said something about drawing banker's drafts for the works, and Dame Yates said something about her money going astray in the abbey accounts. I was rather shocked to hear it, but then I remembered you saying that Mr Bray had lately been anxious.'

Mrs Bray was staring at me rather oddly, arrested in the act of raising her teacup to her lips, and I decided I had better be quiet. 'But, dear me, I am so feather-brained,' I added with much forced cheerfulness, 'I dare say I have got it all wrong as usual. I don't know about you, Mrs Bray, but sometimes I feel quite as silly as a pigeon.'

39

ONEY TROUBLE IN the abbey. Dame Yates's memorial fund gone missing. The stolen grave goods and Blake's stolen drawings. Mr Suckling's unaccountable pantomimes of ghosts and gods and haloed saints. And a young, handsome French antiquary dead of a hideous wound amid it all.

If Dame Yates's fund had gone missing, it wasn't the canon-treasurer's fault, for according to his wife the abbey never had the dame's fund at all. And yet I distinctly remembered Father saying he arranged payment for the memorial. He had certainly said so. It is written down in these pages in my own hand. And Dame Yates also believes the abbey has had her money. Perhaps she is wrong. Perhaps she misunderstood everything. Perhaps she is another hapless pigeon and not a tortoise at all. As I hastened back through the Dark Entry into the East Cloister my mind was spinning.

The cloister lawn was half mown and Michelson, the gardener, was sharpening his scythe. 'Good afternoon, miss,' he said. 'Majesty's in the abbey again.'

I had been going home, but now I hurried on to the south transept door to find that every soul in the place had assembled to bow and curtsey and gawp at the king. He had just arrived with Lindley from Louis Durand's dead body in the lock-up and, despite being a little pale (probably from the smell, which I imagine was by now decidedly *not* beeswax) His Majesty was in fact cock-a-hoop. He waved a benign royal hand at the assembled crowd and then hurried Father off for a private consultation in the quire, Lindley and I hastening at their heels. It was then I realised the king had brought a new gentleman with him, for he followed us at a respectful distance, mopping his forehead with a very large handkerchief.

'Well, Dean,' the king said jovially when we had reached the quiet shelter of the choir stalls. 'Well, Dean, I have found it all out. By Gad, I have! I have found it all out, while you have been fussing and getting nowhere, what, what?'

That seemed a trifle harsh, but of course there was no question of contradicting him.

'Found it out?' Father said, the harassed frown returning to his face. 'Your Majesty, I thought we had *found it all out* already. Mr Suckling . . .'

'Suckling? Oh, him. Yes, yes, I dare say, but that is all by the by, you know. I now understand it all and it turns out the story concerns me, and me alone, just as I should really have expected all along.'

'Indeed!' Father looked astonished and – though perhaps it was my imagination? – the slightest bit relieved. I remembered the abbey's *rocky* finances. Had Father for a moment feared, as I had, that the king's new information related to that?

'Concerns yourself, Your Majesty?' Father said, rather abstractedly. 'But how can that possibly be so?'

'How can it not be so, Dean?' the king countered. 'How can it not be so, when the entire case rests on the corpse of a former king of England, what, what?'

This was certainly a view of the matter I had not previously considered. But the king was now introducing the new, unknown gentleman to us. His name was Sir Horatio Mann, nephew to the government's Envoy Extraordinary to the Tuscan Court in Italy. Sir Horatio was another spoon-faced creature, like the king and Mr Suckling, but in his case he was thin, and his curved nose was beaky like Lindley's.

'My uncle, Sir Horace, lately wrote me a letter,' Sir Horatio explained to us, at the king's bidding. 'It contained some interesting news from Rome.'

Rome! For the first time since we had found Louis Durand's dead body, I remembered the Vatican coin in his pocket.

'It's not common knowledge in England,' Sir Horatio continued, 'but Rome is where Charles Stuart has lately settled his court, after marrying an eighteen-year-old German princess. He tries to persuade the Pope to recognise his claim to the English throne but apparently the Pope is tired of him. He has been pestering His Holiness for thirty years and my uncle judges his chance of success to be very slim.'

'King Charles III, as he likes to style himself, has a very small following these days,' His Majesty put in pityingly. 'They flit from place to place on the Continent, always seeking the support of the king of here and there, to put me off my throne. But no one likes him now. He is no longer a bonny prince but a poor old thing, too fond of his bottle, and very dropsical in the legs. His only companions are a few hangers-on and a few old Scottish clansmen. And the old clansmen are now very old and very few, the original traitors from '45 being naturally very much reduced in number. But they have had some offspring, more's the pity, and Sir Horace sent his nephew word that one of them had lately been seen in Calais.'

'My uncle is always anxious not to allow any Jacobite to reach these shores unseen,' Sir Horatio said.

The king snorted. 'And no wonder, sir, since he disgraced himself in '45 by missing the departure of the entire invasion fleet.'

'He certainly has a bee in his bonnet about it,' Sir Horatio conceded. 'He thought he had lost the Pretender again, a year or two ago, somewhere in the Alps, and there was hell to pay until he found him.'

'In all events, a Jacobite from Charles's court was seen in Calais, and Sir Horace sent his report to London.' The king took up the tale. 'Being very unwilling to let another invasion slip past him, he also wrote to Sir Horatio here and bid him bring the news to London himself, in case his letter went astray. It's lucky he did, for the Ministry with its usual incompetence contrived to lose the message from Sir Horace before they had even read it. And then I recollected that man Delingpole had talked to my equerry about Durand. Said he might really have been a Welshman with some fancy for an old crown hidden in Longshanks' tomb. It all seemed far too fanciful, but when Sir Horatio came up with this Jacobite in Calais, I put two and two together.'

The king looked smug.

'And is this Jacobite still at large?' Father asked, rather slow as he often is.

The king was now shaking his head pityingly at Father's innocence. 'Not at large, Dean. No, not at large at all. He is presently lying in your abbey lock-up as dead as a nail.' The king looked triumphant. 'Yes, Dean! You see, I have solved the mystery all alone, without your aid, what, what?'

Sir Horatio cast his eyes down, evidently not liking to seek any credit for himself. But it was also hard on Mr Delingpole, for without his message to the equerry, the king could hardly have made the connection himself. On the whole, however, I thought the main lesson was that His Majesty had been quite unreasonable to demand Father solve the mystery himself, when his own people had been able to produce answers with such miraculous promptness merely at his own bidding.

Sir Horatio now took up the thread. 'When the man introduced himself to you as Monsieur Durand, a Frenchman, he was lying. Sir Horace's agent, who saw the man in Calais, identified him as a courtier in Charles Stuart's retinue named Hamilton. There are many different Hamilton family lines in the Jacobite movement – an Irish one, a poetical one, an aristocratic one – perhaps even a Welsh one, who knows? – and we cannot positively say to which particular branch of the family this fellow belonged. Be that as it may, the Ministry view is that Hamilton heard of the forthcoming tomb opening and was inspired, in a fit of youthful zeal, to embark on this madcap mission.'

'Mission?' Father asked. 'What mission?'

'Who can say? To steal the body of Scotland's oldest

enemy, perhaps. Or to find this crown, if it turns out he was a Welshman and somehow knew it was buried in the tomb.'

'*I* fancy Hamilton meant it as a gift to the Pretender,' His Majesty added, and it seemed a reasonable supposition. From what we had heard, Charles was probably in need of cheering up, what with his failed life's work to take the English throne, his bottle, and his dropsical legs.

'Our people have traced Hamilton's movements as far as London,' Sir Horatio went on. 'We believe he came to England on the pretext of delivering a letter from the young queen to a lover.'

'A letter from the queen!' His Majesty now forgot to pretend that he knew the *whole story*. 'A lover!' He looked scandalised at the idea of a fellow monarch (however counterfeit) being thus betrayed.

'Yes, sire. It seems a young Englishman lately visited the court of the Pretender and met the eighteen-year-old queen, who is very lovely, they say, and was probably distressed to find her husband – whom she had never previously met – to be such a poor specimen. It seems there was some dalliance between the two young people and Hamilton arrived at the young man's lodging in London last week, carrying him a letter from the newly married young queen. The Runners are at present seeking to find out the name of this young man and the whereabouts of his lodging, in the hope he can tell us more.'

I looked at Lindley, and he looked at me. Light had dawned upon us both, as bright as Apollo's fiery chariot. How many young Englishmen visited the Stuart court on their Grand Tour? How many fell in love with young ladies who had just married a man they had never previously met? How many could have received a letter by the hand of a member of that court last week? But what would be the penalty such a young man with ridiculous spaniel ears would suffer, if his name were revealed to the king and his Runners?

'I would hang the young fool for conspiring with a traitor,' His Majesty said carelessly, 'but they tell me I would stir up more trouble that way than by letting the thing pass. If we can find him and get to the bottom of the story once and for all, then I dare say I shall be content to let him live.'

Lindley looked at me again. I nodded at him eagerly. He took a breath and turned back to the king.

'I am well acquainted with the man you are looking for, sire,' he said to the evident astonishment of everyone present. 'A perfectly respectable young fellow, as far as I know, if a bit of a fool. I am sure he himself has done nothing wrong, but I can bring him here to the Ascension service tonight, to be questioned, if it would please Your Majesty to do it.'

40

THE KING WAS PLEASED enough with the effect of the lamps ascending on their chains to the triforium at the moment of Christ's ascension to heaven, but Father took less pleasure in the success of his spectacle than he might have done had it not been so thoroughly eclipsed by all the electrical showmanship of recent days.

His Majesty also deigned to show a good-natured interest in the new tombs Fidoe had revealed behind the tapestries on the Cosmati pavement, just by the royal family's special seats. He had all his children with him, arranged in order of height from eleven-year-old Prince George, looking exceedingly bored, down to the Prince Augustus, a lusty boy of one, being dandled in his nurse's arms. Only Prince Adolphus, being three months old, had been deemed too young to properly enjoy the event and had been left at home, while the youngest daughter, Princess Elizabeth, was presently swinging on her father's hand.

Mr Delingpole came up and made his obeisance as the congregation departed.

'Ah, Delingpole,' the king said, 'I have a bone to pick with you. I hear you had another look at that mummy without me, what, what?'

As he straightened, Mr Delingpole looked alarmed. 'Yes, sire. It was quite an impromptu affair, when the mummy was found, and I did not think—'

'Did not think, eh? What, what? Did not think your sovereign would care to join you after all the trouble he has taken over the matter?'

'Did not like to take the liberty of disturbing you at home, sire.' Mr Delingpole looked humble, but I thought he overdid it rather, almost in the manner of the sacrist in the company of the archbishop.

The young princess swinging on the king's hand pointed behind us and gave a sudden squeal of delight. When I turned to look, the Deanery footman was approaching across the pavement carrying Cuthbert in his cage, as I now remembered the king had desired. Having never previously ventured into the abbey, Cuthbert was looking about at the candles and the deep shadows beyond with an admixture of interest and alarm.

'Ah, yes, what, what? Good, good,' the king said. 'This is the creature I told you of, children. The creature I taught to speak.'

God save the king, Cuthbert said obligingly as the footman arrived among us and bowed low. *What, what?* And then, perhaps in imitation of the bowing footman, or sheer satisfaction at being admired, he nodded his head vigorously and turned a somersault on his perch. The little princess clapped her hands and squealed again.

'You like it, Lizzie?'

'Want,' she said. And then added in a forceful baritone, '*Want!*'

Mr Delingpole looked from the child to the king and back again. No doubt still anxious to placate His Majesty, he was now struck with an inspiration which sealed my opinion once and for all of his spousal qualifications.

'I think this is the little Princess Elizabeth, soon to be four years old,' he said, in a manner almost verging on Suckling oiliness. 'Your Majesty wanted a gift for her birthday, I remember. Well, sire, I have studied birds and their song – or speech – in exhaustive depth, and let me say I cannot recommend anything more highly to Your Majesty than a talking bird as a very acceptable pet.'

Perhaps he meant *any* talking bird. Perhaps he did.

'A perfect notion, Delingpole.' His Majesty clapped his hands again. 'A splendid notion. Have the bird's cage taken to the second carriage, Desaguliers, and find out what it eats. You shall like it, Lizzie, shan't you?'

'Want,' she boomed again. '*Want.*'

I was awoken from my frozen horror by Lindley's voice coming coolly from my elbow. 'No, Your Majesty,' he said, and I turned to stare at him. His face looked both sentimental and stern all at once, positively like a noble knight of old.

'What, what?' the king said with equal surprise, probably not having heard the word *no* ever previously uttered – at least, not quite in that way.

'I am afraid the Princess Elizabeth may not have my cousin's bird,' Lindley explained, with a tremendous and hitherto unsuspected natural authority, which was as startling to me as my own observations on *refraction* had been to him the night he showed me the magic lantern. 'Cuthbert belongs to Susan, and she is very fond of him. You will understand my uncle's probable feelings on the matter, too, sire, since you yourself once observed that *daughters are a man's delight*. It would grieve the dean almost as much as it would grieve me to see our beloved Susan weep.'

'But she could always get another bird, what, what?'

'I'm afraid she can't, sire. She is attached to this one.'

'And I want this one for the princess.'

'Then I am afraid we are at an impasse, Your Majesty.'

They looked at each other: the tall, well-made king frowning at Lindley, who now looked every inch the lord of his Leicestershire manor. He was standing up for me against the king! My breath almost failed me and Cuthbert said *Good God preserve us*, apparently as much astonished as I was.

I cannot say how it would have ended, if a diffident figure had not at that moment strolled into the lamplight, all spaniel ears and languid manner.

'Ah! Here is Thomas Ffoulkes, Your Majesty.' Lindley indicated the newcomer and simultaneously nodded his head meaningfully at the footman to hurry Cuthbert away to safety. The spaniel ears bowed deferentially and I saw Tom Ffoulkes was, in fact, extremely nervous, likely on finding himself in the shadow of the noose. He was brave to have come at all.

'Tom is the fellow Hamilton was visiting in London,' Lindley was explaining to the king. 'As you can see from his coming here of his own volition, he is quite innocent of murder, but I am pretty sure he will be able to tell us a good deal more about Hamilton and his scheme.'

*

IT WAS QUIET IN the abbey. The royal children had left
and Cuthbert was, I hoped, safely back in the Deanery
parlour. The congregation was gone and the vergers had
snuffed out most of the candles. Only Fidoe's lamps still
glowed above our heads, their wicks guttering as the oil ran
low. We had all adjourned to the quire: we three Bells, Mr
Delingpole, the king, his equerry and Tom Ffoulkes.

'So you knew this dead fellow, what, what?' the king said
brusquely. 'Been dallying with young queens, too, I hear.
Not very creditable, sir, not creditable at all.'

Tom Ffoulkes bowed again. But, I thought, just a shade
less deferentially this time. How had I not recognised he was
a Jacobite when I met him on Saturday, with his ruffled cuffs
and cavalier wig? Hadn't I afterwards thought that Charles
II's plumed hat would have admirably suited him? It seemed
to me now that I had been very slow in putting two and two
together – almost as scatterbrained as Father – especially
considering that Mr Alnutt had raised the possibility of some
anti-Hanoverian chicanery with Llewellyn's crown. After Sir
Horatio's revelations I had thought back to that meeting –
had got out this journal and read it over again. If we had
only known it, Tom Ffoulkes had told us most of it already.
If we had listened, we might even have guessed Hamilton's
business here at the abbey. But we were not listening, and in
this city of near a million souls, why should it occur to any
of us that Ffoulkes and Durand had ever met?

The spaniel ears bowed again, this time on the conclusion
of his explanation about Charles Stuart's young bride.

'Took a fancy to you?' The king's eyes had opened very
wide. 'But how did you permit yourself to be *fancied*, sir?'

'I felt very sorry for her, Your Majesty. The king is such a sad old man.'

'The king?'

'The Pretender, I mean, Your Majesty.'

'And how did you inveigle yourself into his circle at all, to be *fancied*?'

Tom Ffoulkes squirmed under the king's eye.

'Come, come,' His Majesty snapped. 'I shan't bite you. Even if you are a damned Jacobite, I am apparently not to hang you neither.'

The boy hesitated a moment and then said, 'The Ffoulkes are a very old Welsh family, Your Majesty.'

'Welsh!' The king looked at the rest of us significantly and tapped his nose.

'We are not Jacobites, sire. My father does not wish for the restoration of the Stuarts in the slightest degree. If he could, he would go back to a time before the English kings ever came to Wales at all. But he is an unworldly man, an antiquary much attached to lost causes. It was in that spirit he bade me seek an introduction to the Stuart court in Europe if I could.' He hesitated. 'And that is where I met her.'

His Majesty was still rather too preoccupied with the impropriety of flirting with an English queen, whatever he might think of her legitimacy. He extracted the details of their liaison from poor Tom – the squeeze of a hand – a kiss – a fumble in a corridor – but I was thinking back again to that night I had first met the lad. It had been after Lindley's demonstration. My cousin had slapped him on the shoulder and Tom Ffoulkes had kissed my hand. Then Mr Delingpole had buttonholed Lindley and Tom had left alone. I had been seated with a view of the passageway outside the Deanery drawing room and had watched him go out of my sight towards the stairs. Another wave of light broke over me (*Query:* or should I say *refracted?*) and I interrupted the king's interrogation rather abruptly and, I am afraid, probably very discourteously.

'It was *you* that stole the keys to the abbey and let Mr Hamilton in,' I exclaimed. 'It was you, Tom, wasn't it?'

Thomas Ffoulkes blushed a deep and incriminating scarlet. Whatever he was, at least he was no very hardened criminal. Nevertheless, from some instinct of self-preservation he closed his lips and would not answer.

'Stole the keys?' Father exclaimed.

'Let the Jacobite in?' His Majesty echoed.

'Of course, Susan,' Lindley said, staring at me. 'Of course he did. What idiots we were not to remember Tom when we went through every other possible culprit there that night.' He frowned. 'Though how did Suckling get into the triforium in order to accidentally kill himself, if he did not have your uncle's keys?'

'Because it turns out he had a key of his own to the dark vestry and the triforium all along. I saw Father give it to Ede this afternoon.'

Lindley raised an eyebrow at this, perhaps struck as I had been by the fact no one else had thought to apprise us of the fact. But that could wait for later. Now he turned back to spaniel ears. 'Well, Tom, since my cousin has found you out, you may as well tell us everything.'

Tom looked at him but still said nothing.

'I remember it all now,' I said to Lindley. 'Everyone was

milling about upstairs, including the servants. You said your farewells to each other and Mr Ffoulkes went downstairs. Father's keys were on the mantelpiece in his study. It would have been the work of a moment to take them.'

Tom Ffoulkes frowned, took off his spaniel wig and scratched the very short hair beneath. He looked at once about ten years younger, and yet ten times more sensible. 'It was perfectly easy,' he said, with a belated attempt at bravado. 'After Lindley heard from Delingpole that the king meant to visit the abbey and view the mummy the next morning, he seemed suddenly very eager to be rid of me. So I was suffered to leave the Deanery alone.'

He stopped again and we all looked at him.

'Go on,' the king said. 'Go on before I change my mind about hanging you.'

Tom Ffoulkes took a breath and reluctantly did as he was bid. 'I knew Hamilton had been at the opening of the tomb that morning. Once he saw the sceptre was there he brought the whole thing to a speedy end before the rest of you could find out the truth. He had paid the workmen to cause a diversion if he threw down his hat.'

'Sceptre?' the king said, his brow furrowed. 'What sceptre?'

'Edward the Confessor's,' I said, breaking in again before Tom Ffoulkes could answer. 'Blake found it out this morning. The sceptre originally buried with Edward Longshanks was different to the one we found with him yesterday in Elizabeth's vault. *That* was a copy, stolen from the ragged regiment along with one of their crowns. I don't know where the crown has gone. But we immediately perceived that the original must have been the Confessor's real sceptre, hidden from Cromwell

330

along with Llewellyn's crown. I suppose you meant to steal it, Tom, before a Hanoverian king discovered it.'

Everyone was staring at me. 'Never mind,' I said, remembering myself under their collective gaze. 'Go on, Tom.'

'I did not mean to steal it. Not at first.' He was still very unwilling to speak, looking at us all like a truculent schoolboy fearing to confess in case of a caning.

'His Majesty has said he will not hang you,' I said, still breathless and excited. 'He merely wants to find out the truth.'

In retrospect this was probably doubtful encouragement, since hanging was the worst, but not the only possible punishment. Nevertheless, after biting his lip a moment Tom Ffoulkes allowed himself to be drawn a little further.

'I told you my father sent me to Charles's court in Rome. He had discovered the story about the hidden crown and sceptre from his old sources and was delighted with the whole idea. He begged me visit Charles while on my Tour and tell him all about it. It was only a romantic notion – I told you Father is unworldly – but it turned out Charles Stuart was delighted. All the Confessor's crown jewels had been destroyed, so far as anyone knew, and new ones made for Charles II's coronation. The Pretender, being as romantic as my father, decided that his claim to the throne would be much strengthened if he could show he possessed the true royal sceptre of ancient times. Hamilton, being a very active, adventurous fellow, immediately undertook to get it for him. And he suggested I come along and take the Welsh crown back to my father.'

'Remarkable,' the king said. But I don't think he meant it as a compliment.

'And Blake's drawings?' Lindley added, struck with a sudden inspiration. 'Did you take the drawings too?'

Tom Ffoulkes looked unaffectedly blank.

'No, Lindley,' I said impatiently. 'That is all found out. I will tell you about it later.'

'All found out?' Father echoed. 'What is *found out*?'

'Never mind,' I said. 'Let us hear Mr Ffoulkes's story first. Had you already decided to steal the sceptre that night, Tom?'

'No. We had not meant to act so soon. But when I learned from Delingpole at Lindley's demonstration that His Majesty was coming back the next day it was suddenly urgent. If the sceptre was discovered it was all up. It had to be that night, before you all returned. I poked about downstairs – had the devil of a shock when someone said *bonjour* to me in the parlour, till I saw it was only a parrot. Then I found the dean's study and a bunch of big old keys on the mantelpiece which I hoped would get us in.'

He was more fluent now, more like the man he had been the night I first met him, though he had thankfully dropped his foppish drawl and sounded more like Lindley, young and eager. It occurred to me that he had been nursing the knowledge of Hamilton's murder alone, all week, and that it must be a relief to share it.

'And so you came back with Hamilton later,' Lindley said, 'very late, I suppose, and let yourselves in with the keys?'

'Yes.' Tom Ffoulkes nodded. 'It wasn't so very late, in fact. About one o'clock in the morning, but of course the place was deserted when we came in through the north door.'

I was trying to imagine it. Their trying all the keys on the ring until they found the right one. He and Louis Durand, as I would always think of him, whatever his real name, two young rebels on what Sir Horatio had called a madcap mission.

'Was it not very dark?' I asked, glancing about at the shadows now gathering around us as, one by one, the oil lamps died.

'We had a shaded lantern with us. But when we came to the crossing there was a candle burning in one of the chapels ahead, which would have helped us see our way to the shrine even if we hadn't brought a light with us.'

'Dear me,' Father said. 'The vergers are supposed to snuff out all the candles before they leave, lest the abbey burns to the ground. I shall certainly have a word with Ede and Catgill about this.'

No one regarded him. 'Go on, Tom,' Lindley said.

'We found no key to the shrine on the ring, so we went round to the wooden staircase in the ambulatory and climbed over the gate. We had brought a rope and some chocks with us, for Hamilton had said the lid to the tomb was so heavy that scarcely ten men had been able to lift it – and strong, rough men at that, not weaklings like ourselves. We hadn't yet acquired a lever, so we picked up one of the workmen's scaffold poles to use. Even with two of us it was impossible to lift the lid more than a foot or so, and without the chocks we should have been entirely defeated. But we worked away, little by little, and gradually got the lid up, on the chocks, to the height of about three feet.'

'Lucky for you the pole didn't break or you might have lost your fingers,' Lindley said excitedly.

'But then, of course, there was the inner lid to the stone sarcophagus to deal with. Hamilton had hoped we could reach in and open it with the outer lid propped, but we soon discovered that the chocks were in the way, and we would have to find some other means of holding the outer lid open without them. Fortunately, we had the rope, and looped it around the outer lid. At first we thought there was nowhere we could sling the rope to tie it off, but then Hamilton remembered the works which had been going on when he came with the antiquaries that morning – a festoon of chains being hung from the gallery with lamps attached. We slung the rope over the chains and tied it off to the railings beside the tomb.'

'Show us,' the king said. He had been listening to all this with the open-mouthed wonder of a five-years infant. Now, it seemed, words were not enough. He wanted illustrations to the story too. And, to be fair to him, I think we all felt the same. We hurried out of the quire into the ambulatory, where Longshanks' tomb frowned down at us from behind its iron grille. Tom Ffoulkes gestured first to Fidoe's chains above us, and then to the pointed rails of the grille. 'There. We looped it over the chains and tied it off fast to the grille. Then we took out the chocks and set to work on the inner coffin. The lid to that was much easier, and we took it out completely with only a little difficulty.'

'We found it where you left it,' I said, glancing up at the roof of the Confessor's shrine, which was just visible beyond Longshanks' colossal coffin. 'Propped away in a corner, behind the Confessor's tomb.'

'Yes, well – I could hardly put it back myself.' A pause. 'Alone.'

334

Tom Ffoulkes had been speaking bravely until now, but at the word *alone* he turned suddenly very pale and his voice faltered. He put out a hand to steady himself. 'Hamilton climbed up on the outer coffin rim to get the mummy. He dragged it out—'

'Dear, dear,' Father said again.

'And he passed it to me. I'll never forget him sitting there, feet dangling, with such a happy grin on his face.'

Finally, at this, Tom Ffoulkes broke down. He put his hand to his eyes and sobbed three times, dry and desperate.

'Go on,' the king urged him, eager for the horrible denouement we all knew was coming.

'Hamilton jumped down and took the mummy from me. It was so light – like a dead leaf. He said, "Look, here is the sceptre, Tom. Is it not glorious? And here's your crown for the Welsh—" And then, at that moment, there was a terrible sound like a pistol shot. The strain of the rope on the railing had been too much. The rail loosened from the stonework and flew straight at Hamilton like a spear, with all the force of the falling lid behind it. It pinned him through the throat. He fell, unconscious at once, though I tried to speak to him – pulled out the railing from his neck, which only brought all the blood with it – and then he gave a horrible gasp and died right before my eyes.'

41

THERE WAS AN interlude in which Ffoulkes sobbed again in that horrible dry way, and the rest of us remembered Hamilton's slumped corpse with the gaping hole in his throat. I could now see the narrow gap in the grille where the iron railing had once been. The stonework had failed under the weight of the lid, just as the old banister on the high ledge had come loose under my hand yesterday. The vergers who found the rail the next day, lying with the scaffold pole, had thought it another lever and called it *rusty*. Well, we now knew what those red stains had really been.

'But then I heard a sound,' Tom Ffoulkes said, mastering himself with an effort. 'I thought that the terrible noise of the lid falling must have brought the searcher to investigate. I ran to the wooden staircase and peered down into the ambulatory. It wasn't the searcher. It was something horrible. Something terrifying—'

'A ghost,' Lindley said, in a tone of sudden understanding that made everyone look at him. 'You saw a bulging, shimmering, golden light and a ghastly tall figure wrapped in white linen.'

Ffoulkes didn't ask him how he knew. 'First I thought it was Longshanks, angry we had meddled with him. Then I thought, No, no, Hamilton is dead and this is *his* ghost. I nearly died of fright.'

'So you picked up the mummy and ran,' the king said. He had begun pacing excitedly between the steps and the chapel where all this had taken place. 'I see it all now, what, what? Remarkable. Quite remarkable.' And this time there was only admiration in his tone.

'No, sire.' Tom Ffoulkes twisted his fingers together anxiously. 'The ghost disappeared as suddenly as it had come, and I jumped down the stairs and ran. But I left the mummy where it was lying, by the tomb. I left everything, God forgive me. The sceptre . . . the crown, too . . . all of it. Poor Hamilton. He died for nothing in the end. I failed him. And ever since that horrid, reproachful spectre has haunted me. I cannot sleep. I can hardly eat.'

In truth it had always been a boyish jape (quite worthy of Lindley, really) and no one could have supposed they would succeed with so little planning and so much youthful thoughtlessness. They might have told each other that the crown and sceptre were matters of grave national pride, but the image of Hamilton (or Durand as I still think of him) sitting, grinning, on the edge of the tomb will stay with me long after everything else is over. Just a boy at heart – a romantic young idiot.

'Then someone else took the mummy,' the equerry said. He really did have a talent for stating the obvious. But Delingpole was speaking to Lindley over him.

'Bell, how do you know the ghost walked? Has Ffoulkes

already told you this story? I hope you have not been protecting him all this time.'

'God forbid,' Lindley said. 'Frankly, I'd like to horsewhip him for his stupidity, except that he seems to be flagellating himself quite sufficiently, without any aid from me.' But he was looking at Tom Ffoulkes with a new kind of compassion. 'Was that why you failed me at the opera, Tom?'

The lad nodded. 'I have been nowhere. Seen no one. No one, except that ghost, day and night.'

Lindley took a breath. 'Oh, for God's sake. Then I suppose it must all come out. Perhaps I'm a fool to confess to my own idiocy, now, after all this time, but I won't have you starve to death, Tom, for the sake of a stupid joke.'

He crossed the paving to the door of the Baptist's chapel and patted its stone tracery with an affectionate hand. 'It was I that conjured the ghost you saw that night, Tom. The same ghost the others saw the next day. What's the point in denying it now?' He looked at Mr Delingpole. 'When you told me His Majesty was coming for a look at Edward's corpse the next morning, sir, I thought it would be vastly amusing to show the king my tricks. I had just had all the Chapter's plaudits for the demonstration, and I was full of myself.

'Yes, I thought it would be the most amusing game. I got rid of Tom and then, when everyone was abed, I carried the large, concave mirror I'd brought back from Holland into the abbey through the open south-transept door sometime about half past midnight. It was a dreadful fag, as a matter of fact, and took me a devil of a time to carry it, being so awkward and heavy. I set it up in the ambulatory and then walked back and forth adjusting it for an age. I lit a candle in the Baptist's Chapel – you see it is just opposite Edward's tomb – and worked out how I could perambulate up and down the little space without being seen and appear and disappear out of the mirror as if out of thin air. I can at least congratulate myself that I achieved exactly the effect I wanted the next morning.' He hesitated. 'But until now, I had no notion I'd also produced an effect that night.'

'But, then, why didn't we see you when we came in?' Tom Ffoulkes asked him, stung out of his self-recriminations. 'The place was silent and deserted – except for your candle in the chapel. I suppose it was your candle.'

'I imagine so.' Lindley looked about at us with a sudden energy which I feared was – despite everything – a return of his usual irreverent enjoyment. 'But come, Tom, let me show you. Go to where you were standing in the shrine.'

Father made a noise as if to demur, but the king was also getting over the image of Hamilton's skewered corpse and was apparently ready for a new diversion. 'Do, do, Ffoulkes. Let us see exactly how it all happened.'

Ffoulkes obediently vaulted over the gate at the bottom of the wooden stairs to the shrine and then, at the top, turned back to peer down as he had done that night. Though Lindley had dispelled his ghost, I thought he was still trembling. How dreadful must it be to relive all the horror.

Meanwhile, Lindley herded the rest of us back down the ambulatory, to the spot where Delingpole and I had seen the ghost the following day.

'There was a rope strung across the path,' I remembered.

'Certainly there was a rope. I put it there.' Lindley's

enjoyment now evidently warred against his finer feelings. 'God forgive me, I thought it was all an act of providence in my favour.'

He raised a hand to stop us following him as he went to stand in the door of the Baptist's Chapel again.

'You didn't see me when you came in, Tom, for after I set up the mirror I went to collect my costume. First, I went back to the Deanery to fetch the sheet from my bed. I almost thought myself discovered, for when I crept downstairs again there was a light in the parlour and I heard Cuthbert cry out *Here's the Dean!* I paused, frozen in the dark, but really thinking it all a most amusing adventure. Then I saw that the light under the parlour door was only the flickering of the dying fire. And I dare say Cuthbert was dreaming.'

'Then you went to the ragged regiment,' I said, with sudden understanding, 'and took Elizabeth's crown to wear.'

He smiled at me. 'Elizabeth's was it, Coz? Well, it proved a touch too small, and when I walked about the chapel the next day as best I could – the chapel is rather cramped as you can see – I dared not keep it up for long for fear of laughing and dropping the infernal thing off my head.

'I brought my costume here to the chapel, flitting along like a ghost myself, for as I came into the ambulatory I thought I heard voices, and I wondered if Cuthbert had been right and the dean was really at large about the place. What he could be doing here at one o'clock in the morning I couldn't imagine, but of course now I realise it was only your voice and Hamilton's that I heard, Tom.

'I had no sooner got into the chapel and wrapped myself up in the sheet, than there was the most God Almighty crash from outside. I hurried to the door, entirely forgetting to be cautious and saw there was broken glass everywhere and that several of Fidoe's lamps seemed to have fallen from their chains.'

'And Tom saw your reflection in the mirror,' I said. Lindley nodded.

'So it seems. Of course, it never occurred to me that anything else had caused that dreadful crash, so I never went near the Confessor's shrine. If I had, I would have seen the mummy and Hamilton's corpse for myself. To be frank, I'm glad I didn't. The crash alone nearly stopped my heart.

'But on the whole, I thought it a remarkably well-timed accident. The one thing I hadn't considered was how to conceal the mirror until it was time for me to make the ghost walk for the king. There was frayed rope lying amid the broken glass and later, when I had disrobed myself and left everything ready in the chapel, I hung it across the ambulatory to ward folks away from the broken glass – and my mirror all in one.

'I went home to bed, and the next morning carried off my trick with great success. I walked about the Baptist's Chapel and scared you magnificently. Then, the moment you all scattered, I came out of the chapel, picked up the mirror, and lugged it away, congratulating myself on a very cool performance. I fully intended to tell you all about it, later, and impress His Majesty with my brilliance.'

'I asked you,' I said reproachfully. 'I *asked* you if it was a trick of yours and you denied it.'

'Of course I did. The next thing I knew, Hamilton was found dead and Delingpole was saying the ghost was also the murderer. Though part of me was vexed to learn the king hadn't seen my performance after all, I began to realise it was a blessing. Even so, I could hardly confess after that.'

I remembered coming into the parlour that morning and finding Lindley at a late breakfast. He had smiled sunnily when I announced that we had just seen something extraordinary, but then, when I told him about the dead body, his face had changed and he had dropped his bread and marmalade in his lap.

'I was horrified,' he said, apparently also remembering the same moment. 'Everyone thought that the ghost was connected with the murder. My God, I would have thought so too. Of course I would. So I dared not confess *then*, not even to you, Susan, though I wanted to do it more than anything. Not when the murder was still a mystery to all of us, and Delingpole on the warpath.'

'And so you hid the mirror in the triforium?' I asked, finding myself obscurely pleased that he had *wanted more than anything* to confess to me alone of all those present.

'No.' He frowned. 'The mirror disappeared at the same time as the Leyden jar and the generator, shortly before your accident in the Little Cloister, Susan.'

'Then Mr Suckling took it,' I said. 'Even if he wasn't the ghost, that much at least is true. He told me you had been both the ghost *and* the god and had almost killed me with your Leyden jar. He said Father knew all about it and had hidden the mirror there to protect you.'

'Good Lord,' Father said weakly. 'Protect Lindley? Protect him from what?'

'Being in league with Hamilton, I suppose.'

'In league?' Lindley also looked puzzled. 'I didn't even know the man.'

'I suppose he meant me to think you were also a Jacobite, come with Hamilton to steal the crown and sceptre.'

'But that was me,' Tom Ffoulkes said. He almost sounded vexed.

'Yes,' I nodded, 'we know that now. But probably Mr Suckling saw you there, when he came along to steal the mummy after you fled. And knowing Lindley was your friend, he must have thought he could blacken my cousin by association with you.'

Lindley was quite as vexed as Ffoulkes, but for different reasons. 'I met Tom in France on the Tour, just as I told you, Susan. He was returning from Rome and I was on my way to Holland. I have no more interest in dethroned kings than in giants.'

My mind had been racing over all the little circumstances of the past week while Lindley had been speaking.

'When I found both Mary's sceptre and Elizabeth's crown missing from the cupboard I was certain it meant the murderer had taken both,' I said. 'But now, if you are finally telling us the truth, Lindley, it means two separate people visited the cupboard on two entirely unconnected errands. You, to find a crown for your little joke with the ghost. Mr Suckling to conceal his theft of the real sceptre from Longshanks' tomb. It seems scarcely credible.'

Lindley spread his hands. '*Cum hoc, ergo propter hoc.*'

'That is very helpful,' I said witheringly. (It was at that moment I really resolved to learn Latin in earnest since, looking around, I saw all the men present understood him.)

'*With this, therefore because of this*,' Father explained. 'It describes a fallacy in logic, I believe, though it is long since my studies at the University.'

Mr Delingpole nodded. 'Just because two things happen together, it does not mean one is caused by the other, or that both are caused by the same event. They may be entirely coincidental.'

'And so, in this case,' Lindley said, 'we have discovered several men were there in the abbey that night, all set on different objects. A joke on my part, Jacobite zeal on Tom's and Hamilton's, and greed on Suckling's.'

Father waved a deprecatory hand at the latter, harsh word. 'Let us not be too hard on Suckling. It might have been desperation that drove him, not greed.'

'Desperation?' Lindley looked unpersuaded. 'Suckling?'

But Father was now addressing the king. 'The sacrist did not really believe my nephew a Stuart sympathiser, Majesty.' Father had been very quiet until now, only *dear-dear-ing* and *Good-Lord-ing* at intervals throughout Lindley's story. As a result, everyone now looked at him with some interest. 'No, no, he certainly did not.' He looked tremulous, as if about to share a long-held confidence. 'Whatever injury he intended to perpetrate was squarely aimed at me.'

'Aimed at *you*?' the king said. 'By George, Dean, you fancy yourself very important of a sudden.'

'I am afraid it is true, Your Majesty, nonetheless. Suckling and I could never see eye to eye and he was always bent on undermining me.'

'Never see eye to eye?' the king echoed, apparently astonished to find anyone other than himself unpopular, mistreated or in danger of being deposed. 'About what?'

Father hesitated. Cast me a look. And since Tom Ffoulkes and Lindley had both confessed their secrets, I thought it would be missish to be coy about my own. 'I expect it was about me,' I said.

'Suckling was very eager to make Susan an offer, Your Majesty,' Father said, quick to elaborate, now I had shown him I was prepared for my affairs to be discussed. 'I told him I did not think it would be a good match, but I fear he disregarded me and made many overtures to my daughter himself. He was a man who did not like to be rebuffed.'

'I refused him,' I admitted. 'In the end he asked me, and I refused him . . .' I paused. 'Discourteously.' Was that an adequate word for telling him I would rather marry a dog? 'More discourteously than I ought to have done.'

Lindley looked at me, his mouth twitching. 'I can well imagine that. Did you tell him it was lucky he found himself attractive since no one else did?'

I remembered my careless taunt, days earlier, that it was lucky he found himself droll since no one else did. I could not have dreamed it would strike home so well.

I grimaced. 'Far worse.'

Lindley whistled silently. One day, perhaps, I will tell him what I really said, and he will no doubt find it highly amusing. But with poor Mr Suckling dead, I myself was ashamed.

'Suckling had always tried to be a party to all the business of the abbey – desired to be my closest aide and confidant – but I am afraid I also rebuffed him,' Father said. 'He had an unfortunate, repellent manner that was very hard to like. Poor fellow.' Father looked sad. 'I dare say he could not help

346

it. But, be that as it may, I fear all we Bells offended him, in our different ways. Even my nephew was offhand with him.'

I remembered Lindley tell the sacrist to go mind his gowns and trinkets after the first tomb opening. I remembered Mr Suckling coming into the Deanery parlour in time to hear Lindley call him a villain. It was hardly surprising he had disliked us all more and more.

'Of course, none of this would have made an ordinary man act as Suckling seems to have done,' Father added, 'but the sacrist was a real oddity. Perhaps more sensitive than was good for him and certainly, it seems, more prone to offence than we ever realised. I think now he nursed his grievances against us and, in the end, wished for nothing more than I should be ruined and driven from Westminster. If he could do so by implicating Lindley in the murder, whom he also hated, then so much the better.'

I thought back to all our dealings with Mr Suckling, and there was no denying that what Father said was true. And other men than us had spurned him, too – Mr Alnutt had deflected his desire to join the antiquaries from an obscure dislike, he had admitted so himself, and made the sacrist *bad tempered*. And the more we had all recoiled from him, the more hostile he had grown. Where had it begun? Had Mr Suckling been against Father from the first, preferring the archbishop's candidate as I had always thought? Or had we somehow offended him at the very beginning and made him hate us?

'But I still don't see how that made him desperate instead of greedy when he stole the crown and sceptre,' Lindley argued, but no one answered him.

'Yes, an oddity indeed,' the king said after a moment.

'So much an oddity that he nearly killed your daughter, Dean, with your nephew's apparatus and finally succeeded in killing himself. And it now turns out he was a common thief, into the bargain, having come upon the mummy after Ffoulkes fled and stolen it.' The king smiled, some of his good humour returning, now all the horrors were apparently told. 'But see, at last, the whole matter is explained, hey, Dean, what, what? All's well that ends well, and the villains are all providentially punished at their own hands, which saves the rest of us a good deal of trouble.'

Tom Ffoulkes looked as if he were attempting to melt into the shadows, in case the king remembered he alone had gone unpunished – except, I suppose, by his dreams which, since that night in the abbey, must have been fearful indeed.

'I'm not sure the *whole* matter is explained, Your Majesty,' Lindley said thoughtfully. 'If Tom didn't take Blake's drawings, then who did? Suckling? And, if so, why did he do it?'

Now, in retrospect, I would have been wise to keep quiet and only show Lindley what I had found scribbled on the drawings later, in private. But at that moment there seemed no reason for discretion (and in all truth I was intoxicated by being no longer a pigeon, but for once being listened to and answered, even by the king himself). So I spoke up eagerly – and fatally. 'I know all about it, Lindley. I told you. They are no longer lost; I found them, today, tucked inside an old book in the library.'

Yes, I really had everyone's attention in a most gratifying degree. Lindley frowned at me.

'In a book? Who put them there? And why the devil was

he foolish enough to leave them there, for anyone else to see?'

'Hardly *anyone*,' I said. 'I believe I am the library's only patron.' (Oh dear, I was preening far more than I should have done.) 'But it must have been Mr Suckling that stole them from the Deanery. If he had stolen the mummy and swapped one sceptre for another he wouldn't want a record of the original to remain. If he meant to sell the jewels, he wouldn't want evidence of where they had come from. And he certainly did mean to sell them, for the real sceptre is already with the dealer.' And with that I drew Blake's drawings from my pocket and showed them the scribbled note on the reverse.

If I had wanted a gratifying sensation I certainly got one now. Father put his hand to his forehead with a look of shocked surprise. Tom Ffoulkes detached himself from the shadows and stepped forward eagerly. Lindley and Delingpole bent their heads over the paper and the king said, 'Hey, hey? What, what? What does it say?'

'*My dear sir*,' Lindley read. '*As requested: Quantitas: twenty-four troy pounds one ounce; faciam: 2 x 2 x 6. Please let me know if you wish to proceed on this basis.*'

'And who the devil is it from?' the king asked with some heat.

Lindley squinted at the paper. 'It is a dreadful scrawl. But I think it might say Robinson. Or Robertson.'

'There is a man named Robertson in Covent Garden,' Mr Delingpole said. 'I have acted for him betimes. But he is no dealer. He is a goldsmith who makes very fine figurines. I dare say he might be in the market for raw gold. From this paper he seems to have weighed the sceptre at twenty-four pounds one ounce, by the troy measure they employ in the trade.'

'*Quantitas*,' Lindley nodded, 'yes that certainly means *quantity. Faciam* – I suppose that means *will make.* The quantity of gold will make 2 x 2 x 6.'

'That is only speculation,' Father said reprovingly.

Mr Delingpole waved an excited hand. 'But in the morning, Dean, we can go to Robertson and find out exactly what it means.'

'I'll do more than that,' His Majesty said. 'Damn me if I don't send the Runners and have him arrested for receiving stolen goods. By God, I want to hang someone over all this business, and he will do very nicely.'

'I'm afraid not,' Father said, very quietly now. If Tom Ffoulkes had emerged from the shadows, Father seemed to be seeking them instead.

'Dean?'

'Mr Robertson has not received stolen goods, Your Majesty. He acts in good faith on the instruction of a man he has no reason to doubt.'

'Indeed!'

The king looked astonished, and I thought: *Father knows about the canon-treasurer after all. But however did the canon-treasurer get the sceptre from Suckling?*

'And who is this paragon of respectability who has been hawking the sceptre about Covent Garden?' His Majesty demanded.

'Me, Sire,' Father said. 'Mr Suckling did not steal the mummy. I did.'

42

WE WERE BACK IN the Confessor's shrine, all standing around Longshanks' tomb, and I had taken a nunnish vow of silence to last the rest of my earthly existence. I had landed Father in a mess far worse than anything I could ever have imagined – even a marriage to Dame Yates, who had turned out to be a very agreeable woman after all. I had been wrong about everything.

'I had half-realised the sceptre was gold that first Saturday morning,' Father said. He seemed relieved by his confession, and the frown that had creased his forehead all week was gone. 'I might not have realised it, had not Mr Delingpole commented on the lightness of the gilt rod and dove by contrast with the gold-plated iron crown. When he bade me lift the sceptre out of the coffin, I found that it, like the crown, was very heavy. Almost too heavy to lift. The Frenchman – that is, Hamilton, as I must now call him – started forward to help me. I dare say he wished to hide the sceptre's weight from the others, so that he could return and steal it later as Ffoulkes has described. At any rate, in all the following fuss, I thought nothing more about it.'

351

(The others looked as if they doubted this, but I did not, knowing Father's unworldliness so well.)

'But I couldn't sleep that night,' Father went on. 'During the day I had had a very disagreeable meeting with Dame Yates, regarding her memorial to her late husband. She announced she wanted a gold statue to finish the scheme and was quite certain that she had the money to do it. Unfortunately, she did not.'

He looked from one of our faces to the next. 'The dame is a very fine woman, Your Majesty and I . . .' He paused. 'I confess, I admire her. As a consequence, I took a more than common interest in the memorial from the beginning, and often consulted with her man of business as to the progress of its construction. Six months ago, he told me in confidence that the dame had suffered a terrible loss. A dreadful loss – in many ways worse than the death of her husband. Her eldest son had gambled away the entire estate on the turn of a card.'

So much for Father's comfortable retirement, was my first involuntary thought, not yet seeing where the story was bound to end.

'Her man of business consulted with me how to break the news to her,' Father said. 'She will be reduced much in circumstances, I am afraid, having only the settlement her husband made upon her when they were married. I felt so much for the poor woman I begged her man of business to say nothing for the time being, until the ruin was entirely certain. Who knew? Her son might somehow win his patrimony back or fight a duel with the man who won it and shoot him dead. Yes, Your Majesty, I know that is not a very Christian hope to entertain. In any event, her man of business told her that the funds had been transferred to the abbey and I undertook to pay for the memorial out of my stipend until we saw how things stood.' He hesitated. 'My stipend which, as Your Majesty knows, is a small one.'

'Three hundred and fifty a year, ain't it?' the king answered, with the casual air of a man who has a million a year of his own. 'Your predecessors managed well enough.'

'My predecessors had other income, Your Majesty. But this is by the by. I did my best to please Dame Yates with the monument, but she is too sharp to miss the little economies I had to make to afford the thing at all. The stone is not the best, for one thing, and progress has been slow.

'Still, we were managing until the matter of this statue. *It cannot amount to more than a thousand guineas*, she said to me. But where in heaven was I to get so large a sum as that?'

'So, as I say, that night I could not sleep. I came down to the parlour where Cuthbert greeted me – yes, Lindley, I was awake when you crept past. I sat by the fire, thinking it over, until I grew stiff and weary but no further forward in my conclusions. I resolved to make small economies – send back the watch my daughter had bought me that day for my birthday, Your Majesty – but still I knew it was not enough. In the end, as the clock struck three, I went to the abbey, taking a single candle with me. It was very dark and peaceful. God is sometimes hard to find amid the hurry of the abbey, but the Confessor is always ready to hear another man's sorrow. I let myself into his shrine and knelt in one of the old, worn alcoves in the side of his tomb to pray, as so many thousands have done before me.'

'Damned popish carry on,' the king said, but without much force. He was too interested now. For myself, I suddenly knew where the story was heading, and that the king was not going to like it at all.

'At first, I didn't think the Confessor had heard my prayer, any more than God had done,' Father went on sadly. 'I knelt there, very much in despair. I could tell the dame the truth about her money, and her son, but I felt I had meddled too far. I had hoped she would accept an offer of marriage, by which my meddling would be justified, but she had repeatedly refused me – mainly, I believe, on account of the parrot.'

The king frowned but elected to let that pass.

'But then,' Father went on, 'as I turned to go, my candle caught a gleam of gold. I lifted the flame higher – ventured nearer – and realised that the mummy of Edward Longshanks was lying on the floor beside his coffin, with all his grave goods scattered about him.

'I lifted the crown – it was rusty, but there was certainly gold plating on it as Alnutt had told us. I looked at the rod and dove. Gilt too. And then I turned to the sceptre and yes, Good Lord, it was gold, pure gold. Surely, I thought, this will be enough to make a statue from.'

Lindley was frankly incredulous. 'You meant to turn Edward the Confessor's long-lost sceptre into Dame Yates's lapdog?'

'Eh, what, what, what?' the king asked, still apparently somewhat bemused, but none of us enlightened him. All I could think was that it was exactly the sort of thing Father *would* do.

'It was a temptation, Your Majesty,' Father said, not sadly but merely simply now. 'A thief had evidently been there and removed the body from the tomb; but then, for some unknown reason, he had fled empty-handed. No one but myself yet knew anything had happened at all. Perhaps, I thought, it was the Confessor's doing: an answer to my prayer. How could it not be, indeed, when the coincidence was so complete?

'At first I only meant to take the grave goods and leave the mummy lying on the floor to be found the next day. The best thing would be for folks to think it not a theft, but only some act of mischief by the workmen or some such – which, for all I knew, it might have been. I went to the ragged regiment and fetched Mary's sceptre, but to my dismay there was no suitable crown and, Mr Alnutt having made such a fuss about the crown's special character, my nerve rather failed me.

'If the mummy was found lying here, with the jewels gone, investigations would certainly ensue, and it would be much harder to dispose of the grave goods undetected. But when I looked at Edward's tomb it seemed to me in the darkness that the lid was closed again. The thief had done that much before fleeing. It occurred to me, then, that with the tomb closed and the mummy gone, no one need ever know anything had happened at all. Even Mr Delingpole had indicated to me that afternoon that the society had seen enough and did not mean to return.

'Of course, I found how wrong I was the following day. Not only did Your Majesty return with the antiquaries, but it turned out that the outer lid of the coffin was ajar and the inner lid had not been replaced at all but had been left lying in a corner. But ignorant of all this, and thinking myself very clever, I hid the mummy with some toil in Mary and

355

Elizabeth's vault, which we had opened the day before. By then I was very weary, and tucked in Mary's sceptre with the rest, instead of troubling to return it to the cupboard.'

We were all staring at him, but he only spread his hands and then folded them in front of his belly as if to say, *There, I am done. Do with me what you will.*

'But, Uncle,' Lindley said, still more incredulous than he really should have been, having known Father long enough to be acquainted with his oddities by now, 'how did you not see Hamilton's dead body?'

'I came in and out by the left-hand door as I always do,' Father said, reasonably. 'Mr Hamilton was by the right-hand one, as you will remember.'

Lindley was still frowning. 'But if *you* took Longshanks' things, then how did Mr Suckling end up in possession of the crown?'

'Ah. I have omitted the last of my crimes,' Father said. 'And perhaps, after all, the worst.' He hesitated a moment. Folded and unfolded his hands in an anxious expression of remorse.

'Susan was not the first to discover the sacrist's fallen body, Your Majesty. God help me, I had come through the south transept a half-hour earlier and found him lying there, already dead. If I could have saved him I would – of course I would – but he was quite gone, his body all splayed like a dead spider, legs and arms broken horribly. It was clear he had fallen from a great height, and when I looked up I saw the faint blue glow of electricity on the triforium bridge.

'*It must be Lindley's scientific apparatus again*, I thought, as with Apollo, but if I had had any lingering doubts as to my nephew's involvement in that trick, this sight allayed them. I had gone home with Lindley after the inspection of Longshanks' body with the antiquaries, and we had then gone walking out by the river, before taking tea in the Deanery parlour. He could not be responsible for whatever new trick was in contemplation up there. Suckling had been our ghost and our Apollo I was suddenly certain; a thought confirmed later by the housemaid, who told us that the sacrist had been in the Deanery while we were out walking.

'As I reflected on all this over poor Suckling's dead body, a thought struck me, probably no wiser than the one which had made me steal the mummy in the first place. How simple it would be, I thought, to give Suckling the stolen crown – which Robertson had rejected as no earthly use for my own purpose – and make a dead man, beyond all further suffering, seem to be both the thief and the murderer and thereby end the whole sorry business.'

'That was very wrong,' His Majesty observed.

Father hung his head. 'So it was, sire. Suckling suffered at my hands too much when he was alive. I should not have continued to hurt him when he was dead.'

'You were not alone in hurting him,' Lindley said sombrely. 'I killed him by recharging the Leyden jar.'

I must say I felt dreadful, too. If I had encouraged the sacrist's love, he would doubtless have loved us all in turn. If I had not stuck him with a needle, I suppose he might not have launched his campaign against Father and Lindley with quite so much zest. If I had believed his story about Lindley being the ghost (which was indeed true, even if he had added to Lindley's apparent guilt with the Apollo trick, and the artful leaving of Lindley's apparatus to be found in plain sight) he might have desisted then. And if he had desisted then, he would now still be alive. Instead, I had rejected him as less lovable in my estimation than Admiral the dog, and I suppose in a fit of fury he had embarked on that final trick on the high shelf in the triforium, presumably to implicate Lindley once again. Only, horribly, to be killed himself.

Good God, I suddenly thought, *the only true victim of this whole affair was the sacrist, and it was Father and I and Lindley that contrived to kill him between us, without ever intending to do it.*

'I fetched the crown and went up to the triforium,' Father continued. 'It was dark and oppressive and when I saw that the sacrist had placed his equipment far out on that narrow ledge, my heart failed me for a moment. But in the end I crawled out with the crown and laid it beside the other things, before returning to the Deanery to wait for the tragedy to be discovered.'

That dull thud I had heard in the library where I had come in Father's footsteps, and which had brought me to the Muniments Gallery, had not been Suckling's body falling, after all, but Father closing the south transept door behind him on his way back home.

'Well,' said His Majesty, 'I suppose you had better show me this monument for which you have risked your all so unaccountably, Dean.'

We all trooped out of the shrine and along the north ambulatory, past the scene of Lindley's trick, to where Sir Joseph Yates's memorial stood.

His Majesty frowned. 'How the devil has she got him here,

in pride of place amid all this royalty, what, what?'

Father bowed his head again. 'I wanted to please her, Majesty.'

'Yes, yes,' the king said, walking around it. 'It is very bad. Shocking stonework, and very poor gold leaf on that inkpot. But where is this famous statue, what, what?'

'Not yet cast, Your Majesty.' Father was humble. 'It turned out I was wrong.'

'Wrong?'

'To think the sceptre would be sufficient. Those numbers you did not understand in the letter, Lindley. They were the dimensions possible to be yielded by the sceptre's gold.'

'Two by two by six,' Lindley said.

'At first, I thought he meant feet,' Father said glumly. 'But it turned out to be inches.'

'What were you looking for in the library?' I asked him, forgetting my vow to be eternally quiet. 'And why ever did you leave the drawings lying there for me to find?'

'I had just that moment left Lindley in the parlour, my dear. We had been talking about the chanter's dratted exorcism and it had struck me I might not be permitted to perform the rite – though the Abbey being a Peculiar, I certainly did not need to ask the Bishop of London for permission. I went to the library to look for a book on the matter and found an old prayer book I thought might help me. But then – like you – I heard a tremendous crash from inside the abbey. I closed the book with the drawings in it, and hurried down to find Suckling dead, as I told you. I suppose I had been in the library less than five minutes, and in all the subsequent fuss the drawings entirely slipped my mind – until you produced them just now.'

To his own dreadful cost, Father had been his usual absent-minded self – and yes, I too had been very wrong and indiscreet to draw attention to them – but nevertheless I thought at last I saw a glimmer of hope.

'So the sceptre is still with the goldsmith, Father?'

He nodded.

'Then I'm sure Father would be glad to fetch it back and present it to you, Your Majesty,' I said, bobbing a curtsey. 'It would be a marvellous thing to show the world, after all.' I hesitated, remembering William the Conqueror and Longshanks, both as much royal interlopers as the Hanoverians and both very keen to appropriate the Saxon past. 'A very *enhancing* thing to show the world, Your Majesty.'

The king frowned at me. 'Enhancing, eh, what, what? And what do you mean by that, miss?'

I felt unable to elaborate.

'Enhancing!' he repeated. 'I suppose you mean I could prance about pretending to be Edward the Confessor, hey, hey, what, what? Would you call me a prancing kind of fellow, Miss Bell?'

'No, sire.' I was very humble.

'Quite frankly, the press would. Oh, yes, *they* would delight in calling me a prancing fool. They would write whole reams about the Glorious Revolution, and the deposed Stuarts, and before you know it, the Jacobites would be frisking about like spring lambs again. No, no, what, what? Not a very clever idea at all, Miss Bell.'

'No, sire.' I was more humble still.

'I tell you what we'll do,' His Majesty said with some

decision, after a musing pause. 'We'll get the damned sceptre back from the goldsmith and hide both it and that old crown in some other tomb, where no one will find 'em till Judgement Day. Perhaps that new female you have uncovered Dean. What was her name?'

'Lady Aveline de Forz, sire.'

'Yes, yes, let her look after Longshanks' things. Being a woman no one will ever trouble to open *her* tomb, you know. Then we'll rip down this ghastly monument and you can go and build one for the woman somewhere else, Dean, if you must.'

He looked at us, appraisingly, turning his eyes on each of us by turns. 'One Jacobite safely dead and the other silent to the grave if he knows what's good for him. The mummy back in its tomb, the grave goods hidden, and the memorial gone. No evidence, no record. As if it never happened, what, what?'

'Yes, Your Majesty,' Father agreed meekly.

'Except for you, Dean.'

'Majesty?'

'We can make everything else go away, but here you remain.'

'I cannot help that, sire.'

'Help it! Indeed, I think you can, what, what?'

Father looked very small. 'You wish me to—' (For a moment I thought the king meant Father to hurl himself off the west towers.)

'Yes, yes, good, good, what, what? A pleasant retirement in the country. Quite for the best.' The king smiled, but without much warmth. 'You are a dear little fellow and by no means the worst dean there has ever been, I am sure. But human frailty is what it is. And so, it will be much for the best. Yes, it will certainly be much for the best if we draw a veil over your time here. Write you out of the record entirely, would be the best thing, what, what? Though I don't suppose that's possible.'

'No, sire,' the equerry said firmly, though for my own part, I suspect the king can do whatever he sets his mind to.

The king was now looking at Father very sternly. All his old affability had suddenly evaporated like a wet stain under an iron. 'Marry your dame, Bell, if you can prevail upon her to have you, or else go back to your family in Leicestershire if she won't. Someone or other will give you a billet, I dare say, but your time here is ended.'

43

THE KING SWEPT out and all the rest followed him, except for me and Lindley and Father – the Bells of Westminster no longer. The abbey will not much care. I dare say within a month a new dean will be sipping his tea in our parlour and warming his toes by our fire. But where shall we be? Once before I had neglected my proper sphere, so that there had been no refreshments in Jerusalem after the first opening of the tomb. I had thereafter taken it upon myself to quiz Mrs Bray not once but twice, and found things out that, for Father's sake, should have been left undiscovered. If I had been a proper young lady like the canon-almoner's daughters, I would have looked at the fashionable world in St James's Park, not mummified kings. I had put my oar in throughout all these explanations with His Majesty with the direct result we were ousted from the abbey. I really should keep to my vow of silence in future, for everyone's sake. But, with forlorn self-knowledge, I foresaw my new resolutions lasting about five minutes.

'So,' Lindley said. 'So, Uncle – cousin – all in all, and taking everything together, I think we had better go back to Leicestershire. You may bring Dame Yates or Cuthbert, Uncle, but not both, it seems.'

Father blinked at him and I sat down suddenly on the base of the dame's memorial. Lindley had a rather lecturing look in his eye. 'The king has bid you retire, Uncle, and what then could be more natural than that you would come home? There will be no need to go into all the regrettable details. Just a pleasant retirement as the king said. That will sound well enough to my father.'

'But he will not have us,' I said. As predicted, I had broken my vow of silence again. 'We cannot impose ourselves on your father's mercy after all these years of estrangement.'

Lindley frowned at me. 'Mercy? Nonsense. Where else would a man seek a peaceful retirement than in the house of a dutiful son-in-law?'

I was a bit slow again. I think I probably blinked at him. Perhaps there is a little of Father in me, too.

'On the occasion of a happy marriage,' Lindley said impatiently, seeing my blank look. 'A marriage much desired by your father for *donkey's ears*, as Fidoe would say.'

'Lindley,' I said. 'You are very kind, but . . .'

'Excuse me, Uncle.' Lindley lifted me from my seat by the elbow and marched me round the corner back into the north ambulatory and paused, once more, under Longshanks' looming tomb. Something moved in the triforium arch above our heads and a voice said, *Bad bird, bad bird, what, what?* Somehow, Cuthbert had escaped his cage and was at liberty in the vast space of the abbey. He sounded a little forlorn and I must say I felt suddenly the same, for whatever happened now, I was fated to live out the rest of my days under that daunting dome of blue sky after all.

'Are you really going to cause difficulties?' Lindley asked.

'You have never liked me, Lindley. You used to bite me—'

'I was three years old—'

'Though I grant it was because I broke your toys—'

'Less pardonable in a child of five, I admit, but I must bear with you, I suppose.'

'Dame Yates may marry Father, after all, if I ask her,' I said hopefully. 'She would get accustomed to Cuthbert in the end, I am sure. Father and I could move to her townhouse, which is scarcely a mile from here, and we could pool our little fortunes together.'

Who knew, with the dame's remaining settlement in addition to my own, we might rise even to the dizzy wealth of a draper instead of a greengrocer. (And I know everything about fabrics and threads, &c. Perhaps a draper would be the very thing.)

Lindley lifted my chin to look in my eye. 'You really find me so repulsive then? Or is a burial in the countryside what you object to, so much you'd have the dame instead of me?'

'I have eschewed marriage,' I said boldly. 'I once thought Mr Delingpole would do. He is a clever man and I quite fancied a life among lawyers, who know everything about the world, by contrast with all these clergymen at the abbey. But he turned out very unsatisfactory, particularly after that business with Cuthbert tonight. And he said I was clever *for a member of my sex.*'

'I have never said anything like that.'

That was true. 'No,' I said more thoughtfully, 'and you pour your own tea instead of expecting me to do it. You talk to me like a rational being. You have listened to my ideas about all this dreadful business quite as if I were a man.' I paused. 'Moreover, you did very well to confess about the ghost tonight for poor Ffoulkes's sake. No, I don't dislike you at all, Lindley.'

'Well then?' He was frowning at me with his large owlish eyes. I didn't answer and he took my hand. If I was really eschewing marriage, I dare say I should have pulled away, but I didn't quite think of it then.

'In fact, I like you a great deal, Lindley,' I said, now remembering his defence of Cuthbert.

He looked encouraged. 'Excellent. If we can go from *not disliking* to *liking a great deal* in under a minute, who knows where we might be in half an hour?'

'But marriage for a woman determines the rest of her life,' I explained. 'Her pursuits. Her interests. Her friends.' I paused. I had discounted Mr Delingpole despite his interesting friends. Might I not discount Lindley's rural neighbourhood for the sake of his own self – the self that had kissed me in his bedchamber, defended me against the king and called me his *beloved*? I had liked the kissing. I had now entirely forgotten his ears and owlish gaze and only saw the handsome creases around his eyes. And, good Lord, he was finally looking at me the same way Blake did.

'I do not like the way you eat your eggs in the morning.' I said weakly. 'And you are never serious.'

In fact, at this moment, he was looking more serious than he had ever done. But the usual joshing tone was still there in his voice. 'I shall submit to whatever programme of renovating works you require, Susan. But you know, you are not a sour old spinster aunt. You are quite as fond of laughing as I am. Delingpole would have driven you mad with boredom in a fortnight.'

'But Father . . .' I said, still clutching at objections. 'He argued with your father so terribly they have not spoken for near twenty years.'

'My father caught yours pocketing the contents of the church poor box,' Lindley said. 'Your father and mine had fallen out about the use of the funds. Instead of giving a mite to each poor family, your father argued that buying one parishioner a pig each quarter would save his whole family from coming upon the parish, and thereby mean they never needed alms again. My father said if God meant a man to have a pig he would have one, and that a world where no one needed alms was a world in imminent danger of ending. Your father did it anyway, the money was missed and presumed stolen, and after that what else could Father do but banish him? And now, it seems, history repeats itself, and in this case, too, we can at least see his intentions were . . .' Lindley seemed to think for a moment. 'His intentions were good-hearted, in their way, at least as far as the dame was concerned, even if his actions were lamentable.'

'And meaning to melt down the Confessor's sceptre is also quite in his character, you know,' I said, looking into Lindley's face with eager vindication. 'We know that – don't we? – from the evidence of the choir stalls and the tapestries.'

Lindley nodded. 'Yes, yes, I understand him well enough now. Understand him and love him.' He hesitated again. Tightened his grip on my hand. 'And I love you, too, Susan.'

Good God preserve us! Cuthbert remarked from up on his lofty perch.

'Do you really?'

'Yes, even though you slurp your tea like a farmhand. What with that and the eggs I can't see how we are ever to get through a lifetime of breakfasts together. But you are still frowning,' he added, 'which is not a very *ringing* endorsement of my heartfelt declaration.'

'Oh,' I said, finding that my fingers were now somehow comfortably entwined in his. 'I was just thinking it all over.'

'Our ways may not *chime* together all at once. But I hope I may a-*peal* in time.'

I put my free hand to his cheek and then I kissed him.

Above our heads, somewhere, someone sighed. Perhaps it was Longshanks in his tomb, mourning his lost golden sceptre. But no, it had only been the sound of Cuthbert's wings catching a downward draught, for Blake now loomed unexpectedly out of the shadows with the bird on his shoulder.

'Oh holy virgin, clad in purest white,' he said. (He had apparently gathered that a wedding was in the offing.) 'Unlock heaven's gates and with thy buskined feet appear upon our hills.'

There was nothing much I could say to that, so I merely smiled feebly. (*Obs*: I have noticed Blake has quite a preoccupation with feet, which I personally think is highly unpoetical.)

He was looking at Lindley now. 'Deck her forth with thy fair fingers; pour thy soft kisses on her bosom—'

'Dear God,' Lindley said, his ears flushing a rather unattractive purple.

But Blake was not offended in the least, and only wandered away again, still reciting, while Cuthbert nuzzled his ear and murmured *what, what?* in an encouraging manner as they disappeared out of sight around the corner towards the nave.

'I don't think buskins are to be had in Leicestershire,' Lindley said. 'But I dare say we can rustle up some *purest white*. Will you, Susan?'

'Yes, Lindley, I think I will.'

God save the king! Cuthbert shouted out joyfully, from somewhere beyond the labyrinth of statues and pillars and tombs. And then we went to find Father.

He had strayed to the Lady Chapel, where we found him eyeing the fan-vaulted ceiling, the most glorious and intricate stonework in all England – and perhaps in the world.

'Such a shocking repository for dust,' he said, as we came up. 'I shall certainly advise the next dean to have it all pulled out.'

The abbey clock began to strike nine. *The curfew tolls the knell of parting day*, I thought, feeling suddenly as elegiac as Mr Gray, the poet. All in all, it is perhaps as well that we are to go to Leicestershire, but how I shall like it I cannot yet say. The wide dome of blue sky will be a novelty, but I am not sure that it will mean greater freedom than I have had here, slinking about the place unnoticed like the abbey cats. I will miss Blake, too, though I think his labours in the abbey must be nearly over, and sooner or later he will disappear into the streets, likely never to be heard of again.

And meantime the abbey will go on with its endless round of services, round and round as it has done these thousand years, first under the abbots and then the deans, with always some king or other poking his nose in their affairs. The candles will be lighted, and the bells will go on ringing, and perhaps – I like to think – a thousand more dean's daughters will wander the ambulatories, and perch like pigeons in the rafters unseen, until the very end of recorded time.

Historical Note

This story was inspired by the opening of Edward I's tomb in Westminster Abbey by the Society of Antiquaries in 1774; an event witnessed and recorded by William Blake, who was then a seventeen-year-old apprentice engraver. He had been sent to the abbey by his employer, James Basire, to make preliminary sketches of the tombs and monuments for two books, which came out a few years later. The poems he recites are from *Poetical Sketches*, his first collection of verse published in 1783, which covers works composed by him between the ages of twelve and twenty.

Of course, no murder or theft really ensued after the opening of the tomb. The antiquaries are based on some of the real men involved in the opening of Edward's tomb. Daines Barrington wrote on the North Pole, childhood prodigies and birdsong, among many other things. Alnutt is based on the elderly Joseph Ayloffe, who wrote the official account of the opening, and the old man's recital of ancient British history is based on the sources available at the time – as is Quintrel's belief in the temple of Apollo lying beneath the foundations of the abbey. (Rather satisfyingly, during the course of writing this book, an ancient Roman temple was in fact unearthed beneath Leicester Cathedral.) Quintrel is modelled on Andrew Ducarel, librarian of Lambeth Palace, who had a doubtful reputation for cleanliness or sobriety, but was indeed one of the first Englishmen to write on the Bayeux Tapestry.

Thomas Ffoulkes's romance with Charles Stuart's new bride is based on the true story of a dalliance between the young queen and a youthful Sir Thomas Coke, who went on to be a famous agriculturalist and MP.

All my clergymen are fictional, though the abbey servants – the vergers, porter, gardener, searcher of the sanctuary and clerk of works – are named for their real counterparts, identified from the abbey's financial accounts of 1774, and the king's equerries are named for two of his real attendants.

Though Dean Bell is entirely fictional, some of his activities are based on real events. John Thomas, the actual dean in 1774, pulled out the fourteenth-century choir stalls and, having revealed the tombs of Aveline de Forz and Edmund Crouchback, went on to hide them again behind a modern wooden screen. My dean's penchant for digging up coffins is inspired by the activities of the inquisitive Dean Stanley, in the late nineteenth century. For reasons best known to himself, Stanley decided that James I couldn't possibly be buried where the written sources had recorded and embarked on an extensive (and enjoyable) course of excavations before finding James buried exactly where the sources had said he was all along.

A few clarifications for knowledgeable readers may be

useful. Lindley's explanation of Susan's mishap with the Leyden jar is based on the eighteenth-century understanding of the phenomenon of electricity, which differs in many respects from our own. For those acquainted with Church hierarchy, it is worth noting that in this period the sacrist was an abbey servant rather than a minor canon, as today, which accounts for his very low salary. And Trollope lovers like myself may notice that Susan Bell is also the name of the heroine in one of his lesser-known short stories.

Sir Joseph Yates has no memorial in Westminster Abbey, only a modest one in St Dunstan's church at Cheam, outshone by the Lumley tomb with its silver horse and two large green parrots. His widow, Dame Yates, married the real Dean of Westminster, John Thomas, in 1775. And, thankfully, her dutiful son never gambled away her fortune as in these pages.

The Anglican Church in the eighteenth century was going through its latitudinarian phase – a lull in religious dogma between the bloody extremes of the preceding two centuries and the rise of evangelical non-conformism in the next. As we know from Jane Austen's novels, the Church was at this time a profession more than a vocation, and as Matthew Payne, Keeper of the Muniments at the abbey remarked to me, there have been scarcely any histories written about the abbey during this period, due to the general laxity and inertia of abbey life. This being so, I have had little compunction in putting my lackadaisical clergymen in all sorts of compromising positions, without meaning to cast the slightest aspersion on the glorious abbey itself or its respectable present-day incumbents.

Acknowledgements

Thanks as always to my indefatigable first readers, Eloise Logan, Mark and William Nattrass, and my agent Nicola Barr. I am so grateful for all their thoughtful input.

This book would have been very different, and much inferior, without the marvellous morning I spent with Matthew Payne, Keeper of the Muniments at Westminster Abbey. Looking through the account books for 1774 gave me the names of many characters and a much deeper understanding of the abbey at that time. Mrs Bray's explanation of how monuments were commissioned and built is almost word for word what Matthew told me. He also pointed out many of the intriguing hidden corners of the abbey that feature in the book, along with the Muniments Gallery, which he suggested would make a splendid viewpoint on events. Susan duly took note. Any mistakes are, needless to say, my own and, in this gloriously complicated and ancient building, probably legion.

Peter and Harry Little provided invaluable help regarding the scientific shenanigans and helped me navigate the difference between our understanding of electricity today and eighteenth-century ideas on the subject.

Emily Rainsford drew the lovely plan of the abbey.

My editors Miranda Jewess, Charlotte Greenwood and Alison Tulett have wrought their usual magic, along with all the Viper team, especially Drew Jerrison, Robert Greer and Rosie Parnham. Thanks to you all.